Where I'm Bound

A Novel
Allen B. Ballard

Inspired by the true story of a black cavalry regiment in Mississippi, this dramatic debut novel tells the adventures of an escaped slave who becomes a hero in the Northern Army, and of his efforts to find and free his family during the last days of the Civil War.

A stunning and engaging novel by a prominent African-American professor, *Where I'm Bound* is the first work of fiction solely focused on an African-American regiment to portray the Civil War in a manner befitting its grandeur and scope. Combining rousing adventure with masterful storytelling and important historical insight, Ballard allows readers to view the Civil War from the perspective of those African-American soldiers—comprising ten percent of the Union forces—who fought for their freedom.

It chronicles the Civil War adventures of black cavalry scout Joe Duckett as he and his hard-riding regiment roam the Mississippi Delta seeking to free slaves from the Confederates and keep vital waterways open for the Union. As the war winds down, Duckett sets out to return to the plantation he escaped from, unaware that his wife and baby daughter are making their own desperate bid for freedom.

Advance praise:

"Allen Ballard's thrilling drama gives Civil War history real life....A terrific story!"

—Nell Irvin Painter, author of *Sojourner Truth: A Life, A Symbol*

"The important story of black soldiers in the Union army has finally found a writer of historical fiction equal to the occasion."

—James McPherson, author of *Battle Cry of Freedom: The Civil War Era*

Allen B. Ballard, Ph.D., teaches history and African-American Studies at the State University of New York at Albany. He is a Phi Beta Kappa graduate of Kenyon College in Ohio and holds a Ph.D. in Government from Harvard University. Dr. Ballard has published two non-fiction books: *The Education of Black Folk* and *One More Day's Journey*. He lives in Clifton Park, New York.

Where I'm Bound
October 2000
Fiction
6 1/8 x 9 1/4, 320 pages
0-684-87031-2

ALSO BY ALLEN B. BALLARD

The Education of Black Folk

One More Day's Journey

WHERE
I'M BOUND

ALLEN B. BALLARD

SIMON & SCHUSTER
New York   London   Toronto   Sydney   Singapore

SIMON & SCHUSTER
Rockefeller Center
1230 Avenue of the Americas
New York, NY 10020

SIMON & SCHUSTER and colophon
are registered trademarks of Simon & Schuster, Inc.

Designed by Leslie Phillips
Manufactured in the United States of America

1   3   5   7   9   10   8   6   4   2

LIBRARY OF CONGRESS CATALOGING-IN-PUBLICATION DATA

ISBN 0-684-87031-2

ACKNOWLEDGMENTS

I would like to thank all of the following people for their help in bringing Where I'm *Bound* to print. Carson Carr Richard Farrell Craig Hancock, Mars Hill, Suzanne Lance, Leonard Slade. Harriet Temps Stuart Tolnay, Gartrell Turman, and Lillian Williams all read part of all of the manuscript and made helpful suggestions. Two of my then-senior students here at the university, Nyree Busby and Andre Duncan, also read it and made very useful comments. The following scholars in the field of Civil War and Reconstruction history were kind enough to read the manuscript and thus helped me, a newcomer to the study of the Civil War, to avoid major pitfalls: Noah A. Trudeau, Reid Mitchell, and Robert R. Dykstra. And Mr. Trudeau was kind enough to supply me with an area map of the territory in which the Third Cavalry operated. They are hereby absolved of any responsibility for factual error—that still rests on me. My office mate, H. Peter Krosby, also read the manuscript and has been unstinting in his support of the work, as has been Richard Hamm. David H. Wallace of the National Archives responded with alacrity to my request for material on the Third United States Colored Cavalry.

I would also like to thank my colleagues in the Africana Studies Department, particularly Chair Joseph A. Sarfoh, and the History Department, particularly Chair Dan White, here at SUNY-Albany, for their backing over the years. I also received great support at my church, Mount Calvary Baptist, where native-born Mississippians Vera Gray, Ernest Williams, and "Big John" Fontain were kind enough to school me on maters as diverse as the proper techniques for picking cotton to the catching and cooking of catfish in their home state. My pastor, Reverend Robert W. Dixon, himself a former horse soldier who served in the cavalry detachment at West Point during WWII, was generous with his time in explaining technical matters about horses and cavalrymen. I have also benefited from my membership in the Capital District Civil War Roundtable, a group of enthusiasts with a wealth of knowledge about the war and an eagerness to share it with others. Edward Kaprielian, Colonel U.S.A. (Ret.) was of great help with his technical knowledge at critical moments in the writing. Kenneth Botsford, Mary T. Linnane, Susan McCormack, Aimee Tschoop, John Smith, and Bonita Weddle, all graduate students with the distinct misfortune to have offices adjacent to the one where a novelist was writing his book, were frequently corralled by me to read a page or two of freshly typed words and never once refused to give me a minute or two of their precious time and offer valuable opinions as to the flow of the narrative and other vital matters. Departmental secretaries Elaine Sevits, Debby Neuls and Ronnie Saunders were of great service whenever I called upon them for help.

James M. McPherson, Nell I. Painter, Joseph E. Persico, and John A. Williams all read the manuscript and were kind enough to take the time to comment on it for the book jacket.

Finally, Ross Browne, of the Editorial Department put me through a rigorous and intellectually exhilarating "postgraduate" education in the writing of fiction in the course of the past six years. Owen Laster of the William Morris Agency has been as fine an agent as one could find, and my editor at Simon & Schuster, Dominick Antuso, has made sagacious and creative suggestions that have substantively reshaped the manuscript for the better.

Through all these years, my son, John, and my brother Walter and his wife, Gerry, and my brother Forrest have been supportive of my work. Thanks for your love, you all!

For all who served in the United States Colored Troops

WHERE I'M BOUND

A FEW CIVIL WAR DATES

April 13, 1861   Fall of Fort Sumter, South Carolina, to the Southerners

April 15, 1861   President Abraham Lincoln issues call for 75,000 volunteers to suppress the rebellion.

February 16, 1862   Fort Donelson, Tennessee, surrenders to General Ulysses S. Grant putting the Confederates in the west on the defensive.

April 6-7, 1862   The great battle at Shiloh, Tennessee, with 23,746 combined Union and Confederate casualties. General Grant will continue to move south.

January 1, 1863   The Emancipation Proclamation takes effect.

July I –3   Battle of Gettysburg. General Robert E. Lee's invasion of Pennsylvania is repulsed and he and his army retreat back into Virginia.

July 4, 1863   Vicksburg, Mississippi, falls to General Grant, thus splitting the Confederacy in two and opening the Mississippi River to Union navigation.

April 1864   Confederate General Nathan Bedford Forrest captures Fort Pillow, Tennessee.

September 2, 1864   Atlanta falls to Union general William T. Sherman.

December 15–16, 1864   General George H. Thomas defeats the Confederates at the Battle of Nashville, effectively ending the Southern threat in the western theater.

December 21, 1864   General Sherman occupies Savannah.

January 14, 1865   Fort Fisher, North Carolina, falls to Union forces.

April 9, 1865   General Lee surrenders to General Grant at Appomattox Courthouse, Virginia.

MAP:
SPREAD on pp 14–15
or FULL PAGE on p 15

CHAPTER ONE

THE first thing Joe did when he caught sight of those colored soldiers wearing blue Yankee uniforms was to stand staring at them with his mouth wide open till the captain rode up behind him and whacked him across the shoulder with his riding crop.

"Don't go getting ideas, Joe. We're going to run them niggers right off into the river and drown 'em like rats."

But they hadn't.

And now, on this late June day of 1863, he was in a Confederate camp not far from Milliken's Bend, Louisiana, where a Texas regiment was licking its wounds after fighting against colored Union troops.

It was unusually quiet as the men prepared to bed down for the night. The song of the Negro mule skinners attached to the unit seemed to fit the mood of the camp.

"Soon, one morning, death come stealing in your room. . . ."

"Wish they'd stop that," Zack said. "Make me feel funny, what with all we going to do and all."

"Best for us they keep at it," said Joe, shifting in an effort to get all of his six-foot frame underneath a tattered blanket. "You know these white men must expect it—their niggers supposed to be singing like that, all sorry so many of their masters got killed today. And by colored, too."

"With them long-assed bayonets on they guns," Zack said.

"Oh, my Lord, oh, my Lord, what shall I do . . . ?"

The Yankees were good and close now, him and Zack wouldn't have a chance like this again. Joe felt beneath his rough-cotton trousers for the knife tied around his leg. He'd be out of this damn camp tonight. Or dead trying. After what he'd seen today he didn't much care which.

Zack moved over closer to him. "You sure this the best time to go? These Texas mens just like mad wolves now—got a killing fever on them. They was cutting up colored soldiers every whichaway—even ones already dead. If they catches us. . . ."

"And you think if we stay here, they going to sweeten?" Joe said. "I say they'll get meaner. I ain't staying one more night with them. If there's going to be killing, I'm the one's going to do it, not them."

Zack thought about it for a minute. "You right," he said finally. "I'd a heap more rather die fighting with my folk than from some Yankee bullet."

"Hush, hush, somebody calling my name. . . ."

The singers' voices were getting low now. Everybody was tired, and no wonder. Yankee gunboats shelling all day, horses going crazy, pack mules running wild, bumping into trees and spilling food and bullets all over the ground. Then a two-hour march to get away from the river and cannon balls . . .

"How soon you want to light out of here, Joe?"

"Give it another few hours. And don't you be falling asleep like you always do. We leaving soon as the camp's quiet."

❖   ❖   ❖   ❖   ❖   ❖   ❖   ❖   ❖   ❖   ❖

The singing had stopped, and in the quiet Joe could hear crickets chirping. He eyed the sentry closest to him: Massa Clem. Sitting on a log stump, shotgun on his lap, old black hat slouched down over his face like he was asleep. Joe knew better.

Massa Clem liked to brag about how no nigger had ever run away from his mule detail, but he'd not be saying it again. Wouldn't be using that bullwhip of his neither, whipping on them all the way from Texas clear on over to the Mississippi. Well, Massa Clem, you done brought me to just where I want to be—the Yankees. Now I am through with you.

Joe sniffed the air. Rain coming soon. Would make it a little harder for the bloodhounds, if they used them.

"Clem, we took a licking today." That was the sergeant, making his rounds, damn fool talking so loud he might wake some folk up.

"I wouldn't say that. Hadn't been for them gunboats, we'd of whupped the niggers good."

"Except it's us retreating, not them. Stay awake. Don't know what to expect tonight."

The sergeant moved on. The first raindrops fell. Massa Clem's chin fell forward on his chest, his hand still resting on the shotgun in his lap.

Joe nudged Zack. He got up and walked over to Massa Clem, pointed first to his pants, then to the woods. The guard nodded, and Zack went into the trees.

Joe looked around at the other sentries. They were quiet, probably asleep. He pulled the knife out from beneath his britches.

Why was Zack taking so long to pee?

Massa Clem must have been wondering the same thing, for he got up with his back to Joe and took a few steps toward the woods. Joe held his breath. As soon as Zack reappeared, Joe was across the space between him and the sentry, quiet as a panther and just as quick. He threw his arm around the sentry's throat, pulled it tight, and drove the knife into his back—felt the blood spurt out all over his hands. Massa Clem's body stiffened, his right hand releasing the shotgun, then flailing the night air. He tried to straighten up and his hat fell off. He did manage to hit Joe in the belly with his left elbow and was trying to aim another blow when all of a sudden his body relaxed and collapsed into a heap.

Joe pulled the knife out and wiped the blade clean on the dead man's shirt. His hand was trembling. Killing a man wasn't like killing no hog. It was the first time he'd done it.

He grabbed the short-barreled shotgun and Massa Clem's old hat—be better than nothing on the hot days—and followed Zack off into the woods. He hardly noticed that the crickets had stopped chirping.

❖   ❖   ❖   ❖   ❖   ❖   ❖   ❖   ❖   ❖   ❖

They were no more than a couple of hours from the Mississippi and the Yankee lines, Zack behind, Joe in front, and trying to keep the road in sight for a guide.

It was raining steady now, and the water from the swampy ground squished in what was left of Joe's shoes. Of late it seemed like the slightest bit of wet might bring on a coughing fit, and it wouldn't do to have one now. Everybody knew the general kept a lot of his soldiers out on picket duty.

Joe felt Zack's touch on his shoulder and they both hunkered down. Twenty feet ahead of them was a soldier, his horse tied to the branches of a tree. He was facing the river. Thank you, Jesus.

Zack pointed toward the road. Two more troopers, also facing the river. Joe looked to the left, Zack shook his head and pointed again. Joe squinted hard—another trooper was just barely visible through the trees.

Damn. Looked like they'd have to stay put for a while. The soldiers would be moving on in the morning, but once the sun came up he and Zack would be in clear sight. Freedom was on the other side of those soldiers, and that's where he was bound. Only needed a little opening. Joe wasn't part Choctaw for nothing. If they—

A horse came galloping down the road. Its rider pulled up, leaned down, and said something to the trooper at the road. The soldier walked into the woods but was back a minute later. The two still in the woods unhitched their horses, pulled out their guns-six-shot Navy Colts—and started beating the bushes, moving slowly in Joe's and Zack's direction. And far off in the distance, Joe heard the cry of the hounds.

He looked up at the sky. Any minute, dawn would be breaking. He nodded at Zack and held up his hand.

Just another minute or two. Don't jump yet, Zack. Let 'em get *real* close.

One of the horses neighed. The trooper closest to them straightened up and cocked his revolver.

Too late. Zack ran straight into him with his knife held hard out in front. It went clean into the soldier's chest. The horse bolted and Zack leapt for the reins just in time to dodge a bullet from the other soldier's gun. Joe let out the breath he'd been holding. That shot would be the soldier's last.

Joe leveled the shotgun, blasted the soldier in the stomach, and immediately looked toward the road. The two other men must have heard the commotion and were coming into the woods to help. He didn't see their horses, but they had to be on foot, too—even he couldn't ride a horse through those trees.

The sounds of the dogs were closer now.

He turned to Zack. "You lead the horse, I'll stay about ten yards back. I got one more load in this gun, and we got theirs now."

They made their way toward the road, Joe darting from tree to tree, searching the woods in front of him. Just like hunting wolves, only this quarry was a mite more dangerous. But not more smart, and ain't no wolf ever outsmarted me yet.

His finger tightened on the trigger of the six-shooter. He motioned to Zack to stop, and they crept into a patch of bushes not far from the road. Joe kept looking up and down but couldn't see hide nor hair of the other two soldiers.

"You reckon they scairt off?" Zack whispered.

"Scared to go into the woods after a couple of crazy runaway niggers with guns?" Joe grinned. "Shows they got good sense. Now it's our turn. Let's get out of here."

No sooner were they on the horse and headed down the road than two bloodhounds come busting out the woods, baying and growling like all hell was on the march.

Zack, who had the reins, dug his heels in.

"C'mon, boy!"

"Not so fast," Joe said. "We going to let these sons of bitches get right up close to us."

"How close? Shit, I can feel their breath on my feet."

"Don't worry."

The dogs were blade-thin and black as night. And they were close, all right—close enough for one quick leap to bring the horse down. Then they'd have their day, oh yes they would.

Joe looked back into the red throat of the closest dog, took aim and fired. Then he shot the other one. The hellish baying stopped and the only sound left was that of the horse's hooves clattering on the packed-down surface of the dirt road.

❖   ❖   ❖   ❖   ❖   ❖   ❖   ❖   ❖   ❖   ❖

About three miles farther on, Zack and Joe walked into the Yankee lines, leading the horse and carrying one engraved shotgun, one carbine, and three good-looking sets of revolvers.

"Howdy there, young fellow." Joe grinned at the black soldier who had a gun leveled at them. "Don't be pointing that thing so careless-like. Don't want to spoil the day, do you? Just look at that sun rising high in the sky." He tipped Massa Clem's old black hat to the soldier, walked over to him, and fingered the brass buttons on his uniform. "Now tell me, how do a man go about getting him an outfit like that?"

   ❖   ❖   ❖   ❖   ❖   ❖   ❖   ❖   ❖   ❖   ❖

Captain William Stiles, Third United States Colored Cavalry, looked up from his desk at the long line of colored men waiting to enlist. Most had the look of the road—dust-covered clothes patched time and time again, battered and torn hats, sweat-stained bandannas knotted around a couple of heads. They'd been following Union troops, working as cooks, teamsters, and laborers, building roads and digging ditches for Grant's army on its way down the Mississippi to capture Vicksburg.

Some of them could ride—they'd been around horses and mules all their lives. Most of them looked hard and lean—strong the way the cavalry needed them to be. Good thing, too, because they'd be going into the fighting right away. With Grant's main units having to move eastward, somebody had to stay back and protect the hard-won Mississippi River passage from the Confederate troops and irregulars out in the woods and the bayous of Mississippi and Louisiana. The Third Cavalry—along with veteran Union outfits—had gotten the job, and by God he'd see they did it well. They had but two weeks before they took to the field.

Time to get moving.

"Name?"

"Joe."

"Joe what?"

"No last name, Massa."

"Don't call me Massa, from now on it's sir. That goes for all soldiers, colored or white."

"Yes, sir."

"Got a last name you like? Everybody has to have one."

"Duckett, sir. That's a good name, I heard tell it was my grandfather's."

"All right, Joe Duckett. Now tell me how you got here."

The captain wrote it all down. A runaway, captured and impressed by them, escaped . . .

There was something familiar about him.

"You the one busted through the Reb lines up at Milliken's Bend? Rode with General Grant's cavalry escort as a scout up there in the Yazoo?"

A broad smile. "The very same, sir."

Now, this was a piece of luck. The man was practically a legend—a cook for Colonel Osband, one day he begs to tag along with some regulars, they mount him on a mule and give him a musket from the War of 1812, and next thing you know he's come back into camp with five Reb prisoners marching in front of him. The story was that he even had them singing "John Brown's Body," but Stiles wasn't so sure about that part.

"Me too, Cap'n," said the tall man just behind Duckett. "I rode with Colonel Osband too."

"Well, I'm glad to hear it, soldier. I'll get to you in a minute. Now, Duckett, a few questions, and then I want you to go over to the headquarters unit and wait for me. Are you married?"

"Yes, and got three children."

"Names?"

"My wife is Zenobia. She still up at the Kenworthy plantation in the Yazoo with my baby daughter Cally, I think. My boy and other girl—Luke and Milly—they was sold away three years ago. I'll find them someday."

Captain Stiles heard the pain in the man's voice and laid down his pen.

"*After* this war is over, Duckett. You understand that, don't you?"

His new recruit pulled himself erect, and did it right. The days around Grant's cavalry told.

"I will do my duty, sir."

   ✿   ✿   ✿   ✿   ✿   ✿   ✿   ✿   ✿   ✿   ✿

An hour later Joe stood at attention in the tent that served as Captain Stiles's company headquarters.

"At ease, Duckett."

"Yes, sir."

"I've got plenty of sergeants, good ones, who rode with me at Fort Donelson and Shiloh. They went through days such as I never want to see again, and they are true as tempered steel. What I don't have is a sergeant who knows the colored people and the country around here. I want you to be the first colored sergeant in this cavalry regiment."

Now how about that! Joe blessed his lucky stars for landing in the hands of a fellow with sense enough to come to such a conclusion.

"I know the colonel will back me up. General Grant, too. It was you and them colored boys up at Milliken's who brought him around on this whole idea of colored soldiers."

Stiles studied the dark smiling face. The man was clearly of African descent, but his black hair was almost curly, hinting at some Indian blood. He wore it parted in the middle and it fell clear down to his shoulders. He looked to be a few years over thirty, and by all accounts he could ride like a whirlwind.

"I'll be mighty proud to do it, Captain. One thing, can I have Zack Bascom assigned to my troop as a corporal?"

"If you think he can do the job, take him."

The captain wrote their names down on the roll.

"We'll get down to training tomorrow—mainly weapons and firing. The men I've picked can ride, probably better than all of us New Yorkers. But they must learn their weapons and the discipline of drill. That's all for now."

Joe snapped to attention and was about to salute.

"Oh, and one more thing. I heard that while you were up with that cavalry outfit, they did a lot of hard drinking around and with the general. I've found that whiskey and horse soldiering don't go well together. Understood?"

Joe winced, then squared his shoulders and grinned. "Yes, sir."

"Dismissed."

CHAPTER TWO

"ZENOBIA! Oh, Zenobia!"

That was Lisa Mae, so it must be lunchtime. Zenobia straightened up and stretched her back, then looked down the long row of cotton plants she'd been picking. She dropped the bag where it was. About half full. Would it be the second or third she'd filled this morning?

"Come on, honey, time for you and Momma to get something to eat."

She scooped her daughter up with one arm, took the piece of sugarcane out of her mouth, and started walking. It seemed such a long way back to the grove. Long as you were picking, the sun wasn't so bad, but once you stopped, you could feel it beating down on you like Satan was trying to burn you off the face of the earth.

All around her, the women in white shifts—the only folks left on the plantation—had stopped their singing and were calling out to each other as they moved back toward the grove where they would eat.

"Lula Mae, what for you laughing like that? You know something I don't?"

"Doralee, child, you been picking all morning and look at that little bit of cotton you got."

"You always be walking so proud, Rena. Nobody tell you there ain't no men left around here to look at you?"

"Nary a one of them ever looked at *you*, that's for sure."

Zenobia joined in the teasing as they came together at the end of the rows.

"If'n Sammy boy with all them big fine muscles and such was to suddenly show up around here, bet you-all would hush that fussing and make some fast tracks to see who'd be the first one to catch ahold of him."

The girls tittered and Lula Mae said, "Way I be, they could run to him as fast as they want." She threw her head back to one side, put her hand on her hip, and swayed her body back and forth. "I'd wait right here where I be, and that there sweet-loving man would come flying down the field to me."

The little children who'd been with their mothers in the field trailed behind them, buck naked. Looking ahead to the blessed shade of the trees, Zenobia could see that Drayton had the food ready—one thing that trifling nigger was good for. Ever since the white overseer went to the army and Miss Kenworthy put him in charge, Drayton had made sure they had enough to eat. It wasn't like the old days, but Zenobia had heard from folks who passed through, moving from plantation to plantation, how bad things were all over. She was grateful for the corn bread and fatback and corn or string beans they got every noontime. At night there were only the greens she grew in her garden.

Drayton was waiting for them, cooling himself with his fancy fan and sitting on the little log bench where the old overseer used to sit. He even had on a white vest and a brown stovepipe hat with its top cut off. She wondered if he was fool enough to think his fancy clothes made him any less a slave than the rest of them.

"See how I feeds you?" he said, as the youngsters who were serving put the corn bread and string beans with fatback into the bowls. "Ain't I good to you, children?"

Good for nothing was more like it, trying to climb in bed with every woman on the place since all the men were gone. She watched a few of the women go over to him, hugging and kissing him. You couldn't really blame them. He could make it easier for them on the job, get them something extra to eat.

She fed Cally, then dipped the hem of her shift in the water bucket and wiped the little girl's face and neck.

"You mighty warm, honey, think you might could stay up here with the bigger chilluns this afternoon? It be too hot out in that sun for you."

"I don't want to be away from you. Somebody take me."

"Nobody going to take you, sugar. You can just stay up here and play with Ned—I'll come to take you both home when . . ." She pointed toward the long expanse of cotton waiting to be picked.

Cally started to cry, and Zenobia picked her up. "Your mama's life is hard enough without I worry about the sun burning you up. Remember, honey, I ain't going to let nobody take you. Now you stay up here with them other chilluns. Lisa Mae won't let nobody hurt you neither."

"All right, you all!" Drayton hollered. "Time to get back to the fields."

Zenobia called over to Lisa Mae. "Take Cally and keep her with you this afternoon. And make sure she keeps drinking water." She joined the line of women headed back out into the fields, looked at the children following their mothers and shook her head. "They should be staying with you too. Sun will burn them hard."

"Wait up there just a minute, girl."

She turned and saw Rufus strutting up behind her.

"Look mighty pretty this noontime. Your walk is something powerful sweet to see. Makes me feel like the earth is shaking."

"Hush your mouth, I gets tired just listening to you."

"Want to take the afternoon off, come on and take a little walk over to my new place? We could look around, drink some lemonade from the big house."

The sweat was already running down her face again, and she'd only just gotten up from the table. She looked out toward the cotton fields where the other women were already picking. They'd started singing too.

> *All night, all day,*
> *Oh God's angels keep watching over me . . .*

Drayton had caught up to her now. "Zenobia—"

"Told you once, told you twice, ain't going with you."

"You still think your Joe be coming back for you. Well, I'm here. He ain't. I can feed you. He cain't."

The words cut right to the very bone. Drayton was right. Joe had left her all alone. It was a cruel world and getting crueler every day.

"I got some cotton to pick," she said.

Drayton grabbed hold of her shoulder. "I can make you go with me, you know. I'm the top dog now."

"Dog be the right word, I'd say." She jerked away, quickly putting some distance between them with her long easy stride. He let her go, but she could feel his eyes following every step out to the field.

"Someday you'll need me," he called after her.

> *All night, all day*
> *Oh God's angels keep watching over me . . .*

❖   ❖   ❖   ❖   ❖   ❖   ❖   ❖   ❖   ❖

Late in the midnight hour. Cally and Ned were asleep on their wooden pallets, the dog between them. Zenobia wished Brother Caleb hadn't shown up. Every single one of her bones had its own ache, and she wanted nothing more than to climb in bed. But here she and Lisa Mae were, sitting at the old log table listening to the preacher man from the Newton plantation down the road.

It was hard enough just trying to keep herself and the young ones fed and washed up and decent. Now here he come, talking about freedom, about how everybody's leaving. Just make that three days' journey through the swamps and woods to the Mississippi River and they'd be slaves no more. Oh, the way would be hard, but General Grant would soon put an end to all of the colored people's pain.

"No more whips," Caleb was saying. "No more auction blocks, no more children sold down the river. A Mighty Deliverer has come to smite Pharaoh's armies. Just one more river to cross, Zenobia child."

"And when would we be leaving?"

"Tomorrow night."

"That soon?"

"Ought to be leaving tonight. All around us these white folks so scared of losing their niggers, they be running colored folks—putting them in big gangs and taking them far away from the Mississippi River so's the Yankee soldiers cain't free them."

"How many of us would be going?"

"About ten, with those from our place."

"Cally and Ned too little to go," Zenobia said. "There's snakes and wildcats and things out there in the swamps, and—"

"Best to leave them here, anyway. We go, we'll have to move fast, and they would slow us down. The white folks ain't taking children, just folks old enough to work."

Lisa Mae leaned forward. "You sure enough don't know Zenobia or me if you think we leaving Cally and Ned nowhere," she said.

"Aw, Ned ain't even your child, Zenobia," Caleb said. "And I tell you, nothing would happen to them here."

Luke and Milly are out there somewhere. Is there a chance I could find them? And Joe . . .

She looked at Cally, the only one of her children she could still protect, the only one she could still see and touch and hold. And Ned, just eight years old and already done had his folks sold away from him. She got up from the table to get a dipper of water, took her time drinking it, looking off into the night.

"I guess you better go on without us."

"Well, now, Zenobia, the thing is, we was counting on you to lead us." Brother Caleb got up and came over to stand beside her. "See, Joe done taught you all about them woods, how to find old Injun paths through the swamps, how to read signs on them trees."

"I ain't going without Cally and Ned."

"But we needs you—"

"If you needs me, you needs *them*."

Brother Caleb sighed. "All right, they can go too. Be ready tomorrow night when you hears the hoot owl calling."

But come morning, Cally was sweating and whimpering. Zenobia wiped her hot forehead and knew they'd not be going anywhere any time soon.

That night the hoot owl called and called, seemed like all the night long.

❧   ❧   ❧   ❧   ❧   ❧   ❧   ❧   ❧   ❧   ❧

Zenobia had to admit Drayton was mighty good to them when Cally took sick. Miss Sue acted half crazy most of the time now, but somehow he got her to listen to him and give them a room up in the big house, quiet and peaceful, with clean white sheets on their bed. He even fixed it so Zenobia could stay in the house with Cally and take care of Miss Sue's children instead of working in the fields.

A week after they moved into the big house, Cally was well enough to play outside, running all over the big green lawn with Miss Sue's children. Zenobia was watching them from a rocking chair on the front porch when a horseman pulled up wearing a white shirt with a blue bandanna around his neck. He was off the horse and past Zenobia in a minute, like he hadn't even seen her. And before she had time to wonder why he was in such a powerful hurry, he was back out of the house and galloping away.

"Zenobia, fetch Drayton from down the field," said Miss Sue, who had come out on the porch. "And hurry up, it's mighty important."

"It's almost suppertime, Miss Sue. You reckon I could take Cally and stay down at our cabin after I give him your message?"

"Oh, for goodness' sakes! I don't care *where* you stay, just make sure Drayton gets up here in a hurry."

By sundown there wasn't a woman in the long line of cabins who would be able to sleep that night.

"Something bad about to happen," Zenobia had told them. "Feel it in my bones. You pack up everything you care about tonight, or you be sorry tomorrow."

"How you know?" one young woman asked.

"She always do," another woman said. "You heard tell about that shooting star that fell just before the war started? Back before you came here? Well, Zenobia told everybody it was coming and that was a whole week before."

Long after all the children were asleep, a knock came at her door.

"Who that?"

"It's me, Drayton. Come on out here. I got some mighty important news and I don't want the children to hear it."

Was he making it up just to get her outside alone? He *had* been good the whole week. Zenobia looked over at the children and Lisa Mae, saw they were still asleep, then slipped out of the cabin and closed the door softly behind her.

"They coming in the morning, so you got to make up your mind."

"Who's coming?"

"Major Kenworthy, he done sent a messenger to tell Miss to move everybody over to Alabama, away from the Yankees, 'cause they robbing and stealing and killing folks something awful. They burning niggers."

"That ain't what I heard. I heard they coming to make us free."

"Don't matter what you hear, the slave-running gang be here in the morning to take everybody. Miss and me and her chilluns, we're going up to a little town other side of Jackson, stay with some of her kin."

"Why you telling me all this?"

"You can come with me and Miss Sue, don't have to go to Alabama. Miss took a liking to you, said you can take care of her chilluns and bring yours and Lisa Mae with you."

"I don't know . . ."

"They coming at sunup, whole plantation be gone by the time the sun's high."

"And if I don't want to go with Miss Sue?"

"Don't make her no difference, plenty other women here *will* want to go." He looked at her and shrugged. "I'll be by in the morning, hope you got sense enough to leave with us."

Zenobia went back into the hut and shook Lisa Mae.

"Get up, honey, come on outside, we got some talking to do."

Lisa Mae's deep brown face stayed calm as Zenobia told her about Drayton's visit, but she kept tugging on one of the long plaited braids that fell down almost to her shoulders.

"I can't see the chillun making it all the way to Alabama, Zee. Way I see it, we got to go with Drayton and Miss and trust in God. Besides, further away we go from the Yankees, the less chance we got to get free."

"That sorry-assed Drayton think the Yankee soldiers going to tar and feather him," Zenobia said.

"He ain't so bad, Zee. Stop talking so mean about him."

"Then when he ask, you can be the one to lay down with him, 'cause I ain't."

"I'd say you may have to if times get hard. It's you he's sweet on, anyway."

Zenobia sighed. "You right about one thing—it don't make sense to start for Alabama with Ned and Cally, especially with her just over being sick."

"So we'll go with Miss and Drayton?"

"And when the time comes," Zenobia said, "we'll get through to the Yankees."

❀   ❀   ❀   ❀   ❀   ❀   ❀   ❀   ❀   ❀   ❀

The roosters crowed so loud that morning Zenobia thought they must know what was happening. She wanted to turn away from the sight in front of her, but she couldn't. This was something she would have to remember. Brother Caleb had been so wrong when he said they weren't running children over to Alabama. They were taking everybody except them and Miss Sue's old house slaves Linus and Mary.

Out of the cabins came the women, some so light-skinned they almost might have been white, some black as night. They carried bundles of clothes over their shoulders, and some of them balanced another bundle on their heads. They walked oh, so slowly down the path to where Drayton waited with some white men. Some of them held guns and others played with the whips in their hands. Merciful Lord! What had they to fear from a bunch of women weighted down with bundles?

Two old wooden wagons hitched to a couple of mules were being loaded up with water, flour, bacon. Two white men sat with the reins in their hands. The boss of the train stood talking to Drayton, counting out the people and checking their names off on a sheet of paper as they fell in line on the road.

"Rena Mae and two young'uns, Lawrence and Lionel?" The man lifted his head and glanced at the coffee-colored woman kneeling down in the road to fasten her sons' sandals. He checked them off the list a moved on.

"Annie and Ruth . . ." The two sisters were holding hands. One was about twelve, with big doelike brown eyes set in a pool of white, the other fourteen but with a body so like a full-grown woman's that the man looked every inch of it over before he put a check beside their names.

Zenobia lifted Cally up and turned to Lisa Mae. "Take Ned's hand, we got to go down and say goodbye. We ain't never going to see a one of them again."

When she got to the road there were many, many more than she had expected. There were colored folks, mostly women, from plantations down the road and up by the river—a long line of them, stretched back almost as far as you could see. More white men with guns and whips moved along beside the women and children to make sure no one strayed. She walked down to the line, Cally right beside her.

"Matty Lou, you don't lose your faith in God, you hear? Zelma, you look after your auntie Lena real good, you promise? Sarah, don't let your mamma carry that bundle, it too heavy for her."

Up and down the line she went, scolding and hugging and crying, till finally she reached Aunt Garry. The gray-haired old woman had been here when Zenobia came, brought in chains over those same hills where the line would soon disappear. She'd been there when Zenobia and Joe jumped the broom, too, and when Luke and Milly got sold away. She'd sung Zenobia to sleep when she cried like a little baby the night a half-crazed Joe ran off into the woods after the children. Like he could bring them back—the big brave fool. Instead she lost them all at once . . .

She put her arms around Aunt Garry and hugged her tight.

"Now don't you go worrying about me, Zenobia. The Good Lord done look after me over all my long journey this far, I don't reckon He going to stop now. And don't you feel bad 'cause we got to go and you ain't, either. You hear me, child?"

"I hears you." She reached down into a pocket and pulled out some Yankee coins she'd dug up out of a secret hiding place the night before. "Here, take this little bit of money, I got some more. Just in case you need to buy some food on the way."

"Keep it, girl. Where I'm going I won't need no money, and you got to have enough for all of you. Now you better be off, 'fore Miss change her mind and send you along with us."

Zenobia stepped back. Somewhere down the line somebody was singing:

"*Jesus have gone to Galilee . . .*"

And right in front of Zenobia, a smiling Aunt Garry picked it up and sang back:

"*And how do you know that Jesus is gone?*"

A low moaning sound, then the women sang:

"*I tracked Him by His drops of blood . . .*"

Aunt Garry sang:

"*And every drop He dropped in love . . .*"

Zenobia picked up Cally and headed back to the hill top. Right in front of the big house, she put Cally down and shaded her eyes so she could fol-

low her friends' white shifts as they walked down the road, little puffs of
red dust rising in their wake.

Soon—so soon—the last of them had rounded the bend, and she could
no longer hear their voices.

Zenobia lifted her head and sang out, loud as she could:

"And every drop He dropped in love."

CHAPTER THREE

MAJOR Richard Kenworthy was bone-weary of this riding. He had served the Confederacy since the eighth day of May, 1861—how long ago was that? It was now December 14, 1863—that made it more than two and a half years. He should be doing a real soldier's job, should be galloping across open fields charging Union cavalry. Not stuck on patrol over in Louisiana raiding abandoned plantations along the Mississippi where Grant had escaped slaves raising cotton and food for his armies.

It was only when he thought about Clifton, the Kenworthy plantation, and what he'd lost that the raids seemed to make any kind of sense. Grant had taken Vicksburg, but even a fallen city had to be supplied—and too many Yankees still thought they could do it with food from nearby plantations. Just as too many coloreds thought they could collaborate with the Yankees now that their masters had all gone away. An idea like that could cause God knows how much trouble on plantations whose slaves weren't free yet.

Behind the major rode Clinton Adams, Kenworthy's oldest friend and for the past two years captain in charge of the second troop of Caper's battalion of Confederate cavalry. Kenworthy slowed down so their horses were side by side.

"How much farther you think the Ransome place is?" Kenworthy asked.

"I'd say three miles," Adams said.

"All right, we'll stop here for the night. Make sure the men see to the horses. And no fires."

Kenworthy had wondered what kind of officer his old schoolmate and drinking buddy would make, but he needn't have worried. Adams was a trustworthy officer, who had, of late, begun to show the marks of real leadership. The men liked him even though he was hard on them. Seemed to have the knack of getting them to be comfortable with him without being too familiar.

After Adams passed the word down the line and set out the pickets, Kenworthy waited for him to return to the little knoll before going over plans with two other officers.

"After tomorrow," he said, "we'll have to head northwest up along the Boeuf River. The Yankees must be real tired of these raids—just got word they're sending out some light cavalry to wipe us out. We have to do a good job with the Ransome place, then light out of there. Fast."

When he'd finished going over the disposition of their forces, the two lieutenants went off to sleep, but not Captain Adams.

"Something on your mind, Clint?"

"Need to talk with you a few minutes before I turn in."

"Long as it's not hours instead of minutes," the major said. "I remember some long nights at Mississippi College."

"I don't like it," Adams said. "I don't like what we're doing."

"Meaning what?"

"What we got to do to those niggers tomorrow."

Kenworthy began to unroll his blanket. "We didn't tell these Yankees to come down here. We didn't destroy the Constitution, tromp all over the rights of property holders. We didn't—"

"But there have to be limits, Richard. Even in war. And these darkies aren't combatants."

"Don't matter. Vicksburg's gone, and what we do this next few months will tell if we get the Yankees to go home or not. Can't you see? any sign of weakness and it's all over for us."

Adams got up from his seat on a rock. "I seem to remember a friend of mine who used to say maybe slavery was bad, maybe we should gradually abolish it. You didn't say abolish the slaves."

"The Yankees took that option away from us, Captain Adams." Damn, Clint was his friend and he hadn't meant to speak to him from such a height, but war didn't allow for all this second-guessing, thinking, and philosophizing. It was just a job, something to be done. "Catch you some sleep, Clint, we've got to be up early in the morning."

❀   ❀   ❀   ❀   ❀   ❀   ❀   ❀   ❀   ❀   ❀

It was about as challenging as a springtime stroll in the woods. When the sun came up the major's forty men surrounded the plantation, shot the only armed black guard, then rounded up every escaped slave who hadn't managed to run off.

One big yellow-skinned nigger seemed to be in charge of the gang of men who'd been working the farm. He was sitting on the ground in the middle of them, surrounded by five guards with double-barreled shot-guns.

Kenworthy looked up at the sky. The sun was climbing fast, they'd have to get out of there in a hurry. His orders were explicit. Confiscate all the cattle and kill the colored who couldn't be taken along and used as labor-ers. He sure didn't have time to take them with the Yankee cavalry all about.

"Captain Adams, burn the buildings and cotton. Get the cattle moving, we'll get them up the road a bit and run 'em off in the woods, maybe three or four miles away."

"And the niggers?"

"Tie their hands behind. Line 'em up single file, backs to the river. Form a firing squad. Oh, and send that yellow one over to me."

A cavalryman marched the man over to Kenworthy at saber-point. He had a bruise on his cheek. Something about him rubbed the major the wrong way, maybe it was because he had the same arrogant look that Joe used to have sometimes back on the plantation.

"Where you from, boy?"

"Squires plantation, 'cross the river."

"How long you darkies been here, squatting on white folks' land?"

"'Bout three months."

"Heard anything about Yankee cavalry coming this way?"

"No, suh, Massa.'"

"I doubt it. If I had time, I'd whip your lying black ass."

"Yeessuh, Massa."

Kenworthy turned to the guard. "Take him back with the rest of them."

As soon as the men gathered the cattle, Adams assembled a firing squad. The major trotted his horse over to where the colored stood, some singing, some praying. A wretched-looking lot, pants threadbare, shoes broken down, shirts ripped or no shirts at all.

He rode slowly down the line and looked directly into the eyes of each man. He stopped when he saw a boy about eleven.

"Take him out, and set him free."

He brought his horse to a halt in front of the big yellow man, looked hard into his blazing eyes.

"You poor miserable darkies have been tricked into believing you are free. And you've been helping the Yankees against your lawful masters. It's a sin and a shame you've been so misled, boys. Because now we're going to have to put an end to you."

He backed the horse a few steps and looked over at Adams.

"Too bad they didn't stay on their masters' plantations. Prepare your firing squad."

"Order arms!" Adams shouted. "Right shoulder arms!"

A minute passed.

What the hell was wrong with Clint? Why wasn't he giving the aim-and-fire command?

What the—

Adams was turning his horse, riding up so close only Richard could hear him.

"You can't do this, Richard. It's wrong and you know it."

The condemned men were as still as the men on the firing squad.

Kenworthy grabbed the reins of his friend's horse. "Clint, do your duty!" he hissed. He released the reins. "Now!"

Instead, Adams made as if to dismount.

"Captain Adams! Attention!" Major Richard Kenworthy sat bolt upright on his horse, his knuckles white from gripping the pommel so tight and hard.

Adams was a soldier, and the order stopped him. He sat at attention on his mount, his eyes straight ahead.

"Captain Adams, I am giving you a direct order. You will obey it."

Adams's horse was pawing the earth, as if he sensed the tension.

"Major Kenworthy, sir, I will not. If their blood is shed, it won't be on my hands."

In all that damn quiet every man must have heard every word. Now they were waiting, all of them, black, white, condemned, free, for his next move.

Dear God—would it be to execute his best friend?

He unbuckled his burnished black leather holster. Felt his fingers tremble as they touched the butt of his ten-shot French-made revolver.

The sound of a scout galloping into the yard broke the silence. "They're coming. Yankee cavalry's three miles down the road. And they're *colored* cavalry."

"Mount up the men. Leave the niggers where they are." Kenworthy rode up to the yellow man. "Looks like your God spared you today."

"We serves the same one, sir."

"I don't have time to argue theology with you, but somebody's God must have been looking out for you." He nodded toward Captain Adams. "And him."

And me.

✿ ✿ ✿ ✿ ✿ ✿ ✿ ✿ ✿ ✿ ✿

That night—miles, he hoped, from the Union cavalry—he called Captain Adams over. His friend stood at attention before him, and Kenworthy felt the anger rise up in him again over this rotten assignment.

"I expect you see what happened today as God's hand and there I'd agree with you. I'm glad I didn't have to kill them, but by His holy name, I will surely shoot you on the spot should you ever again refuse to obey an order."

✿ ✿ ✿ ✿ ✿ ✿ ✿ ✿ ✿ ✿ ✿

Sergeant Joe Duckett stood up in his stirrups and looked behind him at the long line of black troopers. They'd come a good long way since that first little fight back in October. This would be their first real raid up into

Confederate country in Louisiana, about twenty miles below the Arkansas State Line. Joe was mighty proud that Colonel Osband said he'd be counting on him to be the scout. He spurred his horse and rode up beside Captain Stiles, who was leading the column.

"Horses and men all ready, Sergeant? I'm thinking we're in for some heavy fighting, and soon."

"Couldn't be more ready, Captain."

Stiles looked over at Joe's horse. "You know that roan of yours may be the damnedest sorriest-looking animal I ever saw. A sergeant ought to be riding something better."

"Begging your pardon, Captain, but the day you find a horse anywhere that can beat Hawk running, then I'll get rid of her and give her to one of the bugle boys."

The captain laughed. "If we weren't getting ready to go into some fighting, I'd like to have a run at you myself. In fact, I think I will once we get back in camp."

"Captain, can I ask you something?"

"You can. What is it?"

"We riding together with that white outfit, right?"

"And?"

"Them men been saying niggers ain't going to fight."

The captain pulled down the brim of his hat. The sun was getting hot. "So?"

"You think they going to back us up like they should if the fighting gets hard?"

The captain frowned. "They will, Duckett. Because out there if one falters, everybody falters, and everybody dies. They're Union soldiers, I've ridden with them and seen them in action. They'll fight with you."

"We heard tell that a whole Yankee regiment tried to run off rather than fight with us."

"General Grant took care of that. Anyway, you know you can't do a blessed thing about what other folk think. Just do your best to make sure our boys are ready, and everything will turn out fine. Now I think you'd better go back and prepare to turn the company over to Zack. It's time for you to go up to the colonel for your briefing."

An hour later, at the noontime break, Joe—dressed like a field hand and wearing his big black country hat—rode up to report to Captain Stiles. In front of them was the Mississippi, muddy and swirling.

"The colonel wants me to find where that Rebel cavalry at, sir."

"Where's your weapon?"

Joe smiled, reached down inside his pants leg, and took out a six-shot Colt polished so brightly it might have just come out of the factory up in Springfield.

"Son of a bitch. Good luck. See you tomorrow. And don't forget about our race."

"Captain, next thing you know you be walking around buck naked," said Zack, who'd come to tell Joe good-bye. "Joe done already won himself a heap of money with that sorry-assed horse of his."

Joe stroked Hawk's mane. "Baby, they talking about you mighty bad, but I wouldn't trade you for nothing." He saluted the captain and rode away.

❖   ❖   ❖   ❖   ❖   ❖   ❖   ❖   ❖   ❖   ❖

Traveling in this country, not more than a few days' ride from Clifton, made Joe sad. Zenobia and Cally were over there somewhere. Oh, what wouldn't he give for just a glimpse of his daughter, see those sparkly black eyes . . . give Zenobia a pat on her sweet ass. It was hard being a free man with family near, close as your breath and you couldn't go to them. But he was a soldier man now, he knew where he had to be.

About an hour up the road he came to a path that led down to the river. He guided Hawk down the hill to where an old black man sat on a little ferryboat. A rope ran from one side of the river to the other.

"Morning, Uncle," Joe said. "You got a nice little boat there."

"Makes me a living. Who you be?"

Joe pulled out a dollar coin. "You take me across and wait for me, I give you two more."

The man took the money and waved Joe on board.

"Careful, now. Two horses as much as this little thing can take." He began to draw the ferry across the river. "You with them Yankees, ain't you?"

"I is a free man. And we fighting to make you free too."

"Better watch yourself when we get to the other side. Them grayboys all around, they catching and killing any colored man they don't know. Say any lone nigger by hisself got to be with the Yankees. They sure going to wonder where somebody tall and strong as you come from. You look like you been eating too good."

The ferry came to the other bank and slid to a halt in the mud. Joe rode Hawk onto solid ground and turned back.

"Don't forget to wait for me."

"I'll say you a prayer, too, expect you'll be needing it." He grinned. "But by the look of you some of them folks might be needing a little prayer soon too."

Joe rode off into the woods with the old man's warning heavy on his mind. If they caught him, they'd hang him from one of those tall dark oak trees in the forest he was riding through. He caressed his neck softly with his right hand, then reached down into his pants for the flask of bourbon. He took a good long swig and wiped his mouth with the cuff of his blue cotton blouse. There, that felt better. Good thing Captain Stiles hadn't asked what else he was carrying. But the captain wasn't out here alone in these dark woods, the trees so thickly branched they must block out the sky when they were in leaf. As it was, not much of the weak sunshine could make it through.

He took another long sip of whiskey, got off of Hawk, and cut him a good stout club. Might need it if he couldn't get to his gun.

Squirrels was everywhere, jumping from tree to tree, sometimes stopping to look at him. Wasn't used to having no company in their forest. If Zenobia was here she'd be teasing him about squirrel stew. Always had fun with him about how much he liked to eat, and he'd rather eat squirrel than anything. Zenobia—

Come on, man, you a soldier in the army, ain't got no time to be thinking about no family—you getting back to them the best way you know how. You—

"Nigger, what you doing out here in the woods on that raggedy-looking horse?"

Shit! Put a little whiskey in your belly, take your mind off a job, and you ride right out into a road and a Rebel trooper. With a gun pointed right at your daydreaming head.

"Oh, Massa, you liked to scared this poor nigger to death. I done told Massa George, if he put me on a horse to catch that runaway Amos, then some Yankee soldiers be surely going to catch me and he'll have done lost hisself two niggers 'stead of one. That's just what I told him."

"We ain't no Yankees, boy. Whose nigger are you, anyway?"

"Like I done told you—I belongs to Massa George. He done sent me after Amos. If'n I don't come back soon, he—"

"Well, you ain't going back right now. I'm taking you to the colonel."

"What for, Massa?"

"Just come on up the road with me, boy."

When they got to a fork a little ways down the road, Joe saw more Rebel cavalry than he'd ever thought about, much less laid eyes on. Had to be at least four companies of them. And there, riding beside what must be the colonel, was Massa Richard Kenworthy, standing up in his stirrups, one hand cupped over his eyes so he didn't have to squint to see the black man riding alongside his scout.

Joe's legs gripped Hawk like he feared he might fall off. "That the colonel way over yonder?" His right hand closed around the big wooden stick, and he pointed with the other.

When the scout turned to look, Joe swung the stick. The blow landed just where neck met shoulder and knocked the Reb right off his horse.

Joe spurred Hawk into a gallop, and they tore down the road with three Rebel troopers hot behind them.

Damn, got me a race today!

Joe put his head down alongside Hawk's neck and whispered in her ear. "Don't forget, I knows there ain't no horse lives can catch you."

The Rebels were whooping that god-awful yell of theirs, sounding like a pack of hounds.

"Gonna hang you when we catch you, nigger," one of them shouted.

Joe shouted, too, but not at the Rebs. *"Go, Hawk!"*

When he took a second to look back, he felt like giving a whooping yell himself. They was falling back. Couldn't keep up with him—except, damn, one of them's still there and gaining. Hawk was all wet and lathered. Wasn't no way to get more speed out of her.

"Come on, baby, it's into the woods."

He could hear the lone trooper crashing through the trees behind him.

Good. Come on into my woods. Choctaw woods. Spirits of my ancestors all around me. Big Bear and Little Wolf . . .

He got down off Hawk and threaded his way through clumps of trees along a path that made all kinds of bends. Just past a real sharp one he tied up the horse, pulled out his Colt, and waited for the Reb to round the bend.

That Reb was only a youngster, but his eyes were mean. Joe shot him in the chest.

The Reb's horse bolted away down another path, probably led to the ferry. Joe jumped on Hawk and followed. I ain't *about* to let a horse fast as you go back to them.

They reached the ferry at a full gallop. "Whoa, girl!" He jumped down and grabbed the reins of both horses.

"Let's get going, Uncle They right behind me."

"God have mercy."

"You can pray while you pull on that rope."

The old man suddenly didn't seem so old. He pulled like he was twenty, and with Joe helping him, the little ferryboat made its way not so slowly across the Mississippi.

Halfway across, he heard shots and saw the water pinging up, way to the right of them. He looked back. Three Rebs stood at the river's edge, blasting away with their shotguns.

The old man's hands shook something terrible.

"Aren't even coming close," Joe said. "You keep prayin' and pullin'."

Soon as they reached the other bank, he pulled both horses up the hill, tied them to a tree, and looked around.

"Watch them for me," he told the old man. "Got something I need to do."

He spotted an ax propped against the old man's wood supply, picked it up, and returned to the boat.

It took but four blows to split the hull. He cut the rope, shoved what was left of the boat off into the current, watched it list and then sink. With his hands around his mouth he shouted to the Rebs on the other side.

"Any of you cross this river today, *it ain't goin' to be here!*"

For a moment, the Rebels stopped shooting and the breeze sent their words clear across the water.

"You see how that nigger broke up that boat?"

"Like it were sheet-board!"

"Just like I'd of broke your heads!" Joe shouted back. "If your sorry-assed horses could of caught me."

Now the Rebs commenced calling him everything except a child of God. And Massa Richard Kenworthy stood right there in the front of them, just waving his fist and shouting God knew what, Joe couldn't tell with all of them yelling. Probably that this was the very last time in life that Joe would ever cross him.

The old man was looking his age again, as if he'd shriveled up even more. Joe offered him the last of the whiskey and it was gone in one long gulp. Joe sighed. It would be a long dry ride back to the regiment.

"Uncle, I sure am sorry I had to sink your boat. But I'll tell my captain how you brought that little bitty boat across the Mississippi with them Rebs firing away, and I reckon he'll make it right with you."

"You tell him that? And they might pay me for my boat?"

"I'll do my damnedest to see they does. Now get up on that horse there—she's a good 'un. We better get out of here fast, it'll go hard with you if they catches you."

"You right about that," the old man said with a broad grin. "I be a sure-nuff Union man now."

❖   ❖   ❖   ❖   ❖   ❖   ❖   ❖   ❖   ❖   ❖

"We'll grab us any boat comes down the river today and use it to ferry the boys across to the other side." Colonel Osband said when Joe made his report. "Good a time as any to whip them."

The Union detachment crossed over the river into Louisiana and pursued the Reb cavalry up toward the Arkansas line. Then the Rebs turned on them and counterattacked, the weight of their assault falling on the white Illinois troopers, who fought like wildcats. Joe would never doubt them again. Seeing the fight almost lost, Captain Stiles grabbed a squad of men, told Joe to come along, and led them across the field with drawn sabers. And oh, those Rebel cavalry had no taste for that. By day's end, seventy-five white troopers and a hundred twenty-five colored troopers sent close to five hundred Rebs running off into the woods. Not without a price: a good quarter of the Yankees ended up killed, wounded, or taken prisoner.

But now the Rebs knew the colored enemy would fight. And the white enemy would fight right alongside them. Gave you something to think about.

CHAPTER FOUR

IT WAS surprisingly mild and warm for a February day, even in upper Louisiana. Pauline watched rays of bright sunshine playing over the still muddy ground where, just days ago, a sudden ice storm had covered everything with its rigid beauty. The road that led to the great white house was strewn with broken branches.

The morning after the storm, she had walked around the plantation and marveled at the still beauty of the trees, every branch, every twig encased in glittering ice. When she heard what sounded like shots, she spun around, frightened, looking for the source of the sound—and again was awed by her surroundings. What she'd heard were pine boughs, snapping under the weight of the ice and sending down a shower of shining tubes as the sheaths of ice, one after the other, broke loose. Nature had clothed the branches in that glittering raiment and given them a moment of splendor—then swiftly and cruelly brought it to an end.

Now on this day when she'd have preferred to be outside, Pauline was in the living room of the plantation, watching the woman she called Miss read a letter delivered not five minutes ago by a Rebel soldier.

"I'm afraid you're in for some trouble," Miss said. "Richard's been fighting upcountry. He'll be stopping in here any day now." She saw Pauline shiver. "You can hide out in that hut down by the river, Pauline. You'd better take Milly and Luke with you, he's still angry that we bought them."

"I wish . . ."

"What, dear?"

Pauline sighed. "It's sad, isn't it, that Joe ran off and never got a chance to know his children were safe with us."

"Sad like so much about this terrible war. I wish to God it were over." She took Pauline's hand. "You worry about him a lot, don't you?"

"Joe?"

"Of course."

"I do. He's my only brother and I see his face every day when I look at Luke."

"What a strange world we live in. Richard still loves *you*, you know. Always has and always will."

Little did Miss know just how strange, for much as Pauline had hated it when Massa Richard forced her to his bed, she'd come to accept his love-making. Then, God forgive her, to look forward to it. Though every time, in the next morning's cold light, she'd loathed herself.

There were times when she'd eyed the clasp knife he kept on his bureau and thought about plunging it into her breast. The devil in the form of the flesh had so surely held her in his grip that she'd thanked her God when old Mr. Kenworthy gave her to Miss Dorothy as a wedding present. How else could she ever have escaped up here to Louisiana, far from temptation? Oh, if she'd only not been born with this beauty that drew men to her—nor been so drawn to strong men with sweet charming ways of talk and touch.

She walked over to the window and looked down on Luke, who was washing a horse down near the stables. Milly, his tall and willowy sixteen-year-old sister, stood watching him. The three years Joe's children had spent with the Cannons had brightened Pauline's life in ways she'd never expected. She'd taught them to read and write, loved them, and been loved back.

And now, with the colonel away, there was no telling what Massa Richard would do when he got to the plantation. He must not find them. . . .

She turned back to Miss. "I think I'd better get down to that hut this afternoon and clean it up. Nobody's been there for a good while. I'll come back and start dinner later."

"Stay down there, don't worry about dinner. Times being what they are, we don't know when he might get here or who's with him."

❖ ❖ ❖ ❖ ❖ ❖ ❖ ❖ ❖ ❖ ❖

Pauline spent the night in the slave shack with the children. Milly responded to their situation calmly enough, but Pauline knew better than to expect anything resembling calm from Luke. It wasn't just his looks that reminded her of his father. He had always had a mind of his own, never thought like children his age. Now he was nearly fourteen. His years on the plantation and recent status as blacksmith had made him bold—dangerously bold.

"Aunt Pauline," he said, "this Massa Richard, what can he do to me? We belong to Colonel Cannon, not him. I want to sleep up next to the stables."

"You'll sleep right here. First thing you know, he'll have grabbed you and have you working on some levee."

"Why you always have to argue?" Milly said. "Just do what she says, just once—please? Remember what happened to you when you fought that white boy?"

Two years ago Luke had bloodied the nose of a boy from a neighboring plantation, and the overseer had come over with a gun. Miss Dorothy had had to do some powerful fast talking to stop him from getting killed. He definitely had Joe's temper. Pauline just hoped he never started drinking.

She put her hand on Luke's knee. "You'll do what I say. And you, young lady, just let me say one more time, keep your blouses pulled up on you and don't be wearing those red skirts."

Milly frowned. "But you're the one taught me to care about how I look. And when I do, you get mad and worry how the men will see me. It's not fair—Miss Dorothy's children dress any way they like."

"You ain't her daughter. That's the problem with you being around those white folks all day. You forget you're colored."

"You were raised the same way, Auntie—and look how you talk around them. And treat them. It's almost like Miss Dorothy was your sister. You run the whole house, and you the beautifulest woman on the plantation, ever. Even Miss Dorothy say that, and—"

"That's different. *She's* different. We played together as children, we been through so many things together . . ." She looked from Luke's face to Milly's. She saw the confusion on their young faces and realized they were right, it didn't make sense. She liked how they made her think about things in a different way. But not right now.

"Both of you, listen to me. These will be some of the most dangerous days in your lives. White folks know the end is near—they're mad enough about it to chew up nails and spit out rust. Don't you see what their faces are like when these soldiers come riding through here?"

"Like they looking in our eyes trying to see what we thinking. See if we want to be free, right?"

"That's it, Luke. We've been their property, and they're losing. It's like somebody losing gold. They're going to fight for it."

Luke came over and sat down on the dirt floor between her knees. "You think all this freedom coming mean we ever going to see Mama and Daddy again?"

Milly's face lit up.

"Things are changing so fast," Pauline said. "Runaways coming through here every day, white soldiers leaving their army . . . But I don't know."

"Maybe?"

"It's time for bed. You all keep praying, the Lord might just send them here to you. No way of knowing. One thing I do know—last I heard, your mother was still over at Clifton."

❖   ❖   ❖   ❖   ❖   ❖   ❖   ❖   ❖   ❖   ❖

She spent the next day in the cabin, reading parts of the Old Testament that she loved so well—stories about Ruth and David, the Psalms, and especially the Songs of Songs. She checked every so often to see that Luke and Milly were staying close to the cabin.

"Don't go up by the big house," she'd told them. "But you can visit your friends down here if you want."

At nightfall, she went with them down to the fire where the other slaves were cooking their evening meal. A little food, a few songs, and it was time for Luke and Milly to go to bed. Pauline stayed by the fire and talked for a while. Living up in the big house, she sometimes didn't get to know much about what was happening on the farm, how things were for the rest of them.

"Ain't seen you down here in ages," said a jet-black man with a scar down the right side of his face.

Pauline smiled. She had felt his eyes on her all evening. "I've been real busy. It's a huge house and most of the help is gone. How come you're still around, Woodson? I'd of thought those press gangs would get a man like you the first time around."

"Ain't because they didn't try, that's for sure." His laugh was rich and powerful, seemed to match up with his strong-muscled arms and broad shoulders. "I reckon I be a little too swift for them. Me and my sidekicks, we can smell the grayboys a mile off."

"For a big man, you sure are fast. But one day they might catch you, and Miss won't be able to protect you. Every week she get another order telling her to send men to the army. But she won't do it."

"I reckon we'll have to take our chances. One day I just might run away up into the swamps and stay. They's plenty of colored folks hiding out up there. They got guns, too."

"What are they saying? What have you heard?"

"White folks leaving. Going every which way. Them Yankees, they done taken most of the land along the river, burned down the big houses and stole everything out of them. Won't be long afore they be coming this way, burn down Miss Dorothy's house."

"She's been mighty good to all of us."

"Don't matter. Yankees burn down everybody—the good with the bad. Like the Book say, the just and the unjust." He poked a stick into the embers of the fire. "I'm thinking you and those two children might want to be going off to the woods with me if trouble comes. Them Yankees, they frees the niggers but they makes free with colored women. And you mighty fine-looking, you know. You *and* the girl."

Woodson was a good man, strong and smart and fearless. He'd been after her for years to be his wife. She always said she had enough on her hands raising the children and running the big house, but that wasn't the reason she kept saying no to him.

No, the truth was she somehow still felt herself connected to Massa Richard, bad as it made her feel at times.

She took hold of Woodson's hand. "That's mighty kind of you, to be always thinking about us. I'll keep what you say in mind."

He kissed her gently on the lips. "Even if I didn't love you, I'd want to keep you safe. You're a woman ought to be kept safe. It's time you were."

❖   ❖   ❖   ❖   ❖   ❖   ❖   ❖   ❖   ❖   ❖

Major Richard Kenworthy spurred his horse and galloped ahead of the five men riding with him. He hadn't realized until he was on the path to his sister's plantation how eager he was to see her, how much he'd missed her. And Pauline. He dismounted, tossed his reins to the trooper behind him, and sent them all down to the stables to water and feed the horses.

"Come on back up for dinner," he said. "You can eat out on the back porch."

He wasn't halfway up the stairs before Dorothy ran down with her arms outstretched.

"Oh, it's been such a *long* time." She looked up into his face. "You seem . . . goodness, I don't know what. I might not have recognized my big brother if I hadn't known you were coming."

He linked her arm in his. "Am I so different?"

"Just older—I think."

"Years and years, the way it feels. A lot's happened since . . . can you have somebody get some food together for my men?"

She looked over his shoulder at the men leading their horses down to the stable.

"Lottie will take care of them," she said.

Lottie? Not Pauline?

"I've put out some clean clothes of the colonel's for you. Come on in and let's get you settled."

When he had washed and changed, he said hello to his nieces, made them blush and giggle and delighted them with some Yankee chocolate. Dorothy was waiting for him on the front porch with refreshments, lemonade for her, a tumbler of bourbon for him.

God, but it was good to sit here in the quiet. He stretched his long legs out, felt himself beginning to loosen up. His sister knew to give him time, and it wasn't long before he was telling her about how Sue and the children had left Clifton and were now more or less safe up at Meridian, where Drayton, Zenobia, and a few others were staying with them.

"But what will happen to Clifton without someone to look after it?" said Dorothy.

The major looked deep down into his glass. "Nothing left to happen to Clifton, sis. The Yankees already passed through."

"And?"

He stood up and sat down on the porch railing facing his sister. "I haven't seen it yet, but I've been told that it's pretty bad . . ."

"Oh, Richard. *How* bad?"

He put the glass down on the railing. "Everything's gone. The bastards destroyed everything. All that clearing away of the brush, all those days at the cotton gin, all that trying to buy the best nigras we could . . . When I think how we took care of them, fed them, stayed up all night and nursed them when they were sick—all that's wasted effort. It don't mean a damn thing."

"Oh, I do hope that nothing happened to that little picture of the brook with the deer drinking from it. That was Mama's favorite."

"I honestly don't know, Dorothy. I'm just thankful she didn't live to see this." He picked up his glass and took a deep swallow. "How's Winston? What do you hear from him?"

"Not a thing for six months now. What with the Yankees on the Mississippi, very little mail comes through. As far as I know, he's still fighting with Jubal Early over in Virginia. *Why*, I don't know. Seems to me he should be here, what with the Yankees so close to overrunning us. Oh, Richard, what can I possibly do if . . ."

He got off the railing, bent over and took her hand. "Well, we do need to talk about what you should do. But right now let's go get some of whatever it is that smells so good."

❁   ❁   ❁   ❁   ❁   ❁   ❁   ❁   ❁   ❁   ❁

Close to ten o'clock, with his men bedded down except for a sentry posted in front of the house against the possibility of some Yankee raiding party, Dorothy offered her brother a glass of cognac.

"I don't know if I should . . ." His head was buzzing from all the wine and whiskey he'd drunk, but he took a sip.

"Better you should drink it than the Yankees," she said. "I've heard they drink as much as they can, then give it to the field niggers so they'll go crazy and rape some white women."

"A lot of what you hear isn't true. Them Yankees don't like the nigras much more than we do—I'd say they would shoot a darky if they caught him trying to rape one of our women. Now, the colored women, that's another story." He shook his head. "Enough of all this gruesome talk. How do you propose to survive if the Yankees come by here, which they surely will soon? I wish you'd take the children and leave. Head on over to Texas till we drive the Yankees out."

No point in telling her the war was finished, it was just a matter of time before the Confederacy fell.

"I'm not letting any Yankees drive me from this land," Dorothy said. "Winston will be coming home, and when he gets here I'll be waiting for him. Me and the children. They miss him something terrible."

Lottie came in to clear away the remaining dishes. Where was Dorothy hiding Pauline? She had to know that was why he'd come.

"What about you?" Dorothy said. "Where are you and those men off to now?"

"We're heading up north in the morning. I've been assigned to General Forrest's cavalry, up in Tennessee."

"That Memphis slave trader, that *common* little man."

"There's not a Yankee general living can outsmart him or outfight him, believe me."

She walked over to him, sat down, and took his right hand in hers. "Richard, what's this war doing to you?"

For a moment he saw her perched shakily in the swing, when they were children—when he was the one doing the comforting. Hold on tight to the ropes and I'll push you just a little bit. If you get scared, just yell and I'll stop. You'll see, you can swing so high up some day your feet might even touch the sky . . .

It was getting late. He took his hand back.

"I haven't seen Pauline," Richard said. "Or Joe's boy and girl—they must be pretty big by now. Did you know that ungrateful boy is fighting for the Yankees now? I'm going to fix him good when I catch him."

He read the look his sister gave him. She was remembering how Joe had beaten him at lots of things when they were children together at

Clifton—from wrestling to skipping rocks on the river to telling which birds were making what sounds. But this time it would be different—he was a crack marksman now and an acknowledged master of the cavalry saber, reknowned among his fellow Confederate horse soldiers for his ferocity and bravery in battle.

She picked up a teacup Lottie had overlooked. "Help's getting awful sloppy these days."

"Pauline isn't sloppy," he said as he followed her into the kitchen. "Where is she? Where are Luke and Milly?"

She didn't answer right away, and when he saw her face he knew she was about to tell him a lie.

"I hired them out," she said. "They're at another plantation, about two days from here, close to the Texas border."

He went back into the salon and replenished his snifter.

"I want to see Pauline," he said. "You going to get her, or do I have to find her myself?"

"What about Sue? What about your own children? Do you ever stop to think—"

"I didn't ask for a sermon, I just want to know where Pauline is."

She stood looking at him. Not a word, not a gesture. He picked up his hat with the crossed swords, buckled on his revolver, and walked out to his lookout sentry.

"Think I'll have me a look around down by the niggers' quarters, " he said, loud enough for his sister to hear.

    ✿   ✿   ✿   ✿   ✿   ✿   ✿   ✿   ✿   ✿   ✿

He pounded on the door of the first cabin he got to.

"Yassuh?" An old man's voice.

"Where's Pauline?"

"She gone this morning."

"Where was she staying?"

He pointed to the hut next door and Richard walked right in. A boy and girl lay sleeping on the pallets. He'd impress Joe's kid Luke, put him to work in the regiment. And the girl, Milly—she'd been a pretty little thing when he last saw her. Not so little now.

"Get up and get outside where I can see you."

The two obeyed.

"Shit, you ain't Joe's kids. Where are they?"

"We don't know, Massa. All we know is, they gone."

He went back up to the big house to Dorothy. "If they're really gone, do you know that makes them fair game for anybody?"

"They've got passes."

He laid his hands gently on her shoulders.

"Sis, I love you too much to dispute with you tonight." He kissed her on her forehead. "I reckon it'll be better if I sleep down in the stables with my men—we have to be out of here at first light."

"You'll take care of yourself? I think it's near the end, Richard. That makes it more dangerous than ever."

"I'll be as careful as I can." He hugged her, started off, then turned back. "When you see Pauline, tell her I love her. And that the world isn't wide enough for her to get away from me."

   ✣   ✣   ✣   ✣   ✣   ✣   ✣   ✣   ✣   ✣

He was halfway down to the stables when he saw Sergeant Barclay with his Colt out, pushing a young darky ahead of him.

"Look what we found sleeping in a stall, sir. A good strong boy—we could use him."

"Bring him closer." The major's face broke into a grin. "Well, I'll be damned if it ain't young Luke. Why, you're the spitting image of that father of yours."

The boy stared him straight in the eyes.

"Looks like you got his sass and spunk, too." He turned to Barclay. "Take him back to the stables, bind and gag him—we're taking him out of here with us in the morning. Don't want no fuss from my sister about it."

"Miss Dorothy! *Help!* They—"

The sergeant slugged him with the revolver, tossed him over his shoulder, and hurried off.

Hell, they'd have to keep Luke bound and gagged. Get nothing out of him about Pauline.

The door of the big house opened.

"Richard?" Dorothy was silhouetted in the doorway. "What's going on out there?"

"Nothing, sis, just some varmint noises. Go on to bed, get yourself a full night's sleep. Wish I could."

Two days later, after Woodson had scouted the plantation, Pauline and Milly came back.

"Where's Luke?" Pauline said the minute she saw Miss. "When we went to get him and Milly to run off in the swamps, he was gone. Woodson wanted to sneak up toward the big house to see if he could find him, but I wouldn't let him."

Miss walked up to Pauline and hugged her. "You must be strong, Pauline. He's gone. With the Confederates."

Pauline took a step back. "Gone?"

"One of the troopers found him sleeping in the stables. Richard impressed him."

Pauline wanted to scream. And if she'd had Luke in front of her, she didn't know what she'd have done to him. Milly began to cry. Pauline put her arms around her.

"He was like a son to me, too—you know that," Miss said. "The war's done things to Richard. Made him meaner. I never would have thought that he'd abduct a child behind my back. I didn't even know about it till after they were gone. Just wait till the colonel hears. Stealing a slave off his own brother-in-law's property."

"If only he'd listened to me," Pauline said softly.

✿   ✿   ✿   ✿   ✿   ✿   ✿   ✿   ✿   ✿   ✿

After she finally got Milly settled for the night, Pauline went into the living room where Miss sat drinking a cup of tea.

"Oh, Pauline, I don't know when all this evil will cease. God seems to have taken a dislike to folks in these parts, black and white. I just feel so helpless before it all." She brushed her hair back with her hand. "There's one good thing—and only one—that's come out of all this."

How could she say such a thing? What was good about losing Luke?

"Joe's alive, Pauline. Alive and fighting with the Yankees. Richard told me so."

For an instant, Pauline's spirits soared. Then, like a dark cloud covering the sun, she thought of Luke, a boy condemned to face all the hardships and brutalities a war could bring. Who knew what would happen to him now that he was riding with people famous for their cruelty to colored folks? And with Richard, who had more reasons than the color of his skin to hate him?

CHAPTER FIVE

THE Yazoo River meanders its way from a point up above Greenwood, Mississippi, through Yazoo City, down past Haynes Bluff, and into the Mississippi at Vicksburg. In February of 1864, Joe Duckett and a detachment of the Third Cavalry were aboard the paddle-wheel transport *Mirabelle P,* in the midst of a flotilla steaming up the Yazoo from Vicksburg to raid the upriver plantations, carry off their slaves, and enlist the men into the army.

Joe stood concealed behind one of the cotton bales that lined the deck to protect the troops. There were Reb sharpshooters hiding up there in the pine trees and rocks on the eastern bank of the Yazoo, firing at anything they could get a bead on. Joe's eyes continually scanned the bluffs, his carbine at the ready. He hoped to get him one of those boys before the day was out.

The Rebs' treatment of the flotilla on this the third day of the expedition had been pure torment. In addition to the sharpshooters, they had a couple of light fieldpieces high up on a cliff. They'd let the escorting gunboats, their stacks belching black smoke, sail by unmolested, then as soon as the gunboats were too far up the river to put down a suppressing fire, the artillery opened up on the troop transports. Sneaky bastards. Withdrew soon as the Yankees put a small landing party ashore to destroy the batteries, then led them on until they ran smack up against a Confederate force that drove them clear back to the river.

Now Joe's transport lay anchored on the west bank of the Yazoo, just out of range of the punishing artillery fire from the Reb batteries again mounted on the hilltop. One thing was for sure; they'd need a lot more troops to push those guns inland, out of range of the river, if they were going to reach Yazoo City and move out into the countryside.

So when Captain Stiles walked over to him, he had a pretty good idea why.

"You're going back, Joe—we need help sent up from Vicksburg. If you and Zack can get through to General McArthur there and tell him what we're up against, he'll send the rest of the regiment here."

Joe nodded. The captain didn't need to tell him how dangerous their position was. Give the Rebs a few more hours and they'd either figure out how they could position those batteries so as to blow the transports to bits or bring up bigger guns with enough range to reach the ships. As it was, the troopships couldn't advance up or down the river without being destroyed.

"Same uniform as last time," Stiles said. "and two separate sets of dispatches sewn into your pockets. And lay off the booze should any come your way. The whole outfit's counting on you. That's General Ross's cavalry over there—might near as good as Forrest's."

Joe saluted, then went in search of Zack. The two of them changed from their blue uniforms into ragged plantation clothes.

"Sarge, we taking bets on what kind of hoodoo you going to put on them Rebs tonight, " one of the men said. "You turning invisible or you fixing to fly over them?"

"He's put his money on you going to make it in under nine hours," another man said. "Me, I reckon more. Maybe twelve, thirteen hours. Any longer than that, and it's our asses anyhow."

Zack laughed. "Joe going to throw a haunt on them bastards, freeze 'em good. They going to see us, good as you all seeing us now, but when they go and try to shoot us, they going to be frozen. He be throwing the haunt on them, you watch and see."

"Ten hours," Joe said. "No more. Ain't but sixty miles to Vicksburg." He looked at Donald, the troop gamble boss. "Put ten dollars on me—I pay you when I get back."

"But, Sarge—"

"When I get back."

They started off to the colonel to get the dispatches secured into their clothing. Behind them Joe heard the men's voices.

"Three dollars on eleven hours."

"Dollar on thirteen hours."

"But suppose—"

"Suppose, nothing. He the Wizard."

❋   ❋   ❋   ❋   ❋   ❋   ❋   ❋   ❋   ❋   ❋

An hour later, when dark had fallen over the Yazoo, Joe and Zack dropped down into a skiff commanded by a midshipman and rowed by four sailors. The oars were muffled with rags; the only sound to be heard was water dripping off an oar when it came out of the water. The men stroked softly, letting the boat drift down the river a bit before trying to make it over to the other side. They knew Reb cavalry on the east side of the Yazoo was thicker than flies on a cow carcass and just dying to get some colored troops to kill. The Texans didn't take black prisoners.

The skiff floated down the river for a mile or so. Then the midshipman poked one of the sailors, and they slowly headed for shore, toward a spot with overhanging pines. Didn't seem there'd be any horse cavalry down there, but if there was . . .

A few minutes later, Joe and Zack slipped ashore and dropped to the ground. It was just a little space, about three feet between the trunk of a big old tree and the water's edge. At least their Colts were dry. They stayed still, listening to see whether the Rebs had heard the landing.

After five minutes with nothing but the sound of the river running, Joe tapped Zack on the shoulder and they started up the bank toward the road that ran alongside the river. Joe motioned Zack to stay still and crawled up behind a big bush near the road to take a good look.

Damn. Up and down the road, every twenty-five yards or so, there was a Reb on a horse. He could get through by himself—God made him invisible. But Zack?

Have to find another way.

He crawled back to Zack and pointed downriver. Hugging the bank, sometimes moving through the water by pulling on low-slung branches, they crept down the side of the riverbank.

Now if he just didn't get himself bitten by a cottonmouth—

Wait a minute. Was that a culvert? Sure enough, going right under the road—right under that Reb picket. Sure to be slimy, and there wouldn't be nothing to hold on to. But the boys on the transport needed help, so there wasn't nothing for it but to crawl in.

It stank something awful. And just like he thought, it was slick with slime. Worst of all, it had barnacles all over it that cut their hands and knees. They kept crawling all the same, didn't slow down, and in a minute Joe was through and out on the other side of the road, Zack right beside him.

"Whoa, Star," came a deep voice. "Something got you spooked?"

Joe and Zack froze.

They were in a pile of rushes on the other side of the culvert, nothing in front of them but swampland and levees. Joe heard the man get off his horse, probably to take it down to a tree and tie it up.

Just enough time.

He felt around till he found a rock, stood up quick, and threw it on the other side of the culvert, into the Yazoo. As the Reb hustled across the road and down the riverbank, Joe and Zack cut off into the swamps. Over fifty miles to go—they needed to get them some horses. The colonel had promised them twenty-four-hours' leave if they made it, even put it in the orders. And that would give Joe a chance to do something important he had to do in Vicksburg.

After walking an hour through the swamps, they came to level ground and spied a good-sized log cabin sitting way out there in the woods. There were lights on inside, and they could hear what sounded like singing.

Joe cupped his hand over his ear to hear better.

> *"She's the sweetest rose of color*
> *This soldier ever knew.*
> *Her eyes are bright as diamonds . . ."*

They were men's voices, raised in that pretty song them Texans sang all the time. The words got more distinct as Joe and Zack crept up closer to the house.

> *"Where the Rio Grande is flowing*
> *And the starry skies are bright,*

She walks along the river
In the quiet summer night.
She thinks, if I remember,
When we parted long ago,
I promised to come back again
And not to leave her so."

One man's beautiful voice rang through the chill night air clear and pure as a church bell on a bright Sunday morning. For a few seconds there, Joe nearly forgot what he was there for.

When they were about fifty paces from the house, Joe took out his revolver. "I'm going down there and take a look, be back in a minute."

"Let me go," Zack said. "You always taking all the chances."

He was right. About time he started letting Zack take some responsibilty.

"Go ahead, but be careful. I give you ten minutes to get back."

Zack disappeared into the darkness.

With nothing to do but wait, Joe realized he was shivering from the cold, and his hands hurt from the barnacles on the culvert. A shot of bourbon would be good along about now. He wished to hell he hadn't minded the captain and had brought his flask. Them fellows down at the house sure were having themselves a good time. There were sure to be some horses down there. And some bourbon, what with all that racket coming from the house.

What was taking Zack so long? Should gone himself.

The singing made him think of Zenobia, the songs she loved, like "It's a Good Time in Heaven, Don't You Want to Go?" That was one singing woman. And she couldn't be more than thirty miles away. Maybe she'd had some word of Luke and Milly by now. Maybe. . . . his heart got heavy.

The music from the house stopped. The loud talk died down, then there was silence.

Joe waited another five minutes. No Zack.

Should he go on? Leave Zack and take the chance of finding horses somewhere else? That would be the wise course of action. The Third Cavalry needed help.

But there'd been no shots fired, so Zack was still alive. He could think all he wanted, but there was no way he was going to leave his buddy there. And there wasn't no Reb in this world could capture Joe Duckett. Not while his ancestors watched over him.

He took out his Colt, twirled the cylinder to make sure all six loads were in place, and crept off toward the house, darting from bush to bush until finally he vaulted over a low fence. Tied up at the railing were four of the prettiest horses he had ever laid eyes on, sawed-off shotguns all tucked in their scabbards.

There was a lot of shouting coming from inside the house.

Joe crept up to a window and saw seven or eight women, none of them what you'd call all the way dressed. And he saw Zack.

He was sitting on a table surrounded by four Rebs. The biggest, with gray whiskers and a Union forage cap cocked sideways on his head, had a pistol under Zack's jaw. His left hand held Zack's chin in a claw grip. The three other men, their pistols holstered, were laughing. One of them had a half-empty bottle of whiskey in one hand and an old banjo in the other.

Most of the women had their skirts hiked up and plenty of white flesh spilling out of their bodices. Some stood near the table Zack was sitting on, others sprawled on a couch, and one was in a chair, her legs spread wide open. All of their faces were flushed with excitement and whatever they'd been drinking.

Well, you didn't have to be as smart as Joe to figure out what had happened. All that confounded fool sidekick of his had had to do was get close to the house to see the men and count their horses. Instead he'd looked in, seen all the fun, stared at those pretty women with their hair flowing all down their backs. And got caught. Probably them Rebs didn't know they had a Yankee soldier, thought they had a peeping-Tom nigger.

Hell, he ought to leave him right there. Serve him right if he waited another half-hour just to let him sweat, which he surely would do when they stopped laughing and drinking in there and pulled out their Bowie knives to cut off his dick and balls.

But there wasn't time for no more fooling around. Those boys back up on the Yazoo . . .

Joe went over to one of the horses and drew a shotgun from its sheath. He quieted the nervous horse, reached into the ammunition pouch, and loaded the gun's double barrel.

It was, he had reason to know, a weapon deadlier than it looked. A wild-riding secesh had once cut down half a squad of Joe's men with one.

Pistol in one hand, shotgun in the other, he crept around to the front of the house.

Now.

He took a deep breath and kicked the door open.

For a few seconds after he burst in scarcely anything moved in the log-walled room with its flickering wick lamps and roaring fire. The sound of the banjo hitting the floor with clanging strings and a loud thump seemed to bring everybody to life. The women tried to cover themselves, and one man's hand moved halfheartedly toward his holster. Another stood staring, with his mouth wide open and his hands high in the air.

"It's another one! Where'd all these damn niggers come from?"

Somewhere in all the racket Zack called his name. But Joe, his thumb on the hammer of the Colt, his finger tight on its trigger, was watching the man with the Union forage cap. He hadn't fully lowered his revolver yet. Any second now, he would chance turning that pretty double-action Adams revolver of his, of which there were very few in existence, on Joe.

He never got that chance. Joe blew his head apart with a snap shot from his Colt and aimed the shotgun at the other men. The one whose hand had been edging toward his holster raised both hands in the air quick.

"Don't shoot!"

"Sergeant Joe Duckett, Third United States Colored Cavalry at your service, ladies. Please join them gentlemens over in that corner!" A wave of the revolver accompanied the invitation.

"Corporal Zack Bascom!"

"Joe—"

"Relieve them secesh of their sidearms!"

Zack took the three men's Colts from their holsters and wrapped them in a blue shawl that belonged to one of the women. In seconds the men were lined up with their hands against the wall. One of them twisted his head around to look at Joe.

"Keep your eyes on that wall," Joe said. "You done surrendered your weapons without a fight and give Uncle Sam's army them pretty horses and those sweet shooting shotguns. Whoeeee! They going to put all your asses in the pioneers corps when you get back to camp—that is, if you lives to see camp."

"Why, you low-down stinking polecat of a field nigger, ain't no way you going to get through our patrols. What you going to do with us? "

"Find me a way of teaching you not to call colored folks niggers for one thing."

Using the revolver, he fired a shot that whizzed past the man's right ear and shattered a windowpane next to him.

"Don't! I got kids, I—"

"Nobody else got 'em, right?"

Zack had taken his own Colt from its holster in his trousers. "Joe, I'm sorry—"

"Get them men down on the ground and tie their wrists behind."

When they were secured to Joe's satisfaction, he turned to the women. Five of them were now hunched together on the couch, the other two sitting on the floor in front of it. They had buttoned themselves back up properly, though a bosom or two was having a time of it trying to stay in.

"What you going to do with us?" one of them asked. She had long curly dark hair and a steady gaze. Couldn't be much over twenty.

"Not what you thinking, little miss. I swear you not much older than my Milly. Ain't you ashamed of yourselves, carrying on here like you ain't been raised right?"

"Joe!" Zack said. "We got to move."

One of the soldiers glared at Joe. "Nigger, you lay a finger on them and you'll burn in hell's own fires, so help me God!"

Shit, they'd never learn. Joe drew out his Choctaw knife, walked over to the soldier, and traced the knife's razor-sharp blade across the side of the man's throat, just barely drawing blood.

"No more talk, hear?" He turned to face the young woman. "You, miss, what's your name?"

"Lydia."

"I intends no harm to you, but you all got to be secured so's we can be on our way."

The woman gave him a long look.

"I'll see to it," she said finally. "Jessica, give me a hand tying the others.

When we're done, this nigra . . ." She looked at Joe's tattered shirt. "This sergeant can tie our hands up, too."

Ten minutes later, Joe and Zack were ready to leave.

Joe walked over to the man who'd said he had children, bent down, and cut the thongs binding his wrists.

"You a big family fellow," he said, pushing the man ahead of him and towards the door. "What's the names of your chilluns?"

The man hesitated, then said, "Two girls, Mary Ann and Portia. And, three boys—Tom, Lionel, and Crew."

Joe nudged him out the door with the barrel of his newly acquired Adams revolver and yelled over to Zack, who stood holding the horses' reins.

"Keep a gun on this Reb, I got me one more thing to do."

"Aw, Joe, you ain't going back in there, is you?"

"Just be a minute."

He walked back into the cabin, and over to the two prone Rebs. "Ain't it a mite hot in here for you boys? With all them things you got on, you might be tempted to take a walk outside or something stupid like that."

He rolled them both over and proceeded to pull their trousers off. The women tittered, and Joe had to admit the Rebs were a sight in their dirty long white underwear with plenty of holes to show off their skinny knobby legs.

It was too much for the man who'd already told Joe that he would burn in hell.

"If I ever see your black ass again, I'll burn you to gray."

Joe gave him a sweet smile. "That's all right, one good turn deserve another. Right now, I'm going to burn these trousers and boots of yours in this here fireplace. When they put you out working on those roads in them swamps with them pioneers, you going to be in bad shape." He tossed the clothes into the fire, then picked up the banjo. "You knows how us darkies just love to strum and strut. And you'd look like hell strumming in them nasty old britches of yours, so I don't reckon you'll be needing this no more tonight." His eye fell on the bottle of bourbon. "This, neither."

He took a good deep satisfying swig, corked the bottle, and doffed his hat to all.

"I bids you all a good night."

    ⁜   ⁜   ⁜   ⁜   ⁜   ⁜   ⁜   ⁜   ⁜   ⁜

He stowed the banjo and whiskey in a saddlebag and turned to the Reb Zack was holding a Colt on.

"What your name, man?"

"Andy."

"Do what I say and you lives to see Mary Ann and Portia. Otherwise . . ." Joe laid the six- inch barrel of the Adams in the palm of his hand and kissed it. "Got it?"

The Reb nodded.

"Thought you would. You looks like a right smart man to me, the kind of man what values his life. We sees anybody, you going to give them a good story about what we doing with you. We make five miles to them good roads over past Satartia, then I let you go, so you can see . . . what the name of your wife? Don't recall you told me."

"Felicia."

"So you can see sweet Miss Felicia and lie in a warm bed with her one more time. Don't that sound good now?" He turned to Zack. "Take the reins of the extra horse and I'll keep my gun on our secesh friend here. Looky here, Andy—see? It's right under this saddle blanket. Let's go now. At a fast trot."

They moved out into the dark night.

About two miles down the road Joe signaled for them to halt.

> *Gave her my promise true*
> *Which ne'er forgot will be . . .*

The voices of the men were ragged, and they were messing up the song. Must have been about a half-mile away. Joe looked back. Andy, sitting straight up like a natural-born horse soldier in the saddle, seemed to be thinking up a storm. Zack, on the horse behind him, had a worried frown on his face. Served him right. Hell, if he'd done the right thing in the first place, they'd be past Satartia and on the way to Vicksburg and winning that ten-dollar bet now. Last time, the pool had been a hundred and fifty dollars!

"And for Bonnie Annie Laurie"

Closer now . . .

"I'd lay me doon and dee."

Joe dropped back beside his prisoner. "Remember Felicia, now."

"Don't you worry none, this pilgrim wants shet of you."

Joe could just make out four riders approaching. Not on patrol, for they loudly hailed Joe's prisoner when they got closer.

"Andy, you going the wrong way—we was just coming down to the shindig . . . Hey, what you doing with these two niggers?"

Joe hoped Zack had followed orders this time and had the men covered.

Slowly he edged his horse sideways to the road, never taking his gun off Andy. If he gave them away, Joe would kill him and escape down the road soon as Zack got the others. None of which were paying the least attention to him or Zack.

"Well, boys," Andy said, "these two niggers . . ." He turned and glanced at Joe, then back at his friend. "These two niggers are the best damn buck and wing dancers you ever did see. And that one there"—he pointed at Joe—"he can play that banjo in his saddlebag up a storm. They tell me there's a few more of 'em on a little plantation down the road can come play for us if we ask their missus' permission. That's where we're on our way to now—some of them pretty gals we got down there are just crazy for music."

Joe was glad the Reb couldn't see his grin. Why, that man deserved a place in liar's heaven, bless his seceding soul!

"How many gals?"

"One for each of us. And guess who's waiting for you?"

"Lydia! It's Lydia, ain't it?"

"And she done put on a white dress for you. What there is of it."

"Times a'wasting. Andy, we'll try to keep the girls busy till you get back." The Reb spurred his horse and they were off.

"Save some whiskey for me!" Andy yelled after them.

Joe rode up with his grin still in place. "Andy, you a mighty fine liar, must of had you a whole lot of practice."

Andy sat up even straighter on his horse. "See how good you'd lie if you had some crazy fool nig—crazy fool soldier ready to kill you dead."

Two miles down the road, Joe set him afoot. "We going to leave you here."

"I'm free now?"

"Like I said."

Joe reached down into the saddlebag, pulled out the whiskey bottle, and uncorked it.

"Here, take you a good swig or two, it may be a while afore your boys come back for you, and it getting cold out here."

Andy took a couple of swallows, then handed the bottle back to Joe, who offered it to Zack and then took a couple of good belts himself.

Andy was no more than a few steps down the road before he looked back.

"Thanks, Sarge, you one heap of man for a nigger!"

Joe returned his wave, which was close to a salute.

   ✿   ✿   ✿   ✿   ✿   ✿   ✿   ✿   ✿   ✿   ✿

Using the back roads and cutting across plantations slowed them down, but they galloped into McArthur's camp exactly ten hours and ten minutes after they'd left. Joe's pocket was already getting warm from the money he knew he'd won. He wondered how many other boys had put their money on ten hours, too.

Soon they were in front of McArthur's tent, and Joe was explaining the situation up there on the Yazoo.

"Go get cleaned up and take your twenty-four-hour liberty," the general said when Joe finished. "You've earned it. And the four horses are a god-send."

   ✿   ✿   ✿   ✿   ✿   ✿   ✿   ✿   ✿   ✿   ✿

Late afternoon found Joe sitting on a park bench close to the courthouse building, high up in Vicksburg, looking out over the Mississippi River toward the Louisiana shore a half-mile away. What must General Grant have felt when he stood on one of these hills overlooking the great river and thought about the ten thousand men it had cost them to take this fortress city?

Earlier that day, walking through the town in his blue uniform with its bright brass buttons, Joe had been struck by the destruction the war had wrought. No matter where you looked, you saw houses with windows and doors blown away or living rooms exposed to the open air because their roofs had collapsed on them.

He couldn't stop thinking about what a beautiful place Vicksburg had been when he used to come down here with Massa Kenworthy before the war. City of a Hundred Hills, they called it. Well, the Union gunboats with their huge pulverizing mortars and the massed ranks of artillery batteries up there in the hills above the city hadn't left a yard of ground untouched. The general had called thunder and lightning down upon the Rebs' citadel.

Joe took one last look at the sky, red tinged by the setting sun. Seemed like every time there was no action, every time there were no Rebels to kill or outsmart, he got sad and started thinking about Zenobia, Luke, Milly, and Cally. Had to be some way he could find them, save them—put his family back together again, be a proper daddy and all.

He smiled to himself and remembered the time when he'd taken Luke down to the blacksmith hearth and let him pump the bellows for a while, seen the delight in the little seven-year-old's eyes as the flames leapt up and flickered in brilliant colored tongues of red, yellow, and white. He'd let Luke stick a litttle iron rod in the hearth and leave it there until it had turned almost white from the heat, then put it on the anvil and let the boy pound away at it with a small hammer until he'd formed a hook in the end of it. Then he had shouted with joy along with Luke when the boy plunged the fiery rod into the water bucket and the steam hissed up into their happy faces. Later that day, he'd trailed along behind Luke as he ran to show Zenobia the new fireplace poker that he'd made as a present for her on her birthday. "See, Momma,what Daddy helped me make for you?" Zenobia had swept both of them into her arms. "My mens!"

He got up from the bench and headed down the steep, winding streets toward the little riverfront place where he was supposed to meet Zack. Not much of his leave left, considering that he had to be back at nine in the morning. So far it had been a real bust. They'd slept half their leave away, then took off in separate directions, Zack to see some friends and Joe to a refugee camp to seek out information about his family.

At the camp, old Brother Caleb told him how Zenobia hadn't shown up on the night of the planned escape. "But, you know, it's a funny thing how

God do work. The patrollers caught all of us three days after our escape, shot three of the mens and took off the women in chains. I's the only one made it through. And you sees what it's like here." A sweep of his arm took in broken-down shacks, mud puddles, and children running around in ragged shirts and torn britches.

"Every day we losing a dozen or more folks to dysentery, " the old preacher man said. "Seem like with all these folk together, disease just jump from one to the other, old devil light on one, get strong, look around and say, 'I sees me another one over there,' then go put the death clamp on them."

"But what you doing to try and keep yourself strong?" Joe said. "You looking mighty poorly, Brother Caleb."

"I got work to do here," he said, with a nod toward the bucket of sand he'd been carrying to the sanitary pits on the edge of the camp. "I'll look after my flock long as my strength hold out.

"You see, son, no matter how bad things get, the good Lord don't ever put more on us than we can bear. He grant his chillun a daily portion of health and strength sufficient to their need." He stopped and put his arm around Joe's shoulder. "The Bible say we shall mount up on wings like eagles, run and not get weary. Don't you ever forget that."

Joe took the bucket from him. "Let me give you a hand, I ain't got nothing else to do for now."

"Ain't changed one bit, have you, boy? The Lord's going to bless you real good, but I don't want you spending your little bit of time off here. No, you young still. Go on out and have you a good time."

"I'll finish helping you with that pile of sand, then I'll be on my way."

"Brother Caleb! Didn't I tell you about carrying them heavy pails? Thank goodness that nice sergeant took it from you."

The low musical voice belonged to a good-looking brown-skinned woman somewhere in her twenties, in the blue uniform with the special green markings of the Medical Department. Even the heavy jacket couldn't hide the shape of a fine body. Her eyes were big and slanted, her features sharp and distinct. Those high cheekbones and that tinge of bronze in her skin meant Indian blood, Joe would have bet on it. She walked proudly, her head thrown back, and beneath her fatigue cap he could see that she wore her hair twisted in braids.

She came abreast of the men and completed her conquest with a smile aimed at Joe. "I'm Nurse Betty Ransome, on loan from the field hospital."

"And I is Sergeant Duckett, now of the Third Cavalry but once from the Kenworthy Clifton plantation, up near where Brother Caleb here come from."

Brother Caleb smiled. "He one hell of a man, but do mind his temper."

"And what brings you over here, Sergeant?"

Joe explained, but it was hard keeping his mind on looking for his family when she reached over and took his hand.

"I'm sorry," she said. "I didn't know—"

Her hand was warm, and, Lordy, but she was one fine-looking woman.

"Ain't no way you supposed to know, ma'am. We all got our troubles."

The three of them walked together to the latrine pits to empty the bucket, then went back to the sand pile. While the nurse and Brother Caleb talked, Joe carried bucket after bucket until he'd transferred the rest of the sand to the latrine area.

As he trod back and forth, a distance of about a quarter of a mile, he thought of various ways he could get Miss Betty Ransome to go out with him that night. He knew she liked him, could tell that from the way she'd looked him up and down when she first saw him. Best to just tell her he'd enjoy her company for the evening.

But when he got back from his last trip with the sand, Brother Caleb was standing there alone.

"A messenger done called her back to the hospital," he said before Joe could ask the question. "Would you like to pray with me for a minute before you leave?"

"I don't reckon it would hurt, considering what I got to go back to tomorrow."

They prayed together right there, in front of Brother Caleb's log hut, then Joe said good-bye and set off toward the river. If the place where he was meeting Zack turned out like the rest of his leave, he'd almost be glad to be back in camp come morning.

But Zack had been right. It was a nice place, a little one-room café that couldn't hold no more than maybe about thirty people. And up at the front of the room was a small band.

A colored man with a bandanna around his neck was playing away at his banjo, just plucking those strings, while a little boy, black as could be, beat with two sticks on a wooden tub turned upside down. Over him stood a yellow man, plucking away at one string stretched out on a long piece of wood. And there was a fiddler, too. They were making some nice music, especially when the string-plucker sang. He had a mighty good voice:

> *"Old master's gone away*
> *And the darkies stayed at home*
> *Must be now that the kingdom's come*
> *And the year for Jubilees.*
>
> *"Look up the road and see the cloud arising*
> *Look like we're gonna' have a storm*
> *Oh, no, you're mistaken,*
> *It's only the darkies' bayonets and buttons on*
> *   their uniforms*
>
> *"Darkies, did you see old master*
> *With the mustache on his face?*
> *Left here soon one morning*
> *Says he's going for to leave this place."*

Most everybody was laughing or trying to sing along with him, and by the time he'd put down two tumblers of whiskey, Joe was feeling mighty good himself.

"See, ain't us having a good time?" Zack was eating away at a plate of hot biscuits, chicken, greens, and baked beans. Joe had already finished one plate and was about to start in on another.

Next thing he knew, some women were dancing to the music. Just like that, they came into the room, and started moving their bodies. And one of them was sure enough Nurse Betty Ransome.

Well! Brother Caleb had said the Good Lord was going to bless him, and now look what He had done for him.

Body moving like it was a willow tree, with a soft breeze blowing it. No beginning, no end, just one part of her flowing into the next, smooth as a shimmering ripple in a quiet pond. Hands balled up into little fists, moving up and down to the sound of that music.

The man with the banjo saw her dancing and had to get up from his seat. Up and playing like the devil done took over his hands, up and down, trying to keep rhythm with that gal's body. He got behind her, Betty peeking over one shoulder, making sure he was there, and then the two of them were stepping perfect-like all around that room like they was one person.

Her brown skin was shiny, her braids a-flying, and her white blouse looked like it couldn't hold them titties.

Joe jumped up, moved the banjo player out of the way, and got behind her himself.

She peeked over her shoulder. "Sergeant Duckett?"

"And mighty happy to see you." Matching every step she made.

Every time she twisted that behind, he moved right with her. Next thing you know, she turned around and they were facing each other, banjo ringing and drums beating, and their bodies just swaying back and forth.

Folks made a circle around them and started dancing too, a roomful of men and women shuffling and moving and shaking their bodies round and round in a circle. Finally, Joe's legs gave out. He grabbed Betty's hand, led her over to his table, and sat her down beside him.

"When I got back to Brother Caleb and saw you was gone," he said. "it like to broke my heart."

She smiled. "Mine, too."

Still holding his hand, she rested her elbows on the table. So soft and tender was her touch that Joe felt dizzy. And no wonder. Her leg was right up against his thigh.

"Who you be, Joe?"

Joe briefly told her how he'd come to be in the Third Cavalry.

"And you the first black army nurse I ever seen. How come you to be here?"

She sighed. "We ain't got but so much time, I hate to use it up telling about me. And I'm hungry. Can I have some of your chicken and biscuits?"

Joe had lost all interest in the plate in front of him. She took one of his biscuits, buttered it, then looked at Joe and put it down.

"You might as well know . . ."

Turned out she had been born of a slave-owning Indian father and a black mother. But her father had raised her as if she were free-born and seen to it that she learned to read and write. When he died, his heirs, her blood half-brothers, sold her and her mother away, separating them. From then on her story was like hundreds of others—house slave, two children sold away, the war, escape, and now the army.

By the time she finished, the chicken was cold and Zack and his friend had long since departed. And Joe's hand was on her knee.

"I'm sure glad I met you," he said, "because I think you could stand a lot of care. I don't wants to brag none, but I thinks I be the man for you right now."

"I don't doubt that for a minute. And when you next get back to Vicksburg, we got a lot of talking to do." She kissed him on his cheek and started to get up. Joe glanced over at the table where her friends had been seated. They were gone.

"It's dangerous out there, you can't go home by yourself."

"Corporal Lewis over there, he's assigned to the hospital and he'll see me home. He'll take good care of me."

Joe's heart was doing flip flops. All this time she'd been talking to him, she hadn't said one word about no boyfriend. Not a peep out of her. And what kind of a soldier let his woman sit there all night with another man?

Betty sat back down. "Oh, Joe, you should see yourself, you look like you just lost your last friend on this earth. There ain't nothing between the corporal and me. That's his girlfriend over there, sitting across from him. He takes us both home when we come here."

Joe let out a long breath and laughed. "Tell you what. I'll pay the bill and you just go over there and tell him you got somebody else to do the honors tonight."

   ❖   ❖   ❖   ❖   ❖   ❖   ❖   ❖   ❖   ❖   ❖

As they walked through the rubble of Vicksburg, Joe began to hum a little tune about "Sally, that old sweet gal," and Betty hummed along with him and squeezed his hand tight. When they got to her place—just a little wooden shack behind one of the big old abandoned houses—she turned to him.

"It's way late—time for you to get back to camp and get you some sleep before you go back up the Yazoo. Besides, my place ain't fit to be seen by no first sergeant of the United States colored cavalry."

"I ain't the man to find fault with your place. I sure would like to lay my head down on your pillow tonight." Surely Zenobia would understand . . .

Betty hesitated so long he thought she was gathering up the words to say no. But then she took him by the hand and drew him into the little house. "You got such a pitiful look on your face, ain't no way I'm going to send you back to no Yazoo City looking like that!"

❖   ❖   ❖   ❖   ❖   ❖   ❖   ❖   ❖   ❖   ❖

Joe woke up the next morning to find Betty propped up on an elbow, look-ing down on him.

"You must of had some bad dreams last night," she said softly. "You was tossing and turning all night long, and once you yelled out something about blood on your hand."

"What time is it?"

"You got about fifteen–twenty minutes before you got to go back."

"That's just about enough time—"

She laughed. "No, you 'bout wore me out last night. When you come back from Yazoo City."

Joe kissed her nipple. "You one sweet thing. And you made this poor soldier mighty happy."

"Least I can do for a man like you. You made me happy too. Hope you don't think—"

"Come closer to me I'll show you what I think." Joe pulled her tight against him.

"Didn't you say you had to be back by nine o'clock?"

"Hush." He kissed her and held her close. She was like the sweetest honey he'd ever tasted in his life. Zenobia was far away, and Betty was right here. And he had to go back to a war. But not *right* this minute.

❖   ❖   ❖   ❖   ❖   ❖   ❖   ❖   ❖   ❖   ❖

As a Reb bullet tore off the branch of a tree over his head, Captain Will Stiles was wishing Joe was up here with the unit instead of on temporary assignment briefing the gunboat captain in Yazoo City on currents and depths in the river. Hell, he'd been there ever since he got back up from

Vicksburg and collected that two-hundred-dollar pot. And Stiles needed him badly, because in front of him and his fifty-man reconnaisance squad, still partially concealed from the enemy by trees and rocks, was a whole damn army of Rebs—cavalry, artillery, and infantry. They weren't supposed to be out there, but there they were, regimental standards flying, not more than three quarters of a mile away.

Through his glasses, he could see the small fieldpieces being wheeled into position, and beyond them, clouds of red dust rising as troops of cavalry massed for an assault. Close to the cavalry was a group of dismounted officers gathered in a circle, some standing, some kneeling on the ground, all listening to a tall bare-headed man giving them orders. The Rebs must have been just as surprised to run into his outfit as he'd been to run into them.

Where had they come from, anyway? In the three months since the Third Cavalry had first come up the Yazoo, the Rebs had pretty much disappeared from this area. But here they were, back again, obviously determined to take Yazoo City and drive them into the river.

The only thing stopping them from getting into the town was a little fort about four hundred yards directly behind the captain and his men—really just a heavily built-up mound of dirt, with trenches deep enough for the men to stand in, and wood planking on top. It dominated the approaches to the city. But right now it was undefended, and until the reenforcements he'd sent for arrived, until he was able to somehow or another maneuver his fifty men back into it, the way to Yazoo City was wide open.

The two sides were going at each other strong, but thank God the Rebs didn't know how few in number they were—if they knew, they'd have swept right on by them into the fort. His men would have to fall back slow, buy enough time for the reinforcements to get up.

At least he had Zack. "Corporal! Tell the men to make sure every shot counts. And watch the flanks."

Sure enough, bullets started flying from the woods to his left. But his men were fighting smart, not panicking, keeping their mounts, giving as good as they were getting.

Another half hour of this, and they'd be able to get back to the fort.

Two troopers galloping to reach shelter in the woods went down, almost as though they were twins—the Rebs had shot their horses. Tumbling to the ground, rolling every which way, bodies one direction, guns the other.

Jenkins, a short mulatto from New Orleans, got to his feet. Jones, the other trooper, was still on his knees when the Reb cavalry pulled up. A major, dressed in that gray uniform with its fancy yellow curls, pulled out his revolver as the Rebel color guard rode up beside him, the flag fluttering in the stiff March breeze.

The major cupped his hands and yelled over to the Yankee lines. "Now, hear me, niggers! The Good Book says 'Servants obey your masters. The wages of sin is death.'"

Jenkins and Jones raised their hands in surrender. The major drew his revolver, took careful aim, and shot both of them in the head.

For a moment, silence fell on that section of the battlefield. Stiles closed his eyes, but only for a few seconds. One Rebel yell was followed by another and another till they were all shouting and screaming and blasting away. Seemed to have but one thing in mind—kill the niggers.

Stiles was everywhere on the field, slashing with his saber in one hand and blasting away with his revolver in the other. And right behind him, always, was Zack, handling his saber as if it were a toothpick.

"Captain, the two lieutenants are dead. Don't you join them." He fired and killed a Reb coming in fast on Stiles's right.

They fell back some more, then he dismounted the men, called some horse holders, and yelled, "Back to the rifle pits!" After half an hour, they fell back again. Stiles was the last man into the fort.

Thank God they'd piled those heavy planks of wood on the parapets with little spaces in between so the men could shoot through them At least their heads would be protected from enemy sharpshooters in the hills all around.

"Come on over, you bastards!" a man yelled.

And now they were all cursing and waving their sabers.

"You wants your niggers, come on and get them!"

He was just wishing his men wouldn't swear so much when a loud hurrah went up from the Reb lines. About a hundred of them got up and started charging over the fifty yards of ground that separated them from the Third Cavalry's lines. They ran fast and low, carrying their sawed-off shotguns and carbines at the ready and shouting that crazy Rebel yell. No matter how many times he heard it, a chill still went up his spine. If only he could have him a war where the only thing that happened was that the colored troops would curse at the Rebs and the Rebs would yell at the Negroes. Put them face to face, ten paces apart—first one to ask the other to quit would have to stack their arms and go home. War over! Shake hands, boys, and go back to the farms! And don't ever bring any of that racket around this poor Adirondack mountain fellow's way again!

That Reb lieutenant with a plume in the band of his hat and a brace of Colts in his hands didn't seem the kind who'd quit till he was laid in his grave by a fast bullet or cold steel. His face contorted and twisted, he was shouting loud in a high-pitched voice as he ran. And he was such a fast runner that he'd gotten five yards out in front of his troops.

"Steady, men, fire at my command!" Stiles looked up and down the line of his troops. They were ready.

For a moment his eyes locked with those of the Lieutenant, now about twenty paces away from the Union lines. The Reb raised his pistols slowly to a firing position and kept on coming. Well, if the young fool was bent on a hero's death, Stiles'd give it to him.

Stiles lifted his Colt and took aim at the gray blouse of the lieutenant. "Fire!"

All over the field, Rebs fell to the ground. You couldn't see them well, in all that acrid-smelling smoke, but you could hear their cries for help. Directly in front of him he saw that the Reb youngster was down, but not what condition he was in—the rest of them kept on coming. Too many to count, and every one of them spoiling for a fight.

Then they were at the ramparts of the fort, and all along the line; man to man, they went at it fast and furious, Rebs and Yanks, blasting away with shotguns and carbines, colored and white swinging sabers, screaming and grunting until he lost all sense of time. He heard the screaming loud as ever, but somehow it seemed far off. He dodged bullets and shotgun blasts and slashing sabers—determined to stay alive in the madness and confusion, and just as determined to kill as many of the enemy as possible. Had to, because it looked for sure like the fort would be lost in a few more minutes. Well, they'd make the enemy pay dearly for their prize.

Just as he was about to give up hope, he heard the sound of a bugle blowing the charge. The Rebs in front of him suddenly turned and bolted. Thank God! Four companies of the 11th Illinois—white infantry—trotting at the quick step into the fort. It would hold for the time being.

He walked a little ways outside the fort to where the boy lieutenant lay in the dirt, groaning and holding his intestines in with his hands. His hat, the plume intact, lay on the ground beside him, brown dirt soiling its crown.

"Water," said the lieutenant, his blue eyes once again fixed on Stiles. The life was fast draining from them, so the water would do him no harm.

He took the boy's head onto his right arm and cradled it. "Here, just take a little sip, Lieutenant." He barely wet the boy's lips with the spout of the canteen, then lowered his head to the ground.

"Thanks."

Stiles took off his own jacket, made a pillow of it and placed it under the lieutenant's head. "Rest easy now, son, we'll get help for you soon. That was a mighty brave charge you led out here."

The boy's eyes brightened with pride, then dimmed. He was about to say something when his head dropped down. Stiles gently retrieved his jacket from under the boy's head and rolled it up under his left arm.

From the fort, his men watched him stand at attention for a minute and salute before walking back to join them.

❖   ❖   ❖   ❖   ❖   ❖   ❖   ❖   ❖   ❖   ❖

The week that followed was a quiet one, so uneventful that Stiles had time to write Eunice. Every two weeks or so he was rewarded with a bundle of letters from her, letters full of her softness and love. He could never write such letters, nor would he have had a moment to compose them even if his words were as strong as his feelings. Since the beginning of the campaign up the Yazoo, he'd scarcely had the time even to think of her, what with the bringing in of cattle and freed slaves, the daily skirmishes with the regular Confederate cavalry, or with bands of guerrillas and deserters . . .

Writing had not come easy to him before, but as he began to tell her about the men, he found the words coming faster than he could write them down:

Their countenances may be dark, but a great light glows within them. When I first marched off to Albany to come down here to fight this wet and devilish war in a land that could only have been created as a cruel afterthought by God Almighty, I thought solely of saving our sacred Union. I know now that there is something more. We have a duty, I have come to believe, a great mission to help these poor oppressed people out of the Darkness and Ignorance to which both the unfortunate accident of their geographic origins and the state of slavery has condemned them.

I have come to admire their courage and valor and determination. Did I tell you how they yearn more than anything to read and write? Even when we are all weary after a long day of chasing the pesky Rebs, they still come up to my tent and ask that I teach them to read yet another verse of the Bible. Some of them—like our Wizard, Joe Duckett, are quick to learn and seem to soak up whatever you teach them. Yet there are some for whom it is a painful struggle. It almost broke my heart when a chap of about forty-five came up to me after the eighth lesson with tears in his eyes and said, "Too late, sir, too late."

Eunice, my dearest, of late I have been thinking that when this conflict is over and the Union restored, I would like to stay here, purchase a plantation, settle our men upon it, and teach them animal husbandry, the science of farming, the uses of machinery. This is such a backward land, and such a backward people, even the poor whites. With a little hard work and rolling up of our shirtsleeves, my men and I can make our farm bloom, set an example for colored and white alike of progressive life. Give white and black a place where their children can grow up healthy, and wise, daily glorifying God. It would be a blessed work, my darling, yet I hesitate to commit myself to it, lest you, for reasons of health or otherwise, find yourself unable to join me here. This is one more thing of which we must talk sometime. I boldly and with no apology admit that my love of you and my need of you comes first.

Have you heard any news of—

He looked up as a shell from a twelve-pounder slammed into the dirt about thirty paces from where he sat writing.

The Rebs were really just getting their strength together. Only a week since the attack on the fort, and there were four to five thousand Rebs surrounding the city. They had the Yankees—just twelve hundred of them—in a noose and were hell-bent on driving them from the fort and the city and sweeping them right down into the Yazoo. And what use were the Yankee gunboats sitting there in the river with their cannon when the Union forces and the city lay between the boats and the Rebels? If they fired, the shells might fall on their own forces.

Now here the Rebs came again. He walked over to where Zack was standing in one of the fort's trenches.

"Wish Joe was back up here. We're going to get it today."

Another shell landed, closer this time, and tore a hole in the ramparts. Zack stood beside the captain, his carbine at the ready.

"Sir, I've a request of you from the men."

Will looked out along the long line of his troopers, who stood waiting for the Rebs. What the hell could they want?

"What is it, Bascom?"

"No surrender. Don't care if all hell descends on this here fort this afternoon. We ask you not to surrender, sir. We done talked it all over, and we is sworn to die to the last man."

That major's assassination of Jenkins and Jones had to be behind this resolution. Will sighed and buckled on his sword belt.

"Then that's the way it will be." He shook Zack's hand. "Just like you said, no surrender."

✿   ✿   ✿   ✿   ✿   ✿   ✿   ✿   ✿   ✿   ✿

That was the last word they exchanged for a good half hour, because the skies opened to pour tons of metal into the Third Cavalry's trenches. The Rebs wanted Yazoo City badly.

When the barrage ceased, Stiles looked out with his binoculars. A Confederate major—he'd swear it was the very one who had a week ago shot down Jenkins and Jones and three more later that same day—was advancing under a flag of truce, a Texas Ranger at his side. Stiles ordered his men to cease fire and went out to meet him.

"General Ross sends his compliments and says your men have fought bravely," the major said. "You've seen the forces we have against you. Surrender the fort and you'll have all the privileges of prisoners of war."

"Privileges? You speak to me of privileges. Why did you kill my troopers out there last week after they'd surrendered?"

"Sir, may I remind you of the rules of war? We may only converse about truce terms."

"And what do the rules say about executing unarmed prisoners? I'd like to wring your cowardly neck."

"Me too." The black trooper who'd escorted him whispered under his breath, so that only Stiles heard him. Even so, he'd pay for that indiscretion if he survived this day.

"Sir," said the major, "will you conduct my superior's terms to your commanding officer or not?"

"Do those terms include sparing the lives of the colored troops should we surrender?"

"Yes. You have ten minutes to give an answer. We'll hold fire during that time."

Stiles turned to go.

"Captain, one more thing, before you go."

"Get on with it."

"If you refuse to surrender, General Ross says he cannot be responsible for what happens to your men. Feelings are running mighty high among our men about that armed nigger rabble. And remember, it's four to one."

Zack was waiting at the ramparts. "Well, Captain?"

"I'll be back in a few minutes."

He went up to Major Wickham, the commander of the fort, and reported both the terms and the colored troopers' oath to fight to the death.

"Hells bells, man! What kind of fool!—what did you tell them, for God's sakes?"

"I gave them my word. No surrender."

"Damn it to hell, Stiles, what's the matter with you? That's not for you to decide, it's *my* decision."

"But, sir—"

"But, sir, nothing! There are some white troops and noncoms here and they deserve some damn consideration, don't they?"

Stiles slapped his gauntlets across his open palm. "After what the bastards did to our men last week, you can't—"

"There are *thousands* of Rebs over there. How long do you think we'll last once they come at us full force? Ten minutes? Fifteen, twenty? Come on, man, they wouldn't kill all your troopers if we surrendered. Probably just a few for show. And maybe not even that. They don't have time, they want to take Yazoo City."

Stiles looked over at his men, who were watching intently. "Major, if you decide to surrender, I ask you to issue me an order detaching me and my men from your command so we can continue to fight. I cannot break my word."

Wickham walked over to Stiles, put his arm around his shoulder, drew him to a spot where the men could no longer observe them.

"I'm an old man, Will, and I've lived through too many battles to want to die now because of some damn niggers. And that's what you're asking me to do."

Stiles nodded his head. At this point he knew the major well enough to know he was no coward. He'd simply assessed the odds and made a realistic judgment based on that assessment.

"Then I'll give you ten of my best, sir, and you can try to make it through to Yazoo City. Just leave me here to defend the fort with the rest of my men."

"And leave me coming into the lines while my command is being destroyed by the enemy?" The old soldier stood for a long moment, glaring. "Damn your eyes, you young pup, we'll fight, we'll fight to the death—which is probably what the damn Rebels are going to be dealing. Now go back and tell that Reb."

Stiles walked back out. "No surrender."

The Confederate major's eyebrows went up. "Well, Captain, we'll be sure to bury you with your niggers when it's over."

"We'll see who does the burying honors." With that, he turned on his heel and nodded to his men. All along the Yankee lines, they began clapping their hands and shouting. "No surrender. No surrender!"

❖   ❖   ❖   ❖   ❖   ❖   ❖   ❖   ❖   ❖

The exhilaration of the moment was forgotten in the onslaught that followed. From the dugout he dropped into, Stiles could see Zack swinging his carbine like a stick, crushing heads all around him. He also saw the extent of the drubbing the squadron was taking.

Everywhere lay dead and bloodied men. Over the din of screaming horses, colored soldiers and Rebel soldiers tried to outshout and outcurse each other.

"That's for Jason!" a colored soldier yelled as he ran his saber through a Reb's chest.

"This for Mattie-Lou!" yelled another.

But they fell back. Fighting, yes. Swearing, yes. But still falling back slowly and surely before the enraged Confederate legions.

Stiles felt a bullet whistle through his hat. Then another grazed him hard on the arm, knocking him to the ground. Immediately Zack was by his side, himself bleeding from a cut on his forehead, but ready to help as Stiles struggled to get back on his feet.

"Hold strong, men." His head was spinning—surely he would fall. "Stand fast!" he cried.

A hurrah went up along the Yankee lines.

"The Wizard, he's coming!"

And two seconds later, Joe was in the trenches. "They near broke through in the city, sir, but we held them. Captain Cook, he put a bunch of us together, and we turned them back. In a minute these Rebs in front of you are going to break. When they do the major says give 'em almighty hell."

Sure enough, off on their left flank the Texans began to break and run, and soon all along the line Rebels were turning and running back across the field, some of them throwing their weapons down in their haste to escape.

"Steady, men," Stiles said. "Give 'em a volley to keep them company."

The colored troops poured a withering fire into the Rebs, then with sabers drawn pursued them across the field.

"Kick their asses."

"If they breathe, stick 'em."

It was all he and Joe could do to stop the enraged men from taking the lives of the Reb wounded who littered the field.

They turned back toward their own lines and saw Zack Bascom running toward them.

"Captain, Captain!"

He glanced around the battlefield. Could the enemy possibly have sent a force behind them and attacked from the rear?

As Zack came closer, they saw that he was crying. "Captain! It's the major, sir!"

"Get yourself together, man, what happened?"

"A shell hit near Major Wickham. He dead."

Stiles put his arm around Zack's shoulder. "Take me to him."

Down in the middle of the fort, where the command post had been, almost a dozen men were gathered in a circle swaying gently back and forth and chanting a slow dirge about crossing Chilly Jordan. As he approached, they stopped singing and parted to let him through. Someone had covered the major's remains with a horse blanket and placed his officer's cap on top of it.

Stiles wanted to cry himself. Hell, hadn't he seen the major lead many a charge, like the one outside Jackson that had sent the Rebs packing? Hadn't he seen how day after day he'd forced his tired old body to stay in the saddle when he ought to have been back home in Kingston sitting by a blazing fire with his young wife and three children? Hadn't he traded his life for those of the colored troops when he agreed not to surrender? Well, so be it. It had been his choice, and there were worse ways to die.

The weight of that choice was heavy on Stiles's shoulders, but he looked at the grieving faces of his men, knew that wasn't what they needed. "Cheer, up boys! He'd be proud of you! You sent him off in like a soldier!"

CHAPTER SIX

SUE Kenworthy felt like crumpling Dorothy's letter into a little ball and throwing it at somebody. So Richard had stopped in to see Dorothy, which at least placed him in Louisiana—but *when would he be home?* What about *her?* What about *their* children? It was bad enough having to live here in a house that had once been her cousin's. But now the cousin was gone, leaving just her and the five adult Negroes to manage the little holding and take care of her four children. The Yankees were destroying *everything.*

She called out to the kitchen, where she hoped Zenobia was fixing lunch. "You didn't get the laundry done yesterday. Martha and Debbie have just about *run out* of clean clothes."

"Only got two hands, Miss Sue. Me and Drayton were down all day trying to do some planting for the summer garden. It's already May."

"But that doesn't mean you and Lisa Mae can't do the other work around here. The children come first, after all."

"Children got to eat, too. Miss Sue, we trying our best, but what with the cooking and everything and keeping this big old house clean—"

"Have you forgotten that I saved you and Cally from going on that transport to Alabama? You could at least be *grateful*, I'd think. Instead it seems to me you don't work as hard as you used to."

"I'm working hard as I can, Miss Sue. It ain't your fault there's so much work—or mine, neither."

"You know, the pressing gangs, they're still in operation if you think you're not up to all this *household* work."

Zenobia came into the room, that blue calico bandanna tied around her head. She was a handsome woman for a Negro, her narrow black face almost chiseled, her deep-set eyes smart and knowing. Probably came from royalty over there in Africa.

"Miss Sue, I don't mean no disrespect, but it seems to me you can't hardly find no more faithful folk than me, Lisa Mae Drayton and the old servants been. You know what's happened on all them other places, colored folks running away to the Yankees. Not us, we've stayed right here. Don't seem to me you should be thinking of sending us to no Alabama."

Sue let out a deep sigh. Zenobia was looking *righteous*.

"I'm sorry I was scratchy. But, Zenobia, everything's changing so fast. Sometimes I just don't know what to make of it."

"You been through a mighty lot, Miss. Reckon it hurt powerful bad to have to leave Clifton. I remembers the day you and Massa Richard was married there. I was working in the kitchen special that day and oh, didn't we cook some spread for you?"

Now, *that* was something to remember. Before the wedding, Cousin Fred had sung, "Thou Wilt Come No More, Gentle Annie." Sue looked around the room, smiled at the memory of turkey, chicken, potato salad, candied yams, and fresh green beans spread on glistening white tablecloths embroidered in gold, which covered the table from end to end. Bottles of the finest French wines, brought all the way from Paris, France, and a seven-course meal—a different wine for each course. And the smiling Negros, so *happy* for them, served strawberries with the special whipped cream flavored with a framboise liqueur.

Oh, how they'd danced that night. And as they all sat on the porch, candles lighting up the night, the Negros sang for the wedding party like God had touched their voices in a special way just to bless her nuptials.

"What was that song . . ." She turned to ask Zenobia, but she must have already gone back to the kitchen.

Oh well. Hadn't folks talked about the wedding for *years* afterward? And then the guests had spilled out onto the lawn and . . . She glanced out the window at the scruffy old brown grass, the path from the house to the road *covered* with weeds.

She stamped her foot at the unfairness of it all and called to Zenobia. "Just see to it that the children are taken care of when they finish tutoring. And you'll just have to find the time to straighten out the salon before the afternoon. The ladies will be coming over for tea."

❋   ❋   ❋   ❋   ❋   ❋   ❋   ❋   ❋   ❋   ❋

Later, that afternoon, Sue and her friends Mary Reynolds and Doris sat on the porch and spoke for a few minutes about the latest news, how Lee was still outwitting the Northerners over in Virginia and how gallantly their troops were fighting to free Mississippi of the Yankees. But soon they were talking about childhood escapades, visits in better days to one another's homes, when life flowed so easily compared to now.

"You know what I was thinking about the other day?" said Mary Reynolds. "Remember the night that we left to go down to Vicksburg to the winter ball on the *Janet Rouse*?"

"How could I forget?" said Sue. "Why you'd forgotten two of your bags, and there the boat was, belching smoke and all, bells ringing, and the darkies clapping because we were dressed so pretty and they were so proud of us."

Doris laughed. "Oh, I can see the captain up there on the side of the pilothouse yelling for us to come on board, and dear old Mammy Eunice running down the levee to catch you, hollering, 'Mary Reynolds, don't you dare leave without this!'"

"She like to have jumped out of her skin and fallen into the river when the captain blew the steam whistle three times," said Mary Reynolds.

Sue laughed. "And the next morning, waking up, going on deck, and seeing the flowers all in bloom along the banks of the river—violets, pansies and daisies, bluebells, morning glories, and wild roses *everywhere*, like the Good Lord had made a special show for us because He knew we were sixteen and on our way to our first ball. As if He'd strewn petals before our feet."

"You have such a way of saying things, Sue. Honestly, sometimes I think you should write stories, or poetry, or something."

"Maybe someday, Mary Reynolds, maybe when . . ."

The women fell silent for a moment.

"You remember that very tall, very black man who worked with your grandfather?" Mary Reynolds said.

"Course I do," Sue said. "Why, that was Luther. I could never, ever forget him."

"What a wonderful old darky he was. I don't think I've ever seen so good a worker."

"We called him Uncle Luther, of course," Sue said. "Why, he could rub the silver, polish the glass, clean the boots, saddle the horse, row the skiff across the Yazoo, and drive us around in the pony cart all in one day. And always smiling, too." She thought of Zenobia and frowned.

"What ever became of him?"

"I'd say he died of sadness, Mary Reynolds. When the war came, and all our Negros started running away, getting ornery, he couldn't *stand* it."

"How 's that? " Doris asked.

"You see, we were truly his family. He didn't have anybody *but* us. And when all these bad things started happening, it just went to his heart and broke it in two. He tried to make up by himself for all the runaways, just killing himself with work."

Doris set her cup back into the saucer and shook her head.

"One day he just *keeled over*, dead of some heart ailment out there in that *cruel* sun."

"They are a faithful and good people." Doris said.

"They *were*," Sue got up and walked to the end of the porch and looked down the side of the house, then returned.

"They haven't changed, Sue. Well, I mean, I guess they have, but it's not their doing. It's just that the Yankees have influenced some of them and corrupted them to think they're just as good as white folks."

"You're right," Sue said. "And I think the Yankees did it out of spite. We lived so well and in such harmony with the Negroes! They couldn't understand it and they couldn't *stand* it, either! I'd say they'll find out what harm they've done when they've lived with the freed ones for a while."

Mary Reynolds tucked a stray curl back into her swept-up brown hair and took a sip of lemonade. "I am afraid for the future, Sue. Aren't you?"

"Well, sometimes. But I hear that England will soon join in on our side,"

"Maybe it will. But in the meantime, every day the Negroes become more insolent. I had to call mine together and read them a letter from John where he promised to give them a thrashing once he came home if they didn't mend their ways."

Sue drew her chair closer to the other two and whispered, "I've had to threaten Drayton in the same way. And he was always so *obedient*. As to Zenobia and the other one, they've become impossible—I'm selling them off."

"When?"

"Mr. Salter will be here in a few days to take them away."

Sue went over to close the window that opened out on to the porch and was startled when five-year-old Debbie poked her head out. "Mommy, surprise!"

"Debbie! How many times have I told you not to listen to grown-up talk? Now, go back outside with the others."

How much had Debbie heard? Should she say something to her about it or just hope that either she hadn't heard it, or, if she *had* heard it wouldn't tell Zenobia?

She turned back to her friends. "Sometimes I don't know about that child. We were talking about the Negroes. . . .".

"I'm afraid they're forever spoiled," Doris said. "The spirit of that Haitian Rebellion is among them—you remember Toussaint-Louverture and what he did to the white people in Santo Domingo."

Sue shivered at the mention of the bloody black dictator's name. "I think maybe you're right. Under our wings, they're a kind and peaceable people.. But once the civilizing example of a higher race is gone from before their eyes, they *revert to barbarity*."

"It's so sad," Mary Reynolds said. "Soon it will be as if we had never brought them from Africa, never tried to teach them our Christian ways."

Doris said, "What do you hear from the front? Has Richard written lately?"

Sue passed for the third time a plate of the blueberry tarts Zenobia had made that morning. "He used to write so *frequently*, and now . . . and it's just *hot and heavy* all the time for them. He's still with Forrest's cavalry. But every now and then he'll send a gift for me and the children with a little note."

Doris said, "Then he was with our troops who routed the Yankees at Fort Pillow last month."

Sue tapped her her teaspoon lightly on the side of her cup. "I've heard that ladies from the neighborhood were so relieved those nigra soldiers and whites were defeated, they held a special service of thanksgiving for the victory and set out the most *delicious* spread for General Forrest and his men."

"I would hope so," Mary Reynolds said. "Those nigras and Yankees were going all around the countryside, terrorizing and burning and stealing something awful. I heard that half of the nigras were drunk when General Forrest's troops broke into the fort."

Sue shuddered. "And they were standing up on the parapets of the fort, taunting our troops and . . . and *exposing* themselves!"

"Did you hear . . ." Doris helped herself to another tart. "I swear, Sue, these tarts are just scrumptious. Did you hear how those foolish darkies kept on shooting even after the truce was declared, so that General Forrest had to attack them again?"

"Well, for some of them that will be their last vile act," Mary Reynolds said. "It should show the rest of them that the Yankees are leading them down a terrible path. They'll think twice before they take up arms against us. Leastwise, before fighting General Forrest."

"But the Yankees are calling it a massacre," Doris said. "Why I read in a paper yesterday that the *Herald Tribune* said in an editorial that General Forrest *murdered*—in cold blood—the defenders of Fort Pillow. They said—"

"Stop, I will not hear it, even from your lips," Sue said. "Richard would never murder *anyone*." She stood up. "Where has the afternoon gone? It's time for the children's dinner. I like to sit with them every evening. It calms them. Which is something we could *all* use nowadays."

An hour later, Sue sat down to dinner with her children and was pleased to see that for once Zenobia had set a good table. There were heaping bowls of turnip greens, mashed potatoes with gravy, and fried ham. And piping hot corn bread, with just-churned butter, and peach cobbler for dessert.

Sue looked at Gregory, her eight-year-old. He and the three girls had been running and playing in the yard all afternoon once the tutor went home.

"Open your hands." It didn't look as if he'd been anywhere near soap and water, but she gave him the benefit of the doubt. "Get up this minute and go wash those hands again. The *idea*. And you're the oldest, supposed to be the man of the house."

While they waited for him, she turned to Debbie. Was there a funny look in her eyes or was she imagining it? She might not have heard anything, and Sue couldn't think of a way to question her about what she'd heard without giving away that something was wrong. Oh, it was just *too much*, having to make all these decisions.

When Gregory came back, Sue bowed her head.

"Bless the table, please."

❊   ❊   ❊   ❊   ❊   ❊   ❊   ❊   ❊   ❊   ❊

When dinner was over and all was quiet in the house, Sue went to her room and read once more the lines Richard had written after the battle at Fort Pillow:

> . . . please read these things, then let me know how you feel. My heart is heavy for I saw much blood two days ago. Indeed the river ran red with the blood of the Negroes. We had told them to surrender. And it is the strangest thing with these new, liberated Negroes—as they used to do at corn shucking time, when the whiskey got to them and they started to fight—so it was with those colored soldiers. It was not enough that they would refuse a truce, they found it necessary to engage in the most vituperative abuse against our men, threatening us with everlasting death should we continue our attack on the fort.
>
> They fought hard, indeed some few never even gave up until the end. When we finally got the better of them, our men gave them no mercy, so exasperated were they by the conduct of the darkies. It was a horrid sight, and I hope never to see such again. They begged mercy, still we fired and kept on firing. I attempted to stop the slaughter, but to no avail. General Forrest came over and ordered the men to keep on shooting, even

though the victory was won and the Negroes and their white al-
lies defeated. . . . Worse, after the battle was over, there was a
sort of blood lust in our men. Some found stocks of whiskey and
committed depraved acts of which I heard, but did not witness.
They nailed the bodies of some wounded black sergeants to logs
by their hands and feet, then fired the logs, making of them one
great pyre. And in their drunkenness, someone got the idea that
some of the colored wounded should be killed by fire. So they
were thrown into buildings, and the buildings were fired. I am
told their cries for help were piteous as the flames consumed
the buildings. Pray for me, and ask God's forgiveness on my
soul.

> Your loving husband,
> Richard

Sue sat holding the letter for a time, then put a candle to it and burned
it up. She sat down at the night table and began her letter to him:

> Dearest Richard:
> I have your letter. The less said of the painful events at Fort Pil-
> low, the better. God knows your heart, and your morality, and so
> do I. If there were any sinful acts committed there, I am sure
> that by your action to try and stop them, God has absolved you
> of any lasting moral stain. We serve a forgiving God. May He
> grant our arms victory.
>
> > Your loving wife,
> > Sue

She sealed the envelope and went to bed.

❖   ❖   ❖   ❖   ❖   ❖   ❖   ❖   ❖   ❖   ❖

Zenobia quietly opened the door to the slave hut she shared with Lisa
Mae, Cally, and Ned. Everybody was sleeping, the children as tired out
from playing as she and Lisa Mae were from working. She was grateful
Lisa Mae had fed them and washed their clothes so they'd have something
clean for the next day.

She went over to her pallet and shook her awake.

Lisa Mae turned over slowly. It had to be hard for her, too, working as a field hand, watching the two children, and trying to deal with the demands of Drayton. Damn man tried to make them do all the work, including his. All the time saying do this, do that, "else I tell Miss."

Zenobia nodded her head toward the door, the only opening in the shack, and Lisa Mae got up and followed her out.

"I'm so tired, every bone in my body ache. Why you wake me up?"

"We have to leave here."

"Why?"

"In two or three days, that woman going to put us on a transport to Alabama."

"You crazy. Why she want to do something like that?"

"She tired of feeding us and keeping us, and she ain't too happy with me nor you neither."

'Miss Sue wouldn't do that."

"Listen to me." Zenobia put her right hand on Lisa Mae's face, one finger just under her cheekbone and the thumb under her chin. "This afternoon, Debbie come crying to me about not wanting Mommy to send me away. I shushed the child and told her Miss Sue was joking, so stop crying 'cause her auntie Zenobia wasn't going nowhere. That calmed her down a mite."

Lisa Mae grasped her hand. "You know what it is you thinking about doing? It's near three or four days to the river and the Yankees. How you reckon to get there, just us and them two little children?"

Zenobia nodded over at the bushes . "Let's go over there and talk. Cally need her sleep, elsewise that cough will never leave her."

"That's just what I mean," Lisa Mae said. "We should stay here, take our chances—"

"I know white folks and I know when they intend to do something. She been complaining about running out of money all the time. That woman mean to put us on the road, and that may be the end of all of us."

Lisa Mae said, "It such a long way, and swamps and snakes and bears out in them woods."

"They's worse things," Zenobia said. "You only eighteen and born at Clifton, but you know I was marched here, me and my two sisters that you never knowed, all the way from Abbeville courthouse, South Carolina, down near the Savannah River. It pain me now to think on it, but maybe you'll understand why we got to run if I tell you about what happened when we was just one day outside of Chattanooga. The sun was beating down on us like we was standing right over a forge. We'd been on the road so long that I lost track of the days and nights. And this woman, her name was Mabel and she had a baby—I were only fifteen, but I used to carry it for her some . . . Anyway, they marched us something awful. I just wanted to lay down there and die, but I was young and somehow or other I always managed to get up when the man cracked his whip.

"But Mabel, she say to the man, I can't walk no more, give me some of that water, please, before I die. The man said, 'You'll die, then.' He took the baby from her and give it to me. I won't never forget. For when she lay down, he commenced to beat her with a whip. 'Get up, you nigger, get up, you lazy bitch'—and he beat her and beat her till she quit breathing. And they left her dead, right there in the road. I carried the baby for many a day, till it took sick and died."

Lisa Mae shuddered. Zenobia reached for Lisa Mae's hand and drew her close. "Truth is, I not only think Miss want to send us away, I also think she want to sell me and you away from these children. I do believe that. And the road to the Yankees can't be no worse than that, no matter the danger out there. Even if—"

"What you girls talking about out here in the middle of the night?" It was Drayton. He lived by himself in a shack close by.

"What you hear?"

"Enough, you ain't going nowhere."

"Hush, you'll have somebody down here," Zenobia said. "Let's go in your cabin."

Once they were inside, Drayton said, "Now give me one reason why I shouldn't go up there and tell Miss."

"Well, for one, 'cause if the Yankees win, and Joe alive, he cut your throat, that's why."

Lisa Mae smiled at the prospect.

"I ain't studying no Joe . . ."

"And for another," Zenobia said, "I hear that the colored Yankee soldiers ain't been too nice to no white folks' niggers like you. Been tarring and feathering them."

"My white folks going to protect me, no matter what."

"Their time is over," Lisa Mae said. "You got to know that."

Drayton had walked outside without his shirt and now busied himself putting it on. "All this kind of talk make me nervous, you understand. Miss get wind of this and she sell me, too."

"Oh, so you done heard, Miss done told you." Zenobia waved her finger in front of his face and turned to Lisa Mae. "See?"

"Miss hold me responsible for you," Drayton said. "You run away, she'll whip me something awful. Remember how I saved you all from going to Alabama, neither one of you has repaid me. And it would just have been a little old thing."

Zenobia had had enough of this nigger. "You do what you want, but I'm going to tell you something. Miss Sue ain't got no money left—Mr. Richard ain't got any to send her. And these Confederate soldiers, they be coming every day to take mens away to work for them. They likely to take you away too—you a big strong nigger. Lessen the Yankees gets you first."

"You got any sense, you be begging to go with us," Lisa Mae said. "Yankees ain't that far away. And Abraham Lincoln done freed the slaves—ain't you heard about it?"

Zenobia nodded. "Might be a more better trip if you went with us. You know how to read and write—can make us out some passes."

"This your chance, Mr. Drayton." Lisa Mae unbuttoned the top of her blouse. "Might even think about how I been so mean to you."

Drayton's eyes lit up. "Well, I won't be telling Miss Sue nothing nohow."

He looked back at Zenobia. "How you planning to do this thing? And what you going to do with them children?"

"You'll see if you decide to come with us," Zenobia said. "But with you or without you, we going. We on our way."

CHAPTER SEVEN

JOE sat at the table smoking his corncob pipe. Betty was on the bed, sewing a brass button back on his blue uniform blouse. She'd cooked a dinner of steak, greens in fatback grease, and corn bread with a good brown crust.

"What you thinking?"

"That you mighty pretty, darlin', not to mention a mighty fine cook." Joe didn't know where she'd gotten that steak, but it was some kind of good.

"You always thinking that. But what about the fighting you got to do tomorrow?"

"Ain't going to be no different. We beating the Rebs. Soon won't be no more of them left in Mississippi."

"Couldn't tell that from all the soldiers that keep coming into our ward every day."

"I didn't say that the Rebs couldn't fight, 'cause they can. I'm just saying we ain't found the ones yet that can stop us."

Betty sighed. "I do worry every time you go up the river. I've just seen so much—men with legs gone, arms gone. And worse."

He looked at her head bent over his uniform and felt a wave of tenderness that startled him. "Honey, I think you beginning to get too close to me."

She shook her head, and when she looked up at him she was smiling. But her eyes were serious.

"Too late to worry about that," she said. "Done already happened."

"What I mean is, if I get hurt I don't want you getting all upset about me. Ain't good for you and surely ain't good for me." He put his pipe down, went over and lay down on his side with his head propped up next to her.

Betty put down her sewing and snuggled up to him. "Baby, you got to talk about this thing."

"Ain't that what we doing?"

"Joe. About going up to Clifton."

"And Zenobia?"

She nodded. He ran his hand through her hair and kissed her softly on the cheek.

"It ain't even about her no more. If she still there—and I don't know one way or another—or if anybody's there, then she probably still mad at me, because I let my temper get ahold of me and ran away to try and find my children. She probably think I'm dead."

"And supposing she is there? What then?"

"I don't rightly know." He was quiet for a moment. "I think I'd ask her forgiveness that I left her to carry the burden all alone, leaving her with our three-month-old baby. It was the corn liquor made me run."

"There's a lot more, ain't there?" She got up and poured him a cup of whiskey.

He took a long swallow and coughed when it stuck in his windpipe on the way down. As soon as he recovered, he sat up straight and stared down at the dirt floor, holding the cup in both hands, twisting it round and round.

"I can't never forget the day they come and took my children away."

"What happened?"

"See, Massa Richard, he knew how much I hated what he done to my sister, Pauline, knew I was bidding my time . . .

"Oh yes, I remember about Pauline."

"Well, he run into debt and had to start selling off land, then he finally had to sell off slaves. And things being like they was between us, he started with my kids." Joe walked over to the small fireplace, knocked the pipe against the stone, and emptied the tobacco ashes into the fire. "Massa Richard he liked to be the best at everything. And he was a very strong man—heavy-built and all, but every now and then I used to beat him run-

ning and even shooting, 'cause his daddy used to let us go hunting together. He always held that against me."

"The way you talk, you must have been one troublesome slave."

"I was surely that."

He walked over to her, bent down and kissed her on the neck. She
smiled.

"No, baby, I wasn't ever thinking like some of these niggers that love old
Massa. No, I argued with that man all the time. Told him he weren't no
better than me, had no right to hold me in bondage, nor to take my people's land—I told you Mama was part colored, part Choctaw. And what
right did they have to sell my poor African papa down into Texas a month
after I was born?"

Betty poured herself some bourbon. Most likely she'd never met no colored man that thought like he did, much less one who would put it into
words. "And he didn't have you whipped?"

"No, because his daddy, old Massa Kenworthy, you see, he liked me a
lot, thought somebody like me was good for his own boy to have as a play-
mate. So I got away with a lot of things other boys couldn't."

"It almost sounds like you was free."

"Not hardly. But there's plenty of men like me—even some in the regiment—wasn't made to be nobody's slave. Nothing the white man could do
with us, except shoot us, sell us, or live with us. Because you see a man so
mean he ain't afraid to die, he a hard man to control. Ain't but one way to
do it."

"By doing harm to those he hold most dear to his bosom."

Joe set down his empty glass and got ready to go. He had to be back at
camp by taps.

"Sold Luke and Milly down the river. I don't know where they be, but
when we lands up there near Clifton, I may find out."

He kissed the top of her head and left her sitting at the table. She was
still there, thinking, long after he was back in camp.

❖   ❖   ❖   ❖   ❖   ❖   ❖   ❖   ❖   ❖   ❖

"Come on over behind the tent," Zack said. "Got us a little jug, and the
guys got them a little poker game going. Tucker's dealing."

"You know I don't like that low-down nigger," Joe said. "Always whip-ping on folk littler than him."

"That don't matter tonight," Zack said. "You play, do you good, what with us going into Clifton tomorrow. Cards will take your mind off all that."

"You go on. Leave me be a little while. I might come back there di-rectly."

Six miles outside of Clifton. Damn. Had sure taken him a long time to get back. Three years of mud, mosquitoes, beatings. Now, in a few more hours, he'd be leading the regiment back into the place where his dear mother had borne him—a slave—close to thirty-five years ago. Never once saw the sun rise on that place in freedom, but tomorrow, Lord will-ing, he would. He'd sorta of be freedom's own personal messenger to Clifton.

For some reason the memory came back of the little brook under a wil-low tree where he and Zenobia made love sometimes when the heat was so bad you couldn't even turn over in the bed without sweating. Maybe there was still a high singing mockingbird up in its branches. The clean lines of Zenobia's beautiful face seemed to be in front of him. What did she look like now? And Luke? Was he tall? Did Milly still have that dimple in her smile or had she outgrown it? And Cally, she'd already know how to talk now. Had to make sure she learned to read and write like proper folks.

Hell, why'd he have that little shot of corn whiskey a while ago? Went right to his head, was splashing through his brains, like some kind of moonshine waterfall. Zenobia, you my soul. Wherever the wind and the water have taken you, if God let me live through these cannon and bullets and shotguns, I'll find you and the young 'uns.

❀   ❀   ❀   ❀   ❀   ❀   ❀   ❀   ❀   ❀   ❀

"Joe?" Zack was back. "Man, that ain't no good, just sitting there staring at the fire. Come on back, have you a little drink, then go to bed. This your homecoming."

"Go to hell."

Zack flinched.

"Sorry." Joe got up. "I'm coming."

He had to smile when he got close enough to the fire to see the serious-faced men sitting in their white underwear tops with their suspenders holding up their blue cavalry trousers.

"Hey, Sarge, sit down. We having us a good time." Patton smiled and moved aside to give Joe a place to sit.

"Don't feel like playing. I'll just sit here and watch awhile."

Slater, a young recruit, was softly trilling on the harmonica. The rest played cards without a word or smile, except maybe when one of them got himself a big pot. When Patton finally won a hand he stood up and pranced around the circle, leaning down and jabbing his finger at each of the other players in turn.

"Told you all don't be sitting down with me! One terrible man! Mountain jack hide when he hear me coming! Lose all your money! All your money, I say!"

Joe laughed and stretched his hand out. "Stop running off at the mouth and hand me back that dollar I lent you to get through the month."

The men broke out laughing.

"Talking about some old mountain jack? Better get out of here while you still got a pot to piss in!"

"Strutting like some damn peacock and ain't won nothing else the whole night long!"

"Why don't you sit in, Joe?"

"Give us a chance to win back some of that two hundred dollars," Tucker said. "Ain't right for no one man to be holding all the money in the outfit. Like you some damn bank."

"All right, I'll give you fools a chance to lose some more of your money. Deal."

He looked over at the razor-cut scars on Tucker's brown face. He was big for a horse soldier, and so strong he'd been known to knock out a mule with his bare fist. Mules wasn't all he hit, though. He had already been busted from corporal twice, once for beating up on the little drummer.

Joe took the tin cup Patton handed him and drained it in two quick gulps. "What's the stake?"

"Dollar a hand."

Tucker was looking at Joe as if he knew he had a turkey. Joe put down a silver coin and started playing. At first things went good, then he started to lose.

"Zack, get me another cup of that rotgut."

"You done had you enough, Joe."

Joe put his cards down. "Ain't you been after me all night to join in? Now . . . hell, man, you won't get it, I'll get it myself."

"Sit, Joe. I'll get it, but this the last one."

Joe drank the whiskey down and wiped his mouth with his hand. Man, that stuff burned your stomach. Did something to your eyes, too—looked like there was two of every man around the slowly dying fire. He looked down at the pile of coins at his side. He'd started with ten dollars, now he had three. He was just thinking he'd go to bed after a couple more hands when he noticed something. Nobody wasn't winning now but Tucker and Easely. The later it got, the more they won. And that damn nine card kept coming up in their hands.

He tried hard to focus on the cards in Tucker's hand. Shit. There was so much whiskey in his brains he could barely see them, much less what Tucker was doing with them. But sure enough, when the deal was done, Easely had won again.

Joe stood up quick and almost fell down again, he was that dizzy. But he reached down and grabbed Tucker by the arm.

"Enough of this shit, give everybody back their money."

Tucker looked at Joe like he was crazy.

"Yeah, you heard him," Zack said. "Give everybody back their money. I seen it too. You cheating."

"Man, that firewater done gone to your head." Tucker looked over at Zack. "You better take this loco Indian nigger and put him to bed before he get hisself hurt."

He shook loose and began to rake in the pile of coins in front of him, but Joe grabbed his hand again.

"Said give the money back, and don't be calling me no names—I'm your superior officer."

Tucker jerked his arm away and leapt to his feet.

"You ain't shit, nothing but a drunken-assed piece of shit. Get out of here before I kick your ass!"

Joe punched him hard and quick in the stomach.

Tucker gasped for breath and bent over like he'd been kicked in the balls. Joe put his two fists together and chopped him hard on the top of his head. Tucker fell to the ground, his big body rolling back and forth in the dirt. He was groaning something awful.

Joe reached down for the money pile. "Zack, count this out and make sure everybody gets what's coming to them. I'm going to bed." He straightened up and started to head toward his tent.

"Look out, Joe!" Zack yelled.

Joe turned and saw that Tucker was back on his feet, a Colt in his hand.

Whoa, Suzy! Turned his back on a hurt animal and look at him now. That gun was gleaming in the glow of the fire, and there was no mistaking the sound of the trigger cocking.

First mistake, Tucker, I still got my Adams double-action on me!

Joe fell to the ground, and rolled fast and hard away from the fire, toward the woods.

A bullet whizzed into the darkness over his head, and he heard Tucker cock the Colt for another shot. The big fool was standing right there against the light of the fire.

Second mistake, Tucker!

Joe sighted the Adams and fired. Tucker dropped the gun and reached for his shoulder, where the blood was gushing out like he was a stuck hog.

"Aw, hell!" cried Tucker. "That red-black nigger done kilt me." He staggered toward Joe like he was going to punch him, then fell to the ground.

In a second, Zack was by his side. Bent over him for a minute, then turned to Joe.

"You knows the penalty for shooting, Joe."

Why they could hang him.

With the whiskey in his brain and his blood up from the fight, Joe didn't stop to think, just lit out for the woods fast as he could.

"*Halt!*" A bullet whistled through the trees over his head, and he plunged deeper into the woods. He'd have to keep on running, of course. Hell, there wasn't a man in the command could catch him, drunk or sober.

I done gone and lost me everything now! But nobody's coming into those woods after me, and I still had got my Adams and my Choctaw dagger.

He knew only one place to go, trotting fast and taking all the old paths where he used to come out into the forest to trap birds or track the bears for old Massa. Wasn't a path around here he didn't know.

   ❊   ❊   ❊   ❊   ❊   ❊   ❊   ❊   ❊   ❊   ❊

He stopped for water at the Newton plantation, about three miles from Clifton, scouted around for a minute, then went down to the slave quarters. All of the little cabins were empty. He pushed open the door of one: nothing in there but the old straw bag the folks used to sleep on, now ripped open and lying all over the floor.

He walked a little farther down and saw the pickaninnies' trough—he'd eaten out of one like it when he was little, pushing and shoving with the other kids to see if they could get some of the bread and milk Aunt Garry used to pour into the trough. He'd always managed to get himself enough.

He walked over to the well, then remembered how his own troop, under orders, had been going around cutting the ropes in the wells. Sure enough, whoever had come this way—Yankee or Reb—had cut the rope.

Sometimes trotting, sometimes fast walking, and crouching down in the ditches when he had to, he finally reached Clifton. A couple of times, he had to get into the woods quickly because he heard the sound of horses' hooves on the road. Had to be Reb patrols. Wouldn't be any Yankees up here until tomorrow.

He skirted around the outside of Clifton, satisfied himself that there were no troops about, then went down to the slave quarters. Same thing as over at Newton's. Seemed like the loudest thing around was the pounding in his head. He remembered how at night, particularly when they were picking cotton in the moonlight to keep up with Massa's schedule, the whole quarters would be lit up, a big fire going in front of the row of cabins, people talking and children singing and shouting . . . Now there was nothing. Quiet like the grave.

He reached the cabin where he and Zenobia had lived together for nearly fifteen years. He pushed the door open. The place was a wreck, gourds all over the floor, the wooden table he'd made for her split up—

part of it must have been used for firewood. And the trundle beds where Luke and Millie used to sleep—somebody had taken them, too.

He closed the door behind him, got down on his hands and knees, and lit a match. Cupping its dim light with his hand, he searched every inch of the floor, looking for something, anything, of Zenobia's or Cally's, maybe even something that would give him a clue as to where they had gone. Surely she knew that someday he'd come back and look for her and that pretty little brown-skinned baby of his.

Shit, Zenobia! You should have left something.

But try as he might and search where he would, Joe couldn't find a thing to remember them by, much less a clue to their whereabouts. Then, just when he was about to blow out the third match, he saw something, almost covered up by the dust. It was the wooden comb he'd made for Zenobia, just about the time Millie was born . He ran his fingers over the smooth wood, felt the pretty carvings he'd put on it. Lord, Zee had been proud the first time she put it in her hair.

He held the comb against his heart, closed his eyes, and could just about see her, a little older but still pretty and haughty, full powerful hips, and skin that shone like fine polished furniture. Oh, it was Zenobia all right, but he couldn't quite make out what she was saying, like something was getting in the way. Then she seemed to fade and rise, go floating up high into some trees, finally drifting away up into some pretty white clouds with little black edges around them.

Gone.

Why hadn't she told him where Luke was? And Millie? Should have waited around, tarried awhile. Damn it, Zee—couldn't hear one word you said. Nary a one!

The door opened. Joe drew his Adams.

"Don't shoot, Joe. It just me."

"Uncle Dan? Ain't you got enough sense not to be poking all around at night? I could have killed you." Joe put the pistol away and hugged his friend.

"I knowed it was you, said you'd be coming back someday. Come on over to my shack. I'm the only one left on the plantation."

The old man was bent over, seemed smaller than before, but he still had that same blue-black skin. Leaning on his oak cane, he led Joe to a shack at the very end of a long row of cabins that stood about two hundred yards from the big house. Inside, he waved his arm for Joe to sit down on one of the two oak-stump stools. He went to light a lamp that hung near the door, but Joe stopped him.

"No need of attracting attention tonight."

As Joe's eyes became accustomed to the dark, he saw there wasn't much inside the shack save for the stools, a straw mattress that lay atop a wooden pallet on the floor, and another pallet where Uncle Dan had piled his clothes, boots, and some jars and dishes he must have scavanged from the abandoned shacks around him.

He reached across and put his right hand on Joe's knee. "I'm mighty glad to see you, son. It gets awful lonesome around here all by myself. Just waiting for the angels to come."

"Don't talk that way, you got some good years left in you."

The old man grinned. "Mighty kind of you to say so, but you knows the only reason I's here is -'cause don't nobody think nothing about me. Ain't worth nothing to nobody, that's why everybody leave me alone—the Yankees, the grayboys, and all them thieves and robbers out there. They comes through here most every day and don't bother me none, one way or another."

"But how do you live?"

"Got me a few chickens out there in a special place in the woods, got me some cornmeal and smoked pork meat. Even got me a little garden. We going to have us some good eating in the morning."

"For now, could I have some water?"

"Sure, and I got something a little stronger than that. Way you look I reckon you could use a good belt or two."

"You guessed right, but I'll just take the water. I'm running away from trouble and headed straight for it. Need to clear my head so's I can think straight. Now, how about you tell me what happened to Zenobia and Cally."

Uncle Dan poured himself a drink. "They gone with Miss Sue up somewhere the other side of Jackson, but you got to know that Cally were sick a lot, and Zenobia, she weren't much better. Her gout done got worse, sometime she couldn't even get out of bed."

He took a sip of whiskey from the cup. "I prayed a lot for them. And I still prays for them every night. Cally, she done took a real liking to me before they left."

"What she look like?"

"Joe, that little thing, she got the shiniest black eyes, and she always smiling. And you know, they could be lots of folks around, and she'd always run right up to me and stick her little hand out for me to shake. She beautiful, Joe."

He was silent for a moment, then pointed with his thumb up toward the big house. "You wouldn't believe what it look like up there."

"What happened?"

"Well, them Yankees-you one of 'em now, but these was white boys— they come through here mighty fast one day—looking to catch Massa Richard, they say he a powerful secesh. They got themselves some liquor, and when they didn't find him, they just naturally commenced to tear up everything."

Joe took Uncle Dan's hand. "Have you seen or heard anything of Luke or—?"

"It were something awful. They ripped up the mattresses looking for money, then commenced to burning the beds, and the tables and the curtains. Burnt everything, then pissed on the floor. Lord, it were bad. Finally, a captain come in and made them stop, made them put out the fires."

Joe said, "We trying to punish these slave masters, break them out of their nasty ways."

"Still weren't right to destroy all them beautiful things. Massa Richard, when he seed it, he were more madder than I ever seen him. And—oh Lord, Joe . . ."

"What?"

"He had Luke with him, serving as his orderly man."

"You sure?"

Uncle Dan finished the last of his cup of whiskey and put it down on the dirt floor. "Sure as I'm sitting here. I'd know that boy anywhere—he grown big and tall now, look just like you. He Massa Richard's body man and a blacksmith with General Forrest."

"Did Massa Richard say anything about Milly?"

"I didn't have no time to find out, barely had time to talk with him. They was in and out of here mighty fast."

Joe was completely sober now. And tired.

"Uncle Dan, I'm going up in the pine grove over there and get me some sleep. Be too dangerous sleeping down here. In the morning, I need you to give me some clothes to wear 'stead of this uniform, and some food. Then I'll be on my way."

"Where to?"

"Meridian. That's where Zenobia and Cally is and that's where I'm headed."

He went over to the grove, broke some pine branches off the trees, made a litter, and lay down to sleep.

Several times during the night he awoke to the sounds of night critters astir in the woods around him. And when he looked up from his bed of pine he saw bright stars splashed all over God's heaven way above him. He pulled Uncle Dan's blanket up over his head and fell back to sleep.

"Damn!" A sharp pain in his butt brought him awake. In front of him was a pair of brown boots and gray pants.

His eyes followed the pants upward to the open flap of the black holster on the brown leather belt of the Reb above him. He grabbed for his Adams.

"Wouldn't do that if I was you. Get up."

Standing there with four Rebs, and pointing right at him, was Uncle Dan.

"See, I told you there were a Yankee here."

Joe said, "Praise the Lord! I'se so glad Uncle Dan went for you. I know'd he would 'cause he a good nigger, sure love his grayboys, just like I do. I thanks you, Uncle."

"It were the least I could do for you, Joe."

"What you talking about, boy?" the corporal said. "You take me for a fool or something? And you with them sergeant stripes on you?"

"I'se a deserter, I done run the guards."

"A likely story. We'll see what the colonel says."

They tied Joe up, threw him over the mule's back, and took him over to the woods about a mile away, to a clearing full of Reb cavalry. Their colonel sure didn't look like no easy kind of man, not with that brace of pearl-handled pistols sitting right on the desk while he talked to Joe.

"Like I was telling this lieutenant, sir . . ." Joe pointed to the corporal.

"Damn," the colonel said. "They sure make anybody a sergeant in the nigger cavalry. You don't even know he's a corporal?"

"I'se ignorant, Colonel, sir. Like I was saying, I was with Colonel Witherspoon's Texas Brigade, sir, a mule skinner and a cook, sir. I's a good cook."

"And?" He glared at Joe, his hand toying with one of the pistols.

"Dem Yankees captured us'n, and next thing I knowed, Generals Grant and . . . let's see, who was that other one? Was it Sherman, yeah, de very same, and these two generals is arguing about whether to shoot us or not for they didn't want to have to feed no captured niggers."

"Boy, you ain't never seen them men."

"Ain't lying, Massa."

The colonel leaned forward.

"What'd they look like?"

"General Grant, he de one wanted to shoot me, but General Sherman, de redheaded one, he say, this nigger fought against us, now let him fight against *them*."

The corporal looked hard at Joe. "And?"

"General Grant, he say then I would have to fire against them, and he march me over to a big cannon, make me put three loads of ammunition in it, put in dat big old heavy ball, swab it, and pull the lanyard. It like to knock me off'n my feet. Then he say, now you go fight for us, boy, and they make this poor darky go into a nigger horse regiment."

The colonel roared with laughter. "Sounds just like Ulysses . We were together in Mexico. How came you to be at that plantation over the way?"

"Well, Massa, I was just abiding my time. Just waiting my chance to get away from those Yankees. So now when we gets up here, close to Massa's house, I knowed I could get away 'cause I knows de country 'round here real good."

"So what did you do?"

"Sneaked out the Yankee camp last night, and when the sentry come after me, I shot him square between the eyes and took off in the woods trying to find my white folks. Dat's how I come to be here." Joe fell to his knees in front of the table, rolled his eyes upward in their sockets, and folded his hands together like he was praying. "Oh, Massa, I'se so glad to be back with my white folks, you got to save me from dem Yankees."

"How many times did you shoot him?" the colonel asked, tapping his finger on the table. "How many times did you shoot that sentry?"

"Once."

The colonel motioned to the corporal. "Let me see his Adams."

He broke it, and counted the five remaining bullets in the cylinder.

"No nigger could have made up that story about Ulysses S. Grant. Wait till the general hears it. You say you a cook?"

"Best you ever et, Colonel, sir. Why sometimes old Colonel Osband he let me feed all de officers. They loved my cooking something awful. For a while there, sir, I was his orderly too."

The colonel leaned forward over the pistols on his desk. "We could use a real cook. You know how to polish boots and take care of horses?"

Joe, still on his knees, showed a wide row of white teeth and grinned up at the colonel. "I is the best. Used to race for Massa at Natchez."

"You better be, because I got one of the finest horses in the country out there—and that's why I got rid of that other boy. Couldn't take care of my Princess properly." He turned to the corporal. "Take charge of this man. Show him his duties, and let him prepare the officers' mess for tonight. We'll see how good a cook he is."

"Massa, you ain't never going to regret this. I'm one thankful nigger. You mighty good to me."

"Well now, don't you worry, Joe, you're back with your people, and we appreciate good niggers like you. As a matter of fact, if you're real good, we might let you fight with us, we got one colored boy that rides and fights with us just like white folks. You'll see him when you go get your new clothes."

He motioned to the corporal to escort Joe out of the tent.

"Oh, and, if we get anywhere close to Sherman and his boys, we'll let you

load you up a cannon and take a shot at *him*."

Joe bent over laughing and slapped his hands on his thighs. "That's a good 'un, Colonel, sir. A mighty good 'un."

❀   ❀   ❀   ❀   ❀   ❀   ❀   ❀   ❀   ❀   ❀

That night the colonel and his officers sat down at a tablelaid with a spot-less white table cloth. Dishes of baked sweet potatoes and slow-cooked string beans were at either end of the table, in the center chickens that had been barbecued on a spit. There were good hot pan biscuits to go along with them. And at the side of the table stood Joe, beaming, a white napkin wrapped over his arm.

"Hope it meets your 'spectations, sir."

Behind him were two waiters, bowing and scraping the way Joe had taught them a few hours earlier.

"Gentleman, we've found us a chef. This calls for some good wine." The colonel tossed Joe a key. "Go into my tent, you'll find a special liquor chest. Bring us out three bottles of that red wine."

By the time dinner was over, Joe had made two more trips to the wine cabinet, and the colonel and his staff officers were singing "When This Cruel War Is Over." The way they were bellowing, you'd have thought it was already over. And the singing got even louder when the colonel called for some of his men—his choristers, he called them—to come over and sing with them.

Joe was back in the mess area cleaning up when he heard the new voices:

> When the summer breeze is sighing mournfully
>   along
> Or when autumn leaves are falling
> Sadly breathes the song . . .

A beautiful soaring tenor was all too distinct from the rest of the voices. Damn. Wasn't another voice in the whole world like that one. And the last time he'd heard it was the night he and Zack stole those horses. Must be one of them Rebs that had been in that house. Just hoped it wasn't Andy, 'cause he'd be sure to recognize him.

Didn't his troubles ever end?

The field kitchen area wasn't far from the colonel's dinner table, and it was getting dark. Joe decided to walk over so as to get a better look.

Oft in dreams I see thee lying on the battle plain
Lonely, wounded, even dying . . .

Oh, that man sure could sing. His voice was sweeter than the clear juice from a ripe melon at the close of a hot summer day.

Joe got as close as he dared—close enough to see it was Andy, all right. Standing there along with five other Rebs in front of the officers' table, just singing his heart out.

The colonel looked back over his shoulder, and saw Joe.

"Come here, boy. Some of my officers want to personally thank you for that great meal!"

Oh, Lord. He walked over to the officers' table—not ten feet from Andy, who looked him dead in the face.

Calling but in vain. . . . .

He stopped singing, and raised his hand. Joe stood tensed on the balls of his feet. He'd run if he had to, and maybe they'd had enough to drink that they wouldn't be shooting so straight. . . .

Andy kept singing, God Bless him.

Weeping sad and lonely . . .

✧   ✧   ✧   ✧   ✧   ✧   ✧   ✧   ✧   ✧   ✧

"Best meal I've had since the war started, Joe," the colonel said. "The regiment will be going into the field tomorrow to give that old nigger outfit of yours a whipping. They won't know what hit them. We should polish them off by noon. That should give you time to get my tent in order and give Princess a good grooming."

"I reckon they won't know what hit them, Colonel, sir."

✧   ✧   ✧   ✧   ✧   ✧   ✧   ✧   ✧   ✧   ✧

In the morning, Joe was up early. He helped the colonel into his boots and buckled his saber and saber belt on. When all the troops was assembled and on their horses, he helped the colonel mount up.

"This a fine-looking animal, too, Colonel, sir."

"Never mind about Tornado, just see you take care of Princess. Rub her down good, you hear?"

"Yes, sir. Give those niggers a good licking for me. Stealing me away from General Witherspoon like they did."

The colonel led his regiment out of the camp about an hour before daybreak, and Joe went into the colonel's tent to start the cleanup. He was humming "Dixie," but at the same time wondering how the hell he had gotten himself into such a fix.

He folded the colonel's blanket, then pulled down a brace of pearl-handed revolvers from a peg, and began to polish the holsters. He eased one of the revolvers out of its holster, broke it, and spun the cylinder. All loaded. It would take the Rebs about an hour and a half to reach the place where they planned to ambush the regiment. Knowing the woods the way he did, he could probably make it in forty-five . . .

But what good would it do him even if he did get there first? He was a wanted man. They'd probably shoot him on sight.

He began to polish Colonel Montgomery's camp table. For the moment, he was better off with the Rebs. At least he wouldn't get shot. And he could get away from them any time he wanted.

He went outside. Wasn't one sentry left in the camp. Nothing but the wounded and they were still asleep.

It would be stupid to go back.

He walked over to the tree where Princess was tied. She was one fine-looking sorrel. Fast enough to beat Hawk?

A rooster crowed. Soon those wounded Rebs would be up and about. On the ground right close to Princess was a saddle and bridle.

Zack, Captain Stiles, Patton . . . those Rebs would cut them all down. Wouldn't take no nigger prisoners, nor their white captain.

He went back into the colonel's tent. He loosened his trousers enough to tie the holsters with the guns around his waist, rebuckled the pants back up over them, and went outside. There wasn't a sound from the camp when he walked Princess a ways off into the woods, saddled her up, and took off to where he figured the Third would be.

The sky in the east was dawn-pink. Couldn't be sure he'd get to Brown's Crossroads before the colonel, but—oh, hell he *had* to. His outfit was in trouble.

He reached the crossroads in just over a half hour. He tied Princess to a tree and squatted down to examine the dirt. Nope, no cavalry horses had passed this way yet. He spurred Princess and cut off the road to make better time. That Reb colonel was right about one thing. Princess could fly.

"Halt, or we'll fire!"

Six black troopers, carbines all leveled at him! More behind them. And at the front, Lieutenant Gary.

"Joe?" One grabbed his reins. "What the hell you doing out here, Joe?"

"Don't worry about that. Lieutenant, a whole regiment of Reb cavalry is right behind me, no more'n a half hour away. Maybe less."

"Be that as it may, you're under arrest. Sergeant, get him back to the colonel and let him report to him. The rest of you men dismount and prepare a skirmish line here." He glared at the sergeant. "Get a move on, man!"

Ten minutes later, the main body of the detachment was in motion.

"We'll see who does the ambushing," Colonel Osband said, then turned to Joe. "Report to your outfit and get that Reb jacket off. We're going to meet Colonel Montgomery."

"You mean I ain't under arrest, sir?"

"I'll deal with that after the fight. Now get the hell out of here."

"Yes, *sir.*"

Twenty minutes later Joe sat on Princess, carbine in hand, Colonel Montgomery's Colts still buckled on, watching from the woods, Zack at his side. A small artillery fieldpiece loaded with grapeshot and its crew stood at the ready. A gunner was poised to set it off with a match. Lieutenant Gary's small detachment, firing carbines from their horses, were riding back across the very field where they'd found Joe.

When they got to the far side of the clearing, they dismounted and fired a volley. Now Colonel Montgomery's men were flooding into the open space. Lieutenant Gary and his men grabbed their horses and ran off into the woods.

From his place of concealment, Joe could hear Colonel Montgomery loud and clear.

"After them, men, we'll teach this nigger cavalry a lesson they'll never forget."

The whole Rebel force came into the big field, firing their shotguns into the woods. The only thing Colonel Montgomery didn't know was that on both sides of the field, in the woods there, were the rest of the Third Cavalry, carbines cocked and aimed, just waiting till all the Rebs were in the jaws of the trap.

When Joe saw that saber he'd polished the night before, he felt kind of sorry for Colonel Montgomery. Him and all them officers Joe has fed such a good meal, the way you feed the pigs before the slaughter, they wasn't bad people. Hell, he wouldn't have minded riding with the colonel, if he hadn't wanted him to be a slave.

Here they came, lickity-split across the field, to the awful sound of their Rebel yell. Sounded like a cross between a hound dog baying and a mountain lion's holler.

The woods on three sides exploded with fire and smoke.

Rebs were falling everywhere. And the horses hit with bullets or grapeshot were screaming with pain.

"Fire at will!"

A steady stream of small arms fire poured into the Rebel ranks.

Colonel Montgomery dropped his saber. Was he hurt? If he was, it couldn't be too bad, because he was shouting, "Dismount, form as skirmishers."

These Rebs were some kind of soldiers. In the midst of all that fire, they kept coming on, shooting into the woods, because they would not take low in front of no colored boys.

The little fieldpiece spoke again, and Joe watched first one, then two, then eight Rebs begin to retreat back across the field. Colonel Montgomery stayed forward, near their colors.

"Don't fall back!" he cried.

But even he finally saw that they couldn't stand against the fury pouring out of those woods. They fell back across the field and set up another skirmish line.

Joe knew how good the gunners attached to the Third were. They'd shell them right out of there. And sure enough, it wasn't long—maybe after fifteen more shells from that little artillery piece—before the Rebs broke, got on their horses, and took off back down the road they'd come up just a while ago.

The Third Cavalry followed them, drove them all the way to a bridge.

Joe was right in front, leading his company. He wished he'd been a little quicker about it, though. By the time they got to the bridge, the Rebs were already burning it and taking up firing positions to protect their retreat. Colonel Montgomery was busy directing his troops.

And he almost had a fit when he saw Joe riding Princess—jumped up and down, waved his saber, and swore. You could hear him yelling over all the fire.

"Ten dollars and three bottles of my best corn liquor to the man that kills that nigger son of a bitch! But I'll hang the one who hits Princess."

Bullets whistled all around Joe's head.

"Joe, take that damn horse to the rear," Captain Stiles yelled. "The Rebs don't need one more thing to get their dander up."

When the fieldpiece caught up with Joe's company and began to shell the Rebs on the other side of the bridge, they retreated again. The Third Cavalry quickly threw together a makeshift bridge and continued the pursuit, swept right on through the camp where Joe had been a prisoner that morning. The Rebs scattered into the woods and the bayous.

   ✦   ✦   ✦   ✦   ✦   ✦   ✦   ✦   ✦   ✦

That evening, when the camp was all policed and the Reb and Yankee casualties taken care of, the colonel had Joe brought to his tent, the very same tent where Colonel Montgomery had slept the night before.

"Joe, you're a most fortunate man," the colonel said. "You just winged Tucker. Probably served the bastard right. It'll teach him not to cheat at cards."

"Yes, sir."

"But you were supposed to set an example. You and firewater don't mix, you know it and I know it. I want your word that you'll not drink whiskey again—not while you're in this regiment."

"Colonel, sir? That's a mighty stiff—"

"Stiff? You say anything but 'Yes, sir' and you'll find out what stiff is. Your word, Private!"

"Yes, sir. *Private*, sir?

"I'm demoting you for at least thirty days. And docking you thirty days' pay."

"Yes, sir."

"I'm also putting you in for a citation. That was a hell of an action you engaged in today."

"Thank you, sir . . . Colonel, sir, may I ask something now?"

He nodded, but his look warned Joe to take care what he was about. It told him, better than a demotion, how much he'd disappointed the colonel.

"I was wondering, sir, if you might not like for me to cook you and the other officers a fine victory meal tonight. I know where all the fixings are."

CHAPTER EIGHT

ZENOBIA knew escape would be hard. The dampness in the swamp was bound to make her gout act up. And what would happen when the cold swamp air hit Cally's lungs? Her cough could give them away in the woods.

There were so many patrollers out there, and she'd heard the tales of what had happened to black folk caught by soldiers. On both sides.

That night she prayed on her knees. "Jesus, they about to separate me from my very last child, and I cannot bear it no more. And poor little Ned—all he got is me and Lisa Mae. You a mighty good captain, and I'm calling on you to lead us on this journey."

The next morning, soon as he'd finished cleaning up the yard, Drayton came into the kitchen with a big smile on his face.

"Good morning, good morning . . ."

It wasn't like him to be full of smiles and greetings.

"I've decided to go with you."

"I think you a brave man." Lisa Mae snuggled close up into his arms. "You'll never be sorry for this."

Drayton smiled. "Just don't want to see you two women sold away, that's all."

No, that wasn't all. Zenobia looked at Lisa Mae, then back at Drayton. Had she slipped out during the night and slept with him?

Didn't matter. Probably Drayton had decided that Miss Sue might sell him too.

She slapped at a mosquito buzzing around her ear. There were dozens of them around. "You going to be able to steal some horses and a wagon?" she asked.

"Yes, but that won't get us but a little ways. We going to have to go by the swamps." He frowned. "I still think you wrong to run away. Maybe Miss change her mind."

This man was getting on her last nerve. Wasn't it bad enough that she had decided to go into the marshland with her baby child? She was leaving a place where they had decent food and a sturdy roof over their heads at night. God only knew what dangers lay ahead of them. She didn't need Drayton trying to make her change her mind, weaken her will.

"You going with us or not?"

He grabbed at a fly, caught it, held it in his hand for a second, then released it.

'I'm going. Now, first thing, we got to fix Cally's cough. I'll make up a special medicine—mullein leaves, sugar, and vinegar. Sure to help her some, but she got to take it twice a day."

"I'll see to it. What else?"

"We're in luck, 'cause Miss she going away to Miss Margie's for a few days and she taking the children. And Linus and Mary, they so old, they hardly going to know we gone."

Zenobia smiled. As if the two old house slaves would have said anything anyhow.

"What about the hounds? What we do if they come after us with them hounds?"

"You sure enough full of questions. Tire a man out. Let's sit down over there." He pointed to the pine bench near his cabin. "I done taken my precautions. Took me two pistols out the big house, and some knives. The dogs may be be the least of our troubles." He shook his head. "See, Zenobia, you so headstrong. You don't know like I do about all of them dangers. It ain't only all them varmints in the swamps. There's deserters, Yankees and grayboys, and there's bands of irregulars—they's armed and they don't obey nobody, they the law all to themselves. You don't hear the way these white folks talk like I do. Some of them are scared of their own people."

Lisa Mae put her hand on Drayton's. "You shoot me before you lets them take me. Hear?"

"Me neither. Regular or otherwise," Zenobia said. "Shoot everybody if that happen."

"Everybody, Zenobia?"

She looked beyond Drayton over at the little pond where, sometimes in the evenings, she used to sit beside Cally and watch her kick her tiny feet in the cool water, or try to catch the little tadpoles darting back and forth. She turned back to Drayton.

"Everybody."

"I will think on it." Drayton said.

"You do that. Now, what else we need?"

"I'm packing some tools with me, because what with the swamps being flooded the way they are, I plan to build us a raft once we get to the rivers."

"That's a good idea." Lisa Mae was looking at Drayton like he'd invented sunshine, but Zenobia had to admit he was smarter than she'd thought.

"You two pack enough food for a week for us all," he said. "Corn bread and cooked corn—things we can eat without cooking, for we scarcely going to be able to make a fire. And warm clothes, 'specially for the children."

"All right. And where we heading for?"

"Right back to Clifton. I know where lots of food is hidden. Uncle Dan is still there and he'll find some place for us to hide. We can rest, then figure how out we're going to get down to Vicksburg way."

Seemed like he'd thought of just about everything. Now it was her turn to get busy so they'd be ready to leave the next day.

◊　　◊　　◊　　◊　　◊　　◊　　◊　　◊　　◊　　◊　　◊

"Bye, Zenobia, bye, Lisa Mae." Miss Sue's children started waving even before the wagon moved forward.

"You behave yourselves!" Zenobia shouted after them as they disappeared down the road. "You hear me?"

As soon as they were out of sight, she took Lisa Mae by the arm.

"You go down to the cabin, get the clothes. Me, I'm going back to the cook shed, pick up the children and the food. Meet me down at Drayton's cabin. Hurry now!"

✼   ✼   ✼   ✼   ✼   ✼   ✼   ✼   ✼   ✼   ✼

Drayton, dressed like a proper coachman, was waiting for Zenobia and the children, but not Lisa Mae.

"I sent her down here to get the clothes. You didn't see her?"

Drayton shook his head and threw his hands up in the air. "We got no time to lose."

Confound it! Where was she?

"Here, get the children and the food packed away, I'm going to look for her."

She walked over to their cabin, looked in, saw the sack with all their clothes was still there. Damn. She threw it over her shoulder and went back to the wagon.

Drayton had already stowed the little packages of food in the wagon, and made the children comfortable on a bed of hay. The two brown horses hitched to the wagon were lazily flicking their tails at the horseflies buzzing around them.

"Come on, get up here with me," he said. "We got to go. Just have to leave Lisa Mae."

"Give me a few minutes. I'll find her."

Drayton took off his hat, slapped it across his knee, and got down from his seat. "I'm thinking this a mighty poor way to be starting."

"Drayton . . ." She took him by the arm, and her touch seemed to calm him.

"All right. But hurry. It don't bode no good for us to—"

Lisa Mae ran up to them, breathless and crying.

"What's the matter?" Zenobia said.

"Old Mary catch ahold of me and say she know I'm going and she want to go, too. Stood there asking to go, talking about she want to die free, and all the time I'm trying to get away and saying we ain't going nowhere."

Drayton said, "Where's she now?"

Lisa Mae pointed back up the hill. "She were on her knees begging when I pulled away and come running here."

Oh, Lord. She felt bad about Mary. Worried, too. Would she give the alarm?

"Zenobia, you get up here with me." Drayton said. "Lisa Mae, get in back. We leaving now. Devil take the hindmost."

Drayton snapped the whip, and they were out of the yard and onto the muddy road. After they'd been traveling for maybe half an hour, Zenobia turned to Drayton.

"No matter what happens, I am mighty grateful to you."

"You know why I'm doing this, don't you?"

"Why?"

He covered her hand with his. "Because I want to show you I'm a better man than Joe."

"There ain't no better man than Joe."

"Then why'd he run away and leave you and Cally all alone?"

She pushed his hand away. "Don't let's go into that, now. We got bigger fish to fry and—oh, Lord, look like they straight ahead of us."

The very first patrollers were galloping down the road toward them. Two riders, all covered with dust, one wearing a red hat, and one a brown hat, both carrying guns. One of them pointed his shotgun at Drayton.

"Where you niggers think you going?"

"To Clifton, Massa, take care of Miss's plantation, 'cause the Yankees done left."

"Never heard of it. How far is it?"

Drayton took out a big red handkerchief and mopped his brow. "Three days, Massa."

"How come your Miss ain't going with you?"

"Miss's children get schooling here, sir, been here for most a year now after the Yankees chased us out of Clifton."

"Guy, let's take 'em back where they come from," said the short, stocky one with the shotgun aimed at Drayton.

"Well, now, Massa, that's up to you, but Miss Kenworthy, she going to be powerful mad if you do that. Major Kenworthy, he come by here the other day and told her to send somebody back, tell everybody General Forrest say the Yankees won't be back up Clifton way for a while. He say we rules up there now."

"This colonel, he rides with General Forrest?"

"Yes, sir."

Guy slowly circled his horse around the wagon, stopped in front of Cally and made a face.

"Hi, little 'un."

She waved with her tiny hand and he waved back. Then she broke out in that special grin of hers and pointed at the gleaming silver medallion in the center of the harness of Guy's stallion as if she wanted to touch it. He nudged the horse up to her so she could. "Pretty horsie." Lord, was there anybody on earth who didn't love that child?

Zenobia hoped this man was also thinking he didn't want to be messing with any niggers in any way connected with General Forrest's cavalry. But he had to be thinking, too, about not losing the money due him if they were running away.

"You know, now I think on it, Guy, it don't seem likely to me these niggers would be running away dressed like they are and in broad daylight. Why, Uncle here, he dressed to kill. Let's take a look at their passes."

Drayton handed them over. The one called Guy pulled out a pair of spectacles and read each one carefully, some of them more than once.

"Well, everyone's accounted for, and the passes say they are going to Clifton over in Edmunds County." He looked at Drayton. "Now I know where you mean. You're right, we control over that way now. Reckon I'd best let you go."

The men reined in their horses and turned to ride away.

Zenobia realized she'd been holding her breath and was about to let it out when Drayton spoke.

"Massa?"

What in the world was the matter with that man? Didn't he see they were going away?

Guy turned back. "What'd you want, boy?"

"Seeing as you a big captain, and we don't want us no more trouble today, you reckon you could help us poor niggers and give us a pass that say you done seed us and looked us over? Them other folks up the road got to know a big man like you."

"Matter of fact, they do. Everybody between here and Jackson knows Guy Burr."

"Thank you kindly, Cap'n Guy, sir."

When the man had written out the pass, Drayton handed him a bottle of bourbon. "Don't reckon old colonel would mind if I give you this when you done protected his niggers so good."

"Mighty white of you, Cephus." Guy's wit sent them off riding hard and laughing big. Or maybe it was the thought of that bottle of Major Kenworthy's mellowed bourbon.

*   *   *   *   *   *   *   *   *   *   *

Over the next few hours, patrollers or troops stopped them just about every hour. Zenobia worried each time that they might steal the horses and wagon for some kind of soldier use, but the pass worked like magic, and by noontime they'd covered a good ten miles. They stopped in a willow grove to have something to eat and let the children pee. When they were ready to go, Zenobia put Lisa Mae up front and sat in back with the children.

Cally said, "Mommy, it hurts riding back here."

"I know, baby, come here and sit on my lap."

"What about me?" Ned asked.

Zenobia reached out and drew him close. "I ain't got but one lap. Will a hug and kiss do for now?"

Ned smiled and snuggled up close to her. "Where we going?"

"Don't ask so many questions. Less you know the better."

"But I was having fun back there at Miss Kenworthy's place, they got the best pine trees for bending and springing."

"I saw you, baby, and you was something." Zenobia believed little boys needed to feel strong, so she hadn't said a thing when he went out there in the woods and climbed a slender pine tree that stood maybe eighteen feet tall. When he got high enough, his weight bent the tree backward and he'd come falling down to the ground, holding on tight.

And don't you know, when the tree hit the ground, all that strength in its young trunk made it spring back up and send Ned flying back up into the air with it. Zenobia's heart had most dropped down into her stomach. And just as she thought, he didn't have enough strength to hold on to the tree trunk, flew through the air and landed on the ground right on his little black butt. She let him cry, and in a little while he was right back on that flying tree. Strong, determined little boy. He'd better be, considering what lay ahead of them.

By late afternoon, the children were tired and cranky. Cally would fall asleep, then the jolting of the wagon would wake her up. Ned kept wanting to get out of the wagon to run and play. The fourth time he said, "I want to pee," Zenobia saw she'd have to do some explaining.

"This ain't no game, Ned. You only eight years old, you ought to be running and playing, but you got to be a man now. If these white folks catch us today and take us back to Miss Sue, you ain't never going to see me or Lisa Mae again in life and they'll beat Mr. Drayton to death. So you hush up now. And if you got to, you pee in your pants. Because we ain't stopping no more."

About six o'clock, Drayton pulled over to the side of the road close by a plantation. A smaller road led down toward a big log cabin that stood about a quarter of a mile away.

He started tying the horses up. "Come on up here, we got to talk and make up our minds about some things."

Zenobia covered the children with a blanket. "You all just rest and be quiet."

"We in a mighty rough situation right now," Drayton said.

"Why?" Lisa Mae asked.

"These animals are tired and need rest, water, and food. You all and these chilluns need the same. Night is coming on and we can't afford to be on these roads at night, pass or no pass. And we about to get out of that man's territory."

"So what you thinking?" Zenobia said.

"That we come this far, and got two choices. We can try to find us some colored shacks around here and stay the night, or—"

"You couldn't hide all of us and the horses and wagon from Massa. Niggers would be scared enough to go tell him."

"*Or* we could keep on going, off into the woods, ditch the wagon and bed down for tonight. Take off tomorrow through the forest—on foot."

"That's one more night for Cally to be in the woods," Zenobia said. "And I don't want that. When exactly will Miss Sue be back?"

"Most likely day after tomorrow, in the morning—but she might be back tomorrow night. And we can't be sure about what old Mary going to do. A man galloping on a horse can easy travel three times as fast as us."

Zenobia put her hand on Drayton's. "Supposing we puts our head in the lion's mouth tonight?"

"What you mean?"

"Supposing we shows our passes and ask the overseer at this plantation to let us stay tonight in their slave quarters since we traveling back to Miss's plantation to take care of it?"

"Zenobia, you sure enough something else." He shook his head. "I ain't never disobeyed Miss before and now you got me telling all these lies, just 'cause you-all *thinks* she might sell you down the river. He looked at Lisa Mae. "I thinks we should go off into the woods and—"

"Well, we ain't!" Zenobia pointed down the road to the plantation. Two white men and a colored man were galloping toward them. "You better do the way I told you."

And that's just what he did. Asked them white folks couldn't these poor colored travelers have a place to stay down at the slave quarters. The overseer looked over their papers and told the colored man to see to it that they were bedded down for the night.

After sunup the next morning, and a breakfast of mush, they were ready to move on. The air was still and heavy, working up to be mighty hot as the day wore on. Just as they were about to leave, the colored man who had brought them down to the shacks the night before came riding along the path.

"Massa want you to stop up by the big house before you leave."

The overseer was waiting at the front door for them. "Good morning. How did you sleep last night?"

Zenobia didn't like the sound of the man's voice. Something was wrong.

He came down the steps and patted Ned on the head. "That's a right strong-looking boy you've got there. What's your name, son?"

"Ned, Massa."

"Mighty fine manners, too." He bent down so that his head was level with Ned's. "Where all these folks going this morning, Ned boy?"

Zenobia took Ned's hand. "We told you last night, Massa. He don't know nothing more."

"Let him speak for himself. Where you going?"

"Over to Clifton to take care of Miss Sue and Major's house, sir."

"Well, that's good." He stood up straight again and nodded a few times. Took his time looking at the rest of them, one by one.

Then his glance fell on Cally. "My goodness gracious, child, your eyes are pretty enough to drive away a cloudburst in August." Delighted, Cally stood up, clapped her hands, jumped up into the air, and fell all a-tumbling back down in the hay. "See me!"

"Why I surely do, darling. Now I got to get back to business." He turned to Zenobia.

"I have a guest going your way. His horse went lame, so you all can take Mr. Coursey over to Doylestown—that's about fifteen miles from here." He looked at Drayton. "You wait right here."

Zenobia wanted to scream, but praying seemed to make more sense under the circumstances.

Massa Coursey was a sight to see with an old grayboys' forage cap on his head and the sleeve on his right side pinned up onto his blouse. His white vest with yellow trim looked like it had been made for a stouter man, and the only thing that seemed lively about him was his red face and long black whiskers.

"Morning, folks. My good luck you came along when you did. " He settled down on the seat beside Drayton. "Beautiful day for a ride. Yessiree, you-all come along just in time—old Red let me down. And that horse been dependable as the devil up to now."

Drayton said, "Always give me pleasure to help one of our brave soldiers, suh."

"Used-to-be soldier, you mean." Coursey pulled out a chaw of tobacco from his pocket and offered it to Drayton. "Here, have some."

"I surely do thank you, Massa. Them Yankees should be ashamed of themselves."

Before long they were both chewing and spitting away.

"I reckon I'm lucky to be here at all," Coursey said. "Many of my neighbors will never again see the light of day, but the Good Lord has watched over me."

Drayton nodded at the man's sleeve. "If'n you don't mind, sir, how did that happen?"

"A Yankee cannonball down at Vicksburg done it. It was almost spent but had enough left on it to mangle my arm."

Zenobia leaned forward over Drayton's shoulder. "Way I hears it, we going to get Vicksburg back. Just the way the Yankees was run out of Clifton, that's the way we going to make them leave Vicksburg. Got no right coming down here, tearing up everything like they do."

Massa Coursey smiled. "You-all are just like Lionel. He's my head nigger, real faithful. When that Yankee scoundrel Colonel Grierson came through, burning houses and all, Lionel hid my wife and some of our belongings back in the swamp. Took care of her for three days. I was mighty grateful."

Drayton grinned. "We lives to make you happy, Massa."

"Well, ain't that a nice way of putting it, now? Let's drink to that?" He pulled out a flask and offered it to Drayton.

"Lawsy, Massa!" A wide grin spread across Drayton's face soon as he'd swallowed the whiskey. "That's some mighty powerful stuff!"

Coursey cackled, enjoying the effect. "That's another thing Lionel does good—makes some of the finest corn liquor in the river county." He waved the flask at two passing patrollers on horseback going the other way. "Howdy, boys, top of the morning to you." They grinned and rode on.

Lord, that man could talk. Soon he was pointing out every little thing along the road to Drayton.

"See that house over there? Had many a dance there when I was a youngster."

Zenobia didn't see a house, only a chimney.

"Look over yonder. See them fields?" All she saw was wild-growing weeds. "Used to have cotton all over there before the Yankees come through."

That flask had to be near empty—who knew what Drayton might say with all that liquor in him?

Massa Coursey slapped him on the back. "One thing been on my mind since we started this little ride. How come you taking them youngsters back over to Clifton with you, if your old Miss want you to be taking care of her place? Ain't they going to be in the way?"

That sly white man wasn't as drunk as he pretended.

"Only Miss and a couple of old niggers left with her over at Meridian,"

Drayton said. She can't be worried what no children might get into."

"Been better for us if'n we could have left them there," Lisa Mae said.

Bless Lisa Mae's sweet lying heart!

Coursey drained the very last drops of corn liquor from the flask. "What you got in here?" He pointed to the carpet bag, which lay on the floor between him and Drayton.

Lord have mercy. They could do without the bourbon, but how would they ever explain the pistols and tools?

"That bag right down there between us," Coursey said. "I knowed that stuff were powerful, but I never knowed it to make a man go blind."

Drayton grinned. "Massah, I can't open that bag. That's the Major's! Miss made it up special for when he come riding back through Clifton, said I was to give to him and him only. He in General Forrest's cavalry."

Coursey put his arm around Drayton's shoulder. "Well, now, how's the major going to know I opened that bag if you don't tell him?" He looked back at Zenobia and whispered, "Tell me, how is he to know? You ain't going to tell him, are you?"

She shook her head. "No, suh."

With a quick motion, Coursey reached down toward the bag.

"No, Massah. Major whip me something awful."

"Then let it be so." Coursey struggled with the buckle.

"Well, sir, if you insist." Drayton drew up the horses, then reached down and pulled out a bottle of bourbon. Coursey grabbed it.

"No wonder your Miss wouldn't let you open that. Hell, man, we got us enough whiskey to drink our way into Doylestown and way beyond. When the major asks what happened, you tell him them thieving Yankees got it!"

With all the whiskey he and Drayton had drunk, Zenobia was relieved when he said Doylestown was just little way off now. The sun was almost directly overhead—they'd for sure better get off into the woods soon. They couldn't count on Miss coming home tomorrow morning; they had to plan on her being there tonight and the patrollers and bloodhounds being after them, too. If only they'd taken Drayton's advice and gotten into the swamps last night. Now they had to get rid of this talking fool on the wagon.

When they drew up to Massa Coursey's house, Drayton helped him down.

"Thank you all kindly." He stumbled and almost knocked Drayton over.

"Now you can go to the stables and water and feed the horses. Afterward, come on up to the cookhouse—Malindy'll give you a good meal and start you on your way."

"And we thanks you, Massa, but we'uns will just get the horses fixed up and be on our way. Miss expect us to be there by tomorrow night."

Drayton was none too steady himself, but he wasn't too drunk to know they had to get away from here.

"I'm hungry," Cally said. "I want something hot to eat."

Ned nudged her. "You ain't got to have anything hot, Cally. We need to keep on going."

"Don't poke me. I'm hungry."

Massa Coursey settled it. "Looks like we got ourselves a mutiny in the ranks. You all stay and eat. That's an order."

"Yessuh."

Drayton started the horses down the slope towards the stables. Zenobia got down from the back of the wagon and took Cally in her arms.

"Baby, don't ever talk around white peoples when us grown folks is with them. You can get us in a heap of trouble, hear?"

❁   ❁   ❁   ❁   ❁   ❁   ❁   ❁   ❁   ❁

The sun was already beginning to set when they got back on the road. You could tell Drayton was mad by the way he took it out on the horses, whipping them along. Zenobia didn't blame him, and not just because they'd been delayed. Lisa Mae had talked long with the colored folks back on that plantation, and who knew what she might have let slip? You couldn't tell what even coloreds might do, who they might tell. Only good thing was that Mr. Coursey had given them a note vouching for them

They were riding now on a road with open fields of corn on either side. As soon as they got a decent way up the road, Drayton reined in the horses.

"The very next time I sees a little road we turning off, and finding us a place to hide in one of these cornfields or in the woods."

"I think we should get as close as we can to Clifton before we go off in the woods," Zenobia said.

"You are one stubborn woman. Look, I know the way better than you, and just over near those hills there's a little river runs down toward Clifton, particularly when the water is as high as it is now. We can spend the night over there, and in the morning I'll get to work on a raft."

"But—"

"But nothing, Zenobia. If Miss Kenworthy gets home tonight she'll have the dogs after us before daybreak. Our best chance is on a raft when them hell hounds come."

Zenobia sighed and turned around in her seat.

"Start getting yourselves ready. Soon as Drayton find a spot, we going to go off the road and get out of this wagon."

But how would they hide the wagon so it couldn't be seen from the road? Far as you could see there was nothing but cornfields. Zenobia solved the problem about a heartbeat after Drayton did—he was going to head straight into the fields.

He waited till they came to a spot where he could see nobody was coming in either direction, then steered the horses and wagon off the road and straight up between the rows of corn. The ground was soft, and the horses strained, but on either side the corn rose so high it gave mighty good cover. There was barely room for the wagon to move, and when they got a good ways into the field, he stopped.

"Get everybody and everything out of the wagon. Quick, now."

This was it—the real beginning of the journey toward freedom. Zenobia's heart was pounding while she helped unhitch the horses and gave the reins to Lisa Mae to hold. It seemed as if everything else—all that tricking on the road and the rest of it—was a game. But now, as she helped Drayton pile corn stalks all around the wagon so you'd have to be up real close to see it, she knew they were truly runaways. On their way to freedom and no turning back.

Soon the wagon was all covered up. She picked up one haversack, handed the other to Lisa Mae, and took Cally in her arms while Lisa Mae led Ned by the hand. Drayton was loaded down with what he needed for building his raft—a hatchet, awl, chisel, hammer, and some nails. He'd also brought rope, though he said he'd just as soon use heavy vines, already soaked. They could tolerate the water better.

She watched him lead the two horses by their reins. "I thought you was going to leave them here."

"Changed my mind. Look how low the sun is. Soon as it goes down and we can't be seen, we're going to get on horseback. We'll have a heap easier time reaching those woods that way than on foot—now, don't you start arguing with me, just keep on going. We got to put distance between that road and us."

Zenobia looked up at the sky. It was beginning to look right pretty, with the white puffy clouds and that old sun a fiery red ball behind them. They reached the end of the cornfield at about the time it went down. Drayton got everybody mounted—Lisa Mae, Cally, and Zenobia on one horse, himself and Ned on the other—and off they rode into the dark of the forest. The sounds of the night were all around them, hoot owls and crickets and, far off in the distance, some kind of swamp critter roaring. Zenobia reached down into her dress, glad Drayton had trusted her with one of the pistols.

She whispered ahead to him, "How far you think it be to the river?"

"Never you mind. You just watch that horse, so he don't throw you. Should be there in about an hour."

Zenobia tried to keep her mind on the horse. But all around her was nothing but dark, and trees looking for all the world like haints—sounding like them, too, when the evening breeze rustled the branches. If there were haints out there, she prayed they were the kind that watch over you like Joe said his ancestors watched over him.

CHAPTER NINE

IN EARLY June of 1864, not far from Tupelo, Mississippi, Major Richard Kenworthy sat under a tree reading a letter from his wife. Things were really going to hell at home. Sue had sold off all the slaves she could, trusting that the ones she'd taken over to Meridian would be enough to see to her and the children's needs. And now that damned Zenobia was giving her trouble, talking back and such. Well, he'd never trusted Zenobia—any more than he trusted her son. First chance he got, he'd try and run off. That kind of thing ran in the blood.

He kept going back to one paragraph in the letter.

> Your sister wrote to say she's thinking of moving to Texas with the children and leaving Pauline in charge of the plantation. As it is, Dorothy has entrusted Pauline with the direction of the entire place, and she's doing a fine job . . .

The sight of Pauline's name was enough to excite him. He put the letter down for a minute. Had there ever been a more striking woman? Dark eyes that flashed, a beautiful face, a body that moved with incredible grace and lightness. Long hair that swirled over coffee-brown shoulders . . .

He closed his eyes and saw her as she'd been that day he caught her in her room, bathing in the wooden tub, her breasts and thighs glistening in the water. Heard her cries, felt the intensity of her struggle, then. . . . What right had his father had to give her to Dorothy as a wedding present, take away from him the one woman he'd ever loved that way? Of course he loved Sue, would have laid down his life for her. But for Pauline he would have leapt over high mountains, swum through turbulent seas, walked through fire and brimstone. That's just the way she'd made him feel.

All that talk about how a Southern gentleman didn't sleep with the house slaves—what a bunch of horse manure! Especially from that hypo-critical father of his who'd bedded every good-looking colored woman on the plantation at one time or another, from the high yellows to the ones so black it seemed like the color might rub off on you if you touched them. Richard liked the honey-colored ones himself, but the old man didn't care so long as they . . . Oh God, had *he* ever been with Pauline? The thought made Richard sick. No, she'd fought too hard, seemed to think things should be different for her. But after that first time, she'd given in to him. And left him with a memory that no woman could ever match.

He'd have her, too. He didn't care how this damn war ended—he would get up to Dorothy's plantation and have Pauline again, find some way of making her live with them. Besides, he had something she wanted very badly. What wouldn't she give to have Luke free?

"What the hell you smiling about, old buddy?" It was Clint Adams. "Considering that we're likely to get our asses blown off tomorrow."

Richard folded the letter up, put it back into his knapsack. "I'm not worried about it. The general's plan sounds foolproof."

"How foolproof can it be when Sturgis outnumbers us two to one?"

"Sturgis isn't Nathan Bedford Forrest, and that's the difference," Richard said. "Wouldn't matter if they had us ten to one—Old Bedford would still carry the field."

"I hear it's going to be Grierson's cavalry in front for them, and some nigger infantry behind him."

"I think we've shown what we can do to them. Stop worrying. Sit down and have a smoke with me. Remember that time . . ."

❀   ❀   ❀   ❀   ❀   ❀   ❀   ❀   ❀   ❀   ❀

After Clint retired to his tent for the night Richard went down to where the colored mule-skinners sat talking around their fire.

The letter from home had started some other thoughts stirring. He called Luke out. The boy was getting tall and strong, looking more like his father every day. Could it have been that long ago that a white boy and a black boy played and tuseled, growing up together at Clifton?

"How're you making out these days, Luke? I hear you do an outstanding job of blacksmithing."

"Yes, sir, Major."

The boy had Joe's ways about him. Sounded respectful enough, but there was something in the way he said it . . .

"You getting enough to eat? You a growing boy."

"Yes, sir."

"They feed you pretty good, then?"

"Tolerably well, Major."

"I should say so! I hear you get molasses and corn bread and milk every morning."

"We do, sir."

Richard put his arm around Luke's shoulder. "You miss your sister and auntie?" He felt the tense muscles. Maybe he'd finally get a rise of the sly little bastard.

"Yes, sir, I do, Major . . . Massa Kenworthy, can I ask you something?"

"Surely."

"Do you know where my mama and daddy are?"

"Way things are now, it's hard to know where anybody is from day to day." If the boy knew where his folks were, he might take a notion to run off and find them. "Go on back and get some rest. It's late, and we got a big fight tomorrow."

❖   ❖   ❖   ❖   ❖   ❖   ❖   ❖   ❖   ❖   ❖

Early the next morning, the smell of frying pork and hot bread wafted through the humid Mississippi air. After breakfast, when the horse holders had been assigned, Captain Clint Adams made his report.

"Battalion all present or accounted for, sir."

Richard was aware of the fine showing he himself made on such occasions, tall and proud in the saddle, and he always enjoyed addressing the men before battle.

"Men, today you're going to have the privilege and honor of whipping

Yankee cavalry and infantry with your revolvers. Every man's to carry two of them, and you're going to fight on foot. Wait till they get real close and shoot low—General Forrest especially wants you to remember that. Shoot low and you'll always hit something. They got something hanging down low that's mighty precious to them, ain't it, boys?"

Laughter erupted in the ranks. "You said it, Major!"

"Now, there's something else that's pretty important for you to know. There's a lot of nigger infantry going to be fighting with them."

"We'll skin the black devils alive!"

"Oh, we going to have us a good time roasting them coons!"

The major raised his hand to silence them. "Three days ago, before they left Memphis, these niggers who are going to fight with General Sturgis got down on their knees and swore to avenge Fort Pillow, swore they would die before they surrendered. And a Yankee officer especially got up in front of them and told them they would be coming against General Nathan Bedford Forrest and his men, that they were to expect no quarter and give none!"

An angry murmur ran through the ranks.

"To show you how serious these niggers are taking this thing, they're wearing badges saying Remember Fort Pillow. Our pickets captured one of the bastards last night."

The major took his hat off and waved it around in the air.

"Make them die down on their knees, just like they were when they took that oath. Now, go with God!"

The men raised a cheer. Then he watched them, thin and raggedy but full of determination, marching off to take up their positions. He felt a surge of pride to be serving with them. A renewed sense of the rightness of what they were doing.

❖   ❖   ❖   ❖   ❖   ❖   ❖   ❖   ❖   ❖   ❖

His faith in his men was well justified. By noon, supported by General Forrest's brilliant use of artillery, they had just about destroyed the Yankee cavalry. Richard led charge after charge, and each time they'd hurt the badly.

But now, from behind a fence where he'd called a temporary halt to the pursuit, with his binoculars he spotted a new threat. A brigade of infantry was coming fast down the road. What a sight—darkies in uniform! Shit, they had to be tired, trotting that way with this mean sun blazing down on them.

He turned to Adams. "Pass the word. Drink plenty of water, check out those six-shooters, and prepare for bayonet attacks. Because that's what's coming."

He walked up and down the line, encouraging the men. Most of them were stripped down to their waists in the heat of the day. It was hot enough to make you feel as if you were wearing the heat.

General Forrest came along on his sorrel. He was a big man, six feet tall at least, with piercing brown eyes, heavy brows, and a high forehead made higher by his receding hairline. A well-trimmed mustache blended smoothly into a perfectly manicured beard. On the shoulders of his immaculately tailored uniform he wore the two stars of a major general.

He was the picture of the gentleman soldier, and at the sight of him the men lifted a cheer.

"In three hours," he said, "we're going to have that crossroads and those cannon that have been making it uncomfortable for you up here. Just obey your orders, and we shall have the victory." He smiled at Richard. "Counting on you, my boy, same as I did at Shiloh."

"I'll do my best, sir."

Just after two o'clock, the Yankee artillery started firing and all hell broke loose. All along the line the colored regiments got up, gave loud huzzas that gave way to shouts: "Remember Fort Pillow!" A drum and fife corps came right behind them, in perfect formation, playing "John Brown's Body." Bayonets fixed, they marched across the field, straight to where Richard's boys lay waiting for them on an embankment behind a fence. To the left, an artillery battery, its guns loaded with grape, was ready to give those Negroes a real warm reception.

"Wait till I give the order, men. Aim carefully. And remember—shoot low."

The band played so well it seemed a shame to spoil the sound. Had to give it to them—they looked like they were on parade. In front of the trumpets, a little darky with sergeant's stripes carried the Union colors. A tall one carried the regimental flag.

Well, parading was one thing, fighting another. In another minute, he'd see what they were made of.

"At a quick march, forward."

Not yet. . . . Damn, they were well drilled. The steady advance picked up speed.

"Fire!"

The heavy volley swept over the Union lines like a firestorm. They staggered as if they were trying to walk into a strong north wind. All along the way, men began to go down. The flag bearer was one of the first, and another man picked up the standard.

Richard paced back and forth along the line.

"Aim carefully, Reilly."

"Thataboy, Moten."

"Steady, everybody."

Then the Negroes were among them, swinging their rifles and thrusting with their bayonets. Richard, saber in one hand and a revolver in the other, found himself up against a big darky with red eyes.

"I'se going to kill you dead, *sir*."

How dare he talk to a white man like that? Richard almost dropped his guard, but he sidestepped the Negroe's thrust just in time, then stuck him in the head with his saber.

A number of times it seemed as if it was over and the Negroes were retreating. The six-shooters had to be getting on their nerves . . .

But here they came again, still yelling about Fort Pillow.

And again.

And again.

❧   ❧   ❧   ❧   ❧   ❧   ❧   ❧   ❧   ❧   ❧

Four o'clock. Quiet fell on the battlefield. Men drank rainwater that had gathered in rivulets. The Yankee bands had stopped playing.

When General Forrest came up, Richard wondered if he'd order the retreat. They couldn't take another assault, not in the condition his men were in.

"Men, we've got them licked. You may not know it, but the Yankee cavalry is in full retreat. And we've got some guns and men coming up over that hill there. When your officers give the command, we're going to attack and make 'em wish they hadn't."

Richard had been sure they couldn't take another assault, but the general's appearance wrought a miracle in the men's spirits. Exhausted only a minute before, they now stood up, waved their caps, and gave the Rebel yell.

Twenty minutes later, just as the general had said in the morning, they stood at Brice's Crossroads turning the captured artillery on the fleeing Yankees, white and black. The coloreds had made a brave fight to save the artillery, you had to give them that, but the field now belonged to the Confederacy.

All along the line, General Forrest galloped back and forth, yelling, "We got the scare on them, don't let it off! We'll run them back to Memphis."

The Yankees were running, all right, but every now and then someone would rally some darky troops and they'd turn and make a stand, fighting with their bayonets against the six-shooters. No contest. Soon as the artillery came up, they'd be blasted right out of position.

About four hundred yards ahead, Richard saw a bridge over a river. It was the Yankees' only means of escape, and there were dozens of supply wagons and hundreds of men still on this side of the river.

He yelled back to an artillery lieutenant, "See if you can't blow up that bridge!"

The gunners went to work, and soon shells were falling on both sides of the bridge into the masses of Yankees waiting to cross. A wagon trying to get away from the fire came barreling over the bridge too fast and turned over, dead in the center of the bridge.

"We got them," Richard said. "Right in a box." He raised his saber and led his men forward so that they weren't more than a hundred yards from the bridge. They lay down in a prone position and fired at will.

Richard watched the slaughter with mixed feelings. Those niggers and whites ran every which way trying to get out of that crossfire and away from the cannonballs falling in their midst. Horses were rearing and snorting, wagons were burning, and so many men jumped into the water that the river was soon littered with bodies floating downstream. Never saw anything like it in his life.

Then, on the other side of the river, Confederate cavalry rode up—they must have crossed the river higher up. They charged the poor devils who had managed to make it over to the other side. In what seemed liked seconds, the bridge was captured. When it had been cleared, Richard led his men over. They kept the pressure on, capturing wagons, horses, weapons, men.

As they made their advance, heavy fire came from a clump of bushes. They directed their fire there, and in about five minutes six colored soldiers emerged, led by a corporal and still wearing their Fort Pillow badges.

"We surrender, sir."

They had dropped their weapons and had their hands in the air as Richard's men hurled taunts.

"Wasn't going to take no prisoners, huh?"

"You going to have your own special Fort Pillow this day, boy."

"Take up arms against a white man, would you?"

Richard looked at the Negroes, their faces smudged with dirt and shiny with sweat. What right on earth *did* they have to bear arms? What a terrible and degrading thing it was for the Yankees to have given them the means to kill good men. Why, fifteen of his troopers lay dead back on the hill, most of them killed by nigger bayonets.

Before he could shout an order, shots rang out. Six Negro men lay dead on the ground.

"Come on, Major, we'll find us some more."

He turned away from the scene. "Let's get moving."

Captain Adams caught up with him, "Richard, the conventions of war."

"Shut the hell up. Just keep fighting. We'll talk philosophy some other time."

Wherever his men got the chance, they did the same thing. When he looked back down the road, all he could see was dead black bodies, dressed in blue, sprawled in all kinds of positions on the sides of the road under the blistering hot late afternoon sun.

A little later, they rode into the courtyard of a plantation and found an old white woman, still sitting and knitting a green scarf despite the war all around her.

"I'm glad you gave them such a whipping," she said. "For when they came this way, they shook their fists at us and told us they were going to show General Forrest that they were his masters. When they came back

through here, they were crying and were asking me would General Forrest kill them. I told them that since they had been such naughty boys that
he would surely kill them, that they deserved to die."

They rode on, around a bend in the road toward where another colored
outfit had decided to make a stand. Richard ordered his men to deploy as
skirmishers. As he raised his saber to lead them forward once more, a bullet smashed into his left arm and knocked him to the down.

He looked at the blood pouring all over the ground. The last thing he
remembered was Clint by his side, applying a tourniquet.

   ✿   ✿   ✿   ✿   ✿   ✿   ✿   ✿   ✿   ✿   ✿

Joe could barely turn his head, so thick was the fire pouring into the embankment where the Third was surrounded. This raid up near Yazoo City
looked like it might be their last time out. Nothing but Rebs all around
them. And their commander was none other than Colonel Montgomery.
He had quietly led them on up into the Delta, throwing out a few patrols
here and there as bait, and the Third had fallen right into his trap.
"Why in the hell couldn't you have stolen somebody else's horse?" Captain
Stiles said.
All day long they'd been fighting hand to hand, pistols, sabers, bayonets,
knives. Fought until they were plum tuckered out on both sides. All in
front of him Joe couldn't see nothing but bodies—black men and Texas
Rangers, lying at funny angles, arms and legs every which away.
It was a strange kind of fighting, real personal-like. The Rebs had been
calling over all day about what they were going to do when they captured
them. Talking about how they were going to kill the officers, too.
Why did these white men hate the colored so much? Because they really
thought they was better? Or maybe because they knew they weren't? Hell,
neither reason made any kind of sense.
Toward sundown the firing died down, and a stillness and calm settled
over the field of battle. Most likely the Rebs were done for the day, figur-
ing they'd come at them and finish them off in the morning. There wasn't
too much chance that the Third could hold out. Just one more charge, and
they'd have to fight with their sabers—the men had maybe ten cartridges
apiece. And Joe himself—well, he knew he'd never see the light of an-

other day if they captured this little fort. He'd heard one of those boys holler about hanging "that son of a bitch'n lying double-crossing horse-stealing black bastard."

He laughed. If he was going to hang, it might as well be for something he'd enjoyed as much as riding Princess. Just as soon not, though. He turned to Captain Stiles.

"What do you think we can do? Looks like we going down this time."

"I learned long ago, fighting in the Fourth Cavalry, not to give up hope long as you can still stand up. Many's the time a battle seemed to be lost, but then something happened, and we pulled through."

"Think that's what's going to happen here?"

"I'm counting on it."

"Well, then, I am too, Captain. Counting on it something awful."

✿   ✿   ✿   ✿   ✿   ✿   ✿   ✿   ✿   ✿   ✿

The night came, and with it a storm. Lightning was striking all over, sometimes so hard and bright you could see the battlefield and the bodies—Third Cavalry and Rebs—lying all around. Joe had killed three men himself today, right there on the ramparts.

The Rebs would know they'd been in a fight if they took this fort. Just like the last time, the men had sworn not to surrender. They'd have to kill them to the last man—each and every one of them.

And Captain Stiles right alongside them. Joe watched him go off to officers' call and thought about his good fortune in serving under this man. Good, fair, courageous, and truth to tell, even though he was an officer, a friend. A man you wouldn't mind dying next to.

And here he came back again, not looking happy at all.

"Well, I guess you know what I'm going to tell you, Joe."

"Bet you're going to send him out again," Zack said.

"Only if he volunteers."

Joe was already reaching for the Choctaw knife scabbard under his night pack. "Right with you, Captain. And don't look so grim. I promise not to steal anything that'll get the Rebs' dander up any worse."

"I'm relieved to hear it."

"Unless, of course . . ."

"Get out of here, you crazy son of a gun! The colonel's waiting."

✿   ✿   ✿   ✿   ✿   ✿   ✿   ✿   ✿   ✿   ✿

When he reported to Colonel Osband, he was surprised to see two other scouts. "Yes, Duckett, I'm sending three of you out. That's how bad it is."

"You hoping one of us makes it—right, sir?"

Osband nodded. "Now, listen. The main body should be somewhere down the Vicksburg road, about two hours from here. Only problem is, you got about two regiments of Reb cavalry between here and there. And there'll be lots of patrols out. I don't have to tell you how . . . well, you know the situation. We've only got half the regiment left. If you're not back by daybreak, we're goners."

"Don't worry none, Colonel," Joe said. "Why, come morning you'll not only have reinforcements, we're going to bring along some fresh eggs and bacon so you can have a breakfast what befits the commander of the Third United States Colored Cavalry."

The colonel laughed. "Just bring the troopers, Joe." He shook each man's hand, then saluted them. "Godspeed, boys!"

✿   ✿   ✿   ✿   ✿   ✿   ✿   ✿   ✿   ✿   ✿

Joe crept up to the parapet and quietly poked his head up. Looked like about a hundred yards between him and the Rebs. The colonel had sent them out on foot, but Joe didn't relish traveling that way with fine horse-flesh just standing around in the Reb's camp. Now all he had to do was find a way to get at it without getting the Rebs at *him*. Lord, the captain be some kind of mad if he knew . . .

He slid up over the parapet, nose to the ground, and began to creep along. Every time there was a bolt of lightning, he stopped. He crawled till he came up to a whole pile of bodies—dead Texas Rangers, they were—and moved around among them till he found one just about his size.

Over toward the Rebel lines it was quiet, probably they were thinking about all the niggers they were going to kill the next day. He stripped the

Texas Ranger's body, and put on all his clothes. Nice gun belt, all studded with jewels, so he took that, too, and the Navy Colts with it. Shit, armed like he was, how'd that Ranger get so dead?

He laid his own clothes over the body. Wasn't right to leave him there all naked.

Bent low, he walked on tiptoe toward the Rebel lines, so quietly he couldn't hear his own step if he listened hard for it. It was awful muddy and the rain was running down into his neck, all down his back. He could even feel it in the crack of his ass. He slid down into a ditch right smack onto the body of another dead Reb, this one all covered with mud, open-eyed and staring right at Joe.

✿   ✿   ✿   ✿   ✿   ✿   ✿   ✿   ✿   ✿   ✿

"Keep a sharp eye out, George. Sergeant says they may be trying to sneak somebody by us to go for help."

"Don't you worry. Ain't I done told you I was the champion possum shooter in my county?"

"Hell, you always bragging 'bout how you the champion this and that. You the champion at sleeping, that's what you are. Just don't let no niggers get by you tonight. I'm going on down the line."

The Reb was sitting there, comfortable-like on a saddle, a six-shooter in his hand, and he seemed to be looking directly at him. Joe calculated the distance, figured the chances of getting close enough to get him with the knife before he sounded an alarm.

He wondered how the other scouts was doing. The colonel had sent them out separate ways. Both of them was experienced, he knew that, but this here was a *situation*.

The rain was coming down much heavier now, the thunder booming like the cannon in the battle down at Yazoo City, the lightning making jagged rips in the sky every few seconds. The sentry stood up to tighten his shirt collar, then bent over, as if he was reaching for a blanket or something to throw over his shoulders.

No sooner had he leaned down than Joe was up, quick as a cat, running right past him, then tumbling into another ditch about fifteen yards beyond and to the other side of him. He clung to the ground for about five minutes, knife in hand. Come over this way, and you'll never tree another possum . . .

He gave the sentry another few minutes, then began to crawl toward the Reb camp about a hundred feet behind their sentry lines. Not many guards around the camp itself—that's what all those pickets up close to the Third were for. Didn't expect nobody to get this close.

Joe crawled over the ground among all the sleeping soldiers. He'd crawl a little bit, then rest, crawl some more. Slow-like, doing nothing to stir anybody up. He wondered where Colonel Montgomery was—probably in that big tent over there dreaming about Princess, and how he was going to have her back tomorrow and string up the nigger who'd stolen her. Dream on, Colonel!

He was creeping along at the outskirts of the camp when he spotted the horses in a clump of trees. "And not a soul watching over you," he said softly . . .

Now what horse was he going to take him this time? Had to be fast, though it surely wouldn't be as fast as Princess. She'd just about replaced Hawk in his favor. His eyes finally settled on a fine-looking white mustang, then he looked around to see where the saddles were piled. When he had everything all arranged in his mind, he just walked up to the picket line, took the horse he wanted, and commenced to saddle it, talking quietly.

"Now, darlin', you the prettiest thing. Me and you going to be good friends. Going to get along just fine."

"What you doing out here this hour of the night, friend?"

Joe kept his face turned away from the Ranger. "Had hard luck tonight, partner. Got to take dispatches up to General Forrest. Shit, I was asleep myself. See you."

Before the sentry could say another word or get a proper look at him, Joe was up in the saddle and riding away. He was in his home territory now, knew the way. Figured it was about another hour and a half to where the main body of the troops was. To be safe and sure, he skirted all around the Reb patrols.

He'd just about come to the place where he was going to take the cutoff that led onto the Vicksburg road when two riders he saw coming the other way.

"Halt, soldier! What you doing out here this time of night?"

"Oh, he's just one of the Rangers," the other man said when he was close enough to see Joe's uniform. "Come on in and have something to eat."

What the hell to do? Five to ten miles from the reenforcements and he had to run into these damn—what were they? Hard to tell with the rain coming down so hard and them in ponchos, most likely with shotguns under them.

"I thank you, but I don't have no time for that. Got dispatches to deliver to General Forrest."

The men drew a little closer.

"Hope you don't mind if we get a little closer look at you, do you? Everybody's suspect these days, even the Rangers."

Joe checked out the little space between the two men's horses, his hand on the trigger of the Navy Colt. No time to play with these fools. His boys were in trouble.

He brought the gun up and fired. The short man, whose hat was pulled down funny on the side of his head, gave a cry and fell right down to the ground with one foot still in the stirrup. The horse bolted away, dragging his body along.

At the crack of the pistol, the other horse had whinnied and reared up—almost but not quite throwing its rider. He was trying to rein in the horse and aim his shotgun at the same time when Joe shot him in the belly.

❋   ❋   ❋   ❋   ❋   ❋   ❋   ❋   ❋   ❋   ❋

Now Joe rode like the wind the rest of the way to the Vicksburg road. He stopped just long enough to make sure no Rebs were about, then rode on searching for the brigade. The night was still dark, the rain beating down, so he didn't see the four riders coming fast toward him until they were dangerously close. Damn.

He reined in his horse and waited. Didn't have much choice. They were sure to have seen the mustang. What had he been thinking to take a white horse?

As they drew closer he saw they were Union and raised his hand. "Hey there!"

"Hands up, or we'll shoot!"

"What the hell—" Joe said.

The first soldier, a sergeant, rode up close to Joe. "Just shut up, and keep them hands raised."

Four carbines were trained on him, but like Zenobia always said, he never knew when to keep quiet.

"Listen—"

"Listen nothing." The sergeant removed the Colts from Joe's holsters. "You're a prisoner, so just shut the hell up like I done told you, and fall in!"

"But I'm Third Cavalry!"

The sergeant laughed. "Now ain't that one for the books, caught red-handed in that ducky Texas Ranger's outfit and wants to go for the Third Cavalry, by golly!"

"You don't believe me, you take this hat off and see! I'm colored!"

The sergeant reined up his horse. "If you're lying, we'll skin you alive. Right here."

The detail stopped with Joe in the middle of them. The sergeant rode over and lifted his hat.

"Well, I'll be a son of a bitch, it *is* a darky! Who *are* you?"

"Serg—no, Corporal Duckett, Third Cavalry, carrying dispatches for General McArthur from Colonel Osband. We're surrounded and need help."

"How come you to be dressed up in that outfit?"

"I took it off a dead Ranger."

The sergeant turned to his men. "Well?"

"I don't really know, Sarge," said one.

"Sounds all right to me, " said another. "Last I heard, the Rebs didn't have no colored in uniform."

"All right," the sergeant said. "Let's get on down the road, I think he's for real."

"No, he ain't," said the third soldier, a tall, skinny boy, with thin lips and a know-it-all look in his eyes. "You forgetting that the rangers have a nigger riding and fighting with them, just like he was a white man. Don't you remember the boys in the Second talking about him when we was in bivouac? That nigger's a spy, that's what he is."

The sergeant nodded, then jabbed a finger in Joe's face. "You almost had us tricked, but it ain't going to work. Now, I don't want to hear another word out of you. When we get you back to camp, we'll get to the bottom of this. Get moving."

Joe said, "You're going to—"

The sergeant slapped him. "Shut up and get moving, I said!"

❖   ❖   ❖   ❖   ❖   ❖   ❖   ❖   ❖   ❖   ❖

It was almost two-thirty in the morning before they arrived at the bivouac area, and another twenty minutes before Joe managed to talk his way in to see General McArthur. Thank God, the general recognized him.

"Sir, we're taken a terrible beating. Colonel Osband say he must have reenforcements by morning or they're done for."

"Captain, have the bugler blow Boots and Saddles. Joe, get a fresh mount and some Union clothes—you're leading the way back up."

In a little less than a half hour, two regiments of cavalry moved out. They rode at a steady pace, slowed down a little by the mud and the rain. Joe was anxious, kept turning this way and that in the saddle. Those Rebs was mighty bloodthirsty. And where were Singletary and Childs? Neither of them had gotten there before him, so they should have run into them on the way back.

As dawn broke, the column was about two miles from where the Third was surrounded. In the distance Joe could hear the sound of shooting. The Reb attack had started.

"At a fast trot forward . . ."

Hold out, boys, we on our way. Don't let them run you over.

When the battle scene came into view, all that could be seen were gray uniforms running up the slope toward the little fort. The Rebs were attacking on all sides, and there couldn't have been but a few men left to hold the fort. But Colonel Osband had his trumpeters blowing up a storm. And the Stars and Stripes were still flapping in the wind.

On and on the Rebs came, Colonel Montgomery at their head as usual. He was one brave old boy and he sure must want that horse something awful. *Not today, sir.*

General McArthur raised his saber and called back to the column of blue-clad troopers.

"Sound the charge."

Joe never saw as pretty a sight in his life. The cavalrymen went sweeping down that mountain onto the Rebs like a mighty river roaring and ranting into a levee after a thunderstorm.

A shout went up from the men in the fort, and the buglers blew even harder. The Rebs set up a skirmish line to protect the camp and allow their men to mount up and get away. They fought hard, but they couldn't stand against that cavalry charge, especially after the Third got up out of the fort and charged too.

❋   ❋   ❋   ❋   ❋   ❋   ❋   ❋   ❋   ❋   ❋

Having lost half of the regiment, Colonel Osband didn't have much of an appetite for the eggs and bacon Joe had brought back with him. And neither did Joe, for that matter. Those other two scouts hadn't ever showed up. This war was getting mighty heavy.

CHAPTER TEN

SEATED in chairs on the after deck of the transport *Mist of the Dawn,* Captain Will Stiles and a few other officers were sipping whiskey and branch water and watching the river go by. Also on board were some civilians, including a few cotton speculators who expected to make a fine profit out of the cargo.

The boat was headed south to Vicksburg with a detachment of Third Cavalry men who'd stood guard as a load of cotton was put on board. Though Will tried to explain how important cotton was to the Union's war effort, some of the men said they'd signed up to fight, not stand around and watch over that damned white stuff.

To Will the assignment was a welcome respite. They had taken a terrible battering at the hands of Montgomery's troops outside of Yazoo City, and he definitely didn't feel like going through anything like it soon again. Ever again, for that matter. But one battle had followed another with no break to speak of, the men returning each time with cotton, Negroes they'd liberated, food supplies and, always, the wounded.

He got up from his chair, thought about going below to cheer them up a bit, but instead walked back to the stern of the boat and leaned over the rail. What an ugly river the Mississippi was, muddy as hell, nothing like the waters back home in New York. The town he'd grown up in wasn't far from Lake George—where, of a summer day, you could swim out a ways and look down in the water and see clear to the bottom. It wasn't just plain clear either, it was blue clear.

Even on the hottest days, that lake water was always cool and bracing. He got goose bumps just thinking about how it felt to dive into it. And if you got a little thirsty, why you could drink all of it you wanted to.

The memory of days when he'd taken his canoe down from its rack, put it over his head, and carried it down to the lake, seemed to belong to another life. He'd paddle out to the center of the lake with nothing more serious to worry about than how long he'd have to wait before one of those trout struck the line and leapt out of the water, silvery brown body glistening and wriggling in the bright sunshine . . . Silver spray, clear day, God's way!

Of course, the Mississippi had its own virtues—the sheer size of it, for one thing, and the twists and the turns, the surprises around every bend. And there was something else about the river. It was the spinal cord of this whole huge country. Knitting it together—linking cities with their factories, plains with their farms and carrying its boats and people in a flow of commerce from one place to another. Muddy though it was, this had its own—

"Don't mind, do you, Will?" Major Cook joined him by the rail. "-Couldn't leave you alone to enjoy yourself too much, just looking down there at the water."

"I'd enjoy it a lot more if we didn't have to worry about those bushwhackers shooting at us every time we get in range."

"The sharpshooters we've got posted should keep them occupied if they start up with us again." He slowly twirled the whiskey around in his hand. "Will, I've been meaning to ask you . . . You're close to these men, particularly Joe. What do they think about us—the white officers, I mean?"

"About how any group of men feel about their officers—hell, you and me were noncoms before we came over here, you know how it is. They like some of us and some of us they don't." He took a sip of bourbon. "But whatever's the case, so long as no one calls them nigger, they'll fight for him. We may be catching hell every time we go up the river, but the boys give as good as they get."

"That they do," said Major Cook, who was tugging at his uniform collar, trying without much success to loosen it. "I'd put them up against any I ever fought with. When I first came over to serve with them, I had my doubts as to whether they would fight—or even whether they could. Slavery's a hurtful thing, no question."

"None at all. And there's no denying they're ignorant—damn planters wouldn't let them learn anything. Makes me mad whenever I think about it. I mean, the slaveholders have a lot to answer for, but for some reason keeping them uneducated is what gets my blood up. It's not like they can't learn—just look at the change from what they were eight months ago. Lord, here comes our cotton speculator. Damn."

"Mind if I join you gentlemen?"

Will did mind. Lamar Chew had been up and down the river with them on these cotton-gathering expeditions before, and while his sympathies were clearly with the Rebs, all he really cared about was taking advantage of the war to make a fortune. He reeked of whiskey and had a full glass of it in his hand.

"Mighty nice view up here, isn't it?"

"That it is."

Will moved away, but Chew sidled right up to him again.

"You'd be Captain Stiles, right? Been watching you the last couple of days. It's estra . . . extraordinary, how you get along so well with those nigger troops of yours. I must tell you, I never saw anything like it."

"Mr. Chew." Major Cook stepped between them. "Perhaps you could be of some assistance to us. How navigable are the upper reaches of the Yazoo this time of the year?"

"Can't help you, Major. I'm just a cotton broker, I don't skipper the boats."

Will had moved even farther down the railing. Chew downed more whiskey and went after him. "Like I was saying, you got a real way with the nigger boys, almost like you were one of us Southern folk."

Will straightened his uniform and turned to face Chew squarely. "Mr. Chew, I have to tell you, I don't appreciate your calling my troopers niggers."

"Now, Will," Major Cook said. " I'm sure Mr. Chew meant nothing by it, that's just their way down here."

Chew patted the captain on the back. "Didn't mean to get you all riled up. Tell you what, my man—let me get you another drink. As a matter of fact, drinks for both you and the major."

They protested, but Chew lurched off in search of a waiter.

"He's drunk," Cook said. "Don't pay him any mind."

"Drunk or sober, I want no part of him."

"Will, you know our orders. We're to be courteous to all civilians, particularly these cotton brokers. We need the cotton. So—"

Chew returned, trailed by a waiter with a drink-laden tray.

"Gentlemens . . ."

"That's right, Uncle. You stay nearby in case we want some more."

They'd had only a sip or two from the fresh glasses before Chew started in again.

"Captain, seeing as you're so friendly with these nigras, how do you find their soldiering?" He leaned in closer and lowered his voice. "Do you ever think they might run out on you? I'm asking this as a close observer of human behavior, if you can call nigra behavior human."

Major Cook stepped between them again and took hold of Will's arm. "That's not a question you should be asking, Mr. Chew. If you want to stay here and drink with us in peace, that's one thing, but if you continue in this line of conversation, we'll have to leave you here."

Will shook off the major's restraining hand and glared at Chew. "My men have never quit on me yet—and never will!"

"Now, Captain, I didn't mean anything, no need to get so worked up." He took another sip of whiskey. "But tell me now, didn't I hear that up at Brice Crossroads old Bedford Forrest had the *nigras* running like rabbits, turned them every which way but loose?"

"Mr. Chew . . ." Will saw the glance Major Cook threw his way and gave a little nod of his head to show that he was in control. "Mr. Chew, sir, I'll have you know they gave as good an account of themselves up there as anybody else."

Chew slapped the rail with the open palm of his hand. "And I'll have *you* know I've supported Abe Lincoln all the way, but he went too far when he armed these . . . these nigras. Maybe Fort Pillow and Brice's Crossroads will give him and General Grant and. . . . and . . . the rest of you some second thoughts about all this."

"Mr. Chew, I bid you good day. This conversation is over."

Chew stumbled, trying to grab him by the arm, but Will just sidestepped him.

"It's over because you know it's wrong—these armed nigras are a menace to white civilization, yours as well as ours."

With every drink, his voice had gotten a little louder. Now a small crowd of officers and civilian passengers was looking on.

"They'll want revenge for slavery," Chew said, "and they'll take it—on our women and children. You've already had to court-martial some of them for rape down in Vicksburg. White men should fight white men. When a white man arms a nigra, he's put himself on the level of that nigra."

"Captain Stiles, just walk away. That's an order." Major Cook turned to Chew. "Sir, my hands are tied since I'm a military officer, but if I were a civilian I'd boot you right up your civilian ass."

Chew raised his fist and shouted after the departing officers. "Say what you like, and fight with the niggers if you will, but I wish the Rebs had ten Bedford Forrests. They'd soon put an end to this race treachery!"

✧   ✧   ✧   ✧   ✧   ✧   ✧   ✧   ✧   ✧   ✧

"That man is through," Major Cook said at the officers' table. "He'll never go up the river with us again. It's hard enough to keep the morale of the men up without this kind of thing."

"I'm glad to hear you say that, sir." Will put his fork down. He was still too annoyed to eat. "But one good thing—it's got me thinking it's about time we stopped equivocating. These soldiers aren't paid as much as the whites, and they have no Negro commissioned officers. I for one know of four men in the regiment who are officer material, proved it in combat, by any measure."

"I hear that one has already been given a field commission in the Fifty-fourth Massachusetts," Cook said. "I want you to look into this matter, Will—first identify the men who are officer material, then find out what we have to do to have them commissioned."

"Major Cook, sir!"

"What is it, Joe?"

"Better get up on deck quick, sir. The men are about to riot."

The officers, led by Major Cook, got up from the table and headed up the ladder.

On the foredeck, where just an hour earlier the men had been quietly repairing their equipment, dozens of them were now milling around. And a small group of them, urged on by Tucker, were pounding with sledge-hammers on one of the doors leading below to the passenger quarters.

"I say kill the bastard."

"Throw him in the river."

"Get me a bayonet, somebody!"

"Captain Stiles, call them to order," Major Cook said.

"Attention!"

Joe looked for a bugler but couldn't see one in the confusion.

"*Attention!*"

"Go to hell!"

Will pulled out his Colt and fired it into the air.

The noise stopped.

"Now fall in, right there on the deck."

They obeyed, slowly forming into six ranks. A sea of sullen, angry faces looked up at Major Cook standing on the bridge.

"What the hell is the meaning of this? I just finished saying you're as fine a fighting unit as any in the whole Delta, and you start acting like a liquored-up bunch of field hands . . . I'll get to the bottom of this, then I'll deal with whoever's responsible. Captain Stiles, get them to their quarters."

❖   ❖   ❖   ❖   ❖   ❖   ❖   ❖   ❖   ❖   ❖

Half an hour later Will reported to Major Cook, Joe and Zack at his side.

Will nodded to Zack. "Tell the major what happened."

"Well, sir, you knows I'm a sharpshooter—one of the best in the regiment, sir, many's the time I won the contest—"

"Get to the point, soldier!"

"And, and—"

With his forearms on the desk in front of him, the major leaned forward as if trying to get the words sooner.

"I was on sharpshooter duty, because Sergeant Duckett here, he want the best man to be in the bow of the boat, be the first man to get a shot at them bushwackers up there in them rocks." He turned to Joe. "Ain't that right, Joe?"

Joe nodded.

"So I was on duty, just watching them rocks, each and every one of them, 'cause you never can tell which one is going to be hiding them bushwackers—can you, Joe? And they especially likes them little cracks where there be a pine tree covering the rocks, and it take a very special kind of man with a very special kind of eye to see—"

"Corporal Bascome, get to the woman!"

Zack took a deep breath and plunged on. "Well, there I was on duty, and this high-yellow gal that been hankering after me, Rachel her name, she come and sit down on a cotton bale near me and commenced to talking."

"Your orders were not to talk to anyone while on duty," the major said.

"But, sir, I didn't. She took a seat and started talking and I just kept my eyes on those cliffs, looking out for the Rebs. But she kept on teasing me about playing soldier."

The major looked at Will. "For this we had a near riot?"

"There's more, sir. Zack, get to the point."

"Well, everybody was all sitting around just watching me, not saying nothing, just watching. And this drunk white man come up to me, had a glass of whiskey in his hand, and he say—right in front of them all—that a nigger soldier, he ain't got no rights in this world, and the least right he got is to talk to a white woman."

'What did you do?"

"I knows my duty. I just kept looking over at those hills, but next thing I know, this white man is waving around a dirk—in broad daylight, sir—and he say he going to kill me dead it I says another word to that woman."

"You'd said nothing to her up till then?"

"Well . . . she mighty pretty, like I said." Zack looked at Joe again. "Maybe just a couple of itty-bitty words."

"This man thought you were talking to a white woman and he openly threatened to kill you. Is that it?"

"That's pretty much it, sir."

"Well, is it or not?"

"Yes, sir," Joe said. "That was it, sir."

"And then what happened, Sergeant Duckett?"

"You know that troublemaker Tucker, he starts shouting at the white man and next thing you know the men are all worked up, say we'd see who did any killing, and I had to hustle the man below deck, and all the way he's yelling, 'Nigger, get your filthy hands off her.'"

"I take it this man's name was Chew?"

"Why, it is, sir. That's him all right. I was just barely able to get him away. If they'd got their hands on him, they'd of thrown him to the fishes. But how'd you know—"

"Where is he now?"

"Locked in his cabin, sir."

"Good work. Leave him there for the present." Major Cook got up from the table and looked at Zack. "You work in the mess all next week. No leave when we get back to Vicksburg. You think it's a game with those sharpshooters up there?" He sighed. "You and Sergeant Duckett are dismissed."

"What a mess," Will said when they were gone.

"There are a hundred brave United States soldiers lying in their graves up beyond Yazoo City where they fell three days ago, and I *will not* permit their deaths to be in vain. Get the salon emptied out, Will. I want an officers' call there. As for Chew . . ."

Will almost smiled. He knew a pause for dramatic effect when he saw one. He also thought he knew what the major wanted with regard to Chew.

"Go up to his quarters, the sooner the better. You're to place him under arrest for making a death threat to a Union soldier while on official duty."

❖   ❖   ❖   ❖   ❖   ❖   ❖   ❖   ❖   ❖   ❖

The officers sitting around a long table in the salon listened intently as Major Cook explained what had happened.

"Under the Articles of War and in the absence of the commanding officer, Colonel Osband, I am convening a court-martial to deal with the seditious behavior of Mr. Lamar Chew."

He stood up and rested his hands on the table. The men looked at one another, then back at him.

"Had Mr. Chew drawn a dirk on a white soldier," Cook said, "he would have been immediately shot. In this case we're going to give him the benefit of the doubt and provide him with a trial. The jury will be made up of each and every officer on board."

He paused for a second. Except for one. "Captain Stiles, you'll serve as counsel for the defense."

"But, sir—"

"You started to read for the bar, didn't you? Go see your client and prepare the defense. Court convenes at two o'clock."

On the way to Chew's cabin, Will called Joe aside and filled him in.

"And I'm to defend him," he concluded.

"You, sir? But the men trust you, believe you're on their side. How will they ever—"

Will glanced skyward, then back at Joe. He'd known this would happen the second the major gave him the assignment.

"Look, Joe, there's a lot you and the men have never been taught about the way the law operates, and I don't have time to educate you on it right now. It's just that in our kind of country every man deserves a fair hearing, and the only way to do that is to give him the best defense we can. That goes for rich and poor, white, red, and black. It's got to be fair—even in the army. And I'm the only officer on board who ever cracked a law book, so I've been ordered to do the job. Now, what's the temper of the men below?"

"They just waiting to see what's going to happen, sir. Don't you worry about this none. I'll go down and explain to them about how you got to defend that man. You just following orders, doing your duty. They'll understand that."

    ✿   ✿   ✿   ✿   ✿   ✿   ✿   ✿   ✿   ✿   ✿

Will found Chew on his bunk, smelling of whiskey, his eyes bloodshot but defiant. A neat pile of business papers—invoices, Will figured—lay on the desk alongside a black top hat. Chew could probably cut a pretty dashing figure in that hat and his white felt shirt and black trousers. His brown boots with their intricate Indian designs were highly polished.

He got up quickly." Now you listen to me, Stiles. Governor Johnson, he's a personal friend of the family and he's going to see to it that you and all the other officers in this nigger outfit are court-martialed. That's a mob you've got, not a regiment."

"Sit back down, Mr. Chew, we have a few important matters to discuss."

"Discuss?" Chew advanced on Stiles, wagging his finger. "Discuss, you say? There's only one thing to discuss. Why have I, a free white man, been locked unlawfully in my cabin and denied the run of the vessel? Oh, I'll have your head for this, just you wait and see."

"I'm sorry—"

"Sorry, are you?" Chew was right up in his face. "Oh no, come with apologies to me now, and expect me not to take this up with the governor? Even if you came on your damn nigger-loving Yankee knees, I wouldn't accept an apology. Now, I'm asking you to leave—time for me to start writing my account of this matter for the governor." He pointed to the door.

"Sit down, Mr. Chew. That's an order!" Will grabbed him by the arm and forced him back onto the bunk. "Now listen to me. Damn it, man, you're in no position to make threats. I'm sorry about this whole incident, but I didn't come here to apologize to you, I came to let you know that you must stand before a court-martial in an hour—and that I'm your defense counsel."

"Court-martial? Me?"

"You."

"For calling that boy a nigger? *For calling a nigger a nigger?*"

"I'm afraid the charges are more serious than that. You threatened him with a deadly weapon while he was performing his official duty."

"What deadly weapon?"

"The dirk, sir. And for that, unless I can find an acceptable excuse, you'll hang."

Chew stood up. "You're having me on, aren't you? Just trying to get back at me for all those things I said up on deck?"

Will shook his head.

Chew slowly eased back down on the bunk, then dropped his head in his hands. "I got three little children at home, and a wife," he said when he looked up. "They're all depending on me."

Will sat down next to him. "I'll mention your family before the court.

For now, I want to know whether you did it or not. They have the dirk, you know. And witnesses."

"You mean to say they'd take the word of a . . . Hell, man, I was defending the honor of white womanhood."

"Then it will no doubt pain you to learn that the woman in question is not white but a mulatto."

Chew's eyes widened. "A nigra?"

Will nodded.

"And I could *die* because of that?"

"I'll do my best to see that you don't, but it's going to be a rough haul. We took a terrible pounding up the Yazoo while we were getting this cotton for you—he glanced over at the papers—"and that's going to make it hard." He got up to go. "Wash your face and clean yourself up. You don't want to appear before the court in this condition."

"When the governor hears about this he'll have every nigger regiment in Mississippi busted up, you just wait and see."

"I'll be back for you in twenty-five minutes."

❖   ❖   ❖   ❖   ❖   ❖   ❖   ❖   ❖   ❖   ❖

Half an hour later, the court convened. Twenty, now in dress blues and presided over by Major Jeremiah B. Cook, sat in judgment on Lamar Chew, Esquire, cotton broker, of Memphis, Tennessee.

Captain Will Stiles, resolved to defend his client as best he could, stood up as soon as the charges had been read and addressed Major Cook.

"I move for dismissal of the charges. I—"

"Dismissal? On what grounds?"

"Lack of jurisdiction, sir." With that, Will picked up a book containing the rules and regulations governing court-martial. "Nowhere in here will you find one sentence, not even one word authorizing a military court to try a civilian so long as any possibility exists that he may be brought, in . . . uh . . . a timely fashion before a civilian tribunal. Therefore this court lacks the . . . lacks jurisdiction in this matter, and I hereby request that the court . . . I hereby request that the presiding officer dismiss the case."

"Request denied." Major Cook banged the gavel. "Proceed."

Witness after witness—Joe, Tucker, even one of the other cotton brokers on board—told the same story. Mr. Chew had threatened Corporal Bascombe with the dirk. And there was no denying that Corporal Bascombe had been performing an official duty at the time, although there did seem to be some question about just how well he had been doing it. Then Chew took the stand.

"Tell them, Mr. Chew, *why* you approached that sentry."

"Because I was firmly convinced that he was insulting the virtue of a Southern white woman."

Will drew closer to Chew. "Why else, sir? Why the threat and the drawing of the dirk?"

"Because I believed that he intended to touch her, embrace her, and I'd die before I'd see a nigger touch a white woman." He glared at the assembled officers. "And you all ought to, too."

Will raised his hand, but his client wasn't about to be silenced.

"Is it not absurd that this civilized nation, the creation of some of the greatest minds the world has ever known—Jefferson, Washington, Madison—is being defended by the most degraded race of all—the Africans? You come into our territory and unleash cannibals and headhunters against us, then expect—"

Major Cook banged his gavel.

"Your own officers say they cannot stop these savages from slaughter and defilement, I've heard it with my own two ears. And you accuse *me*—"

Major Cook pounded the desk with the gavel and stood up. "Mr. Chew, get control of yourself or I'll have you restrained. We've heard the witnesses. Now we need your account, and in an orderly—"

"My witness should be a hero like General Forrest—"

"Bind and gag him. Captain Stiles, do you have anything further to offer in this man's defense?"

"No, sir, but . . . if I could just make another point about the question of jurisdiction—"

"You may not. This ship and all on it are governed by martial law. If you have no other witnesses to call, make your summation."

Will rose and faced his fellow officers. "Gentlemen, my client, Mr.

Chew, is upset. Which of us would not be, facing the penalty he faces. I beg you not to allow his remarks, offensive though they may have been, to influence your decision." He put the manual back on the table. "In view of the refusal of the court to deny jurisdiction I ask that if you find my client guilty you punish him by means other than death. If you cannot find it in your hearts to have mercy on him, do it for his wife and children. Banish him to Rebel territory, take his cotton broker's license from him, confiscate all of the cotton he has on board, but don't condemn him to die for a failure to understand the situation he was in."

He pointed at Chew. "We don't deny that he cursed at Corporal Bascombe and threatened him with a dirk, but this was a reaction to a situation he'd never been in before—a colored soldier talking on an equal level with a woman mistakenly perceived to be white. Nothing in his experience had prepared him for such a moment. In his mind, raised as he has been raised, he had no choice but to defend her honor. Don't send him to his death because he couldn't tell the difference between a quadroon and a white woman. Hell, the poor man may have a touch of color-blindness—"

The officers erupted in laughter. Major Cook pounded the gavel for order.

Will continued. "Haven't we seen enough of death for a few days?" The room was quiet. "God knows I have."

It all seemed to have gone too fast. Will wished he had more to say, but he didn't. He sat down.

After the prosecution's summation, the major declared the court in recess and retired with the other officers to the mess to reach a decision. While they deliberated, Will sat with Chew, still bound and gagged, the four colored sentries looking on.

"When the court comes back," Will said, "I'm going to request that these restraints be removed. I'd like to at least have you treated as a man. Can you promise me there'll no more outbursts?"

Chew nodded.

"Attention!"

When the major and the other officers were seated, Will made his request, and the gag and restraints removed.

"Have the prisoner brought before the court," Cook said.

Will moved forward with Chew. Had to give the man credit, he was standing tall.

"The court finds the prisoner guilty of assaulting and threatening with bodily harm a soldier of the United States of America while in pursuit of his official duty."

Will felt Chew tense and took him by the elbow. And just in time, it seemed, because with the phrase " . . . hung by the neck until dead" Chew seemed to wilt and would have fallen without support.

"To be carried out in one hour on the taffrail of the ship."

❖   ❖   ❖   ❖   ❖   ❖   ❖   ❖   ❖   ❖   ❖

When they were back in Chew's cabin, accompanied this time by guards, Will asked Chew what he could do for him.

Chew was sitting on the bunk. "How much time?"

"About forty-five minutes, I reckon."

"Not much time to get my affairs in order."

"The major told me to give you every consideration in that matter," Will said.

Chew picked up a pen and began to scribble away. His hand trembled as it moved across the pad of paper.

"This is for my wife. It informs her where she can find my will and lists the other provisions I've made for her and the children." He looked at Will. "Reckon a condemned man could have a few shots of bourbon at a time like this?"

Minutes laters, a sentry delivered a bottle of the best, courtesy of the ship's captain.

"Would you join me?" Chew said.

"I will, sir."

After his second drink, Chew put on his jacket. He looked every inch the proper gentleman.

"You know," he said, "something's changed in this country of ours. I can't exactly put my finger on it now . . ." He laughed and pointed to the bottle. "Because it's a mite unsteady, but it's like we white people, you and me, we're being made to fight each other—by the niggers. Like they've turned the tables on us."

Will listened in silence. Death has its privileges.

"You know I always knew my big mouth would be the death of me, but I still can't believe I'm going to be hung over what I did to a nigger."

"It's a brutal war and you, my friend, just got caught in the middle of it. I truly pity you. Because there's some truth in what you say. The times changed, fast, and you didn't change with them. That's what happened." He poured them another drink. "Better get yourself ready, now. Do you want to pray? "

"I reckon I should. Will you pray with me?"

Will nodded.

"Our Father . . ."

     ✣   ✣   ✣   ✣   ✣   ✣   ✣   ✣   ✣   ✣

Will accompanied him up to the deck to the sound of drums rolling. Dusk on the river was a sight to see, the red of the sky reflecting off the water with a deep coppery glow. On the deck, row after row of Negro cavalry-men stood like their officers, ramrod-straight, eyes ahead. Up on the bridge of the ship, colored and white passengers watched a sergeant form a noose to put around the neck of Lamar Chew.

Will gripped the poor devil's elbow to steady him, for with his hands bound in front and his arms and legs lashed with rope, he was having trouble keeping his balance.

Stiles snapped to attention beside Chew as the first lieutenant in command of the execution said, "Does the prisoner have a last word?"

"I do. It's a sin to hang a man because he had one drink too many and wanted to protect the white womanhood of the South!"

At a glance from the lieutenant, the roll of the drums diminished.

The sergeant put a black hood over Chew's head, then—almost gently, it seemed—fitted the noose in place around his neck. Chew was moved into position. The drum roll got louder, but everybody heard the last of his last words:

"*Damn your eyes and damn you all to hell!*"

"Execute!"

The sergeant pushed him off the ship.

The line uncoiled, stiffened, and seemed to come to rest for a split second before commencing a pendulum-like swing. The ring to which it was attached made a creaking sound every now and then as the body below reached one end or the other of its arc.

The lieutenant peered over the stern. He snapped to attention, marched over to Major Cook, and saluted. It was done. The troops were dismissed and ordered below.

And the *Mist of the Dawn* made her way on down the river with a load of cotton, the Third Cavalry, and the body of Lamar Chew as supercargo.

CHAPTER ELEVEN

ZENOBIA woke to the long whistle of a red-winged blackbird perched on a bush nearby. The sun was just rising. She left Lisa Mae and the children sleeping and headed down to the river to see how Drayton was doing.

He was doing good. Spread out on the ground were eight good-size logs, each near long as he was tall. He was chipping away at one of them, shaving off the rough edges so it would fit in with the others. On the ground lay vines for binding them together.

"Ain't that heavy thing going to be hard to get in the water?" said Zenobia.

"And good morning to you, too, sister, you-all have a good rest?"

She laughed. "Sorry. My temper's none too sweet after sleeping on that hard ground. Probably more better than working all night, though. You doing good. Got a way with them tools."

"Maybe. But you right, it's bound to be heavy. I need something to push us off with. Look over there in the woods where I've got the horses tied, see if you can't find me a long pole."

Zenobia found a good strong limb and dragged it back. He put his awl down for a second and wiped his brow with the sleeve of his shirt.

"You got some kind of figure on you, woman. And your eyes are something to behold."

"We got no time for that foolishness. Just get that raft finished so we can leave."

"Don't you worry none. I be finished long before it's dark enough to set out."

"Dark? I think we should get out on the river as soon as you finish."

"There's going to be traffic on the river, Zenobia—small boats or something, folks is always out fishing." He looked up from his work. "Try explaining what we'd be doing with children on a raft. Don't make no kind of sense."

"And it makes sense to wait for the bloodhounds?"

"We going to have to chance they won't find us here during the day. You a big praying woman—now the time to do it."

"I reckon that's all we *can* do."

✿   ✿   ✿   ✿   ✿   ✿   ✿   ✿   ✿   ✿   ✿

By the time the sun was high, the raft was finished. Drayton stood up and kicked it in a few places, testing its soundness.

"It look mighty good, don't mind if I say so myself. Come on, Zee, let's get it covered up with some weeds so won't nobody see it from the water."

When that was done and the horses fed, everybody sat down under the shelter of a big pine tree deep back in the woods to wait for nightfall. Drayton dozed off, Lisa Mae stayed with the children and Drayton, Zenobia leaned on a tree from which she could keep an eye on both the raft and the cornfield where they'd left the wagon.

She looked up into the green leaves over her head. What was she doing out here in the middle of nowhere? Didn't even know where "here" was. And where was Luke and Milly—and Joe? Where was that lovable man of hers? Did he miss her as much as she missed him?

"What you doing here, Auntie?"

Zenobia jumped. A tall, pretty girl with her hair in cornrows stared down at her.

"Where'd you come from? I must have fallen asleep." Zenobia looked up at the sun. It was mid-afternoon. She shook her head and got to her feet, keeping a hand on the tree to steady herself. "You by yourself?"

The girl nodded. "You running away?"

"What's your name?"

"Helen."

Zenobia put her arm around the girl's shoulder. "What you doing down here all by yourself? Where the rest of the colored folks?"

"Ain't none left but me and some old aunties. And old Miz Jeffers. I just come down to see if I could catch us some fish."

"Ain't no white mens that live on the place?"

"They all gone to war. Was some mens come today while we was eating out in the cook shed, patrollers looking for some runaways. They—"

"Where are they?"

"You ain't the one. They was looking for a man and some women and children."

Zenobia put her hands on Helen's shoulders and turned her until they were face to face. "Where they at now?"

"They left. Miss told them to check at the Rankin plantation just down the way."

"How long ago?"

"A little while."

"Did they have dogs with them?"

"Yes, Auntie, up in the wagon."

Should she take this child back to the others? Or send her off with a warning not to tell on them? Either way, they had to get out of here now. She took Helen by the hand.

"Come with me, honey."

Drayton was already awake, making sure their food was wrapped tight in cloth bundles.

"What do we have here?" he said.

"Little sister says the patrollers is close, we got to leave now."

Drayton looked up at the sun. "Done told you, Zenobia, we can't go out on that river while the sun's still up. They'd catch us for sure." He looked at the girl. "You know any place in the river we could hide a raft?"

She pointed downriver. "Right around that bend, there's a little place where I fish sometimes, set back from the river, trees all over it. But . . ." She looked at Cally, then back at Drayton. "Where you going?"

He was already moving off. "Get the children and the food down to the raft, Zee. I'm going to run the horses away. Might throw the dogs off."

Zenobia and the others went down to the raft and pulled away the weeds. She looked out at the open water, tried to figure how long they'd be visible to anyone coming down the river before they were safe in Helen's hiding place.

Drayton came back with a rope in his hand. He tied it around one of the logs, then grabbed the other end. "Give me a hand." He turned to the two women. "Grab ahold of this rope and pull."

Zenobia and Lisa Mae each put the rope over their shoulders and pulled hard with Drayton behind them. The raft didn't budge.

"You-all got your feet planted solid?" Drayton said. "When I say pull, pull hard. One, two, three—*pull!*"

The raft moved just a little ways on the dirt.

"Pull again!"

Two feet forward.

"Let me help." Helen put the rope over her shoulder. "Please?"

"Me too, Uncle," said Ned.

"Me, Me! " Cally tottered forward and got under the rope.

"Pull!"

At first the raft moved an inch at a time, then it began to pick up speed. Soon they had it down by the riverside.

"All right." Drayton patted each of the children on the head. "Don't know as we'd of got it down here without you." He lowered himself into the water and held the raft tight against the slowly moving river while the women and children got on, then called back to Helen. "You go on with your fishing, child, and act like you ain't seen nobody if they ask you."

"Don't tell her that," Zenobia said. "They going to see we been here and they'll whip her if she lies. Just tell the truth, honey, only not where we going to be hiding."

Helen stood looking at them. "I want to go with you."

"No, you stay with your own."

"I ain't got no own no more."

Drayton shook his head. "Too many already."

"If we leave her here," Zenobia said, "they'll whip her anyway, just because she saw us and didn't come running to them."

Drayton sighed and reached his hand out to Helen. "At least you can show us where that hiding place is." He shoved the raft out into the river.

"Lord have mercy!"

"Help, Mommy!"

Water was coming up through the cracks between the logs. The river was running a lot faster than it looked like from land.

"Zenobia, move over this way quick, before it turns over."

Drayton was dragging the pole in the water in an effort to slow the raft down. But the river had gotten ahold of the raft and was spinning it around so fast Zenobia got dizzy. Their clothes were soaked through in no time. Thank the Lord Drayton had built four little posts on the raft—they were the only things they could hold on to.

Helen had said the water was shallow enough here for Drayton to pole them over into the hiding place, but it seemed like no matter how far he stuck the pole down into the water, he still couldn't reach bottom.

The bend in the river was coming up so fast, it looked like they were going to end up flying right past the place where they were supposed to hide. Then they'd have nothing but open river in front of them—and three hours of daylight. She must have of been crazy to get them in this fix. A bunch of field niggers, not a one of whom could swim, out in broad daylight on a raft they couldn't handle.

Helen nudged her and pointed ahead. "There, just behind where that big old rock and that long tree branch down near the water is."

They were bound to miss it by the length of a man's body.

Unless. . . .

She tied a big loop in one of the ropes Drayton had brought and motioned to show him what she was going to try to do. He must have understood, because he tied a knot in the other end of the rope and secured it to one of the posts.

"You're going to have to lean out to reach it," he said. "For God's sakes be careful."

"What you talking about—falling overboard?" Lisa Mae said. "You never seen the way she walk with them cotton baskets on her head?"

The limb Zenobia had spotted was coming up fast.

"Hold on tight," Drayton said. "When Zenobia loop the rope over that tree branch, this little thing going to come to a stop mighty quick."

Zenobia eyed the branch and waited. Closer . . .

Now! At first the rope slid back along the branch toward her, like it wasn't going to hold, then all of a sudden it tightened up and caught. And just like Drayton said, the raft came up tight against the rope and there was water everywhere—like the whole river was mad at them for stopping the raft and was going to sweep them all right off.

Lisa Mae lost her grip on Cally. Zenobia reached out and caught her hand, but not fast enough. Cally's wet palm slid right out of her grasp, and she tumbled off the raft into the river.

"Mama!"

Zenobia's heart had been ripped right out of her breast.

She watched as Cally's head disappeared below the surface of the muddy water, felt Drayton's strong arms around her own shoulders. "-Don't, Zenobia."

She shook him off, determined to leap into the river after her daughter. But where? The river had swallowed her up whole. Zenobia brushed Drayton's arm away again and rose to jump into the river. Then she heard another splash. Helen was in the water and swimming fast to a spot about ten yards downstream. She too disappeared below the surface of the dark river.

Oh, Sweet Jesus, part them waters!

Just twigs and branches floating along on the surface like nothing had happened, like her soul wasn't suffocating down there along with Cally's. Behind her she could hear Lisa Mae praying softly. And Drayton, too.

"There's Helen, Auntie," yelled Ned.

And Cally?

The child's head slowly broke the surface of the water. She was safe in Helen's arms, but crying "Mama" between coughs and grasping for breath.

Helen pulled Cally ashore, which made them safer than the folks on the raft. With the river running so fast, that rope wouldn't hold long.

Helen put Cally down on the shore, ran up on the bank, and called across the water to Zenobia. "Throw me that other rope—I'll *pull* you in."

And bless her heart, she did. When the raft was tied to land, Zenobia hugged her tight. "God sure enough sent you down to the river today. He never forget His own."

❀   ❀   ❀   ❀   ❀   ❀   ❀   ❀   ❀   ❀   ❀

It seemed quiet under the trees, after the rush of all that water. Zenobia looked around her. Lisa Mae was holding tighter than ever now to little

Cally and Ned, trying to warm their shivering little bodies with her own, which was soaking wet. Drayton was checking his revolver. Helen lay flat on the raft, looking up through the tree leaves over her head.

"What you see up there, child?" Zenobia asked.

"Nothing particular, Auntie, just waiting to see some signs of sunset so we be on our way."

Zenobia shuddered. "Lord, I don't even want to think about getting back out in the middle of that old river . . ."

She opened one of the packets of food, only to find that the water had soaked right through the wrappings. The corn bread was nothing but mush, so she passed out mussel spoons and began to feed Cally. After a few spoonfuls, Cally left Lisa Mae's arms and attached herself to Helen.

"She know how to swim and you don't," Zenobia said. She searched through the packets of supplies. "Anybody seen the cough medicine?"

"Reckon it's gone," Drayton said. "Probably went over with some other things when that rope caught and we stopped so sudden-like. Mercy, but that was something to see—you throwing that rope."

Didn't he ever stop? Silly to be making up to her when she had so much to worry about. She looked around and trembled. Cally was coughing, and there on the bank, not even twenty feet away, a pair of water moccasins slithered in and out of the water, like they were playing. At least there were no alligators. She hated their ugly leering faces. That little bitty raft wouldn't do much more than slow them down if they attacked.

"Sun getting low in the west," Helen said.

Good. The patrollers might not risk losing their hounds in strange country at this time of day, might wait until morning to let them loose. By then, according to Drayton's reckoning, they'd be at Clifton.

He held his finger up to his mouth in a signal for silence, and in a second they all knew why.

"What you figure we can catch this time of day?"

The voice came from somewhere on the opposite shore.

"Oh, I don't know, maybe some brims or mud cats. Who the hell cares? It's a good chance to get away from the house, ain't it?"

"You right about that."

"Then don't complain. Here, have a swig."

Zenobia couldn't see them, so they must be upriver a little. She took Cally from Helen's arms and pressed the shivering, soaked little body tight against her chest. Soon they were both shivering.

Time passed, what with the men fishing and talking, and every now and then breaking out into some song or another. She didn't recognize the tunes and couldn't make out the words.

The sun was almost gone.

"Reckon we'll see the niggers them patrollers is after?"

"I'd say we're as likely to see them as them patrollers. They didn't seem none too eager to me." A cackle. "The dogs were, though. Raring to go. Course, dogs ain't no good on the water. Bet those boys are going to stay down at the Pennypacker place tonight, rent them a boat there, and start down the river after those niggers in the morning."

"So what do we do if them runaways was to come floating by? Right now, I mean?"

"Me, I'd keep on fishing. Ain't going to let nothing spoil my day."

The sun had been down for a while, and Zenobia's teeth were chattering. They were lying on the raft now, warming each other with their bodies. Drayton was the only one sitting up, looking over everybody, pistol in hand. More and more, it seemed like he might sure enough be able to protect them and see them through to Yankee land.

"Well, Jeb, you ready to call it a day?"

"Day? Hell, we done run out of day."

"Womenfolk will be fussing if we still out here much longer."

Once they were gone, Zenobia could hear the whipperwills and the crickets. And somewhere upriver, a dog barking.

Time to be on their way.

Drayton had tied ropes to the posts, four of them, and put loops in them, so everybody now had something better to hold on to. He looked over at Zenobia.

"How's Cally?"

"I'm dry now, Uncle," Cally said. "But I can't get warm."

"We'll find us a warm place by morning," Drayton said.

Zenobia hugged Cally close to her as Drayton slowly poled the raft out into the river. The current caught hold just like before, but this time it wasn't as strong. So the raft floated calm-like right on down the river. And thanks to those little ropes, there was no tossing and turning of folks all over the place.

If only the moon wasn't full, she might almost feel safe.

"Everybody lay flat down," Drayton said. "We just have to hold on now and trust God."

The raft was moving fast, the logs wet and slippery, the water bubbling up and slapping around the sides of the raft. Zenobia couldn't even remember what it felt like to be dry.

Drayton was right beside her, his leg against hers. She couldn't move away more than an inch or two—wasn't any place to go, and his leg was making hers warm. When she moved closer, he put his hand on her ass. Oh well, it felt good through the wet skirt.

They were going along just fine when the first hound dogs bayed. Zenobia squeezed Drayton's hand.

"This must be where them mens supposed to be staying for the night."

"Quiet."

The dogs soon were howling fit to wake the dead. And now a light come on in the house on the hill.

Oh, Lord . . . She looked toward the shore and saw a big rowboat tied up to a tree. The door to the house opened, and light flooded out.

"Quiet, you waking these good folks up here."

Zenobia knew it would take more than yelling to make them stop. Those nigger dogs knew they were out there.

"All right, that's *enough!*"

As they floated at last past the house, she heard a whip crack again and again. The yelping that followed was loud enough to cover Cally's first cough of the night.

❖   ❖   ❖   ❖   ❖   ❖   ❖   ❖   ❖   ❖   ❖

Way before sunrise, Drayton poled the raft into the little landing at Clifton. Although the air had already warmed up some, Cally was still shivering badly.

Zenobia left everything to Drayton and Lisa Mae and took Cally up to their old slave shack. She lay Cally down on the bare ground and commenced to rubbing her legs and arms. They were cold, terrible cold, even though her forehead was burning hot.

> Ring around the rosie
> Pocket full of posy . . .

Cally didn't even know she was singing the song.

The others came in from the raft and Drayton looked down at Cally.

"I'm going up to the big house to see if I can find some old blankets or something. We hid some things before we left. Ned and Helen are cold too, even if they ain't complaining."

In less than a halfhour, they had blankets and dry clothes. He made another trip with Lisa Mae and this time came back with cornmeal, bacon, and dried apples. A hot meal.

"Use hard wood," she said as he set off to start a fire in the old cookhouse. "It won't smoke so much."

"This ain't the first fire I ever built," he said over his shoulder.

But what if grayboys showed up? Or bandits?

She sighed. Whatever the risk, Cally had to have something hot. And if the rest of them didn't get something to eat soon, they'd end up as sick as she was.

❧   ❧   ❧   ❧   ❧   ❧   ❧   ❧   ❧   ❧   ❧

The good, hot food soon had the children and Lisa Mae off to sleep. Zenobia and Drayton sat on the ground outside the shack and talked. The way he saw it, they had to get down the Yazoo. And the best way to do that was just to keep floating at night and hiding by day.

"Only thing is," he said, "Cally don't seem fit to travel with that fever."

"You think the patrollers will keep after us still?"

"They might, but I'm beginning to think that man up there fishing was right about them not being too eager. I'm more worried about outlaws, what with there being deserters from both armies."

"And Cally?"

"I don't propose to leave her or you," he said. "By noontime today, we can go into the woods back of the north cotton field—remember the old slave arbor?—and stay up there till she get better."

"What about the raft?"

"Don't you worry about it, ain't nobody going to see it. I want to fix it up a little bit, meantime I'll keep it hid during the day."

"Well, since you fixing it up, I did notice one or two things that could use some improving . . . Now don't go getting your feelings hurt—it's a fine raft."

She reached up to kiss him on the cheek, but he pulled her close and covered her mouth with his. Hard to say which of them was most surprised when she pressed her body into his and kissed him back. But it was Drayton who finally broke the embrace.

"Who's that way up on the hill?"

Zenobia looked where he was pointing.

"Don't you recognize him? I wonder how long he's known we're here."

She stood up and waved. "Uncle Dan! It's me—Zenobia!"

CHAPTER TWELVE

SUE Kenworthy was standing on the porch, her arms around Laura and Gregory, when she heard the coach coming up the path. Richard was *home!* Too bad that Debbie and little Martha had been sent away to live with relatives in Alabama.

She ran down the steps to meet her husband, but the children got there first. A young colored driver helped him down. Richard put his good arm around her and drew her close for a kiss.

"We've missed you terribly, " she said when he finally let her go.

"Good grief, Laura, you're almost up to my shoulders!" He held their ten-year-old daughter at arm's length, then got all tangled up trying to embrace both mother and daughter with one arm. Once disentangled he turned to Gregory, who gave a proper Confederate salute followed by a wild Rebel yell.

Richard laughed and so did the bearded sergeant who was just getting down from his horse.

"I don't know about the Yankees, son, but you sure scare the life out of *me.*"

The only one not laughing was the Negro. Sue looked at him, then took a step closer.

"Aren't you Luke? Zenobia's and Joe's boy."

"Yes, ma'am."

Sue looked at Richard. "How did—?"

"Tell you about it after dinner. Where the devil's Drayton?"

"That'll have to wait for later, too," she said, taking his arm. "Come on inside." He was bound to be angry, but she couldn't help it if they'd run off to the Yankees. That spiteful, *deceiving* Zenobia! It was all her doing, Sue was sure of it.

❖   ❖   ❖   ❖   ❖   ❖   ❖   ❖   ❖   ❖   ❖

Sue and Richard sat together in the living room after the children were in bed. It was so good to have him here even for just a few days, right next to her, close enough to touch.

"Hold me?"

"Come here, sweet Sue."

She sat in his lap. "All those nights alone, I can hardly believe you're *here*."

He nuzzled the bare skin just above the line of her dress and shifted his body so that she rested—oh, so perfectly—in the crook of his arm. They stayed that way for a few moments without talking.

"Richard?"

"Yes?"

"Remember when I first met you?"

"With the greatest of pleasure."

"You were so handsome, all dressed up for the ball, the *rising star* in the state legislature. All the girls were praying you'd pick them for dancing, and then you asked *me* . . ."

"I didn't have a choice, you know. The way you looked at me."

He'd been so light on his feet, she'd danced more gracefully than ever in her life. It was the way they fit. Perfectly. She'd known it that first five minutes, dancing in that ballroom . . .

There would never, ever again be balls with women in beautiful dresses and champagne flowing like water and smiling Negroes passing trays of delicacies. She looked into Richard's face. He looked bigger, seemed older than before he went off to war. And there was something in his eyes. . . .

She began to cry, softly at first, but before long her cheeks were wet and she couldn't seem to stop the tears.

Richard held her tight. "Oh, my poor Sue, you shouldn't have had to deal with all of this on your own. And you've held up things wonderfully with the children and all, with so little help and me so far away. I'm very proud of you."

"But, Richard, I've . . . we've lost *everything*."

"That's just not true." He took out his handkerchief and dabbed at her eyes—dried her cheeks.

"We have too! You're being so understanding about Zenobia and the rest. But her and Drayton, and Lisa Mae and the two children—I know that's five thousand dollars' worth of property, not to mention the ones we lost in that march over to Alabama. We're practically *destitute*, only ten slaves, and one of them that worthless Uncle Dan over at Clifton."

"We'll get them all back when we drive the Yankees out. The nigras will have nowhere to go."

Sue sat up and looked at him. "You surely don't believe that, do you? Why the Yankees are *thicker than flies* around here, raiding up and down the Mississippi and Yazoo like they owned them."

"We whipped the hell out of them at Brice's Crossroads."

"And I'm proud of you, glad you were part of it, but that devil Sherman has got people chasing our poor boys all over Tennessee and—" She stopped, resolved to get back to happier subjects. But somehow the anxious words kept pouring out of her. "I'm sorry, but between having no money, and Clifton gone, and *begging* from your relatives, and now having to go to Mobile to live—it's just too much for a body."

"I know, honey," he said. "It's not easy to see everything we've worked for destroyed, or take charity from kin, or—"

She put her hand up to his mouth as if to quiet him, but he took it away and kissed it.

"Let me finish. You need to know, we've not given up. We've had setbacks, defeats, even desertions, but don't you worry. There are still men like General Forrest and me, plenty of them, who'll die before we see colored—"

She put her hand over his mouth. "Stop! I won't hear the least reference to you *dying*. Now, tell me how come you've got Joe's boy with you? Wasn't he over at Dorothy's place along with his sister—what's her name? Merry or Milly or something?"

"He was, but I had duty over that way, found a chance to stop over and see Dorothy. Luke's a blacksmith and the cavalry needs them, so I took him."

"Seems to me you treat him like a body servant."

"He's that, but mostly he's a blacksmith. Since Joe ran away and joined the Yankees, I find it kind of fitting to have his son serve in his stead."

"Why didn't you write and let me know you'd seen Dorothy? You know how much I love her. I should have written to let her know how things were with us, maybe even invited her to come over here and stay with us instead of up on that *barren* plantation all by herself."

Richard took his arm from around her waist. "I can't think of everything, you know. I did have a battalion of troops to think about, and—"

"Pauline. You had time to think about Pauline, didn't you?"

She felt his body stiffen and knew she'd caught him. Pauline was what he'd gone up there for.

"Well, how is she? Still the kind of woman that makes grown men call out her name in their sleep?"

He got up so abruptly that she almost fell to the floor, but he hardly seemed to notice! She stared at him for a moment, then turned away.

"I'm going to see about the children," Sue said.

When she got back downstairs, Richard was slumped in the chair, staring at the floor. He looked forlorn, like a little child whose favorite puppy had died—oh, why did she have to taunt him his first night home, and with his poor arm in that condition? The hero of Brice's Crossroads looked exhausted. She knelt in front of him and took his hand in hers.

"I'm sorry, Richard. Really sorry. Come on now, let's go to bed." She led him into the bedroom, stood on tiptoe, and kissed him. "You'll not hear *one other* unkind word from me." She patted the bed. "I'll help you out of your clothes."

When he was down to his underwear, she sat beside him on the bed, stopping at each button to play with the hair on his chest. He put his arm around her so that it cupped her breast, then leaned over to kiss her. She sat there for a moment, his mouth on hers, his hand on her breast, oh, Lord . . .

"Mary drew a hot bath for you while we were downstairs." She had unbuttoned his long underwear about halfway, so that her hand rested just above his waist. She pulled back. "Now I'm going to have the great and distinct pleasure of scrubbing you clean."

His hand moved down from her breast, down along the side of her skirt.

"I have to say, Mrs. Kenworthy, scrubbing isn't exactly what I have in mind at the moment." His hand slipped between her thighs.

"Mmmm . . . Oh, Richard, I've thought about this every *single* night you've been gone."

"Me too . . ."

What was he saying? She couldn't focus on anything but what his fingers were doing. She grabbed the front of his underwear and tried to find the buttons.

"I *will not* get into bed with an unbathed heathen."

His hand was still kneading her through the skirt. "Shall I stop?"

She took a deep breath, gently pushed his hand away, and stood up.

"Think I have no willpower, do you? Think the great hero has come home and I'll cast myself at his feet . . ." She giggled and did just that. She was trembling all over, on her knees now, her fingers tearing at the last buttons on his underwear. "Think I have no control over myself, that I'm a slave to my passions?"

As soon as he was free of his underwear, she brushed his penis with her cheek, first one cheek, then the other. Kissed it right on the crown. She looked up at him.

"Your turn, Colonel." Her voice dropped. "Want me to stop?"

She took him into her mouth and pulled down her blouse and bodice. As soon as her breasts fell loose, she felt his hands playing with her nipples. She struggled with her skirt and petticoats, and when he dropped to his knees to help her she drew back and put her fingers on her nipples and rubbed them.

"*Now* look what you've done," she said.

Then his mouth was all over her face, on her eyelids, at one ear, down her neck and over her nipples . . . When he sat on the floor and drew her onto him, the shock and pleasure as he entered her made her grab at him. She dug her fingernails into the flesh of his shoulders—and remembered his arm.

"Oh, Richard, am I hurting you?"

"If I can mount a horse, I reckon I can deal with this right easy." He began to move slowly back and forth. "Know what you are, sweet Sue?"

"*Don't* stop."

"A Georgia peach. A sweet, ripe little peach."

She answered him movement for sweet movement until it was just him and her, nothing else but the two of them in this whole wide world. Their world. That fiery, lush, gorgeous place that was always beautiful, *always* just the same.

She gave Richard his bath in the morning.

❖   ❖   ❖   ❖   ❖   ❖   ❖   ❖   ❖   ❖   ❖

There were no more cross words between them. He took the children on hikes in the countryside, taught Gregory how to aim and shoot a Navy Colt, cut fresh flowers for Laura, and showered Sue with gifts—something new every day for seven days. Porcelain cups with her name on them, a silver medallion, a daguerreotype of a rose, and, best of all, a photograph of him in his new colonel's uniform. They had so much fun that she hardly thought of Pauline.

The only thing that bothered her was Joe's son. Richard treated him as if he were a trophy, a prisoner of war, and you could see from the way the boy's eyes moved that he hated his master.

"I wish you'd get rid of Luke, place him with another unit," she said one evening. "He always says 'yes' and does what you say, but he scares me. Why do you want him around you, when it would be so easy for him to get hold of a gun?"

"I told you about that day Joe stood across the river from me and taunted me. Well, I can't hurt *him*, he hasn't fallen into my hands—yet. But fate has given me his boy. He'll do for the time being."

"What about Milly? Why didn't you take her too?"

"She wasn't there. But if I can get my hands on her, I'll—"

"Bring her to me, Richard . . . I could use her to replace Zenobia."

"Just what I had in my mind."

"But you *will* keep an eye on Luke, promise me? He means you harm, I'm certain of it."

"Don't bother yourself about him. Sergeant Barclay watches him like a hawk."

"Even in the heat of battle?"

"Especially then."

❖   ❖   ❖   ❖   ❖   ❖   ❖   ❖   ❖   ❖   ❖

The following morning a courier rode up to the house with orders for Richard.

"Well, you're going to have me around the neighborhood for a while now. I've been ordered to take command of a reinforced cavalry troop to back up the infantry regiments guarding the Big Black River Bridge. Guess the wound means I can't be galloping around the countryside with General Forrest anymore. For a while, anyway."

"Richard, that's wonder—oh, I'm sorry, darling. I know how you love your cavalry, but I'm just so happy you'll be nearby. Are you *very* disappointed?"

"Well, no. It's actually one of the most important assignments I've ever been given. The Mississippi Central railroad bridge on the Big Black is crucial to the running of supplies from Mississippi to General Hood's army over in Tennessee. If Hood can retake Nashville and drive the Yankees out, they'll be forced to withdraw from Tennessee and Mississippi. And that could end the war."

"Good heavens, Richard. Do you really think that will *happen*?"

"I do, because that tottering Abe Lincoln regime can't stand one more big defeat."

❖   ❖   ❖   ❖   ❖   ❖   ❖   ❖   ❖   ❖   ❖

Richard, accompanied by Luke and Sergeant Barclay, was on his way to his new command early the next morning. Sue was relieved that he'd agreed to delay moving her and the children down to Mobile. And his optimism was infectious. With the bridge intact and under control of the Confederacy, Hood would *crush* Thomas.

"I have no intention of losing that bridge," Richard said as he got into the coach. "We've already wrecked two Yankee regiments who tried to take it. And by God we'll destroy as many as necessary to hold it."

Gregory gave a Rebel yell, and Richard put his head out the window of the coach and returned the yell.

Sue laughed and hugged Laura. "Aren't they *something*!" Yankees, beware!

❖   ❖   ❖   ❖   ❖   ❖   ❖   ❖   ❖   ❖   ❖

"I don't think that there's much use even trying to make a crop next year, Miss Dorothy." Pauline held out a list of seed supplies to her. "Everything's gone. No seed, all the tools on the place stolen." Either by deserters or by Confederate regulars or by hands who'd run away. "Come on down to the stables, I'll show you what I mean."

A premature frost had left a white crust covering the earth.

Pauline showed Dorothy the one mule left on the place. "It's so thin they didn't take it." She walked over to the cow, the only source of milk and butter. Downright scrawny. And the loft that used to be filled with hay was empty—all taken by the army for fodder.

The two women, hand in hand, walked back to the big house.

"I didn't know it was this bad."

"But I been telling you every day. You need to look around you—in a few days, when that stock of wood Luke cut in the spring runs out, we'll have nothing left to warm the house. And soon it won't just be chilly at night."

The two women sat down in rocking chairs in front of the fire in the living room. Finally Miss Dorothy seemed to be paying attention. She *did* look around.

"Oh, Pauline, when I think of what all we've lost . . ."

"I know it's sad, Miss, and I hate to worry you, but if you don't count me and Milly, there are just two able hands left here."

"It's true—something must be done. The children keep catching colds, and they're not used to eating mush every day."

Pauline poked the fire she had built that morning. "How much longer you think the teacher will be able to keep the school open?"

"It's a wonder he's still here. That old man hasn't been paid in two months, and I don't know how we can find the money to pay him. So many people have fled to Texas."

"We could shut off parts of the house. If you move the children into your room, we'd only have to heat it and the kitchen. We could save a lot of wood that way. Me and Milly can move our things into the kitchen and live there, for the time being."

Dorothy sighed. "Everything you're saying is kind and helpful, but I can see now that we're going to have to leave this place before long. The colonel is too far away to help us, and what with Atlanta gone, I doubt he'll be able to spare us any of his attention any time soon."

"I think if you *are* going to leave, you better do it right soon. I hate to say this, but there are some slaves up in the hills who've been raiding other plantations, stealing things out of them. They're bound to come this way sooner or later. And I wouldn't want nothing to happen to you or the children."

Pauline didn't say that the only reason they hadn't stolen everything already was because Woodson—out of love for *her*—had held them back. And she didn't tell her Miss that some of them were colored Yankee deserters, who were saying it was all right to burn down the mansions. Hadn't General Sherman told them to do that? There was even a white soldier among them who'd been captured by the Rebs and escaped.

"Do they hate us so? Neither the colonel nor I have ever done any harm to them. We have treated our nigras well—haven't we, Pauline? And I thought most of the danger was from our own Confederate deserters, not our own faithful nigras."

"But, Miss Dorothy, they ain't your faithful nigras anymore. That's changing. The Yankees are putting different notions into their heads. Believe me, many of them would delight in being able to destroy this place. And it's sad to say, but indeed they would laugh as it burned."

"Oh, Pauline, you can't . . . I just don't believe it."

"Let me tell you a story an old lady told me once, maybe it'll help you understand how my people feel."

"Your people, Pauline? How can you talk like that? We love each other, you're more like a sister than—"

"But I'm not, Miss. I love you dearly and I do know you love me, but the colored are my people."

"How can you say that? What makes you say that?"

Pauline had been looking into the fire, but now she turned around.

"No matter the reason, sisters don't own each other." When she saw the tears well up in Dorothy's eyes, she reached for her hand. "I didn't say it to hurt you, I just—"

"That's not why I'm crying. I should have freed you long ago. And if it hadn't been for the war, I would have by now. But to give you free papers would only have placed you in more danger from *my* people. Now it's too late for all that, the Yankees will do it for us. I would rather I had done it myself, but I'll never have that chance." She blew her nose, sat up straighter. "Now tell me the story."

Pauline drew her shawl more tightly around her shoulders.

"Once upon a time, there was a mean old slave driver named Duncan, who carried the biggest, meanest whip for miles around and took great delight in making the slaves do *anything*. Well, one day his hound dog—its name was Glover—died. Many's the nigra it had caught in its lifetime, but Duncan called all the colored folks on the plantation to come to the funeral and mourn Glover's death."

"Oh, Pauline. Surely not!"

"It's true, Miss. Not everybody is as good and kind as you and the colonel. Or has as much sense. So anyway, that dog was the dearest thing in life to Duncan, and he wanted the colored people to pray and cry over this dog who'd treed so many of them when they tried to run away. You see, Duncan was convinced they had a special way of praying that would reach God—you know, pray on Glover's behalf, ask God's forgiveness for all the colored folk he torn to pieces. Duncan didn't think he could get in touch with God all on his own."

"So he had *some* sense, then."

"So the colored people came to the funeral, just like he asked, and they had little pots of water they hid from him, and they used the water to wet their eyes, and they prayed and shouted up a storm. Old Duncan caught the Holy Spirit, and broke down in front of them and started hugging and kissing them and calling them brother and sister. He was so happy, he gave them a special ration of whiskey that night."

"So then what happened?"

Pauline's face lit up. "Well, that night, after Duncan was gone, they drank his whiskey and all night long they kept on bringing Glover's name before the Lord. 'Poor old Glover—that dog done gone and died and can't catch us no more. Give me another drink! Poor old Glover! May the gates of hell open wide! Amen, Amen!'"

The story had a different, more violent end, but Pauline knew she'd been right to change it when her mistress laughed out loud for the first time in ages.

They were quiet again for a while, though every now and then one of them would say "Amen! Amen!" Or "Poor old Glover!" and they would both start laughing all over again.

✧   ✧   ✧   ✧   ✧   ✧   ✧   ✧   ✧   ✧   ✧

A week later Miss Dorothy gave Pauline legal papers so she and the few others left behind would not be harassed by the authorities. When the day came for her to leave, she lingered on the porch with Pauline even when the children were in the coach.

"I can't imagine waking up tomorrow without you nearby," she said. "We've spent practically every day of our lives together."

"I know, Miss. But I don't know what else we can do. You've done all you can for me and Joe's children, now you have to see about yourself." They walked to the coach arm in arm. "Seems like everything's changing, but the love for you and the colonel in my heart . . . well, that won't ever change."

✧   ✧   ✧   ✧   ✧   ✧   ✧   ✧   ✧   ✧   ✧

Pauline watched until the coach was out of sight, until she could no longer see Dorothy's face framed in the tiny back window.

"Who's going to take care of us now, Auntie?" Milly asked when the coach rounded the first bend.

Pauline put her arms around Milly's shoulders and pointed to the grounds around the big house.

"See all that out there? You see how empty it looks—remember how all our folks would be working and running to and fro for Massa and Miss? That's all over now."

"They're leaving it to us?"

"Well, in a way. Come on, let's go inside."

The mansion's furniture was all covered with linen, the central fireplace dark and silent. Pauline led Milly out into the kitchen and put on a kettle of water for some tea.

"You're free now, honey. No matter what happens, slavery is finished."

Milly smiled. Lord, she was a pretty thing. Had Joe's eyes and his way of smiling.

"Oh, Auntie, everything seems so . . . It's funny, but I feel more danger now than I felt when Miss was still here."

"That's because you ain't used to standing on your own feet. It'll take a little while, but you'll get used to it. You're going to do just fine."

"Who's going to protect us now?"

The teakettle began to boil. "We're going to take care of each other. Brother Woodson and some of his people, they're going to come in tonight, going to live in the big house. The men have got guns, and they've decided that it's better to be here than out in the woods."

"What if the graycoats come by?"

"The men going to keep a sharp lookout for them. The main thing is to get all those folks in out of the cold and the rain."

Woodson and thirty other people, mostly runaways, filed into the building toward evening, looking up in wonder at the crystal chandeliers that hung from the ceilings. Most of them were young and strong, men and women who'd taken to the woods over the past two years or so and banded together. Their clothes were ragged and some had only cloth wrapped around their feet to protect them from the cold.

Soon they had a fire roaring in the main fireplace. And the kitchen was bustling with folk happy to find a real stove to cook on. Somebody began singing, "Glory, Glory, Hallelujah, When I Lay My Burden Down," and the song spread through the house

> Gonna put on my shoes
> Walk in glory
> When I lay my burden down . . .

Pauline admired the way Woodson set things up so quick. He gave everybody an assignment. Some in the kitchen, others cleaning, the young men chopping wood, the older men—including the wounded Union veteran they had rescued—setting up defenses, sentinels around the place for a good two miles. He even laid out his plans for evacuation in case any grayboys came their way.

"And one more thing," he said. "Other folks are going to find out about us and want to come join us. Well, we're going to let them. The more of us they is, the better able we be to protect ourselves. These grayboys are on their knees now. Yankees whipping them every way they can. Our job is to save ourselves, protect these children till the Yankees get up here. Won't be long now, we just got to hold on."

"Speak on, brother," a man said. "When we get strong enough, we ought to go out and *bring* folks in."

"That's just what I have in mind. We going to be a beacon of light in the darkness, my brothers and sisters."

Somebody began to sing, "I'm Going to Sit at the Welcome Table, One of These Old Days."

Pauline got the fiddle out. "Anybody know how to play one of these?"

Before long most everybody was dancing, and nobody seemed to mind when the children got out of their beds and came down and joined in. Who could sleep on such a night as this?

    ✧   ✧   ✧   ✧   ✧   ✧   ✧   ✧   ✧   ✧   ✧

When the house was quiet at last, Pauline left the pallet next to Milly's in a room where the women slept. As she walked through the house, she wondered where Miss Dorothy was tonight, hoped she and the children would be all right.

Most of the men lay asleep, their weapons nearby. Woodson was still sitting up, staring at what remained of the fire.

"Want to talk?" Pauline pointed to a little room off from the big hall, and they went in and closed the door. She put her hand on his knee.

"Do you really have confidence in the sentinels? We'll all be slaves again if they don't sound the alarm in time."

"We've been out in the woods for almost a year now, and they ain't caught us yet. We be all right." He put his arm around her shoulder and drew her close to him. "Long as I'm able to hold you like this, I can deal with whatever come."

She snuggled up to him. "You think the others would mind if we stayed in here together? Think they would take it unkindly, like we had privileges?"

He kissed her. "I think nobody here going to hold any happiness we make for ourselves against us."

"Then wait, I'll go get some blankets and we can make us a pallet on the floor."

"Don't be long. I got something important to ask you."

When she came back, undressed, and lay down beside him, he pulled her close to him.

"I want to care of you. Marry you. Will you have me?"

His body was very warm against hers. He was a strong man, and they were good together.

"That's a hard question to ask me on a night like this. Things changing so much—this is my first night free, remember?"

"There's no one else, is there?"

"No. Please, can't we just love each other tonight?"

CHAPTER THIRTEEN

FOR three days and nights, except when Lisa Mae or sometimes Helen would take over for a little while, Zenobia sat by a pallet where Cally lay twisting and turning and sweating.

The lean-to in the bush arbor wasn't much of a shelter. The wood planks on the muddy ground and the canvas outer covering did little more than keep out the rain that had been coming down for four days. They had a little fire in there, and a way for the smoke to get out. What they didn't have was a way to make Cally well.

"Dear God, oh God, sweet Jesus, take my life if it has to be, but let Cally live . . ." Not gone like Luke and Millie, both of them maybe dead by now. Jesus knew all about the pain and the emptiness and the fear deep down there in her soul. And Zenobia had kept on praying, hadn't she, when Joe went away and left her and Cally behind. Had stayed on her knees day and night and sang every morning:

> *When I saw that bright sunshine*
> *I didn't have no doubt!*

She took a damp cloth and wiped Cally's brow. Why, oh why, had she taken her on this hard, long journey to freedom? If she'd been sold down into Alabama, away from Cally, maybe she'd be someplace warm and dry now instead of in this damp, smoke-filled hiding place.

"Here, get up for a moment." Drayton put his arm around her shoulder. "I made some more of the medicine. Let's see what it will do."

He bent down and gave Cally two spoonfuls. She stared up at him and didn't even move her eyes.

Zenobia looked around her. Ned, his eyes all mournful, was poking a stick in the little fire. Lisa Mae was patching some clothes. Old man Dan, leaning on his cane and wearing those patched blue pants of his, was by the door. He came up to the arbor twice a day to see how Cally was.

Zenobia handed the damp cloth to Lisa Mae and beckoned Drayton to follow her outside.

"I want you to take the others and go on," she said. "It's dangerous here, and even if Cally gets well she won't be able to travel for days. Go."

"Think I could make any of them in there leave you? Would Ned leave you? You been his mother since they sold DoraLee away. And Lisa Mae? She stick closer to you than a sister. Helen? She done decided to be your daughter." He took her hands. "And me?"

She stood tiptoe and kissed him full on the lips.

"What you smiling about?" she said when they broke apart.

"I love you, Zee."

She let herself be held for a minute. "You making me feel things I ain't felt for a long time. Let's go back inside. It's cold out here."

She lifted Cally out of the bed and held her while Drayton put a blanket around them both. She and Lisa Mae took turns rocking Cally's slight little body.

>   *When I got down on my knees*
>   *I didn't have no doubt!*

Such a long night. Around midnight, Uncle Dan came back. He knelt in front of Cally and Zenobia and commenced to pray.

After a while, Cally opened her eyes and smiled.

"See, Zenobia, she always do that with me, she love her uncle Dan." He waved his hand. "Hi, sweetie pie."

Cally closed her eyes again and seemed to sleep. But she breathed heavy, and Zenobia kept wiping away the sweat beading on her little forehead and soaking through her clothes.

Drayton took off his cotton shirt and wrapped it around her.

I knew the Lord would take care of me
I didn't have no doubt!

❖   ❖   ❖   ❖   ❖   ❖   ❖   ❖   ❖   ❖   ❖

Uncle Dan bent down next to Zenobia and kissed Cally on her brow. "I be back first thing in the morning, going to pray all night, the old African way, good and loud down in my hut! Going to turn them hellhounds back!"

Drayton sat down on the floor in front of Zenobia. "Always a good sign when somebody sweat, mean the fever coming out."

"I seen it happen many a time," Lisa Mae said. "So, Zee, why don't you just lay down and sleep and let me hold Cally the rest of the night?"

Zenobia shook her head and kept on rocking. Soon Lisa Mae was sleeping on her pallet, and Drayton dozing off with his head against Zenobia's legs. And as the night wore on, Cally seemed to be resting easier. Breathing mighty fast, but she'd stopped sweating.

It was getting lighter in the hut. Far away Zenobia could hear a rooster crowing. Soon another joined in, then another. Must be Uncle Morris's birds. She bent low over Cally, couldn't hear her breathing, it was so soft. Her face looked peaceful.

> *The little baby gone home*
> *The little baby gone home*
> *The little baby gone along*
> *For to climb up Jacob's ladder.*

Through a crack in the door, she could see the sun rising all red—orange between the earth and sky.

She kissed Cally on her brow, her eyes, her little mouth, took her up, held her tight, rocked her gently.

> *For to climb up Jacob's ladder . . .*

Cally's eyes opened. She smiled pretty, just like she had for Uncle Dan, then closed her eyes. Zenobia held her breath, waiting for Cally's next one. It didn't come. And when Zenobia did breathe again it came out with a sob that woke Drayton. He held them both, mother and daughter, rocked

Zenobia, who kept on rocking Cally. Rocking and crooning. Rocking and crooning.

❖   ❖   ❖   ❖   ❖   ❖   ❖   ❖   ❖   ❖   ❖

There was a tall, spreading pine tree at the top of the hill at Clifton. Birds of all kinds liked the spot; in the springtime a red cardinal perched on the pine tree's highest branch and sang the song he used to sing when Joe and Zenobia walked up the hill and looked out over the bend in the river. "Someday we'll be free." Joe had said it so many times they'd ended up calling the place Someday.

That was where Zenobia told Drayton to dig the hole.

There was no wind. They stood around the grave, heads bowed, while Uncle Morris said a prayer.

"Oh Heavenly Father, we come before thy presence humble as we know how to come, calling upon you to have mercy on us poor sinners. And especially on the soul of your departed servant child, Cally. She ain't never done nobody wrong, were just a little bitty thing who loved to take her uncle Dan by his hand. Now we down here asking you to let her into your kingdom so she can play up there around King Jesus' golden throne.

"And, Father, we begging your mercy on us who still down here on this hard and tedious journey, asking you to look down on this grieving mother, beseeching you to console your daughter Zenobia. Put your love all around her, be unto her a fence all around, clarify her mind, give her strength for the journey. You an all-seeing God, an all-knowing God, a Burden-Bearer, Heavy Load Sharer, Mighty Waymaker. You Our Bright and Morning Star, our Wheel in the Middle of the Wheel, Our Shelter in the Time of Storm, Our Rock in a Weary Land, I say you our Rock in a Weary Land . . ."

Lisa Mae began singing soon as Drayton tossed the dirt over the little body wrapped in cloth:

> *Oh—Grave yard! Oh—Grave yard!*
> *You must give over to the body,*
> *Dig my grave with a silver spade*

You must give over to the body!
Let me down with the golden chain
You must give over to the body!

Drayton pounded a cross down into the earth.

Cally
Born 1861
Died 1864
"Let the Little Childrens Come Unto Me."

It was over. Drayton took Zenobia by the arm and led her down the hill, Lisa Mae, Ned, and Helen trailing behind. Uncle Morris stayed up on the hill, like he wanted to pray some more, maybe hold Cally's hand on her journey home.

   ✿   ✿   ✿   ✿   ✿   ✿   ✿   ✿   ✿   ✿   ✿

Two days after they buried Cally, Zenobia knew it was time to go on their way. Drayton spent the morning checking out the raft again. It seemed like every day he thought of a way to make it stronger. The way Zenobia saw it, the longer they waited, the more chance that somebody would come and capture them.

She gathered up the bundle of food she would be carrying.

"You all go down to the raft," she told Lisa Mae and the others. "Drayton's down there already. I want to go up the hill one last time, then I got to stop by and tell Uncle Dan good-bye. Go on, now. I'll be along soon."

   ✿   ✿   ✿   ✿   ✿   ✿   ✿   ✿   ✿   ✿   ✿

When she got to his shack Uncle Dan was sitting there, staring down at the floor. "I reckoned you'd be to see me before you left."

Zenobia hugged him. "You was the first person I met when I come here from South Carolina, remember?"

"I got something I ought to tell you, and I been meaning to do it but couldn't seem to find the right time, what with Cally passing and all."

"What is it?"

"It's about Joe. He come back here about six moons ago."

"He's *alive?*" Not dead, not drowned in the river when he tried to run away?

"Was the last time I saw him. Them grayboys come and captured him."

"How did he look?"

"He were a soldier with them Yankees. He against us."

Poor old man. "Did he ask about me? About us?"

Uncle Dan looked away. "I told him you and Cally gone with Miss Kenworthy over Jackson way. And he say he was going to fetch you all."

She'd known it all the time. Joe would never give them up for lost!

"What happened then?"

"Like I say, them grayboys on horses come by and caught him."

The story sounded mighty strange.

Uncle Dan reached over and took her by the hand. "If I was you, I wouldn't be going with them on that little old raft."

"It's too late for that now. It won't be long before we reach the Yankees."

"Them grayboys all around."

"We won't be leaving until dark."

"God bless you, child."

Zenobia got up to leave the hut.

"Zee?"

She turned back to him. Seemed like he was trying to say something, but the words were stuck in his mouth.

"Yes, Uncle Morris?"

"Them grayboys . . ."

"You already done told me about them, we be careful."

"But—" He was holding her by both hands, like he didn't want to let her go.

"Uncle Dan, if they knew we was here, they'd have come by now, but all the same I appreciates your worrying about us. Unless you knows—"

He released her hands. "Oh no . . . ain't nothing. You'd better run along now. It getting late."

❈   ❈   ❈   ❈   ❈   ❈   ❈   ❈   ❈   ❈   ❈

When night came, they were all ready to go. Drayton pulled the raft from under its cover of leaves and showed Zenobia all the things he'd done to make it stronger. Proud of himself, and why not? He'd even put some planks crosswise on top so the water wouldn't come through so much. Doing his best to make it better for her, Lisa Mae, and the children.

The raft was heavier now, but with everybody pulling together, they were able to get it in the water. It looked sturdy.

"You done good." Zenobia kissed Drayton, but knew that she'd never lie with him now that she had some hope that Joe was still alive.

He tied the raft tight to the dock. "All right, everybody, get on—careful-like." He handed Zenobia the long pole. "Here, put that right there in the holder. Everything here?"

Zenobia looked around. "No, wait, I left the extra food bundles up at Uncle Dan's. I'll go get them."

"No, you won't. I don't want any more getting in and out of that raft than is necessary. I'll go up and get them, just wait here."

"Hurry."

Zenobia busied herself with arranging things on the raft. She put the foodstuffs in a little box Drayton had built to keep them dry, then checked to see that Ned and Helen were bundled up good for the night trip. Drayton had said they would need to be on the river at least two nights, then they might start running into Yankee boats.

Strange he wasn't back yet—it was only a little ways up to Uncle Dan's house.

"Lisa Mae, if he doesn't get back in a few more minutes, I'm going after him."

"Oh, Zee, you worry too much. If ever a man could take care of himself, it's Drayton."

The minutes dragged on. Full night had fallen, and Zenobia checked to see that the revolver Drayton had given her was in its special wrapping. When she drew out the gun and started to get up, Lisa Mae grabbed her arm.

"Don't leave us here all alone. If he in trouble, you the only one can get us out on the river."

"She's right, Auntie," Ned said. "If Drayton and you both gone, who going to take care of us?"

She sat back down on the raft and made herself wait, her eyes straining to see something through the dark. They all jumped when the sound of gunfire and flashes of light came from up toward Uncle Dan's house.

"Uncle Drayton in trouble?" Ned said.

"I don't know, we have to wait and see." Her grip on the gun in her lap tightened.

The firing and the noise were closer now.

"I think we got the nigger!"

"Oh!" It was Drayton's deep voice.

"Drayton, Drayton!" Zenobia screamed his name into the night.

More gunfire, then he shouted through the darkness. "Go, Zenobia, I'm shot—can't make it. I'll hold them off."

"No, we'll wait for you."

Three more shots.

"Zee, I did love—"

The sound of the shot went right through Zenobia.

She put the revolver back in its wrappings, cast off the rope, took the pole, and pushed as hard as she could.

The heavy raft barely moved.

She could hear the sounds of galloping horses and shouting men nearing them. She pushed again, harder, praying they would make it out into the current before the men reached the docks. By now she could make out the shapes of the men's horses.

She gave one more shove, then lay down on the raft. Lisa Mae had her arms around the children.

"Stop your crying. You got to be quiet. There ain't no moon, they might not see us. If we catch the current, we be gone before they know it."

The raft seemed to stand still, like it was stuck in a pool of molasses. Someone on shore shouted:

"All right, you niggers, the game's up. Come on back before we have to shoot!"

The raft wasn't even a hundred yards from the docks, just bobbing up and down in place. Zenobia took the revolver out and sighted it in the direction of the land.

"I know it can hardly reach them," she said, "but it might put some kind of a scare in them, anything better than just laying here."

She fired and was immediately answered with a ragged volley of shots.

"Now you niggers are dead for sure!"

Zenobia pointed the gun to fire again, but Ned tugged at her arm.

"Auntie, don't you feel it? We *moving*."

She looked at the water and could just see the white bubbles behind and to the side of the raft. First slowly, then faster and faster, the current drew them into the dark void of the river.

The men on shore kept firing and filling the night with their curses. They could curse and shout all they wanted to, God did have some mercy on His people.

When they were well out into the river and the noise had died out behind them, Zenobia turned her attention to her flock. They were sitting up, blankets wrapped tightly around them, all crying, holding on to each other for dear life.

Ned said, "We ain't never going to see Uncle Drayton again, Auntie?"

"Not in this life, you ain't," Zenobia said. "Only thing you can do, and me too, is pray for him. He were a good man." How good she'd never find out now.

"I used to hate him when we lived at Clifton, " said Lisa Mae, who was crying. "Zee, you remember how every time you turn around, he'd be beating on somebody or another, saying Massa made him do it? And he'd always whip full measure."

Zenobia drew a hand across Lisa Mae's wet eyelids, then her own. "The Good Book say judge not lest ye be judged." she said. "We got to say a prayer right now for Brother Drayton, forget the bad things he did and remember how he brought us over this long way and give his life out there in the field to protect us. Lisa Mae, pray a little for his soul, then I wants you all to get to sleep." When all was quiet, her mind drifted back to the words of Uncle Dan's—he must have known about the graycoats, maybe even told them.

❖   ❖   ❖   ❖   ❖   ❖   ❖   ❖   ❖   ❖   ❖

Through the rest of the night, Zenobia watched the shore. Now and then, there'd be a light, then it would vanish. The raft was mostly dry, thanks to Drayton's good work. She wiped away the last of her tears. She could almost hear his voice: time to figure out how to reach the Yankee ships, Zee.

✿   ✿   ✿   ✿   ✿   ✿   ✿   ✿   ✿   ✿   ✿

Early in the morning, just after daybreak, she picked up an oar when the raft rounded a bend at a narrow point in the river. She used it the way Drayton had taught her, fixing it so it bit down deep. At first, it didn't seem to make no difference, then it caught and the raft started to go in toward shore, into a clump of trees like the ones they'd stayed in when they first started out.

Soon as the raft got close enough, she poled it into the bank.

"Where are we, Auntie?" Ned asked.

"Not far enough away from them, and not close enough to the Yankees. Give me a hand, we going to try to pull the raft up here on the bank so we can hide it real good."

Ned stepped down into the water and helped her. When the raft was well covered, Zenobia climbed up the bank to see if she could find them a good hiding place for the day.

They were in luck. There must have been a big plantation here—and a little way back from the river, she could see a shack probably used for cooking meals for the hands when they were out in the fields. When she was sure there wasn't anybody about, she got the others, and they settled in for the day. By the time the sun came up, they were snug as could be.

Zenobia fixed it so one person was outside looking, especially when the others were asleep. They passed three days and three nights like that, hiding in bushes or a shack by day and floating down the Yazoo at night.

✿   ✿   ✿   ✿   ✿   ✿   ✿   ✿   ✿   ✿   ✿

On the fourth day, while they was hiding up on a little hill in a clump of trees where they could see down to the river, some grayboys come riding down the road on horses. They were noisy, shouting to each other and singing songs and riding along like they didn't care who knew it. Like Drayton had said, the grayboys still controlled the land around here, Sherman close to taking Atlanta or not.

Behind the line of them came two pairs of horses, and they was hauling two big guns. They stopped right near where Zenobia had hid the raft and for a minute there, she thought they might find it. But looking for a raft seemed to be the farthest thing from their minds. These men were after bigger game. They drew those cannon right up to the riverbank, aimed them out at the water, then covered them over with branches and leaves.

All morning they stayed down there, not doing much, just lying around. Now and then one would go down to the river with a spyglass and look up and down. Around noontime, the one with the glasses started jumping up and down and shouting. The others come running fast as they could and started aiming the big guns.

"Look, Auntie!" Helen pointed to a long, gray boat floating down the river, with no decks for anybody to stand on and look out. "It's a Yankee ship, you can tell by the flag."

"And it's got big guns too," said Ned, who'd stood up.

Zenobia pulled him down. Thank God the soldiers were looking toward the river.

Pretty soon the air was full of smoke and noise, with some of the gray-boys shooting off their big guns and some others who'd gotten up into the trees firing their rifles down at the boat.

The whole side of the Yankee boat seemed to turn into fire and smoke. Zenobia could see how the balls from its guns were plowing right into those grayboys, but they kept on shooting—until, suddenly, it was over. The Yankee boat steamed on down the river away from the Rebel guns.

The grayboys who were up in the trees came down and ate with the others, then they packed up their guns and rode off in the same direction as the boat.

"Lord, that was something to see," Lisa Mae said.

"Do you know what I know?" Zenobia said.

"I know we going to have one hard time getting out to a Yankee boat."

"Even if we gets to see another one," Zenobia said. She called the children over. "You're going to have to do exactly what I say from now on, especially when we're on that raft. It's the only way we're going to escape to the Yankees."

They promised.

After two more nights of floating on the river and seeing three big Yankee boats go by, Zenobia made up her mind to stay in one place. They had a good place to wait, right behind a little island.

"We going to have to take our chances getting out to one of them boats,"

ALLEN B. BALLARD

she told them. "And we ain't got no guarantee the grayboys ain't going to be around."

"What you getting at, Auntie?" Helen said.

"We going to stay right here in this place, ain't going to move no more, and when the next Yankee boat come, we going to shove off on that raft, shout to high heaven, and pray they stop and pick us up. That's the only way. If we quick enough, we might make it."

✾   ✾   ✾   ✾   ✾   ✾   ✾   ✾   ✾   ✾   ✾

Two more days passed. Then, just after daybreak one morning, Zenobia heard the distant rumble of big boat engines coming down the river. She got up off her pine needle bed and shook everybody awake.

"Quick, now. Down to the raft."

Lisa Mae was up in a minute, but the children were tired. Helen yawned and stretched her arms. Ned started to wipe the sleep out of his eyes. The drone of the engines was getting louder. Zenobia dipped water into a bucket and splashed some of it into the children's faces.

"What you do that for??" Ned cried.

"Boats coming. Hurry!" Helen, who was already on her feet, grabbed her little bag. "I'm ready, Auntie."

Zenobia snatched up her own bag. "Run! And when we get there, don't bother with the leaves, just get on."

The boat engines were very loud now.

She ran to the edge of the little island and looked up the river. Sure enough, it was one of them Yankee boats with the guns and the big old wheels on the side.

She raced back to the raft. Her stomach felt funny. And they were leaving all the food and most of the clothing behind.

She poled the raft out into the muddy river. Lord, it was a big boat. And didn't that red, white, and blue flag snapping in the morning breeze look pretty?

"You got that white flag ready?"

Lisa Mae nodded.

"Then start waving it!"

Ned and Helen were on their knees, waving their hands.

"You two lay down before you tip the raft," she said. "You be safe soon."

They got down, but kept on shouting and waving their hands.

"Hey, boat, stop for us!"

"Auntie, can't they see us?"

Zenobia had never seen anything as big as that boat. Nor as fast. Why, it was already abreast of them and no more than a field's length away. And it was making waves big enough to send the raft sliding up one side of them and down the other. Zenobia, now on her knees, had to hold on tight to one of the ropes. She could see soldiers in blue uniforms standing on the decks. And lots of them were colored. Lord, she never thought she'd live to see the day.

The river was taking the raft fast downstream and toward the boat.

Were those men blind? How could all them eyes miss a raft with four people on it?

Another bow wave from the boat hit the raft so hard it almost tossed Zenobia overboard.

"Watch yourself, Auntie!" Helen yelled. "You can't swim!"

Zenobia clung to the rope, her feet dangling in the water.

Helen tossed a rope to her and she pulled herself up toward the center of the raft, just in time to be thrown back by the blow from another wave.

One more like that, and the whole raft would go over.

Suddenly the men on the boat started waving and yelling. Up at the top of the big boat, a man with a white hat on waved too, then turned around and yelled something to some other men in blue.

Bells clanged, whistles blew, and a big cloud of steam belched out of the smokestack.

The ship slowed, then the big wheel on its side started to turn backward. And praise the Lord if it didn't come to a stop right in the middle of the river. Somebody could sure steer that boat.

The waves still rocked it, but now the raft had floated up to the back of the boat. A colored man in a blue uniform yelled down.

"Catch this rope when I throw it and tie it to the raft! We can't stop long and can't put a boat down—they's Rebs all around."

He tossed the rope down. Zenobia reached for it, and missed. The man recoiled the rope.

"Better catch it this time, sister, we can't wait for you."

He tossed the rope again. This time Zenobia kept her eye right on it, caught it, and tied it between a couple of logs.

The deck of the boat was thick with soldiers.

"Make sure it's tight!"

"You all lay down!"

"We'll bring you on board a few miles down the river!"

Ned and Helen waved at the men. Lisa Mae was crying.

"Look sharp, the captain's going to start the engines." The sailor who'd thrown down the rope never took his eye off them. "You all hang on, now, no matter what happens. It's likely to get a mite rough."

They all lay down on the raft and took a good hold on Drayton's ropes.

"Well, we done made it to the boat," Zenobia said. But any relief she felt vanished when bullets started whizzing over their heads and striking the wooden hull of the boat. One bullet crashed into the side of the raft itself.

The rope connecting the raft to the boat got real tight, then came a hard tug on the raft as the engine speeded up. Zenobia felt the sudden surge of power as the paddle wheels took hold. The boat began to move.

Too fast! So much water was coming up over the edge of the raft, it was being pulled under. The whole front part of the raft was already submerged, and so were Zenobia's legs.

"We going down!" hollered Lisa Mae, trying to scramble to the other side of the raft.

"Auntie, save me!" Ned was in water up to his chest.

Helen had been swept off the raft and was holding on to one of the ropes Drayton had made.

Zenobia grabbed Ned and held him close, but she could feel herself slipping off the raft. Couldn't hold on, not fast as that ship was going.

"Don't let go of that rope, Helen!"

Lisa Mae screamed, "I can't hold on no more." The water was up to her neck.

Zenobia said a quick prayer and prepared to die. The whole raft was under water, covered over by a mass of big white bubbles thrown up by backwash from the rudder of the ship.

But now she felt the raft lift itself back out of the water, rock a few times, then steady itself and begin to drift.

Helen crawled back on.

Lisa Mae just cried and cried. "We *almost* made it," she said between sobs.

Zenobia looked up and saw a sailor waving a knife in the air. Must have used it to cut them free of the transport ship.

"Thanks, mister."

Most of the soldiers who'd been waving to them were now busy returning the fire of the grayboys. But two or three of them kept on waving and one yelled, "We'll be back for you someday!"

When she looked back down, she saw that the raft was floating toward shore. It wasn't long before they were close enough to make out the guns of the white men standing on shore, waiting for them.

CHAPTER FOURTEEN

Second Report
Headquarters Cavalry Forces
Vicksburg, Miss., December 4, 1864

Capt. F. W. Fox,
Assistant Adjutant-General

Captain—I have the honor to report that, pursuant to orders of the major general commanding, I moved with my command to Big Black railroad bridge on the morning of the twenty-third of November. On the morning of the twenty-seventh of November we marched at daylight, and the advance of a column under Major Cook, Third U.S. Colored Cavalry, cut the telegraph on the railroad below Deasonville, and in sight of Vaughn Station, at 12:30 P.M.

The railroad bridge across Big Black lies four miles below, without any approach save the railroad track, and artillery cannot be taken to it.

I am, Captain, very respectfully, your obedient servant,

E. D. Osband
Colonel Third U.S., Colored Cavalry
Commanding Cavalry Forces, District of Vicksburg

"I tell you," Joe said, "them infantry boys has seen some things, but the way they talked about them poor colored women and children on that raft that was cut adrift . . . well, it must have been one sad sight."

He stopped pacing long enough to take the cup of coffee Betty handed him, then sat down on the bed.

"Said it made them feel mighty bad, like they was slaves again. There wasn't nothing they could do but stand there and watch the family float over to the Rebs."

"I'm sure they did everything they could, Joe."

"One of them said he kept wishing he had wings so's he could fly down there and pluck them off the raft, bring them safe back onto the boat."

Betty sat down on the bed beside him and rested her hand on his thigh. "Bet it got you to thinking about Zenobia, didn't it?"

He nodded.

"If it's God's intention, he'll bring her back to you."

"You think?"

"What I think is you don't have no control over what's happening, any more than me."

He leaned against her, rested his head between her breasts while she stroked his neck and back.

"All I know is I love you more than I've ever loved anybody, Joe Duckett. I hate to see you looking so down."

"Don't you ever get to feeling low, Betty?" He raised his head and studied her smooth brown face. "You don't never complain, you just go to work every day, and set here and wait for me every night, even when you know I ain't getting no leave. I'm getting mighty sweet on you."

She snuggled up close to him. "Don't you be mocking me, honey."

"I ain't, trust me, I ain't. Sometimes I feel like I'm almost going crazy— like you and Zenobia is all mixed up in my mind, like you is one woman."

Betty kissed him, then took a step back and began unbuttoning his shirt. "Don't really matter to me, honey . . ." And his trousers. " . . . long as I'm the one in your arms right now."

He pulled her to him and kissed her belly, ran his tongue up, between, and around her breasts. Beneath his tongue he felt her skin contract, felt the long shudder that seemed to run the length of her.

He laid her down gently so that she was beneath him. She locked her legs around him and drew him down deep into her, moving back and forth and up and down in a way that made him think of the first time he saw her dancing.

What old war?

❧   ❧   ❧   ❧   ❧   ❧   ❧   ❧   ❧   ❧   ❧

Joe sat at attention on Princess while Captain Stiles rode back and forth inspecting Company A. Damned if they weren't back up on the Yazoo again—by now Princess pretty much knew the way by herself once they got off the boats. Hadn't had a single easy time of it, and by the look on the captain's face this one wouldn't be no different. They'd see in a minute.

"Top of the morning to you, men!"

"A good morning to you, Captain, sir!"

"Well, now, it is my great pleasure to tell you that your Uncle Sam thinks very highly of your conduct on the field of battle. You've been good and faithful fighters, and the story of your exploits on the Yazoo has echoed through our great nation, near and far. So great is your fame, in fact, that the army has given us the distinct honor and privilege of going to destroy that very same bridge that General McArthur's boys tried to take back in June."

A groan came from the men.

"Sounds like you know the one I mean," Stiles said with a grin. "That one up there in the swamps. We're going to take that railroad bridge on the Big Black River and take it Third Cavalry style. I don't need to tell you how heavily defended it is, or how important it is to our men in Nashville that it go down. The Rebs up in Tennessee are getting all their cotton and corn and hardtack over that bridge."

His horse skittered for a second and the captain paused long enough to settle him.

"We'll just follow Major Cook's orders like we always have and carry this one off in our usual style. He's never let us down once, and we won't let him down this time."

The captain had told Joe there were close to six thousand Reb troops up here in the Delta to protect the bridge and the town of Jackson. Command must have done some heavy planning on this thing.

That very same morning, their horses had gone clattering across the pontoon bridge on the Big Black River, but they headed east toward Jackson instead of upriver and north toward the Big Black River Bridge. Just like the army to tell you they wanted you to do one thing, then change around and do another.

But the captain said Jackson, and that's the direction they took, Joe leading the column. There was less resistance from the Rebs than they expected, so they moved a good ways that day. Come nightfall, the orders were to set up good strong bonfires, and soon the whole night was lit up. Bonfires every which way you looked.

Then, around midnight, the captain has come down the line and told everybody to be quiet, and make sure the horses didn't neigh. In the dead of night they skedaddled out of there heading back west, leaving the bonfires burning behind them.

Looked like the plan was to fool the Rebs into weakening their forces at the bridge, make them think the Third was headed toward Jackson so they'd concentrate their forces there. Joe was sure of this by morning when the Third led the column up the east bank of the Big Black River, north toward Benton—back once again in the country near Clifton.

After two days of marching, the regiment was ready to make the assault. At the first sight of the bridge, Joe had taken a quick sharp breath. Holy shit! An awful lot of colored men must have died building that thing. From the hill he was standing on, he could look down and see the railroad tracks stretching far off into the distance. And there, far away—he could barely see it—was some kind of building, perched on a hill that overlooked the bridge.

The railroad track bed was broken at several points by high trestlework, maybe sixty to seventy feet in the air. The trestles were real narrow, and the ties weren't much wider than the tracks. There was a whole lot of space between each tie, and a long way to fall if a man, running hard, tripped on one of them. And to top it all off the whole damn shebang was built on a swamp. Into which he'd bet anything the Third Cavalry would soon be descending.

For there wasn't but two ways to get to that bridge—either march directly over the railroad tracks, or go down through the swamps. Couldn't get artillery close enough to blow it up, either. The wheels of the guns and caissons would sink in the marsh.

The way Captain Stiles explained it they were going to go both ways— over the tracks *and* through the swamps. The captain got all the officers and sergeants down from their mounts, then here Major Cook came to draw the details in the dirt. A company—that was Joe's—was going to go through the swamps on the north side of the railroad—B company was going to do the same thing on the south side of the railroad, and Major Cook himself would lead a company straight down the railroad track.

"But, boys," he said, "we've got one little problem when we reach that bridge. The Rebs have built a blockhouse that commands its approaches. Now, we've got us a pretty good plan, but this is not going to be like your morning promenade."

He scratched a few more lines in the dirt, two straight ones about an inch apart, and a big square where the lines ended. Except the major couldn't draw too well, so the square was a little lopsided.

"See, here's the bridge, and me and an assault company are going to go straight over it, right direct at that blockhouse."

He pointed the stick to the sides of the bridge he'd drawn. "And here, while we're keeping them busy on the tracks, is where you other boys are going to come up from the swamps and fire at them when they come out of the blockhouse to get us."

He stood up and grinned. "Once you give them a good dose of the carbines' medicine, all the companies will re-form on the tracks, charge them, and take the blockhouse. Simple as that. Any questions?"

Joe had one big question, but he didn't figure there was any point in asking it. If that was all there was to it, how come the Rebs done throwed back two attacks already?

°   °   °   °   °   °   °   °   °   °   °

It was noon before everything was ready. Joe assigned two men to stay behind with the horses and had the rest check the Sharps carbines, and their Colts. "You got to act like infantry now," he told them. "Like Sherman's boys at Chickasaw Bluffs."

Finally, Major Cook waved Joe's company off, with Captain Stiles leading. Joe looked behind him. The men, some with their hats slouched over to one side, others with brims turned up in the front, slipped one by one down into the marsh until they were knee-deep in mud. Soon they were clawing their way through a god-awful tangle of vines and slimy moss-covered limbs long ago broken off from the trees towering above them. Here and there you could see where a bolt of lightning had struck and left its jagged mark on the shattered trunk of the tree. Thorny brambles tore at their uniforms.

For a November day, it was mighty hot. Mosquitoes hummed all around them, and even though you couldn't see them, the chiggers was probably having a feast. Seemed like every time Joe looked, Zack was scratching somewhere or slapping away at his face.

"Better watch it, you might slap the little sense you got right out of yourself."

"Still leave me with more sense than you—I ain't been captured by the Rebs no three times."

"They likes my company and my home cooking. Done come to expect it."

"And they expecting you to fall into their hands one more time, Sarge," Logan said. "And when you do—"

"Whee-ho!" said another. "Whee-ho! Them Rebs going to fight to see which one gets to stretch Sarge's neck first!"

"And don't let that Colonel Montgomery win," Zack said. "Oh no. He going to have all of his boys lined up to see what he going to do to Joe. Might even call a truce so's everybody can see he done caught him the Wizard. And then—"

"Silence back there." They still had a mile to go, but Captain Stiles didn't like any horseplay come fighting time.

The mud pulled so hard at Joe's foot his boot almost came off. The water was all the way up to his waist now.

"How'd they ever build that damn bridge?" Zack whispered.

"What I want to know," Joe whispered back, "is *why*." God didn't intend for no bridges to be built on such land, 'specially no railroad bridges. Just weeds and muck and buzzing insects everywhere. Be glad when this war was over. Now, at home—

He almost laughed out loud.

Home? Hadn't had no home since . . . He closed his eyes and saw Zee's face, those deep-set twinkling black eyes that knew all . . .

"Pass the word back. We're stopping here."

They were right under the bridge on the side opposite the stockade. If they moved a little higher on the riverbank, up into the thick clumps of bushes that dotted the hillside on their side of the bridge, they'd have the stockade—a hundred yards away from them on the other side of the river—right in their gun sights. Same for Company B on the south side.

The captain pointed to where he wanted the troops placed, just like he'd gone over it with them before. Joe nodded, gestured with his fingers, his head, sometimes his whole body, until he had the men moved quietly into position, right where the major wanted them. They had every sally port of the stockade under their guns. Only thing they could do now was wait for Major Cook to come along the railroad track.

A few rifle shots rang out from the blockhouse.

The major and his men must be coming into sight, the Rebs probably wondering if he was a fool or just plain crazy, coming down that track on foot, high up in the air, where they had a clear shot at them. Where would they be able to hide?

Wasn't no place. Joe was glad he wasn't the one coming up those tracks.

A heavy fire came out of the stockade, then the Rebs did just what the major wanted. Thinking they had old Major Cook on the run like they done the other Yankee regiments, they stormed out, all hot to chase the major and his men back down the railroad track.

"Steady, men!" Captain Stiles held up his hand. One mess-up and the Rebs would run right back instead of whooping it on down the tracks, shooting off their guns and their mouths.

"Come on back, niggers, we'll let you have the stockade for nothing, or near about—just a little lead."

Joe and his men were looking slightly down on the Rebs, spread out all along the track, when Captain Stiles gave the order.

"Fire!"

Caught in a crossfire that had them cursing and shouting and running, the Rebs managed to get back in the stockade, leaving a lot of dead and wounded men on the tracks. But it was all they could do to get a shot off, because the Third was pouring lead into that fort. Which meant it was only a matter of time before it fell.

Back on the hill on what was now the Third's side of the bridge, Major Cook had the bugler blow assembly. Led by Captain Stiles, half the boys who'd come through the swamps scrambled onto the railroad tracks and joined Major Cook's men to form three assault companies. The rest of the men kept peppering the blockhouse with a steady crossfire.

The major yelled over to Joe. "Come on with me! Your squad will lead the way. We've got to storm that blockhouse." He turned to the bugler. "Sound the charge!"

Lord, but he was a sight to see, running over those railroad ties with his saber pointing the way. And Joe—carbine strapped across his back, and a pistol in each hand—wasn't no more than a couple of steps behind, so he could see him good. Who'd of thought the major could move that fast?

Barely a shot came out of the Reb firing ports. Thank God for the troopers up on the hill.

The feel of the ground when he reached the other side of the bridge was solid and reassuring. Another minute and they'd be at the sally ports, then into that fort.

The bugler was blowing to beat all hell. That boy sure could blow that thing.

The Rebs had abandoned the firing ports and were now up behind wooden picket fences on the parapets of the fort firing down at Joe and his troops. But Third Cavalry was pouring off the railroad track and onto the ground. Soon as a hundred or so of them were there, Major Cook raised his saber again.

"Follow me!"

He ran right through a sally port the Rebs hadn't been able to close. Joe was now no more than a half-step behind him with nothing but Rebs in front—just as fighting mad as he was, and shouting to beat all hell.

A big-assed man in a red shirt, his bayonet fixed, came right at him. His eyes were smoking and he was yelling, "Nigger! Nigger! Nigger! Triflin' son of a—"

Joe sidestepped and shot him twice in the back.

Didn't have no time to think before two more were in his face, one of them swinging his rifle. Shit, that little-assed boy belonged home with his mama. Joe leveled the Colt in his left hand and shot him, then shot the other man dead between the eyes. The Rebs were fighting hard—some swinging rifles, others thrusting with bayonets,—but everywhere he looked, they was giving ground.

✳   ✳   ✳   ✳   ✳   ✳   ✳   ✳   ✳   ✳   ✳

Captain Stiles was putting his saber to good use over there. But it looked like he needed shooting support, so Joe moved up behind him. Zack must have had the same idea.

"See behind them sandbags over there?" he said. "That's where most of the fire coming from now. What say we knock 'em out?"

"Captain?"

"I heard. Do it!"

Joe turned and called back. "Tucker, Logan, Johnson, Mendenhall, front and center!" He pointed over to the sandbag cover: "Let's take 'em."

They ran across the courtyard, bullets whizzing all around them. One burned Joe's head, he felt it go right past his ear.

They hit the sandbags at a dead run, were up and over in no time.

Seeing Joe and his boys come over the sandbags—yelling like crazy, running through bullets like they didn't mean nothing to them—must of put a scare into the Rebs. They threw down their rifles every which way and took off like the devil himself was after them.

And when they ran, damned if the rest of the Rebs didn't, too. Right on up the hill behind their stockade, scattering like a bunch of flushed ducks.

"Bugler, sound Recall!" Major Cook said. "Captain Stiles, Sergeant Duckett—they'll be back soon and with plenty of reinforcements. Take fifty men, advance as far up that hill as you can, and set up a skirmish line. We need enough time to soak the bridge with coal oil. We'll sound Recall when we're ready to burn it, and then you'd do well to get your asses back down here real quick."

They formed into squads and marched up the hill behind the stockade till they met fire coming from the woods less than a hundred yards away. From a position in the grass about halfway up, the Third poured a steady fire into the woods.

Then things got quiet for about half an hour. Joe hoped the hell they was hurrying with that oil stuff. Some fifty men were filling their canteens with it. That should be enough to do the job.

The fire from the woods started up again thick and heavy—reinforcements must have arrived. A trumpet sounded, drums started beating, and a line of Rebs came marching out of the woods.

And who was that leading them, saber in the air?

"It's my old master, Captain."

"We have to protect that bridge. If you kill him in a fight, well and good."

The Rebs were moving steadily forward. By now, Joe could see that their drummer boy was colored.

"Get behind our line and direct the firing," the captain said. "Keep them steady now."

Joe dropped to one knee behind the center of the Yankee line. He was surprised at how steady he was, what with Massa Richard Kenworthy marching on him, proud as a peacock, looking like the cock of the walk. And mean.

"At the order only, Joe."

The Rebs were maybe forty yards away. What was the captain waiting for?

Massa Richard whooped and raised his saber. "Charge!"

The Rebs broke into a run.

The captain said, "Fire!"

The Reb line staggered and wavered, but kept on coming with Massa Richard close enough now for Joe to see how old he looked.

The men waited, disciplined and ready for the captain's next order, and when it came, the Rebel line wavered again. Massa Richard's shoulder was bloody, but he was still running toward them, hell-bent on breaking their line. He'd dropped his saber now and was waving a pistol.

Joe lost sight of him when the Rebs crossed into the Yankee lines and the hand-to-hand began. No time now to worry about anything but keeping himself alive and the Rebs away from the bridge. He pulled out his Choctaw war knife and just went to work.

Saw one man out of the corner of his eye aiming a pistol at him. Ducked down low and sprang at him like a mountain cat, stabbed him quick three times, felt him drop to the ground. Turned around in time to throw the knife into the chest of a gray-haired man who was trying to bayonet Zack. He helped Zack up, retrieved the knife, and ran on.

And there was Massa Richard. He had three Rebs around him, but Joe could get to him. Yes, he could.

"Joe, I'm hurt!" Captain Stiles called out. "Take command!"

What about Massa, there? Ready to take him back into slavery, and close enough to kill. But Joe knew his duty.

"Fall back, men," he said, calm as could be. "Right down there behind those rocks. Form a new line. Zack, get the captain."

A bullet tore through his sleeve. He ducked behind a boulder and looked around to see Massa with a Colt aimed in his direction.

"I got your boy, Joe. Come get him."

Did he mean Luke? No time to think about it now.

"Steady, boys, them Rebs are hurt bad, ain't going to be asking for much more."

He detailed two men to get the captain back to the bridge and got his men into a rhythm of firing again. And sure enough, the Rebs retreated back up the hill. For the time being, they'd had enough of the Third's carbines.

Joe kept his eyes up there on the woods where the Rebs had gone, thinking, hoping it was all over now—surely it was, with Massa Richard wounded. No, there was the sound of that drum beating again. That little colored boy had been so small and they'd tried not to shoot him but here the little feller came drumming again, a line of Rebs right behind him and Colonel Kenworthy behind them.

This time he didn't have a saber, couldn't have carried it nohow. But what the hell *did* he have?

Joe knew the answer when he heard first one bark, then two, then . . . shit! Sounded like a whole pack of dogs. The colonel, this time on a horse, was leading a bunch of men forward, and each of them had five or six hounds on a leash.

Hellfire and damnation!

Listing to one side on his horse, Colonel Kenworthy raised his hand, and advanced on Joe's lines at a trot, followed by his pack of hellhounds— must have been thirty or forty of them.

The colonel wasn't able to keep up with his men. A sergeant took the lead, breaking into a run. Just behind the dogs was a line of infantry. They was going to use those dogs like they was cavalry.

Joe had seen his men face a lot and stand strong. But dogs? Probably nigger dogs, trained to attack colored.

"Man, do you see what's coming?"

"Sarge, them's some mean-looking bastards."

"Shut the hell up! Them ain't nothing but dogs." Joe moved along the line. "You men that's got sabers, stand up right behind the men lying down with the carbines. Dogs get in here, hack them up. We ain't letting that bridge fall!" That damn Tucker was getting up like he was going to run. "Zack, put your pistol aside Tucker's head. If he move any way but forward, shoot him."

The barking was louder, and the Rebs was about twenty-five yards away. Colonel Kenworthy had to be way back now, but he wasn't so far that his voice didn't carry.

"Joe? Can you hear me, Joe? The nigger dogs are going to chew your black asses up."

"I hears you, all right. They going to try, just the way you tried to whup me under that pine tree that day. Come on, Colonel, I ain't scared of you and I ain't scared of your damned dogs!" He dropped to his knees. "Steady, men, fire when I give the command."

They were twenty, fifteen . . .

"Joe?"

He gave the command to fire at the same time the Rebs released the dogs.

"Sic 'em, boys, make the niggers run!"

The dogs leapt forth, yelping and barking like they'd been thrown a whole pailful of bloody red beef. When the volley from the carbines hit the dogs, there was a wild confusion of yelling and barking, men and dogs all tangled and wrestling in pools of blood on the slippery grass. A hellish mingling of screams and howls, punctuated by the sound of pistols and carbines exploding with quick flashes all over the field.

Joe tried to shut it out, worked with his Choctaw knife and his Adams, tried to ignore the coppery odor of blood mixed with smoke. Everywhere he looked, was nothing but hand-to-hand fighting or hand to throat. And the worst thing was, there wasn't no line no more.

A brown and white hound leapt for his throat. He stuck his knife right in the bitch's belly, but she had no more than fallen to the ground than another one was tearing at his arm. Joe swirled around so hard the dog went flying. He shot him in mid-air with the Adams.

"Fight, you poker-loving bastards—we the Third Cavalry!" he yelled. "Take more than hellhounds to finish us."

And now he saw that a group of his men had formed around him again, that there *was* a line. And little by little the barking got fainter and the firing seemed thinner, till he turned and saw only one bloodhound left, standing over a fallen Third man, tearing away at his throat. Joe threw the Choctaw knife right into its side and heard his own savage yell as the dog collapsed.

The Rebs were retreating at a trot, nary a dog in sight, and Colonel Kenworthy barely keeping up with them. Must be hurt pretty bad. That bastard wouldn't be back today.

But oh, what damage he had done. All around men lay dead and dying, torn and mangled and side by side with the dogs' bloody red carcasses strewn across the green field. The baying of wounded and dying dogs filled the air.

It was another long fifteen minutes before he heard them blow Recall down there at the bridge. Gradually, what was left of his men made their way down the hill, firing back at the Rebels as they went.

Major Cook was waiting. "Was that dogs I heard?"

All Joe could do was nod, but his grim look and the men's torn and bloody uniforms said the rest.

"God will have to forgive them, for I cannot. You and the men did yourselves proud, Sergeant."

"Sir? Captain Stiles?"

"He'll live. He's on the way back to the main unit. You'll take command of the company in his absence. Dismissed."

"Yes, sir."

❖   ❖   ❖   ❖   ❖   ❖   ❖   ❖   ❖   ❖   ❖

Fifteen minutes later he watched the bridge burst into flames. The men were cheering.

Not Joe. Too many lay there on the field amid the dogs. And glad as he was they had succeeded, he finally had time to think about what Massa Richard had said. If it was true, that bridge burning over the Black River was cutting Joe off from his son.

He turned away at Major Cook's command to march. "Zack, did you hear what Massa said about my boy?"

"Don't worry, we get him someday—me and you alone if we have to."

"We got a war to fight, Zack. Get the men lined up. Major wants to tear up the railroad line to make sure that bridge is finished good and proper, and that's what we going to do next. Right?"

"Right. But I ain't forgetting."

The dust kicked up by the lifting of the railroad ties must have been visible for miles around. But thick as it was, the smell of the dirt couldn't take away the metallic stench of battlefield blood that stayed in Joe's nostrils.

CHAPTER FIFTEEN

"HEY there, you all, won't be long before we can have us some fun!"

Zenobia and the others on the raft faced six men, every one of them waving and shouting.

"That pretty little one with them big titties, she going to be mine." The man cupped his hand over his mouth and shouted out over the water. *"Ain't you, honey?"*

Helen squeezed Zenobia's arm. "I'm scairt, Auntie."

Zenobia hugged her tight. No sense in telling her that in another few minutes, when the raft drifted in a little closer to land, they would be delivered into the hands of deserters and irregulars. She could tell that's what they were from the way they was all dressed different from one another and from their wild shouting and yelling. They didn't obey no man's rules.

"Here, throw me that rope, I'll pull you ashore." One of the men came splashing through the water with his boots on, his hand outstretched for the rope.

Did she have any choice? The raft had been bobbing up and down on the river for the longest time, maybe an hour or two, before drifting in close to the little inlet bordered by tall pine trees. She'd kept praying the current would pick up, carry them on down the river and away from these men. But without the oars they had no control, no way of steering.

She tossed the rope, and the man put it over his shoulder and pulled. When the raft was about ten feet from shore, he stopped and turned around.

"You all get off now and wade the rest of the way. It won't come in any closer with all that weight on board. And watch yourself, don't want none of you pretty ladies getting hurt."

Zenobia had no more than set her foot on shore when a short man in a red woolen shirt lifted the hem of her skirt with the long barrel of his rifle and nodded.

"I'm mighty pleased the good Lord sent you and your fine-looking legs floating my way." He put his hand under her chin. "Now, you didn't have no intention of going nowhere else today, did you? Who you belong to?"

"Colonel Richard Kenworthy," Zenobia said. The truth could get them sent back, but by the look of these men that might be less dangerous.

"Once upon a time I used to ride with the colonel," one of the men said. "But he don't have no plantation left, way I heard it."

"Don't make no difference nohow," the short man said. "We ain't got no practical way of returning these niggers to him even if we planned to, which we don't." He turned to a long skinny man with a patch over one eye. "Take them back to camp—we'll decide later on what we're going to do with them."

Helen was trying hard not to cry. She had grabbed Ned's hand, and now Zenobia grabbed hers.

"Don't worry, honey. They take care of us, now they know we belongs to Colonel Kenworthy."

"She got that right, children." The man was smiling, but all the smile did was twist his ugly features. "We sure enough going to take care of you. Now get a move on, you niggers."

   ✦   ✦   ✦   ✦   ✦   ✦   ✦   ✦   ✦   ✦   ✦

Seemed like they walked all afternoon long, but it was still light when they came to a big opening in the woods with tents all over, and lots of white men. There was a little stockade for their horses. The man led them across the camp to a big fire where some colored men and women were cooking.

"Nichols, these some niggers we picked up off the river this afternoon. Take care of them till Captain Odom decides what we going to do with them."

"Yessuh, with pleasure, suh."

The white man snatched up a piece of barbecued chicken and walked off.

Zenobia glanced around her. Looked like about ten colored folk here, mostly men, except for two old ladies. It was probably their job to cook and do the laundry, take care of the horses for the white men.

"My name is Nichols Brown—what's yours, now?" His skin was yellow, and his head bald and shiny.

"Zenobia. This here's Ned. And Lisa Mae and Helen. You got any dry clothes we could put on?"

He said something to one of the colored women, who walked away and returned in a few minutes with a pile of clothes.

"Come on." She led them into a tent with eight pallets on the floor. "When you all get dressed, come outside, we give you something to eat."

"Zee, what we going to do?" Lisa Mae was trying to find a way to hold up a pair of baggy trousers.

Zenobia rummaged on the floor in the pile of rags and handed her what looked like an old sash. "Must be something in here for Ned. All of you got to put on as many extra clothes as you can. Be cold here at night, and it might be even colder where I'm thinking about going."

"You're not—"

"I surely am. We among some evil people, best to get away from them."

The woman poked her head back into the tent. "Come on out and eat."

The corn bread and bacon Nichols Brown fed them was as good as anything Zenobia had ever eaten. But even telling him what a good cook he was didn't seem to make him happy. Zenobia wondered if he ever smiled.

"Tell me about these white men," she said. "Not a one of them in uniform Who are they?"

"Thieves and robbers, that's who they are. They ain't in nobody's army. Fight everybody that come near them. On the run from everybody and stealing from everybody."

"How long you been with them?"

Nichols put his hand under his chin. "Seems like forever. I were the head man's driver for many a year, then followed him off to the wars. I been everywhere, my sister, anyplace you can think of. Up in the Tennessee mountains, over in them Arkansas swamps, and last year up in Virginny. That were the prettiest place I ever did see."

"You talk about it mighty nice," she said.

"Well, when you travels a lot, it do something to your thinking. Make you want to live other ways, do other things." He looked at her for a moment, then shrugged. "Anyways, while we was in Virginny—you know it ain't as hot up there as it is down here—the Yankees was shooting cannons at us every day."

"They does a lot of that down here too," Zenobia said.

"And finally, old Massa just got tired. Said, 'Nichols, my African friend, we going home, find us another way to pass our time. I come up here to fight Yankees, not sit here in a fort and let them fire away at us with them big guns.' Had some ideas, he said, 'bout how we going to make a living now that the plantation's gone. So we got on the railroad train and come home."

Zenobia looked around the campsite at the stacks of rifles and boxes of ammunition.

"Yep," said Nichols, following her glance. "He got the notion to stop fighting and start robbing. Done made me into a thief. And I fears my God!" He mopped his brow with a white towel he had tucked under his belt. "Feel sorry for you and the young'uns. I'se going to do my best to help you, now he done put you in my charge. But you got to help me, too. Pull your share of the work and do what I say and it *might* not be so bad for you here."

He studied her face for a long moment. "Sister, you ain't even listening to me—you trying to figure a way out of here. And there ain't none!"

"I respects what you said, Nichols Brown, and I don't want to cause you no trouble, but I got to consider the children."

"Then you'll stay right here and let me figure out a way to help them," he said. "You done fell into the hands of Captain John Odom. Onliest chance you got is if he decide to sell you to some slave speculator."

He pointed with his thumb back over his shoulder to where five hound dogs were tied up.

"That man just love chasing niggers," he said. "Wait. I want you to see something." He hollered out to one of the colored men. "William, come on over here and show them your back."

From neck to waist it was nothing but big, thick scars. Looking at them, Zenobia shuddered.

"He tried to run away," Nichols said. "See now, Captain Odom, he just love the runaways. Back on the plantation, he might let folk go for two or three days just to make it harder for him to catch them. Say he don't like no easy game. But he ain't never failed to catch one yet, and when he do— once he gets his hands on you, that man sure know how to play a whip."

Some men galloped into the camp. Nichols Brown pointed to the short one in the red shirt leading them. "There he be. The one and only Captain John Odom."

"That little one in front?"

"Don't be fooled by his size. I reckon he about the meanest man alive. If they's any meaner, I hope I never meet him."

Captain Odom and his men left their horses with William and another colored man and sat down at long tables in an oak grove a fair distance from the cooking area.

"Nichols, where's the damned food?"

"Coming, Massa." He looked around at Zenobia, Lisa Mae, and Helen. "You girls stay back here and dish the food out. Better that way. Me and this boy here—your name Ned, right—we'll take these plates over to them."

"Corn whiskey!"

Nichols stumbled over himself in his haste to pour the whiskey and get the cups to them.

"Hurry up, Ned, Massah don't like to be kept waiting."

Once all the food and the whiskey were on the table, the men quieted down. Thieving and robbing all day must be hungry work. Zenobia and Lisa Mae washed bowl after bowl, stealing glances at men eating with their fingers just like they was field niggers.

They sure could drink. Seemed like no sooner had Nichols taken one jug over to them than they were hollering for another. Zenobia counted twenty men, more ugly white people than she'd ever seen together at one time. Some had scars, others had hair like nothing on earth, and one man's beard was might near down to his belt. A few of them wore old grayboy pants. And there was one who looked like a full-blooded Indian. He wore a big round hat with a feather in its band and a big Yankee belt buckle on the front.

Captain Odom fired his pistol in the air. "Nichols, where's the music?"

"Coming, Massa. William, bring the guitar, I got the banjo. Mitchell, you get the bones."

By now other men were shooting off their pistols into the air. Must be mighty happy they'd caught some colored folks today.

"You all get in the tent and stay there," Nichols said. "He loves his women something awful."

Zenobia thanked him, then led the others into the tent where they huddled together on a cot. The men started their singing with "Dixie," and must have sung it ten or fifteen times, a little louder each time. The banjos and guitars were twinging and twanging and the coloreds was singing as loud as the whites. After a while it seemed like they were quieting down, then the captain called out: "Sing "John Peel," Nichols."

> *Do ye ken John Peel*
> *With his coat so gay?*
> *Do ye ken John Peel*
> *At the break of day?*
> *Do ye ken John Peel*
> *When he's far far away?*
> *With his hounds and his horn*
> *In the morning."*

Sounded like all the white men joined him for the second verse.

> *Twas the sound of his horn*
> *Called me from my bed*
> *And the cry of his hounds*
> *Hath me oftimes led*
> *For Peel's view halloo*
> *Would awaken the dead*
> *Or a fox from his lair*
> *In the morning!"*

Nichols's voice floated above all the rest. Poor old Nichols, she hoped they didn't shoot him—though that might be better than . . . she remembered the fear in his voice when he talked about that whip.

"Lisa Mae, we got to get out of here right now. All of us."

"But, Zee, you heard what Nichols said. If we—"

"I heard, but I heard too about mens like these—know what they going to be hollering for in a few minutes."

"But, Zee—"

"And after they gets it, they's going to beat us and likely kill us. We better off with the dogs tearing us up." She was quiet for just a few seconds, busy cutting a hole in the tent with her knife. "Grab that extra blanket, and give me your feet, you-all. Quick!"

Ned giggled. "That tickles, Auntie. What you doing?"

"Hush! It's cayenne pepper. Dogs hate it. I stole it while Nichols was cooking up those barbecued ribs."

She stepped out into the darkness and looked up. Thank goodness, no moon, but there was the North Star. Which way to go? Should they try to go back to the raft? They could make it to the river in about an hour and a half. But that's the way the white men would figure they'd go. Besides, what use was it without some way to steer it? No, they'd go the other way, off into those woods there. And trust in God.

"Come on, quick now, they's starting another song."

With Ned at her side, Zenobia started walking as fast as she could, pushing bushes aside as she headed into the dark woods.

If there was a path, they never found it. The branches of the trees kept tearing at their faces, and when Zenobia touched her cheek, she found it was bleeding.

"Auntie, don't go so fast," Ned said. "I can't go so fast."

"Don't get tired, honey, don't you hear how that singing is lower now? We getting away."

They were deep into the woods before she finally looked back. No campfires in sight. No singing within earshot. But they had to keep going, put as much space between them and those men as possible.

She was sweating something awful, even though it was cold. Like the children, her feet were bare, but she was used to that. She wasn't used to being in charge of others, even herself, but God had given her Lisa Mae and Ned and Helen, and she had to lead them to freedom.

Of course, right now she was leading them all back into the land of the grayboys. But hadn't she just walked right out of that camp? And wouldn't they be some mad white boys when they came looking for their colored women?

❖   ❖   ❖   ❖   ❖   ❖   ❖   ❖   ❖   ❖   ❖

They arrived at a little clear spot in the woods as day was breaking and sat under a big magnolia tree, its trunk spread out thick and wide, like a little seat for them. She put her arms around Helen and Ned.

"First thing we got to do this morning is thank God that He done watched over us—brought us this far. Ned, you can pray."

"But I don't know what to say."

"Just close your eyes and God will give you the words."

He scrunched up his eyes, but it took the words a while to come.

"Jesus, it was real scary out here in the woods last night. I didn't tell Zenobia, but I seen devils leaping out the trees at us with pitchforks and all. But the angels, they was dressed in white, kept telling them devils not to touch us, we God's childrens—don't touch them. And they sure enough didn't, so I thanks you. Amen, Jesus."

"I know for sure God going to hear such a sweet prayer," Zenobia said. "I don't know where we are now, and I don't know where we going to go from here. But you was *all* strong during the night, and I got a little surprise for you."

She pulled out some corn bread she'd wrapped in an apron and hidden under her skirt last night before they left.

"See, you learned something last night, Ned. You was tired, but you didn't give up. Now that man Nichols, he ain't no bad man, matter of fact he a good man. But them dogs and that old captain done scared him to death, so's they don't even have to worry about him running away. But we looked at them same old dogs and wasn't scared. And we ain't nothing but some womens and a little boy." She stood Ned up. "I want you to take a good look all around you, now. You see any dogs here?"

"No."

"You see anything after us?"

"Yes."

"What?"

"A lot of soldiers."

Zenobia pulled him down quick. She crept up to where he had been and sure enough, right down there next to a road was a big camp of grayboys just waking up.

As she watched, a man came out and blew a bugle to make sure they all got up.

Zenobia sat back down. They'd just wait till . . .

"*Look,* Zee." Lisa Mae was pointing down where they'd just come from. That Injun with the Yankee buckle on his hat was headed straight for them, a rifle in one hand and the lead for one of them bloodhounds in the other.

He shaded his eyes, looked up right where they were.

"Only one thing to do," Zenobia said.

They started running down the hill, straight for the grayboys' camp.

CHAPTER SIXTEEN

WILL Stiles raised his hand to ask a question, but Colonel Osband waved him off and continued his briefing of the officers assembled in front of him. They were on the transport *Morning Star* and would be landing in Memphis shortly.

"Gentlemen, we've got these Rebs right where we want them, and now we're going to rip the state wide open, from the Tennessee border straight down to Vicksburg. Tear up every foot of railroad track we find, destroy anything that can be used to feed or clothe the Rebs, and free every Negro we can. Every able-bodied colored man will be enlisted into the army." He nodded at Stiles. "Now, Will."

"You think that will stop all those pesky cavalry raids on our supply lines, Colonel?"

"You bet your boots it will. General Grierson's going to throw three brigades of cavalry against them. I'll be in command of the Third Brigade, and together we are going to bring these Rebs to their knees."

✵   ✵   ✵   ✵   ✵   ✵   ✵   ✵   ✵   ✵   ✵

Three days later, Will Stiles led his company out of Memphis as part of the column. Sickness and wounds and death had depleted their numbers badly, and Will was still wearing a bandage around his head where a bullet had creased him—knocked him unconscious at Big Black Bridge.

December 21, 1864. So close to Christmas, and yet he'd almost forgot-

ten there was anything like Christmas still left in this world. Eunice had
sent a special package—Lord, he missed that sweet woman—and he had
shared the cookies with Joe. And she wrote him most every day. Joe was always teasing him about her writing him so much. Probably because he
never got any letters himself . . . of course he didn't. How could he? He
and most of the men were just beginning to learn to read and write.

And even if he had been able to read well, who would he hear from?
His Zenobia? His daughter? Joe had no idea where either of them was, no
way of letting them—or his son Luke—know where he was.

A voice sang out:

> *"If you see my mother*
>   *Oh, yes!*
> *Won't you tell her for me*
>   *Oh, yes!*
> *I'm a ridin' my horse on the battlefield*
>   *Oh, yes!*
> *I want to see my Jesus in the morning!"*

Will looked back over the long line of colored troopers behind him.
They were freshly mounted on horses recently procured from anywhere
the army could find them. Fine soldiers, strong and good-natured men—
but practically every one of them had a story like Joe's. Mothers, fathers,
sisters, brothers, children, scattered to the wind. All they really had was
the army—the United States Cavalry. And maybe that was the way the
army should function. Be their family till the real one came along.

All along the column they took up the melody.

> *"Ride on King Jesus*
> *Ride on, you conquering King!"*

They sure loved to sing. Seemed to give them a sense of peace and
strength. Well, they were sure going to need it on this trip. From what the
colonel had said, they'd be stirring up a hornets' nest. Easy enough to say
the Rebs were almost beaten, what with Sherman about to take Savannah,
but that didn't seem to make them any easier to fight. And they were particularly fierce when they were fighting colored troops.

But his men would be ready for them. This was going to be a swift-moving column—each man had two days' worth of rations and forty rounds of ammunition, with the other supplies on pack mules. They were going to live off Mississippi land. What they didn't eat, they'd destroy.

"Damn."

He felt the raindrops on his hat. Rain would make it hard on the new horses, not used to the wear and tear a trooper put on them. Will tightened the green scarf he wore around his neck and prepared for the long uncomfortable ride ahead.

❖   ❖   ❖   ❖   ❖   ❖   ❖   ❖   ❖   ❖   ❖

That first night they camped out in a bare field. It was already a wet and soggy mess, and then the sleet started up. Since they'd packed light the men didn't have any protection from the weather except to sit around the few fires they somehow managed to get going, shivering even with blankets over their shoulders. Will was accustomed to the cold, didn't mind it so much, but what must it be like for these men so much more used to dealing with unbearable heat?

He saw Joe and Zack huddled with a group of troopers around a fire.

"Mind if I join you, men?"

"Not at all, sir," Joe said.

Will knelt down beside them. "I want you to hear this news from me. This is my last time out. I'm being reassigned to Washington for some staff work with the Bureau of Colored Troops. They seem to think my experience will come in handy."

"What?" Joe said. "When did the orders come, sir?"

"Just before we left Memphis. I told Colonel Osband I didn't want the assignment, but the army's not much interested in what I want."

He rubbed his hands together to warm them, put them to his mouth and blew on them.

"Something else. They've commissioned a colored soldier, name of Swails, in the Fifty-fourth Massachusetts. Something I've been thinking ought to be done for some time. I'm recommending that Joe take over the company as a second lieutenant. You can pass the word around. Naturally, there's a lot of channels to be gone through before he can be mustered, and Joe will remain a top sergeant in the meantime, but I thought you'd like to know."

Joe and the others sat quietly. Had to be quite a surprise to them.

"I think Joe can handle things pretty well—don't you, Zack?"

"Lieutenant Joe . . ."

They all laughed then and began patting Joe on the back.

"Yes, sir, I believe he do just fine, but we're going to miss you something terrible."

Joe looked embarrassed. "I feel the same way, but . . . well, see you fellows in the morning. Sorry I couldn't arrange better weather on this first night out." He got up. "I'll walk with you a ways, sir. I don't hardly know what to say, sir, how to thank you . . ."

"No need to, Joe. You earned it."

"All the same, I . . . I thanks you."

They walked on in silence for a bit.

"Going to be rough without you, sir. You know, I don't mean the fighting, because we can do that, but you been a good friend, too."

"I'm not leaving forever. Remember? I'll be back when the war ends. You haven't forgotten what I talked about, have you?"

"No, sir, I ain't forgot. I reckon what with the other things on my mind, I just don't think too much of what it's going to be like when the war is over. There's a heap too many Rebs between me and that day, Captain."

"Well, I'm not forgetting. I'll be back."

    ✿   ✿   ✿   ✿   ✿   ✿   ✿   ✿   ✿   ✿

By Christmas Day, not having met any serious resistance, the column was in Tupelo, Mississippi, dead in the center of Forrest's country. But much of the venom had been drawn out of that particular rattlesnake's mouth. While the Third Cavalry stayed in Tupelo, one of the other regiments hit the town of Verona, about seven miles away. Hit it around nightfall, and Forrest's men just disappeared. Left the town and all their supplies right there.

So while the men didn't have a real Christmas, they did have a spectacle of sorts. The whole town burned, and it was something to see, close to three hundred tons of ammunition going off, and bullets and shells exploding all over. Old Bedford Forrest must be crying somewhere. You could see the explosions easy from Tupelo. In the midst of the miserable weather it gave the men something to cheer about.

The next few days were spent tearing up the railroad tracks in every direction around Tupelo. Still no enemy resistance. Will thought it all seemed too easy, especially when they reached Okolona. Intelligence had intercepted a dispatch saying the Rebs would make a stand there, and with the railroad running into the town, General Grierson expected a hard fight.

But then the close to three thousand colored and white cavalrymen came winding out of the woods and fell smartly into formation. Line after line of blue-clad men, horses pawing the ground, the Stars and Stripes flapping in the cold December wind, and regimental standards held proudly aloft by color sergeants. Second New Jersey Cavalry, Fourth Missouri Cavalry, Seventh Indiana Cavalry, First Mississippi Mounted Rifles, Third and Fourth Iowa Cavalry; Tenth Missouri Cavalry, Fourth and Eleventh Illinois Cavalry, Second Wisconsin Cavalry, and the Third United States Colored Cavalry. When the men in the garrison saw all that, they had to have become weak of heart. Still they didn't show the white flag.

Then the trumpets—all twenty of them in the Third Cavalry—blew the charge. Will, sitting high in the saddle on his brown bay, raised his saber. At the command the bay began to trot, then canter, and with the shout "At a gallop!" the long column swept right at the town, yelling and whooping, expecting the Rebs to open fire any minute now.

Will was riding so hard his hat blew off. He took a quick glance back and saw his men galloping as fast as he was, their sabers raised high in the air. At the edge of the town the Union column split, the Third Cavalry with those going to the left. Had to sound to the Rebs like all of Hades was riding down on them, and the next thing he saw was a white flag fluttering from the ramparts of the Rebel stockade. They hadn't fired. Not a single shot.

That night another bonfire lit up the sky for miles around as the Reb supplies and ammunition, including wagons captured from the Union Army at Brice's Crossroads, were destroyed and rendered useless to the enemy. In the days that followed, they tore up more railroad tracks. And took prisoners, scores of them. By now, just a few days before the New Year, they had almost five hundred of them, including many former slaves who had been impressed into service by the Confederates.

But despite such heavy losses, the Rebs weren't finished. It was like you can be wrestling a man, and think you've almost got him, then he pulls some kind of move or you feel some strength there you didn't at first, and you know you're in for a battle. Will heard it in the hostility and smart comments of the white prisoners, sensed it in the way bushwackers hung on the flanks of the regiment. You could just feel these Rebs, whose domain had been invaded, getting together to destroy the Yankees running loose in their backyard.

You had to give them credit. They definitely made a stand at Egypt Station. Will and Joe watched from a spot where the Third Cavalry was being held in reserve. These Rebs had no intention of allowing the 1st Brigade of the Union Cavalry to advance. It took some serious fighting to drive them out of the woods and into the open plain that surrounded Egypt Station.

"I'd say those boys in the 1st Brigade are lining up just like they did back at Okolono, Captain."

"I just hope we get the same results. That's a lot of open space to charge across. Get the men ready. We're going right behind them as soon as the colonel gives the signal." Will raised his binoculars: "There they go."

The Union line swept forward at the trot, then the gallop. The captain swept the glasses along the fence of the Rebel stockade. It seemed unnaturally still.

The 1st Brigade was very close to the stockade when what sounded like thunder exploded from the front of that fort. It was awful. Close to a thousand men in the charge and at least that many Rebel muskets all going off at the same time. Not since Shiloh had Will seen anything like it. Union horses and men down all over the field. The charge was broken.

No time to think about that. He looked down the front of his own line. Colonel Osband had raised his saber. Will followed suit and the Fourth Illinois and the Third Cavalry moved at a fast trot to a position on the south side of the fort—away from the crushing gunfire coming from the front, where the 1st Brigade was trying to re-form itself.

The Fourth Illinois swept around the side of the fort, and Will ordered his men to dismount. Their orders were to assault the fort from the south on foot.

"Sergeant Duckett, get the horse holders up here."

The men, shouting now, moved into a long line, ready for the assault. Somebody in the fort must have decided to pay attention to them, because scattered fire began to fall among them and two or three men went down.

"On your knees, men! Make a smaller target."

Why didn't the colonel give the order for the assault? They were sitting ducks.

"Bugler, sound the charge!"

The men gave a loud hurrah and began advancing on the fort just as a white flag was raised over the stockade. A few minutes later, the men of the Fourth Illinois who'd ridden into the rear of the stockade were running up the Stars and Stripes. They'd saved the Third Cavalry what would have been a costly charge.

One minute he was saying to Joe, "Our luck seems to be holding up," and the next wishing he hadn't. A shell burst right in the middle of the company.

He swept his glasses over toward a train on the railroad track. Damn, a whole trainload of Reb infantry was jumping off it. They began to form up in a skirmish line about three-quarters of a mile away, lining up smartly as their band played "Dixie." Definitely regulars.

He wasn't surprised when Colonel Osband said the Third Cavalry was to be the rear guard, hold the Rebs off while the rest of the column moved off with the prisoners. So many times, out of all the companies in the regiment, his was asked to be the first one out there.

"Joe, get the men off the horses and deploy them as skirmishers. We've got to keep those Rebs off the main column. The rest of the regiment will back us when they form up."

Smooth as clockwork, the men fell in and began advancing. When they were about a hundred yards from the Reb line, Will ordered them to their knees and they commenced rapid fire.

The train must have been carrying close to four companies of men and they kept on coming. With the music going, they seemed to pick up their steps And their fire.

Joe, behind the line, was steadying the men as usual. "We men of war—we the fighting Third."

Zack was loading, aiming, and firing like he'd been a soldier all of his life. To a man, the company was making those Sharps sing. But it wasn't stopping the Rebs. Joe saw his men falling right and left. There wasn't any cover.

Finally, at the last minute, when it looked for sure like the Rebs would overrun them, the regimental bugler sounded Recall. Will looked back and saw the whole regiment, all eight hundred of them, lined up behind him, sabers drawn. A beautiful sight to the remaining men in his company, a signal to retreat for the Rebs!

"Let's get the hell out of here, Joe."

   ✦   ✦   ✦   ✦   ✦   ✦   ✦   ✦   ✦   ✦   ✦

That night, long after the rest of the column was in bed, the Third Cavalry, still acting as rear guard, came into camp.

At officers' call the next morning, Colonel Osband assigned Will to ride along the entire length of the column and report its general condition. The colonel was interested, in particular, in the prisoners and the colored refugees.

Will rode off early in the morning. First thing he saw was how few horses had survived yesterday's action. Many cavalrymen were doubled up and some were even on foot. The Third Cavalry alone had lost nearly a third of its mounts. But the friendly waves he got from the men—both black and white—as he made his way down the column was reassuring. The Third Cavalry and its officers had definitely earned their spurs, and they knew it.

Nothing he'd ever seen had prepared him for the condition of the prisoners. Even the ones who weren't obviously sick or wounded were a pitiful sight, and up close, he could only marvel that these men had offered such fierce resistance. They looked half starved, walking along in rags, most of them without shoes, some lucky enough to have Union blankets around their shoulders. They didn't look like they'd washed in months. Well, neither had the Union boys, but at least their clothes were intact.

They were marched along, guarded sometimes by colored troops who treated them with a forbearance, even kindness, that surprised him. More than once he saw them sharing food or gear, extending a hand to help a prisoner who had fallen. Will wasn't sure he would have been able to do the same if—

What the devil was that commotion up ahead? As he got closer he saw it was hogs, must have been a thousand of them, snorting and rolling in the mud while a bunch of cavalrymen tried to drive them along.

He rode up to a sergeant: "What the hell is this?"

"Orders, sir. To deny food to the Rebs. Colonel said to drive them down to Vicksburg to feed our army."

"To Vicksburg? Good God—that's at least a hundred and fifty miles from here."

"Don't I know it, sir. And these some ornery critters—got their own sense of direction."

"From what I can see, their only sense of direction is down in the mud."

The sergeant said, "Well, sir, if all else fails, we could have us one hell of a barbecue."

A little farther along Will heard a long-drawn-out moaning sound that seemed as if it was coming out of the earth. A deep sound—not a moan, a song. He reined in slightly, listened intently, and recognized the tune.

> *"Oh, freedom, oh freedom*
> *Oh, freedom over me*
> *And before I'd be a slave*
> *I'd be buried in my grave*
> *Go home to my lord*
> *And be free!"*

His boys sang it all the time—but there weren't hundreds of them, there weren't women and children singing. It sounded like a heavenly chorus, and when he rode over the crest of the road and saw the mass of black men, women, and children coming behind the army, he came to a complete halt, as stunned by the sight as the sound.

Stretched out before him was what seemed to be an endless stream of

Negroes, as if the Mississippi earth had opened up and borne this fruit. As far as the eye could see there was nothing but the peoples of Africa.

He edged his horse forward. Many of the men were carrying picks and shovels. The army was already making pioneers, construction men, out of them. Women, in white night shirts, their hair twisted in long braids, carried infants and led toddlers by the hand. Young boys and girls wore the same long shirts of coarse cotton or burlap. He looked at their feet and saw how few of them had shoes in this forty-degree weather, looked at their faces and saw the eyes of old men and women. But they pointed and smiled as he rode past, called out, "Yessuh, Yankee soldier!" And at the sight of a passing colored trooper they shouted and clapped their hands.

He rode slowly along the long column, stopping occcasionally to smile at a child. And at a woman, one he was sure he would never forget. She was tall and beautifully made, figure and face. But what drew him to her wasn't her beauty so much as her bearing. Even here in the midst of what had to be a wilderness to her, in plain cotton and shoeless as the rest, she carried herself as if she was at home with everything. With her were a young boy, a pretty girl of about fourteen, and a young woman about twenty.

The woman looked up when Will spoke to her, but only for a second.

"Where do you come from?" he asked her.

"We was washing clothes for the grayboys in Okolona."

The thought of a woman this lovely among the Rebs made him flinch.

"Is there anything we can do for you right now?"

She looked at him for a moment before answering. "Nothing that don't need to be done for everybody here." She waved her hand to embrace the whole column. "We all needs warm clothing and more food, but you boys are doing your best. At least we free—and that will do us just fine for now."

Will tipped his hat and rode on. He just hoped they'd be able to get them to Vicksburg safely.

❖   ❖   ❖   ❖   ❖   ❖   ❖   ❖   ❖   ❖   ❖

When he returned that afternoon and gave his report, his voice shook a little when he described the long line of refugees and their singing. As for the hogs, he had strong recommendations. They had to be killed—they were holding up the progress of the column and could not be left behind for the Rebs. The colonel agreed to arrange it. But Will and his men wouldn't be around for the barbecue.

"Your regiment is breaking off. I want to free up the Third Cavalry for offensive action. The other two brigades will escort the refugees and the prisoners. We'll meet down in Yazoo City."

CHAPTER SEVENTEEN

JUST before going off to inspect the refugee column, Captain Stiles detached Joe to serve as a scout for a white company ordered to make a side raid on the town of Bankston, Mississippi. Said Captain Gomillion had requested him by name, because he'd heard Joe knew the country thereabouts.

Wasn't there any other man in the regiment who could scout? And in such cold weather!

He could think of lots of things he'd rather be doing than riding down the town's main street alongside Gomillion on this quiet, powerful cold night. At least the Rebs weren't shooting or otherwise raising hell.

He led a detachment on through the town, past a big cotton mill, a flour mill, and a shoe factory, scouting the area just beyond the town and posting sentries all around to give the alarm should any Rebs be coming down the road.

When he returned, Captain Gomillion was standing in front of the cotton mill. Nearby, pacing back and forth, was a tall skinny white man in nothing but his nightclothes.

"Oh, God . . ." The man stopped pacing. "Why are your men lighting those torches, Captain?"

Gomillion took no notice of him, turned instead to one of his men.

"Sergeant, take a squad through these buildings, make sure nobody is in there."

"I repeat, sir, what is the purpose of those torches?" The skinny man moved in front of Gomillion so he was between him and the building. "I demand an answer. Is it your intention to burn these buildings?"

The sergeant returned with another man in tow. "Found this fellow in there, sir, but it's all clear now."

"Thomas, you're the mayor, can't you make them stop? They're pouring tar oil all over the floors in there."

Joe almost felt sorry for the mayor. Hard to exercise authority without your clothes on. But the guy kept on trying.

"By what authority do you intend to commit this act of arson? I can have you arrested for this, you know."

The captain didn't look the least bit worried. "It's cold out here," he said. "My men have been riding all day, they need a fire to keep them warm."

"You're mad, sir, a pyromaniac. Would you burn down two buildings to keep your men warm? Take a people's livelihood away from them?"

Gomillion turned to the sergeant. "Burn them."

"I'll report this, sir, to the proper authorities. You'll be held legally responsible."

"Well, that's as may be, sir. But next time old Bedford Forrest comes this way looking for supplies, you give him General Grierson's compliments and tell him he and his men are welcome to anything we leave behind."

❖　　❖　　❖　　❖　　❖　　❖　　❖　　❖　　❖　　❖　　❖

By morning there was nothing left of the factories but a pile of smoldering ashes. When Joe rode by with the cavalry on their way south to tear up more railroad track, the mayor was still standing there.

"Damn you, damn you all to hell!"

Joe trotted right on past him without a trace of the pity he had felt last night. Everybody loses something in a war.

❖　　❖　　❖　　❖　　❖　　❖　　❖　　❖　　❖　　❖　　❖

Richard Kenworthy was back where he wanted to be, protecting the lines of communication against the Yankee raids. He had been transferred, along with a regiment of men from the bridge, to General Adams's cavalry. It wasn't the same as riding with Bedford Forrest, but it was cavalry all the same.

He looked around the pretty little church in the small town of Franklin, Mississippi, and wondered if it would still be standing at the end of the day. He'd just received word that they'd practically burned Bankston to the ground and were on their way here. The loss of those factories was sure to make a bad situation even worse. Without a way to keep the troops supplied, there was no hope of slowing the tide of desertions that were hurting them worse than anything. The boys who remained still had a lot of spunk, thank God. They'd need every ounce of it, with Grierson's boys tearing down the railroad system mile by mile and destroying everything in their path. Damn Yankee locusts. They'd get a warm reception when they came down this way.

He turned his mind to the task at hand, put his hand on Captain Johnston's shoulder.

"You take over here, I'm going outside to make a final check, see that all is in order. Those Yanks are going to wish they never laid eyes on this town."

He left the church and rode around the other positions. The troops placed just as General Adams wanted, several companies hidden in the woods, and the junction of the road where the church stood well covered. When the Yankees came up, they'd be driven off the road and into an open field. The two companies of cavalry he'd concealed across the bridge stood ready to break the point of the Union column when they came into view. Panic them and send them scurrying back to Memphis like the rats they were.

He looked over his column. He'd fought with these men so many places now, the names had become a blur. One battle after another—didn't matter which way you turned the Yankees were always there—losing men, losing horses, but always coming back at you strong as ever. They wouldn't be satisfied until Mississippi was a barren land, smoking from one end to the other. He would never, ever understand how Christian men, white men, could harbor such malice in their hearts.

He looked at his watch. Twelve-fifteen. Wouldn't be long now.

He turned to Sergeant Barclay. "Send somebody back there to check on our body servants—especially Luke. Some of them boys are looking mighty restless. Make sure he keeps a sharp eye on them when the battle starts, and when they catch sight of those colored troops—"

A scout galloped up. "They're coming! A column of nigra cavalry about two miles down the road."

Good! Probably Joe's bunch.

He rode forward to where the two roads came together and took a quick look up the road with his binoculars. They were coming, all right. And they were coloreds. This time he'd be the one doing the surprising.

He rode back to his column. "Ready, men. Just like General Forrest taught us. No sabers, just the Colts. Going to put so much scare in those boys, they'll wish they were back on a peaceful plantation shucking corn and eating watermelon."

He knew it wasn't much of a joke but wasn't surprised to hear laughter all along the line—more from tension than his wit, most likely. When the coloreds came swinging around over the bridge and down that road . . .

"Any of you see a nigra top sergeant with what looks like Injun hair, leave him to me." He raised his revolver over his head. "Column forward." He heard the sound of the pounding hooves behind him and settled into that old rhythm. He loved the smell of hot horseflesh, loved the feel of the moist skin under his hand. God, it felt good to be cantering again. Right on over the bridge.

As he passed the church, Captain Johnston waved him on. "Tan their hides good, Colonel."

The colored cavalry came into view about three hundred yards away, the Third Cavalry banner waving over them.

"Bugler, sound the charge!"

Richard spurred his horse and the entire column picked up the pace. Now the men began to yell, Richard right along with them.

The officer at the head of the coloreds held up his hand and shouted a command. The Yankee troopers broke from column formation into a solid front of at least a hundred men, carbines aimed facing his charge. Another command and they fired in unison.

At the cries of shock and pain behind him, he pulled up fast and looked back.

About fifteen of his men and even more horses were lying in the road.

The rest of the men were milling around, although they were uncertain what to do.

"Forward, men, let's put them to the run." He raised his pistol again.

Another volley echoed from the colored cavalry. Beside him, a lieutenant fell and his horse bolted off to the side, away from all the smoke and fire. It was no good—more men and horses down.

"Blow Retreat." Not a moment too soon, because now the Yankee buglers were blowing their charge, and here came the Third, shouting and yelling like all get-out. Hell, one man was handling his saber as if it was nothing at all.

Richard turned his horse and galloped back down the road, barely able to keep up with his men flying right back where they'd come from, the colored troopers close behind them, shooting and yelling. On the far side of the bridge, he dismounted.

"Come on now. Damn it, you're white men."

Gradually the men settled down and began a rapid fire. They had to get that bridge back. Better wait until reinforcements arrived before making any more charges. In the meantime, his men in the church and the woods at the convergence of the roads would give the Yankees something to think about.

He rode up a little hill from where he could get a view of the whole battlefield. Damn, that little column he'd charged was nothing. There must be a whole regiment behind them—all coloreds, and they were dismounting. Instead of being driven into the open field for the crossfire he'd prepared for them, those colored devils were going to head right into the woods and try to flush his men out of there. Which meant the trap wouldn't work—*couldn't* work if they outflanked him. And that's exactly what it looked like they were planning to do.

Where the hell were his reinforcements?

Slowly but surely the coloreds cleaned out the woods, forcing his men into retreat, then they went to work on the detachment in the church and rooted them out. And they were still on the Confederate side of the bridge.

He scanned the position with his binoculars one more time. No question about it. When the reinforcements showed, they'd definitely outnumber the Yankees, probably about two to one. But right now his troops were taking a licking.

When a bugle sounded in the distance, he looked and saw the main body of his regiment. Thank God. Those coloreds holding the bridge had just plain overextended themselves.

He swung into his saddle one more time. "All right, men, we're not stopping till we run them back down that road."

The counterattack swept them off the bridge and out of the church. Had them on the run now, all right.

About fifty yards ahead of him, he saw that a Union flagbearer had been unhorsed, left alone by his retreating comrades. He was sitting on the ground still trying to hold the Stars and Stripes upright.

"There, men!" Richard shouted. "Grab those colors!" He spurred his horse and pointed his saber toward the fallen man, heard the sound of his troopers galloping after him. He saw the man clearly—jet black, head upright, and blood all over his blue blouse, one arm fumbling to reach the Colt revolver that had fallen to the ground beside him.

Richard fixed his eye on him and with a maneuver of his horse that astounded even him, cleaved the man's chest open with a stroke of his saber and grabbed the flag.

"Here, Barclay, take this back to our lines!"

The sergeant went to take the flag. Richard saw the warning in his eyes before he heard him shout, "Watch out, Colonel!"

About ten troopers, sabers drawn and led by Joe, had broken away from the mass of retreating Yankees and were bearing down on him. Joe had to have recognized him. The look on his face was hard, determined, and confident, nothing like what he'd looked like back at Clifton. Hell, that was a strong-assed man galloping down on him now, and he'd damn sure better deal with him that way. That wasn't a toy saber in his hand.

"Get that flag out of here!"

Barclay grabbed the flagstaff, but by now the coloreds were on them, and Richard was face to face, saber to saber with Joe.

"It's your last day, Joe!"

"Don't let it be yours, Colonel!"

They went around and around, the horses twisting and turning, skittering off to one side and the other as the two men slashed away at each other without either one drawing blood.

The sergeant aimed his pistol at Joe.

"No! Barclay, leave him to me."

He'd noticed something on the last two passes they'd made at each other. Joe had a habit of raising that saber, lifting it high as if he wanted to get the leverage to lop off his head. Let him try it just one more time!

The next time Joe lifted the saber in that peculiar way of his, Richard spurred his horse and met the downward blow with a hard upward movement of his own. The force of his thrust combined with the horse's extras burst of speed sent Joe's weapon flying and left him openmouthed, his eyes following its flight until it was lost in the swirling mass of men and horses fighting around the flag.

"It's all over with you, Joe!"

"I'll see you in hell, Colonel!"

Had to get to him before he got his revolver out . . .

But he wasn't going for the gun!

He was coming at him again, low down on his horse now. Damn savage had a *knife* out. Richard raised his saber to cut him down when he rode by, but he'd forgotten about Joe's riding tricks. Joe slipped down beneath the belly of his horse and ran his knife blade right along the side of Richard's horse, ripping the animal wide open. The noise the horse made as it stumbled and collapsed on the ground was pitiful to hear, and it was a moment before Richard realized that his legs were pinned beneath it.

He looked up to see Joe grabbing the Stars and Stripes from a stunned Barclay, then galloping back toward the Yankee lines, the flag flying high.

Barclay recovered and helped get Richard free. "Here's another mount, Colonel. Better hurry up. Lots of Yanks coming back at us."

Richard shook his head to clear it, just in time to see another regiment of white enemy cavalry come into view. Led, this time, led by a wild-riding redheaded captain. Back over the bridge they came. There was no stopping them. No end of them.

Driven back once more on this side of the bridge, Richard's men settled into a strong defensive position. As always he walked back and forth, trying to rally his forces to drive the Negroes from the bridge once again.

"Hell, men, this ain't no day to give up fighting. I *know* what you can do."

They were avoiding his eyes. "Crenshaw, remember Brice's Crossroads? Simpson, remember Tupelo? And you, Creighton, you were king of the hill at Shiloh."

They'd had enough, and when the coloreds withdrew of their own free will, and departed with the rest of the Yankee column in another direction, Kenworthy let them go.

The casualty report was bad enough—a major, a lieutenant, and fifty men dead—but there must have been something else for Barclay to be looking so nervous.

"You have anything else to report?"

"Yes, sir . . . You know when that white cavalry broke us down on the flank? Well, sir, they overrun the staging area."

"Did they get any horses?"

"About ten."

"Anything else?"

"Some of the nigger teamsters, sir."

Richard drew a deep breath. "Luke?"

The sergeant was silent for a moment. "Expect we'll be getting us another blacksmith," he said finally.

"Hell's bells! I specifically gave the order that Luke in particular was to be watched."

"One of the men winged him as he was running away. I don't know how bad he was hurt."

Wounded or not, he was Joe's son and he was running. Long gone by now. Richard rubbed his eyes. God, he was tired. Tired of all of it.

"Colonel? Is there anything I can do for you?"

"What? No, Bark, no thank you. Tell the men they fought bravely today. We'll have another go at the Yankees in a few days. Dismissed."

❖   ❖   ❖   ❖   ❖   ❖   ❖   ❖   ❖   ❖   ❖

The day after the fight at Franklin, Major Cook called Joe in. Captain Stiles had been wounded again, this time in the leg, and was in a hospital convoy on the way down to Vicksburg along with the others wounded in the battle, including some Rebs and their black teamsters.

"First I want to congradulate you, Duckett," the major said, stepping forward and taking his hand. "What with Captain Stiles being wounded, we'll have to advance the timetable a bit, so I'm officially placing you in command of Company A. Colonel Osband and myself have the utmost confidence in you."

"I won't let you down, sir."

"And now I have your first assignment."

Assignment? The regiment was supposed to be on its way back to Vicksburg.

"There's a lot of bandits and irregulars out there, riding around and raising hell with everybody and anybody. In particular, there are a couple of bands that make a practice of shooting up the Union convoys on the Yazoo. I want you to take a detachment of fifty men out in the countryside and see if you can't put a stop to some of that. You'll rejoin the regiment at Yazoo City in five days."

"Yes, sir."

"And, of course, you're under standing orders to confiscate any property of the secesh and destroy anything that can in any way be of use to them militarily. Any questions?"

"No, sir."

"Then you're dismissed."

Joe saluted and made for the door of the tent, but before he reached it the major called him back.

"Joe? I just wanted you to know that every officer in this regiment wants you to be commissioned. Let's hope the war's not over before those folks in Washington approve it."

CHAPTER EIGHTEEN

SUE Kenworthy leaned on the porch rail and looked down the long empty road. Oh, how she missed having Richard's unit nearby. Every now and then he'd send an officer by with a few men to check on her and the children, but the little messages and things they brought . . . it just wasn't enough.

Ever since her cousin had left for Mobile, all she seemed to have enough time for was worrying. What was she doing here on this little plantation with nothing but two darkies—and one of them that worthless Mary—to look after everything? The grounds and the house, chopping the wood and . . . just everything.

She *dreaded* the long scary nights. Gregory might be just a little boy, but he knew. He'd taken to wrapping himself in a blanket and curling up at the foot of her bed. She wanted to cry every time she saw him lying there, curled up with that toy sword in his little hand. Laura had slept beside her off and on whenever Richard was away, and now she was there every night.

About the only contact they had with people was when the sheriff, an old gray-haired man who'd lost an arm at Sharpsburg, came to pass the time of day with her. Most everybody else had left. It was him she was expecting today—probably wouldn't be here till this afternoon, though. Good thing, too—Mary was *supposed* to be cleaning up in anticipation of his visit.

She found the old woman right where she'd left her, sitting on a stool rinsing glasses in a round, wooden tub.

"Honestly, Mary. It's been a half hour already, and you've only washed six of the glasses. If you keep on at that pace, it'll be afternoon before they're ready."

"Yes, Miss."

"And you still have to get lunch for the children and bake some biscuits for the sheriff. You know how much he likes them."

"Yes, Miss."

"Now, tell me just how do you expect to get it all done?"

Mary kept her eyes on the water in the tub, carefully wiping down and drying each glass, and putting it on the cupboard.

"Mary, I'm *speaking* to you and I expect—"

"Ain't got enough help around here."

"What did you say?"

"Too much work for one soul."

This was intolerable. Mary had been a slave for fifty years, and she ought to know better.

"What has gotten into you?"

"I does my best, but you asking too much from me. Want me to make up the beds, wash all the clothes, cook all the meals, help Linus in the garden. Used to have thirty niggers to work this place, now it's only me and Linus. Ain't fair."

"*Fair?* Who taught you such a word?"

"And Linus, he old and crippled, can barely take care of himself."

Sue stood over Mary with her hands on her hips. "Who feeds you? Who clothes you? Who gives you a place to sleep? Who has to put up with your insolent lazy ways? *Me!*"

"Everybody else done left you, gone to the Yankees."

"Well, you might just as well have gone with them for all the good you are to me. I just wish you had to live *one day* as a mistress, then you'd see what it's like trying to . . ." She reached into the cupboard for some flour. "Never you mind about the biscuits, I'll do them myself."

✤   ✤   ✤   ✤   ✤   ✤   ✤   ✤   ✤   ✤   ✤

"Mighty good biscuits, Mrs. Kenworthy."

The sheriff had slathered on so much hot butter and honey Sue wondered he could taste the biscuits.

"Really worth the trip over here." He wiped his sticky hands and took a long sip of lemonade.

Well, he was better than no company at all. "I'm just tickled to hear you liked them as much as usual—I baked them myself this time. Mary's been . . . out of sorts." She glanced back toward the kitchen. "I suppose that's the case with them all these days."

"As a matter of fact, it is. Them that remains, that is." He took out his pipe. "Mind?"

"Go ahead and smoke if you wish."

"I don't like to presume. Wouldn't want to offend a lady such as yourself. And while I'm on the subject, I think a lady such as yourself, like I said, and your children . . . that is, as a matter of fact, as the sheriff . . ."

"Whatever are you trying to say?"

"Well, ma'am, I'm thinking of ordering you to leave this place."

"*Ordering* me? My goodness!" She folded her hands in her lap. "I see no reason to do so now. It seems that one way or another, the war is about over."

"That may be, but right now things are mighty dangerous around here with these bands of irregulars robbing and plundering and . . . I don't know what all. I got no means of stopping them, just don't have enough men."

"But what about our regular forces?"

"The Yankees are a handful, and with so many slaves running loose, well, I hate to think of a lady such as yourself so unprotected."

Sue walked to the window and looked out at the children. "If Richard . . ." She took a deep breath. "I'm grateful for your concern, Sheriff. I'll begin making arrangements."

"I'm relieved to hear it, Mrs. Kenworthy, ma'am, and I'm sure it'll make the colonel rest easier."

    ✿   ✿   ✿   ✿   ✿   ✿   ✿   ✿   ✿   ✿   ✿

Sue was very busy the next few days, burying jewelry and coins—it wouldn't do to travel with them. For once Mary seemed eager to help her, as a matter of fact seemed to enjoy it, almost like it was a game. And Gregory showed her some of his favorite hiding places—behind rocks, and under little hillocks up by the creek. He kept playing with his toy popgun, dropping down every now and then behind a rock, giving the Rebel yell, and shooting at an imaginary advancing Yankee skirmish line. A few times Sue even let him shoot the revolver Richard had left behind for her protection.

On the evening before they were to leave, Sue was reading to the children, a chapter from the *Tale of Two Cities*. Mary was out in the kitchen eating with Linus after having served the evening meal. A good-sized fire was burning in the fireplace and Jonas, the only hound dog left now, lay in front of it. The children were sitting on the rug, Laura with her head on her mother's lap, and Gregory leaning against her legs.

> So does a whole world, with all its greatnesses and littlenesses,
> lie in a twinkling star . . .

Jonas's ears stiffened, and he began a low growl.

"Hush, Jonas!" said Laura. "What Mother's reading is so pretty."

Sue remembered the sheriff's warning. She began again, only slightly uneasy. A raccoon or a possum was enough to set the hound off . . .

> Château and hut, stone face and dangling figure, the red stain
> on the stone floor, and the pure water in the village well—thou-
> sands of acres of land—a whole province of France—all France
> itself—lay under the night sky, concentrated into a faint hair-
> breadth line . . .

Jonas leapt to his feet with a growl and ran barking to the front door.

Oh, why hadn't she left right away? Who could that be at this hour of the night? But then maybe it *was* the sheriff.

She called Linus from the kitchen and told him to answer the door. He obeyed quickly, he wasn't like that no-account Mary.

A short man in a fur jacket with a pistol strapped around his waist pushed Linus aside and stepped right into the foyer.

"Captain Odom, to see the Miss of the house."

"But, Massa—"

Odom froze Linus with a look and walked into the large open space in front of the fireplace, then bowed to Sue and the children.

"I'm sorry to have to inconvenience you this way, but me and my men have been battling the Yankees for the past two days and are sore in need of food and shelter."

She looked at him. He wasn't wearing any kind of a uniform, except the gray pants. But then, times were hard and many of their men were ill-dressed.

"Get up, children. Mary will see you to bed." She kissed them. "I'll be up to tuck you in before long." She turned to Captain Odom. "How can I be of help to you?"

"Well, ma'am, I got about eighteen men left in my outfit now, and I'd be much obliged if you could put them up."

"We have plenty of room for them down in the stables—I'll have Linus show your men the way. You, of course, will do me the courtesy of staying with us in the house. Mary will prepare the guest bedroom for you." She beckoned to Linus. "Help the captain get his men settled down there."

The captain nodded to Sue and followed Linus out.

In fifteen minutes he was back again, this time accompanied by three men, one of them an Indian. With a wave of his hand, he presented them to Sue.

"My bodyguards and yours this evening."

"What—"

"Oh, you needn't worry about finding accommodations for them, they'll sleep right there by the fireplace. Won't you, boys?"

Sue was not reassured by their grunts. "But we have never . . ."

"Had an Injun to sleep in your house."

Sue nodded.

"Well, you needn't worry about this one. He's a fine soldier and a real gentleman to them he holds dear. And faithful as they come. Why, he wouldn't let me sleep in a strange house by myself! No, we'll all be safe as houses what with him here. " He smiled at Sue. "No thieving Yanks tonight."

Nevertheless, she locked the door behind her when all was settled and she was finally in her bedroom.

"Mama? I don't like those men. They don't look like the men that ride with my father," Gregory said.

"They are fighting for our freedom, Gregory. This is the *least* we can do for them."

"That Indian looked at me real funny. And did you see those scars on his face? Maybe he wants to scalp me."

"Hush. Some of our *finest* sharpshooters are Indians. I won't have you speak of them like that."

Laura was awake, too, sitting up on the bed. "Do you have the gun in here?"

"Yes, silly. But there's no need for it."

She got into bed, and drew Laura close to her. The child was trembling. Even their little warrior left his post at the foot of the bed, and the three of them fell asleep in a tangle of arms and bedclothes.

❖   ❖   ❖   ❖   ❖   ❖   ❖   ❖   ❖   ❖   ❖

Awakened by a scraping sound, she carefully moved her arms so as not to wake the children.

The sound was coming from outside. Somebody was shoveling.

What were Captain Odom's men doing? Did he know? She slipped out of bed and put a night robe on.

When she opened her door, she saw that Captain Odom's was open too. He must have heard the same sound and gone downstairs to investigate.

She was near the bottom of the stairs before she saw how mistaken she'd been.

Linus and Mary both sat bound and gagged on the rug The Indian was taking the fireplace apart, stone by stone, and other men were searching every corner of the room. And Captain Odom seemed to be directing the entire operation!

She had to get back to her room. And the revolver.

"Ah, Mrs. Kenworthy. Come on down—no need to alarm the children."

That odious man was aiming his pistol at *her*.

The Indian turned away from his project in the fireplace and smiled. Captain Odom moved to the bottom of the staircase.

"I'm sorry my men woke you. It was my intention to have been out of here before dawn without disturbing you." Still aiming the pistol, he offered his other hand and laughed when she hurried past him, head high.

"You traitor!"

"Oh no, ma'am, don't call me that, please. I've never lifted an arm against my sovereign government."

"Sir, you have taken advantage of my hospitality—and a woman's vulnerability."

He lowered the pistol. "Please sit down, ma'am. You may be able to speed us on our way. A person of your station surely has more assets than have so far surfaced here."

"We have *nothing* here. No gold, no jewelry, so there's *no use* in trying to get them from us."

"It grieves me to have to contradict such a lovely woman as you, but we both know there are things of considerable value concealed here—or somewhere nearby."

She gripped the top of her night robe and pulled it tight around her neck. All of the real money they had left was buried out there. She would *not* tell!

"Come now, Mrs. Kenworthy, I'm sure you don't want me to wake those children up or have my men beat the secret out of your old niggers over there." He waved the pistol in the direction of Mary and Linus. "It's only money, and what's money beside a human life? Of course, this Indian here, he don't have the same feelings about human life as us. And the worst part's that once I tell him to do something, there's no stopping him. Why, once he took a pot of scalding hot frying grease and—"

"All right."

What a mangy-looking bunch of hoodlums they were! "Just wait until daylight, and I'll show you where everything is buried. But you'll pay for this. The colonel rides with General Wirt Adams."

"I had the pleasure of riding with that gentleman myself at one time. There is naught to fear from him." He glanced at his men. "We'll wait until morning. Mrs. Kenworthy, I'll accompany you back to your room to see that you get there safely."

As she walked up the stairs, she could *feel* his eyes going right through her robe, so she wasn't surprised to feel his hand on her buttocks when they reached the landing.

"Would you like to sit up for a while and talk? Perhaps in that very nice guest room of yours."

She turned and with both hands shoved his shoulders so hard he would have fallen down the stairs if he hadn't grabbed the railing.

"You'll regret that." He touched her cheek with the pistol and walked into his room.

❖   ❖   ❖   ❖   ❖   ❖   ❖   ❖   ❖   ❖   ❖

Sue awoke to a smell so delicious that she almost forgot her situation. Mmmmmm, bacon. Neither of the children was in the room. She dressed hurriedly and rushed downstairs.

That man Odom—she had no intention of honoring him with the title of captain any longer—was seated in Richard's favorite chair, drinking a cup of coffee.

"Looking for your children? They're in the kitchen eating. My men have already eaten and they're waiting down at the barn for us. Why don't you have something to eat and then we'll get to the matter of the jewelry."

Sue went into the kitchen. Mary and Linus were cleaning up after Odom's men, while the children finished their eggs and bacon.

"Mary told us these are bad men," Laura said. "Are they going to hurt you?"

Sue sat down at the table with them. "There's nothing to worry about. We're going to give them what they want and then they'll leave. I want the two of you to stay up here with Linus and Mary." She got up from the table. "I'm going now."

It was chilly outside. A touch of frost had left a light coat of white on the lawn, now overgrown with weeds. The sight of the men assembled at the stables made Sue tremble. They had already taken the shovels out of the barn.

A hound dog leapt up and down with joy when it saw Odom, who went over and patted it. "Morning, Cornpone."

These men had no right to be doing this. They were nothing but *highwaymen* who would run away to Texas with every last thing she and Richard had accumulated and never be heard from again.

"Sir, I implore you in the name of Southern chivalry—"

"Let's go, men. Mrs. Kenworthy will lead the way."

The odious Odom made a deep bow. Odious Odum . . . Sue remembered what her friend had said about her writing poetry. Merciful heavens! Was she coming unhinged, thinking about such things at a time like this?

❋   ❋   ❋   ❋   ❋   ❋   ❋   ❋   ❋   ❋   ❋

She watched dry-eyed while they dug up the boxes of gold coins and jewelry she had buried so carefully just a few days ago. But she couldn't hold back the tears when the men passed around the diamond wedding ring made especially for her in London. She had cried when Richard gave it to her at the ceremony . . .

"All right, men," Odom said. "Don't play with that stuff. Take it back up to the house, make a regular inventory of it, and we'll divide up fair and square before we leave."

Sue glared at him. "You said you'd go if I gave you the valuables."

"Did I? Well, we'll see. Have to count what we have, then we'll decide when we're going to leave."

When they got back to the house, he ordered Mary and Linus to go upstairs with Sue and the children. He locked the door to her bedroom from the outside and posted the Indian as a sentry.

"If you-all need anything, Mrs. Kenworthy, just call."

Sue thought about the revolver. But there were too many of them. Even if she killed some of them, the rest would brutalize her and her family. She was truly at the end of her wits.

Linus and Mary lay down on the floor and slept, exhausted from the night before. Sue began again to read to the children, and soon they were engrossed enough in the story that they seemed to forget about the danger downstairs. She tried to forget, too, but the memory of her wedding ring in the hands of those men wouldn't let her.

Several hours passed with barely a sound from downstairs. When the children finally went to sleep on her bed, Sue peeked through the keyhole. The Indian was asleep on a chair.

❋   ❋   ❋   ❋   ❋   ❋   ❋   ❋   ❋   ❋   ❋

What could be taking them so long? They had what they wanted. Why didn't they leave?

Another hour passed before Odom finally unlocked the door and marched right in without so much as a knock.

"We've finished distributing the shares and have decided to accept a little more of your hospitality. We've been doing a little scouting—there's a bit of military activity going on in the vicinity that might make it unwise for us to be on the highways right now."

"I hope they catch you."

"Now, Mrs. Kenworthy, you don't mean that. They're Yankees."

"Doesn't matter."

"Nigger Yankees."

"What?"

"Yes."

"I want you out of here, sir."

"Send the two niggers down to make lunch. And tell them to get the liquor out. We're just going to settle in here and have us a little party till the darky soldiers go away. Might even invite you to come down and join us."

Gregory walked over and stood between her and Odom. "You're a coward, sir, and my father will punish you for all of this."

"He'll have to catch me first, son, and that ain't real likely. Mrs. Kenworthy, get those servants, moving, please."

❀   ❀   ❀   ❀   ❀   ❀   ❀   ❀   ❀   ❀   ❀

By two o'clock, they were loud and raucous. Never had such profanity reached Sue's ears. They had no respect for either God or man.

By three o'clock, their singing was punctuated with the sound of breaking glass.

When would this end? Reading Dickens no longer calmed the children. Sue sat on the bed with her arms around them.

"When are they going to stop?" Laura asked.

"Never you mind. I think it's time we prayed together."

They were on their knees saying the Lord's Prayer when Odom appeared at the door with the Indian behind him, peering over his shoulder. At the sight of them, the children screamed.

And no wonder! Odom's eyes were red and his cheeks were glowing like polished apples. He had removed his bow tie and had grabbed hold of the doorknob, which he seemed to need in order to remain upright.

"Mrs. Kenworthy, my men and I beg the pleasure of your company below."

Sue had anticipated this moment and knew she had to go if the children were to remain unharmed. If she could just keep herself calm, maybe Gregory wouldn't do anything foolish.

"Sir, I'll sit with you and you alone in the guest bedroom, if you'll bring Linus and Mary up here so that they can give the children something to eat."

"Why, I'll be pleased to do that . . . I'll be right back with them."

"Don't go!" Gregory said. "Don't leave us."

Laura clung to her mother's dress, and began to sob. "You can't go with that awful man, he'll kill you."

Sue bent down and put her arms around both of them. "Now, don't worry. I don't like him either, but . . . we're just going to talk for a little while. I'll come in to check on you every now and then, and Mary and Linus will take care of you."

When she walked into the guest room, he was at least enough of a gentleman to get up from his chair. A tiny hope stirred. She watched him open a bottle of the wine Richard had had shipped from Bordeaux itself.

"These red French wines seem to be a favorite of our Southern ladies." He poured some and offered it to Sue. It wasn't even a wineglass—just a tall glass like the one he still had filled with bourbon whiskey.

She held the glass tightly, barely restraining herself from tossing its contents right into his red face. The whiskey smell on his breath hit her full blast as he took her by the elbow, trying to maneuver her over toward the bed.

"My men must have scared you with all of that racket, but there's no harm in them, just kind of playful at times."

She edged away from him. "How do you expect to live again in this territory when this war is over? Either the Yankees or our own will put an end to you."

He moved close enough to take her elbow again, the arm holding his bourbon stretched outwards so that when she retreated she was forced to move back towards the bed.

"You've got beautiful skin, Mrs. Kenworthy."

She felt the gnarled wood of the bedpost pressing into her back. When he bent to kiss her on the cheek, she recoiled.

"Now, you don't want to go making it hard on yourself. Your children are in there, and we don't want my men to forget themselves, do we? I wasn't exaggerating about how wild that Injun is when he's riled up, especially with all that liquor he's got in him now. Just be sensible, and we'll be gone in a while."

Sue fell to her knees before him, folded her hands together, and began to cry. He put his hand on her shoulder.

"Now there, I'm not such an ugly man, am I? Just take a good look at me." He grabbed her chin and twisted her head so that she had to look up at him.

She stopped crying. Who was she to be spared? How many times had Richard suffered grievous wounds? Did not over half of the young men who'd formed his wedding party now lie in their graves, dead for the Cause? Yes, the rain fell on the just and the unjust alike. With the little dignity she was able to muster, Sue stood up.

"Turn your head around so that I may undress."

"That's a sensible girl. We'll have us a jolly good time, and then I'll be on my way." He unbuckled his belt.

"Captain Odom!" She heard footsteps on the stairs, then a sharp knock at the door. "Yankees! They're right down the road."

He was buckling his pants and his pistol belt on the way to the door.

   ✿   ✿   ✿   ✿   ✿   ✿   ✿   ✿   ✿   ✿   ✿

Sue thanked God every step of the way to her bedroom.

"Look at them run, children!"

She joined them, along with Mary and Linus, at the window—just in time to see the gang mounting up. Odom was the last, but once he had mounted they all took off down the road. The hound dog was yelping and running in circles by the stable.

They were barely out of sight when a whole bunch of Yankee cavalry came just as fast down the road right behind them.

"Look, Mama—nigger soldiers."

Sue didn't know whether to cry or cheer, but considering what Odom had been about ready to do to her—

"My God! The jewelry and the gold!"

If anything had been left behind, it mustn't fall into Yankee hands. That's who she'd hidden it from in the first place. They all rushed downstairs and looked around.

"Glory, Miss Kensworthy, your wedding ring still there."

Glory, indeed. In their haste to depart, the scoundrels had left a good half of the loot on the table.

❊   ❊   ❊   ❊   ❊   ❊   ❊   ❊   ❊   ❊   ❊

An hour later, Sue watched through the windows as the Union men wended their way up the roadway to the house. What a sight! Darky soldiers in blue uniforms with yellow piping that made their faces look even blacker, sitting astride those horses as if they had been accustomed to riding all of their lives. And not a white man with them.

Was there no end to the evil acts resorted to by the Yankees? Sending black men out on their own to *devastate* the land.

She stepped away from the window and went to change out of her night robe and into a dress.

"Mama, look at that nigger sergeant leading them." Gregory prided himself on knowing all the insignia in both armies.

❊   ❊   ❊   ❊   ❊   ❊   ❊   ❊   ❊   ❊   ❊

She was ready when the knock came at the door. In her chair, with her children at her side.

"Linus, answer it."

"Joe!" she heard him say. Then, "Mary! It Joe, Zenobia's Joe, we safe!"

With a big smile on his face, he led the sergeant into the living room. At least this was a *familiar* Yankee. Sue smiled, too. Then she remembered.

"How do you do, Miz Kenworthy?"

Joe's uniform was dusty, but there was no mistaking the stripes on his arm or the authority in his walk. The ex-slave carpenter on their estate was now a Yankee noncommissioned officer.

Mary had slipped up next to him. "Joe, you done come to free us, ain't you?"

Joe *hugged* her! "Sure have, honey. Me and President Abraham Lincoln."

He released her and bowed to Sue. "You don't have to worry about nothing from us, just going to see to it that those secesh are run out of this territory, then we'll be moving on. Some of my men are still chasing them."

Sue remained silent. Her children clung to her.

"Don't worry, little chilluns," Linus said, "Joe my friend."

"That'll do, Linus." It was time for Sue to show her authority. "How long do you propose to be here?"

"We going to be confiscating those two horses down in the stable, and my men will kill the cow for dinner tonight. Any livestock we can't take will be destroyed." His speech had changed some—it was more like that of a white man.

"We were counting on those horses to get us to Alabama."

"Sorry, Miss, the needs of my command comes first."

The *nerve* of him! Another one appeared at the door, grinning. "Excuse me, sir, we got him, we got the leader."

"What's the joke?" Joe said.

"See, he almost got away. Left his horse and tried to run away down in the swamps. Onliest thing were, he didn't take that nigger dog of his with him. So we lets it loose and he tracks down the old master! We come up on him, standing there trying to shush that old dog of his'n away. Then he tried to shoot his way out."

"Where is he now?"

"He ain't going to be doing any more shooting. Ever."

"Good. We're bivouacking here tonight. Post the pickets and get the men fed."

"You surely don't intend to spend the night in this house!" Sue stood up. "Under my roof?"

"I'll post a sentry at the bottom of your staircase. Now I must see to some things."

❖   ❖   ❖   ❖   ❖   ❖   ❖   ❖   ❖   ❖   ❖

She was sure she wouldn't sleep a wink, but they all went to sleep without even a page of their book. When she came downstairs the next morning, the revolver was concealed in the pocket of her gown. The children were eating breakfast with the Negro soldiers, Gregory examining the Yankee weapons. After breakfast, Joe asked Sue to come into the living room and sit down.

"Miz Kenworthy, I understands you sent the patrollers and the hound dogs after Zenobia and my child Cally. What did they report?"

That Mary had told *everything*. "I don't have to answer you," she said.

The muscles in his face were twitching.

"They were my legal property."

"And Milly and Luke—they was your legal property too, right?"

"I *will not* answer any more questions."

She started to get up, but Joe nodded to a sergeant by the door. "Be prepared to restrain her if we has to."

She sat back down. "Don't you *dare* put your black hands on me."

"The colonel done made my son a body servant."

Sue's upper lip began to tremble. "I bear no responsibility for his actions."

"Mary done told me about your treasure, and now I needs you to bring it downstairs. It's Federal property. Zack, you go with her."

*   *   *   *   *   *   *   *   *   *   *

They spread all the gold coins and the ring on the table in the dining room. Joe carefully itemized everything "confiscated from the secesh," then signed his name and title at the bottom.

He turned to the one he'd called Zack. "Bring those children in here."

Sue's heart sank. And when they saw the look on their mother's face, Gregory and Laura burst into tears and ran to her side.

Sue slipped a hand into her right pocket, hooked her forefinger around the trigger of the revolver. This time she was prepared.

"Get me that wedding ring out of the bag," Joe said.

What was in that evil African mind of his? What revenge was he seeking for his children and wife?

"Give it to her."

The other sergeant slowly rotated the ring in his hand.

"That's an order."

"Yes, sir."

"Miz Kenworthy, I need you to sign this receipt for the wedding ring's return," Joe said. "If you be so kind."

She signed and he folded the receipt and bowed.

"We leaving now. Mary's going with us, but Linus wants to stay with you. Good day, ma'am, and my compliments to the colonel. His money going into the treasury of the United States Government."

From a window Sue watched him speak to another sergeant, then walk back to the house.

Joe never looked at her face this time. She could have sworn he was looking right through her shawl at the pistol as he handed her a bag of coins and another piece of paper.

"I've decided to leave the horses with you. And a hundred dollars. Your children has done us no harm and won't be made to suffer. Now I got to trouble you to sign one more time. . . ."

CHAPTER NINETEEN

ZENOBIA woke up with pain shooting from the calf of her leg straight through the rest of her body. Oh, Lord, she could barely turn over. Wouldn't be seeing Freedom Land any time soon.

They'd been walking for eight days, and the swelling had just crept up on her over the last twenty-four hours—slow at first, like always. There was no way to get heat for it, no way she could rest proper at night with nothing but that little bit of a blanket between her and the cold damp earth. And no sweet Joe to snuggle up against her real tight or rub her leg with that special oil he made up.

Lisa Mae and Ned and Helen were bundled up together, sleeping their weary young souls away. How could she ever make them go on without her? The only thing she knew to do was pray.

❖   ❖   ❖   ❖   ❖   ❖   ❖   ❖   ❖   ❖   ❖

Lisa Mae woke up first. "You already wake, Zee? Why you not up finding us some breakfast like always?"

"Afraid this the end for me. I can't walk."

Lisa Mae laughed. "Ain't no time to be fooling with me like that, big sister."

"Get Helen and Ned up. You all got to get ready for the walking. They be leaving soon, and—"

"Wait a minute. We ain't going nowhere without you." She shook the youngsters. "You stay here and watch Auntie Zenobia. I'm going to find a soldier to help."

"Give me that bag, Ned." Zenobia reached in and took out some pieces of hardtack the soldiers had given out the day before. "Here, eat—you all need lots of strength today."

"What's wrong, Auntie? Why's Lisa Mae fussing?"

"Well, you know I been having some pain in my leg. Now it's swollen up like a big ham. No way in the world I can leave."

"You can't *walk?*" Ned asked.

"I think God got other plans for me today."

Helen looked like she was about to cry—in fact, they both did—but bless her heart, she took Ned by the hand. "Come on, honey."

Around them folks in the camp were up, singing and packing their little bundles for the day:

> *I'm sometimes up, I'm sometimes down*
> *Trouble going to bury me down!*
> *Oh brethren! Poor me! Poor me!*
> *Trouble will bury me down!*

Everybody was pretty much ready to go by the time Lisa Mae returned, riding on a horse with her arms wrapped around a white cavalry soldier. She slid down from the horse, talking a mile a minute.

"Looky here, Zee, I done fixed it. John here, he going to let you ride behind him. Lots of folks doing it up the line."

"You think you can get up here, sister?"

"Soldier man, I try anything once."

The line began to move.

"If you're coming, you got to hurry," the horse soldier said. "The Rebs ain't far behind now."

Helen and Lisa Mae took her by the arms. Zenobia tried to stand up.

"It burn like fire when I move." Beads of sweat broke out all over her face. "Too much. You all go on."

The soldier leaned down from his horse. "Sister, this is your last chance, I have to get back up the line."

"Then go. And please take these young folks with you."

She could see now that the end of the line was not far away. *God, give me the words to make them go.* She looked up into the circle of worried faces.

"If you love me, you'll go," she said. "Break my heart if we come all this way for nothing. You got to follow the soldier man."

Helen knelt down beside her. "You my mother."

"I know it, my baby. I love you, I loves you all. But you got to obey your mother and go on like I tell you. I be all right."

"Come on, you-all, start walking," the soldier said.

"Lisa Mae, you the leader now," Zenobia said. "Be one."

Lisa Mae took their hands. "Come on, you two."

"Don't you dare look back," Zenobia said. "You hear? Don't look back!"

"May God keep you in his care, sister." With that, the cavalryman spurred his horse and rode off down the road.

❖   ❖   ❖   ❖   ❖   ❖   ❖   ❖   ❖   ❖   ❖

"Come on in," Betty said. "The captain's right over here."

"Hello, sir."

Captain Stiles sat up. "I'm mighty glad to see you, Joe, the colonel told me you did one hell of a job after I got it."

Joe put his cap on the night table. "Was all right I guess, but we missed you like the devil. And I got a lot to learn about military tactics."

"If a general store clerk like me can learn, so will you," Captain Stiles said.

"How's my woman been treating you?"

"Couldn't have had a better nurse. Don't see how somebody pretty as her hooked up with you."

Betty said, "Now, Captain, he got a few good points."

Joe laughed and put his arm around her. "One thing for sure, I'm a lucky man."

"How're things going with the company?"

"Going good, sir. We brought down a lot of new men from those plantations up in the Delta. Zack's keeping busy whipping them into shape, but he don't have much time. We're going up to Arkansas and Louisiana soon to wipe out some of the Reb bands operating up there."

"I probably won't be here when you men get back, they're sending me home as soon as I can walk again. They think I'm too banged up to go to Washington."

"Do you think . . . You still going to be able to farm, sir?"

"Well, with that bullet where it is, I'm going to have to take it easy. But you don't think I've forgotten, do you?"

Joe grinned. "Just checking, sir. How long you think before all this be over?"

"With Savannah and Fort Fisher gone, the Rebs won't be able to hold on much longer. I'd give it another five or six months. But don't you get careless, now—a bullet can't read a calendar."

Joe squared his shoulders and shook the captain's hand. "Sir, I just want to tell you how proud I am to have served with you. If you don't never come back this way again, me and the men, we won't never forget you."

"You made me proud too, Joe. Plenty of times."

❖   ❖   ❖   ❖   ❖   ❖   ❖   ❖   ❖   ❖   ❖

Betty walked out with Joe. "Come along with me while I make my rounds. Might make some of them a little jealous, but still I'd like to show you off a bit."

A long shed housed all the sick and wounded who had come down the Yazoo with the brigade.

Almost as far as Joe could see, there was nothing but soldiers, colored and white, lying in those beds. For the first time he realized all the work this woman of his had to do. He thought back on the men who had started out with the Third and were now lying in their graves somewhere up there in the Delta. What a wonder he'd been spared so far, hadn't had more than a few scratches. Now he looked down the long row of beds, saw the faces, some empty, some eager, waiting for Betty's touch, her voice.

"Harrison, this my friend, Sergeant Duckett . . ."

"Corey, how you today? Let me see that bandage . . ."

"William, I brung you some candy today, made it special myself . . ."

She paused by one bed. "Brother Roland, let us have prayer together."

It wasn't long before Joe was longing to breathe some fresh air. But when Betty had finished with the short prayer, she nodded toward a far corner of the shed.

"Some real sad cases over there. Colored boys who've been with the Rebs, and they ain't had too much to eat when they come in. You boys been doing too good a job cleaning out those plantations."

One man was lying in his bed, a blanket over him, facing the wall. He had a big bandage on his shoulder.

"He like that all the time. Won't even tell me his name. So young, but he seen a lot and he pretend to be sleep all the time. He don't believe he free." She leaned over him, her voice even gentler than before. "Turn over, honey, let me feel your brow."

The man didn't wake up, didn't turn over, but Joe knew.

"Luke!"

"Oh, my God! And he been here almost a week." She reached out to wake him.

"No," Joe said. "Let me."

He touched his son's temple.

"Daddy!"

Joe was on his knees beside the bed now, stroking Luke's forehead, then kissing it. Hugging him tight when he sat up.

❖   ❖   ❖   ❖   ❖   ❖   ❖   ❖   ❖   ❖   ❖

Betty sat on the bed and wiped away their tears—and her own—with a corner of her apron.

"Be careful, you-all, don't want that wound to open up."

Before the day was over, she had arranged to have Luke moved into her room. And now Joe had a special reason to go up into Louisiana on the raid—Milly and Pauline were there.

❖   ❖   ❖   ❖   ❖   ❖   ❖   ❖   ❖   ❖   ❖

A few days later, just before the regiment was due to leave for Memphis on the boats, Joe asked Zack to go with him to the refugee camp just outside of Vicksburg. He'd heard there were thousands of colored folks the government was trying to put back together with their families.

He walked into the camp real slow. Being on the battlefield was a whole lot easier than to having to deal with his life and everything so scattered.

What would he find in the camp this time? It was mighty scary, considering that all these folks came from right up there in the Delta where he'd spent so many years.

There were tents all over the place, set up in rows. In front of some of them, toddlers in night shifts followed after their mothers, who were gathering wood, cooking in big iron pots over fires, or mending clothing. Stray dogs darted back and forth, their barking almost drowned out by the loud and often shouted conversations of people gathered in dozens of small groups around the camp. A banjo player sat on a stump chair, surrounded by women and children who were stomping their feet and clapping their hands as his fingers plucked out the melody of "Camptown Races."

"Look at them soldier boys."

A woman with a red turban around her head was pointing at them.

Some young boys ran up. "We know you, you got that three on your collar. You from the Third Colored Cavalry."

Joe reached down and lifted one of them up. "That's right, sonny boy."

An old man, his trousers held up by a string, reached out to touch the buttons on Joe's jacket.

"Them buttons mighty pretty. Never thought I'd live to see it. Praise God!"

At the far end of the camp, where you could see down over the river, there was a big tent. As Joe and Zack approached they saw children sitting on benches trying to draw the way the teacher was drawing on the board. When she started asking them questions, they jumped and shouted to show her they knew the answers. A mighty fine thing to see them. Colored folks was on their way up, all right.

The teacher wore a tight gray dress with a high white collar. Every time one of the children gave the right answer, she clapped her hands as much as they did. Joe felt like clapping himself—he knew most of the answers. Not like two years ago. Now he could read up a storm and so could a lot of men in his company.

He and Zack had been standing watching the children for a few minutes when the teacher motioned for them to come in.

"Us?" Joe said.

"Yes, you and the sergeant there."

They took off their hats and walked over to her desk.

"Children, we're going to do something very special today." She took hold of Joe's and Zack's hands. "These men have been out fighting so that no one will ever again beat you, or call you little niggers, or sell your mothers or fathers or sisters or brothers away from you. Many lost their arms or legs or been killed by the Rebels so you can grow up as free children. Now, who wants to come up and thank them on behalf of this class?"

Every hand went up. "Me! Miss Francis!"

She looked out over them, beckoned to a girl in the back with a thin, serious face, and turned to Joe.

"It's the first time Helen has ever wanted to speak in front of the class," she said.

The girl looked up at Joe and Zack, then back down at the floor. Some of the other children tittered. Miss Francis put her fingers to her lips. "Shush!"

Joe bent down so that his face was level with the girl's and took her hands in his. "Say whatever's on your heart, darlin'."

She glanced over at Miss Francis, then back at Joe. "We is so proud of you. Most of us, we ain't knowed nothing but hurt . . ."

Joe squeezed her hand gently. "Go ahead, baby child."

"I ain't never known my mammy, never had a daddy, and my little brothers and sisters, they been sold long ago down into Alabama. Grandmama raised me and that old overseer, he would tie her to a tree and whip her. She dead now."

Joe put his hand gently on her head.

"Onliest other person I ever had were Zenobia, and now she gone too."

Joe looked at her. Could she mean *his* Zenobia? He didn't remember this child's face from Clifton.

"We going to study and work real hard to make you proud of us like we proud of you soldier boys. We thanks you from the bottom of our hearts."

She kissed each of them on their cheeks.

"Now our song, children," the teacher said. "Sing it good for them."

> *"Walk together, children*
> *Don't you get weary!*
> *Walk together, children*
> *Don't you get weary!*

Pray together, children
Don't you get weary!
Pray together, children
Don't you get weary!"

"Now it's our turn," Joe said. "Me and Sergeant Bascombe here, we just wants to tell you how proud we is of *you*." He turned to Miss Francis. "Can I have a word with Helen outside for a minute? It's mighty important."

"Is that all right with you, Helen? Class is almost over."

She nodded and followed them outside.

"Now, Helen, this Zenobia, what she look like?"

"She a mighty pretty lady. She take care of everybody."

"Was there anybody else with her?"

"Lisa Mae and Ned, and Cally and Mr. Drayton at first, only they . . ."

Joe looked at Zack. "It's her."

"You know Zenobia?" Helen said.

Joe took her hands. "Yes, darlin', I surely do. Now tell me what happened to you all."

"She can tell you better." Joe looked in the direction Helen was pointing and saw Lisa Mae walking toward them.

And she saw him and hollered at the top of her voice.

"Joe!"

They ran across the field and Joe lifted her off her feet for a hug. How many times had Aunt Garry's granddaughter stayed over in their cabin, chattering away the night with Zenobia, so tired the next morning that she could barely go back to the fields? He held on to her like if he let go they'd never see each other again in this life.

By now class was over and Miss Francis came out to join them. "Your wife?"

"No, ma'am, but she my wife's best friend." He let go and took a step back. "Now, Lisa Mae, tell me what happened . . ."

❁   ❁   ❁   ❁   ❁   ❁   ❁   ❁   ❁   ❁   ❁

That night, the last one before they shipped out, Joe stopped by Betty's house. Luke was asleep, so they sat at the table and talked quietly.

"Want some coffee, Joe? You look like you could use it."

"No, just come on over and sit in my lap. I think this about the confusingest week of my life, don't really know which way to turn."

"Anybody wouldn't know, what with all that's happened."

"But somehow I got to make sense of all these things. See, I love you, and I love my Zenobia, too. Now, ain't that sinful when she's lying out there on some road up there in the Delta, maybe froze to death? And my little Cally gone on home to glory . . ."

"Joe—"

"How the hell am I going to tell Luke about all this? Life done dealt us a rotten hand."

She ran her fingers over his clenched fist. "I never heard you talk that way before."

"It's true, ain't it?"

"No, it's dealt a rotten hand to all those men in the sick ward. You got your health and strength and lots of people to live for, starting with me. I'm going to boil you a fine cup of coffee, then we can lie down on that pallet for a little while and maybe I can take some of that hurt out of you."

She started setting up to make coffee.

"Your men depending on you. All kinds of folks loving you and depending on you. You got to get yourself together, Joe."

"Betty?

"What is it, honey?"

"Look." He stretched out his hands.

"You shouldn't have started up drinking again, baby. You promised me—"

"Ain't had no whiskey. I'm scared. First time."

CHAPTER TWENTY

ZENOBIA watched the last soldier spur his horse and move off.

Well, that was the last of the Yankees.

She looked up the road. The Rebs, now, that was something else. She'd heard many a time how grayboys killed colored folks who tried to run off with the Yankees and failed. Once the Yankees had left so quickly they burned a bridge and left a hundred freed colored on the other side, some on their knees praying, others running into the water. The cavalry boys had a field day, cutting and slashing away at those poor souls with freedom in their heads. Killed so many it was said water from the river could have dyed a dozen bolts of white cloth crimson red.

Now here she was, watching for them. Sitting by the roadside waiting for the death angel.

Well, let them come. She didn't have any real hope of living to see another day. Didn't know if she even wanted to. Joe gone, Cally gone, Milly and Luke God knew where. At least Lisa Mae and the children were freedom bound . . .

In her head, she heard a voice. Brother Caleb's voice, at prayer meetings down in the bush. "When your burdens get heavy, my sisters and brothers, lean not to your own understanding, for He will always give you a song. May not be a song that come out of your mouth, 'cause all of us can't sing good, just may be a night sky when He make the stars to shine all at once, light up His whole big kingdom for all His chillun to see and praise His name. *He will always give us a song!*"

Wasn't nobody in sight, and she wouldn't care if there was. She opened her throat wide and sang the song He gave.

> *"I couldn't hear nobody pray*
> *Oh, I couldn't hear nobody pray!*
> *I was way down yonder by myself*
> *And I couldn't hear nobody pray!"*

She was still singing it when she saw the first clouds of dust down the road, heard the sound of the galloping hooves like the low rumble of far-off thunder. Not so far off, after all. Through the thickening cloud of dust she saw the flag and the horses and men, all coming right at her.

When the column was abreast of her, an officer raised his hand.

"Halt!"

His uniform was in tatters and his thin face was all splotchy and scraggy-bearded.

"Auntie, your Yankees left you here, didn't they? How long ago?"

"A long time, Massa."

He shook his head. "What's that mean, Auntie? An hour? Two hours?"

"Don't know. Long time, Massa."

The officer looked back toward his men. "Sergeant Riggins, come over here. A bite of the lash may loosen this darky's tongue, help her to re-member better."

The sergeant uncoiled his whip. Zenobia winced as its hateful snap bit into the tree right above her head.

What had she to hide? Nothing she said could either help or hurt the Yankees.

"About an hour, Massa."

"That's better. Now, how come they left you here?"

"I got a sickness in my leg. Can't walk."

The sergeant unsnapped his holster and waited for the order. The cap-tain nodded his head, the sergeant drew his Navy Colt out of its holster and pulled back the hammer.

Zenobia looked into their eyes—first one, then the other. "You mighty young boys to be killing womenfolk. How do it feel afterward?"

The sergeant placed the muzzle of the gun on Zenobia's temple and pressed. "Why, you ornery bitch!" She tried to move away from the pain, but he just pressed harder.

"Just a second there, Sergeant!" The captain put his hand on the gun. "What plantation you from, Auntie?"

"What do it matter now?" She twisted her head to look at the sergeant. "Go ahead and shoot, you look like you done had lots of practice. Too bad there ain't no more women around. And nary a child. If there was, you could let my blood flow in the same stream as theirs."

The sergeant raised the revolver again. "Sir, just let me get rid of this—"

"Not so fast." The captain smiled. "Hell, I ain't never seen nobody stand up to a gun like that. Now, dammit, woman, we ain't got time to fool with you. Tell me where you're from."

"Clifton. I'm from Clifton"

"Put away that gun, Sergeant, and let's get moving."

"But, sir—"

"Hell, man, that's Colonel Kenworthy's place. He's riding somewhere back behind us and wouldn't take too kindly to killing of his property." He looked at Zenobia. "You know Clifton's only about ten miles away from here, don't you?"

"Don't know nothing about that, neither."

"You're a real smart one, ain't you? He turned to the sergeant. "Let's get after them Yanks."

He retook his place at the head of the column and raised his hand. "Forward!"

Zenobia wrapped herself in the blanket and watched the long column of cavalry pass by. The ribs of the horses looked about ready to push through their skin, and many of the soldiers were riding barefoot. Every one of them was ragged and dirty, and they wore all kinds of things on their heads—Reb caps, farmers' hats, bandannas, and some of them even had on Yankee caps.

A few looked at Zenobia when they passed, but most never even glanced her way. Toward evening, the number of calvary thinned out, and when nightfall came, a small detachment stopped and made camp.

A short, clean-shaven soldier came over to where Zenobia lay beneath the tree. His right eye kept blinking, like it had a mind of its own.

"Well, Suzy Mae, what you doing here?"

"Waiting till my leg get better."

"To do what?"

She pulled the blanket over her so it was almost up to her chin. "To go back to my plantation. Yankees stole me from it."

The man laughed. "One of them runaways, huh?"

They built a good-size fire and soon had a pot boiling. The smell of corn mush made her mouth water, but when they brought some over to her, it didn't have no taste. Even so, the warmth of the thin mush seemed to spread down into her leg and ease the pain some.

She awoke to a hand shoving her shoulder.

"Wake up, Suzy Mae! The night's young and we ain't even had a chance to get to know you. Tomorrow we got to be pushing on."

The man who had spoken to her earlier was holding out a cup of whiskey. "Here, take this, it'll be good for you, make the pain go away."

She took a swallow.

The rest of the men were sitting around the fire drinking and singing. "She ain't in no pain!" one of them hollered. "You know niggers is always playing sick."

He sat down next to her, that eye of his blinking up a storm. "You right good-looking, you know. What's your name?"

"Zenobia."

"Comes from the Good Book, don't it?"

She nodded. The warmth from the whiskey was spreading through her body.

"Here, have some more. You been out here all day."

He watched her take another sip.

"Zenobia, me and the boys been fighting the Yanks for the last three weeks, and we're feeling mighty poorly, just about the way you're feeling with that leg. We going to pick you up and move you over closer to the fire for the night, so's you can be good and warm."

Zenobia pulled the blanket back up to her neck. "I'm just fine here."

"Now, don't be arguing with me. Some more of that whiskey and some heat from that there fire, and you'll be right as rain." He yelled over to his comrades. "A couple of you boys come on over here and give me a hand getting Zenobia over where she can be near us and the fire."

They lifted her up, and she felt their hands all over her thighs and breasts.

"Easy with her, boys, don't want to damage the goods."

They laid her down on a bed of pine branches not far from the fire, and she pulled the blanket back around her.

"Going to need a little time to get used to our company, ain't you?" The man with the blinking eye was mighty eager to share his whiskey with her. "We ain't no bad fellows, just looking to have us a little fun tonight. Cheer you up and us too."

Some of the men were lying on their backs, others with their legs hunched up close to their chests. One was strumming softly on a guitar while another sang in a high clear voice that seemed to float into every part of the night:

> *Where the Rio Grande is flowing*
> *And the starry skies are bright,*

"We'uns don't want to hurt you . . ."

> *She walks along the river*
> *In the quiet summer night.*

One of the men by the fire kicked dust into it, making sparks fly up. "What the hell you doing, treating her like she's a white woman or something? Go ahead and do what you got to do. We can't be up all night if we're chasing Yankees at daybreak."

Another man said, "You ain't man enough to take her, get the hell out the way and let us have her."

> *She thinks, if I remember,*
> *When we parted long ago,*

"Aw, hell." He jerked the blanket off. When his hands hit her swollen calf, she cried out as pain shot through her body. "Don't fight me, girl, you'll just get the others riled up and then you don't know what they might do."

He unbuckled his belt and bent over to take his pants off.

"Touch her, and I'll shoot!" The man with the beautiful voice had stopped singing and was standing about five feet away with a revolver in his hand. "Put her skirt down and cover her up with that blanket."

"Andy, have you gone plumb out of your mind? This ain't nothing but a nigger."

"Be that as it may, you heard what I said." He had drawn another revolver, had one in each hand. "I'm sick and tired of all this killing and raping and pillaging—and I ain't having none of it tonight from you, Ben, or"—he pointed in the direction of the campfire—"any of you others."

They all stared at him. The only sound was the popping of the fire.

With a grunt, Ben pulled his pants back up and stomped off.

Andy rolled a log over to where Zenobia lay, propped his back up against it, and sat with his guns in his lap.

"I'll be watching over you tonight, Auntie. There won't no harm come to you."

Zenobia said, "I thank you kindly, Massa Andy. God bless and keep you."

❖ ❖ ❖ ❖ ❖ ❖ ❖ ❖ ❖ ❖ ❖

In the morning, he fed her hot mush and a cup of something made out of leaves and grass.

"We're going to be on our way. Maybe somebody will come by and help you today." He gave her a gold coin. "This could come in handy."

Zenobia smiled. "That's mighty kind of you. And what with the sun coming out, this pain might go away soon."

He didn't need to know she was getting the shivers, had sweated all the night long. Let him think he had saved her.

She waved as he walked off.

❖ ❖ ❖ ❖ ❖ ❖ ❖ ❖ ❖ ❖ ❖

She lay there for another two days, as troops, deserters, and stragglers rode by. Occasionally, somebody would leave her some hardtack, a piece of fatback, a cup of water. But nobody else tried to harm her.

She awoke every morning shivering, her blanket soaked and dreams of Aunt Garry and Cally still in her head. And Drayton shouting, "run, Zenobia, run!" Seems like that was all she'd been doing. And Clifton no more

than ten miles away! Yet so far away, so long ago. Head so hot, body so
cold . . .

She propped herself up and leaned her back against the log where Andy
had sat guard over her. The sun was high, driving the mist off the bare
fields that stretched out in the distance on the other side of the road.

She couldn't remember ever being so thirsty before. She drained the
last drops of water from the canteen Andy had left her. She wiped her
brow, then looked at her hand: soaking wet.

✧   ✧   ✧   ✧   ✧   ✧   ✧   ✧   ✧   ✧   ✧

"Zenobia? Zenobia, is that you?"

Slowly she opened her eyes, then closed them again as the sun almost
blinded her. And felt again a gentle nudge on her shoulder. "Wake up,
Zenobia."

A thin white man with a heavy beard and bloodshot eyes dropped to his
knees beside her. "That's it, Sergeant, put the compress right on her forehead."

The coolness from the damp cloth seemed to spread through her body.
And the man's voice . . . she knew that voice.

"Thank you, Sergeant. Here, Zenobia, take some water, do you good."
He put his hand under her neck and lifted her head so she could drink.

"That you, Massa Kenworthy? How you doing?"

"It's me all right. I'm tolerable well, but you don't seem to be."

"How you find me?"

"I didn't. The sergeant drew my attention to a woman lying here under
the tree, and I came over to take a look."

Zenobia tilted her head so she could see him better. "What you going to
do with me now? Send me back to Jackson?"

"I'm going to get you a wagon and have a couple of my men take you
back up to Clifton. At least you'll have Uncle Dan up there to take care of
you. I'll write out a pass so nobody will bother you. Once you're up there,
you'll be on your own."

He turned to the sergeant. "We'll take a noon break here and move on
in an hour. Get her some hot grub, then leave us alone for a bit. And make
sure the wagon has lots of pine branches. She's a mighty sick gal."

He sat down in the dirt beside her while she ate. "Zenobia, you got swamp fever. Don't reckon I have to tell you how much rest you're going to need once you get back to Clifton."

"I know." She felt like she was burning up.

He shifted his position and picked up a twig, broke off a small piece, and then broke it into two smaller pieces.

"I got some things to tell you, Zenobia, and not much time to do it. I've been thinking a lot about things of late. Not much liking the way I feel about them."

It was hard to hear him over the ringing in her ears.

" . . . anyway, I want you to know that your boy, Luke, is with the Yankees now. I think he's all right. He's hurt, but not bad enough to keep the little hellcat from running. Yankees'll know how to help him. And last I heard, Milly was safe with Pauline over in Louisiana."

"And Joe? You heard anything of him?"

"Heard of him, Zenobia?" The colonel took a deep breath and looked off into the distance. "Why, Joe's been as close to me as I am to you right now. Not more than a week ago, we liked to have killed each other. As a matter of fact, he did kill my horse."

Blood rushed to Zenobia's head, now pounding so badly she couldn't tell if the ringing had stopped or not. Joe had been so near?

"He's a soldier now, a sergeant in the Yankee cavalry—and I don't mind telling you that he's a handful when he's in battle. Don't reckon I've seen many his equal in this war."

A *sergeant!* "From what Joe told me, you and him been fighting from the time you was little."

The colonel laughed. "True enough, Zenobia, true enough. And you'd think we'd have learned to live peaceable once we grew up, but it's not like that. Hell, I guess we both got a kick out of having at each other out on that battlefield last week, and neither one of us would have hesitated to kill the other if we'd gotten the chance. That's the way it is out there . . ."

"You mens been through a lot, Massa."

"I have, for sure. What I want more than anything now is a good night's sleep. And maybe a chance to go to a church all by myself. Remember the stone chapel up at Clifton? I tell you, some of the things we've had to do to survive, I need to . . . There's nothing like a long and serious conversation with the Lord."

He was talking just like she should understand him, know how much hurt he felt. Maybe that happened when sudden-like you run into somebody you ain't seen for a long time and they from your same home place. Even if it was a darky you'd never had much use for.

He looked at his watch and hollered over to the sergeant. "Fifteen minutes!" Then he turned back to Zenobia. "And Cally, the pretty little girl with those black eyes, where is she?"

Zenobia tried to tell him. Couldn't.

"I'm so, so sorry." He reached down and took her hands, not bothering to wipe away a tear on his own cheek.

✿   ✿   ✿   ✿   ✿   ✿   ✿   ✿   ✿   ✿

A half hour later, Zenobia was on her way back to Clifton. As night fell, they drove her up to a shack. An old colored man came out, lantern in hand.

"You Uncle Dan?"

"Yes, sir!"

"Colonel Kenworthy sent this woman for you to take care of. She's sick. Here, put the lantern down and come give us a hand."

"Wait a minute, " Uncle Dan said. "I got to clean off a pallet and lay some fresh straw down for to make her an easy lying place."

The three men gently transferred her to the newly made pallet. Just before they left, one of the soldiers handed Uncle Dan some Yankee greenbacks.

"Use this to buy food and medicine for her. Courtesy of the colonel."

✿   ✿   ✿   ✿   ✿   ✿   ✿   ✿   ✿   ✿

Once they were gone, Uncle Dan hung the lantern up by the door and sat down by her side.

"Baby child, I'm so glad they brought you back here so's I can watch over you. What you need is to have some of my bark tea and some mush. Make you feel better, you just wait and see. Mmm-h*mmm*."

He got up and started collecting things for cooking outside over the fire.

He returned with a steaming bowl of porridge and a cup filled to the brim with his special medicine.

"Here, take this, baby child."

Zenobia ate and drank, and whether it was that or being off the hard ground after so long, she did feel a little better.

"Uncle Dan? What happened to Brother Drayton? I got to know."

He stared down at the floor for a long moment before he looked back at her.

"Oh, he didn't suffer too long. Six grayboys shot him, still he managed to kill one of them before he died. A right brave man, according to my way of thinking. Some of the niggers come out of the bush the next day, and we buried him."

Zenobia propped herself up on one elbow. "Is there something on your mind, something else you want to tell me about what happened to Brother Drayton?"

"Ain't I always treated everybody right? Ain't I always tried to do the right thing?" He was rubbing his hands together.

"You have. None could fault you."

A tear rolled down his cheek. "Zee, I is an old man. Gets confused sometimes . . ." He was bent over, head almost to the ground, not looking at her anymore.

He'd turned Joe over to the Rebs and betrayed Drayton, sent two women and two children down the river without a man to protect them. Could she forgive him? She looked at his white head bent over like so many times in the past, remembered all the guns and whips and dogs. And his wife, Aunt Sarah, sold off by Massa many years ago. All those long hurtful years without her . . .

She laid her hand gently on his shoulder. "Well . . . don't worry yourself, Uncle. The good Lord knows what's in your heart, reckon I do, too. Where did you bury Brother Drayton?"

"Up aside Cally."

"Oh, if I could only get up from here and go up there on that hill and pray a minute. If I had the strength . . ."

"I goes up there every week and prays for her and him . . . and when we got flowers, I puts them up there. You know I loved that child something awful." He smiled. "I'd be standing there with a lot of other people and she'd walk right up to me and take my hand, yes she would! Out of all them standing there, she'd come right up to me." He saw the look on her face and laughed. "Guess I done told you that a time or two before. Yessir, I'se a old man . . . a foolish old man."

He took her hand. "Now, you got to sleep, get your health and strength back. Swamp fever be a powerful foe."

Zenobia began to shake. "Could I trouble you for another blanket, Uncle?"

"I ain't got no more, Zee, but I'll cover you with my coat. Now you go on to sleep, child." He began to sing softly.

> *"There is a balm*
> *In Gilead*
> *To make the wounded whole*
> *There is a balm*
> *In Gilead*
> *To heal the sin-sick soul!"*

✿   ✿   ✿   ✿   ✿   ✿   ✿   ✿   ✿   ✿   ✿

A warm Sunday afternoon in early spring. Massa and Miss Sue had let all the folk worship with the whites that morning, sitting right outside on the colored folks' porch while the minister preached the gospel. They walked back to the quarters, singing and shouting and having a fine time in the Lord's name. Then, after a good Sunday dinner, she and Joe left the children with Aunt Garry and walked hand in hand up to Someday.

"Zee, do you know how glad I get when I wakes up in the morning and see your face next to mine? It makes up for a whole lot of pain."

Far in the distance, she could see where the river curved down toward Yazoo City. The birds were singing in the trees that spring day with the air still light and fresh, not heavy and damp the way it got in the high summer.

"I know," she said. "And how you think I could live this life of ours if it wasn't for knowing that you're always there to take me in your arms."

She shivered as he put his arm around her and brushed his fingers against her breast, loved it a little with his fingers, right through her yellow blouse.

"Let's lay down here, baby, right in the soft grass."

It felt so good when he touched her, rubbed his fingers back and forth so slowly against her skin. She liked that about him, that he took his time loving her.

"Joe, I—"

He said "Shush" and put a finger against her mouth, kissed it and talked to her body with his gentle, slow-moving fingers . . .

❉   ❉   ❉   ❉   ❉   ❉   ❉   ❉   ❉   ❉   ❉

Wasn't till later in the afternoon, lying warm in his arms, that she turned her head toward the river.

"See that path down there?" she said. "I want to go down it a little ways. Can we?"

They meandered hand in hand along the bank.

"Joe, you been way down there riding horses for Massa in them races. Where do this river go?"

"To the Mississippi."

She squeezed his arm. "And then where?"

He grinned. "Straight on down to New Orleans."

"And then?"

He stopped and thought for a minute.

"Into the Atlantic Ocean, I guess."

"Joe, you ever seen the ocean?"

"A couple of times."

"Do the ocean go to Africa?"

He just looked at her.

"I want to know. Do it go to Africa?"

"I suppose. What's got into you, Zee?"

"Did you ever want to be a fish?"

"Now, that's enough!" He swatted her on the bottom and laughed.

"No, wait. Listen." She ran out a few paces ahead of him and was walking backward now with her black skirt swirling around in that way she knew made men stop and watch her as she went around the quarters of a Sunday morning. "If you was a fish, you could swim right down this river, into the Mississippi, past New Orleans, all the way to the ocean, then go into the deep blue sea, and swim anywhere you wanted to, anywhere . . ." She clapped her hands and shouted. "Anywhere! I know it!"

❀   ❀   ❀   ❀   ❀   ❀   ❀   ❀   ❀   ❀   ❀

"Here, Zenobia, drink you some of this." Uncle Dan lifted her head with one hand, brought the cup to her lips with the other. "You must of been dreaming, baby child, now you . . . Zenobia?"

Very gently, he eased her head back down.

CHAPTER TWENTY-ONE

PAULINE awoke early that morning, sat up, and slowly rubbed the sleep out of her eyes. When she realized how high the sun was, she all but leapt out of the bed. The hogs! They should have been fed by now. Then she spied the long white dress laid out on a chair, smiled, and lay back down for a few moments. There'd be no feeding of the animals for her today—

What would Miss Dorothy think if she knew?

Hard to believe she'd been gone almost two months already. The patrollers in the area made a habit of stopping in now and then, but each time Woodson had been able to get everybody into hiding. And since Pauline had the proper papers to run the place, nothing had happened so far.

A soft knock came at the door of her room.

"Auntie?"

Must be Milly. The door creaked, then her dear face appeared, eyes sparkly with excitement. Well, a seventeen-year-old girl on the morning of a festive occasion *ought* to be excited.

"Can I come in?"

"Of course, baby."

"Oh, how pretty it looks!" Milly clapped her hands. "How did you make something so beautiful out of those old dresses?"

"Oh, there's enough fancy stuff up there in the attic to make wedding dresses for plenty more women—none of it good for anything else. Now let's have a look at *you*. Turn around."

Milly pirouetted and made a little bow.

"Good gracious, honey, you're so pretty you're going to have to beat the boys off with a stick."

Milly giggled. She had a sweet and lovely face, but it was the way she carried herself that drew your attention. She was Zenobia's daughter all right.

Milly had left the door open and the odors of baked sweet potatoes, ham, black-eyed peas, and apple pies all mingled and drifted upstairs. They were going to dine in style to mark this special Christmas and her wedding day. Even going to have biscuits!

Milly sat down on the bed and helped Pauline finish arranging her headdress.

"Auntie, I've been thinking . . ."

"Yes, honey?"

"When all this war is over, and the Yankees come . . . do you think you and Mr. Woodson can come back and live with us all over at Clifton, or someplace? You know, so everybody could be together?"

It would be good to live once again where she could see her darling brother Joe, every day.

"We'll just have to see about that when the time comes. Right now, why don't you run and get Ann and Jill. It's almost time for us to march in."

❖   ❖   ❖   ❖   ❖   ❖   ❖   ❖   ❖   ❖   ❖

Pauline stood at the top of the stairs with Milly and the two little girls and looked down. A small table covered with a white cloth had been dragged to the middle of the living room. On it were two red candles; in front of the table was the big bearskin rug. A fire burned in the fireplace, and stockings stuffed with apples and homemade toys and gifts hung from the mantel. The tree Woodson had brought in was decorated with strings of berries and pine cones and any little pretty shiny thing the children could find. Pine boughs crisscrossed the mantelpiece.

The living room was so big it didn't seem as if forty people were really standing down there waiting for her, all looking up as she started down the stairs, then clapping and stomping as they parted to make an aisle for her. Everybody had dressed up their best for this day. For most of them it had been years since they'd had anything new to wear, but they'd washed and scrubbed and smoothed what they had till everything was neat and clean.

Tears came to her eyes as she took in the beauty of the many tones of color in the faces smiling at her: coffee brown, honey yellow, mahogany red, plum black, earth brown—colors made more vibrant by the glow of the fire.

And there next to old Preacher Williamson was Woodson, the only one not smiling. He looked serious and proud. Well, *she* felt proud to be loved by this dear good man.

When the words had been spoken and the vows exchanged, two people held the broomstick so Woodson and Pauline could jump over it together.

"I now pronounces you man and wife."

They kissed. And at last Woodson smiled and kept on smiling while they ate and drank—there was good corn liquor aplenty. When the fiddler began to play, Woodson grabbed Pauline's hands and they joined the men and the women lining up in rows facing each other. After the women curtsied, the men bowed and began to clap their hands and shuffle their feet in time to the music.

> *Come along little children, come along*
> *While the moon is shining bright*
> *Get on board, down the river shore*
> *Gonna' raise ruckus tonight*
> *Now my old mistress promise me*
> *Raise ruckus tonight!*
> *That when she died, she'd set me free*
> *Raise ruckus tonight!*
> *She lived so long that her head got bald*
> *Raise ruckus tonight!*
> *I thought she wasn't gonna die at all*
> *Raise ruckus tonight!*
> *Oh, come along little children, come along . . .*

Woodson bowed in front of Pauline, offered his arm, and began the promenade down the aisle between the lines of the men and women. He could really do that walk! He took a step and then jerked his face to the side, as if he were saying, "See that?" Then he stuck one leg out, bent it in mid-air, and twirled it around. Every time he did that, the folks would break out shouting and clapping and Pauline would look at him in mock amazement.

Then it was her turn. She'd shake her hips a little, throw her shoulders back, move her arms to and fro and wave her hands in the air at the same time. It took them a long while to get from one end of the row to the other, but when they finished, everybody clapped and started strutting their stuff right behind them, little children at the rear.

"Make your circle!" cried the fiddler. He sat in a rocking chair, a jug of whiskey at his feet.

Woodson led the way, going around and around that great big room. The fiddler was feeling so good, he walked right into the middle of the circle, found the prettiest girl he could—Milly, of course—and played along right beside her, making a sweet and special sound with the bow every time she twisted that young body of hers.

It was the wildest dance that Pauline, raised as a house slave, had ever seen. They'd dance all in step together, then freeze their bodies, shake their shoulders, take another step, shake their hips, take another step, clap their hands together—then everybody would twirl around in place, and start all over again.

For a while it looked as if they'd never get tired, but once a few started finding somewhere to rest, it wasn't long before all of them were sitting in various places around the room. A big man who was sweating and out of breath from the dancing held up his hands. "You all be quiet a minute, I wants you to hear this little thing I made up:

> "Run, boy, run, de pat'roller' ketch yo'
> Run, boy, run, it's almos' day.
> Dat boy run, dat boy flew,
> Dat boy tore his shirt in two.
> Dat boy cried, dat boy lied,
> Dat boy shook his old fat side,
> Run, boy, run, it's almos' day."

They clapped and hollered, "More! More!" but Preacher Williamson broke in.

"Well, it's getting on to midnight now and we done had us a real good time. Tomorrow we be up and back to work, fixing up this place. It's the only home we got now and we going to keep it nice. Besides, Woodson and Pauline, they got to go to bed. Come forward here so you can face the folks and tell them good night."

Pauline walked up with Woodson, then turned around and looked right down the length of the room. "At the window!" she shouted.

A white man's face was pressed right against the glass at the far end. His eyes were big and protruding, and his beard long and bushy.

Woodson was already on his way out the door, followed by most of the men. By the time Pauline got outside, the only trace of the man was the sound of hooves fading into the distance.

"We'd never catch him in the dark with that head start," Woodson said. "Best thing for us to do is get ready for an attack. Either that or go back out into the woods. And with all these women and children—no, we'd freeze to death."

They worked the night through. Boarded over the windows, leaving openings so the men could fire through them with what muskets and carbines they had. Put great big tubs of water in the middle of the floor in case the assailants—whoever they turned out to be—decided to burn them out. Got all the livestock into a stockade at the rear of the house. Stored powder and cartridges near the windows. And brought hay in to make pallets. From now on everybody would sleep in the big house.

They set up firing posts to cover most approaches to the house and brought the pickets in closer. That would shorten their warning time, but out in the woods they'd be easy pickings for Rebs or deserters.

Toward dawn Woodson sat down with Pauline and took her hands in his.

"I'm going to mount up and do a little scouting around the neighborhood, me and Josh." He smiled and kissed her. "Not exactly what I had in mind for our wedding night."

✿   ✿   ✿   ✿   ✿   ✿   ✿   ✿   ✿   ✿   ✿

When they returned that afternoon, he called everyone together. "We didn't see no sign of large forces out there, and the tracks of last night's visitor go off into the woods. Right now it don't look like we're in danger. Not tonight or maybe even tomorrow night. But that one white man knows we all here and they will surely come to capture us sooner or later. Josh, here, he's volunteered to take a horse and try to get through to the Yankees and tell them where we are."

He reached down and picked up a little boy who'd been pulling on his pant leg. "That's about the best we can do for now, so I want you all to pray Josh gets through. You know how to pray, little man?" He looked down at the boy, who answered by folding his tiny fingers together and leaning his head against Woodson's chest.

Woodson handed him over to Pauline and put his arms around her and Milly.

"We family here, and we going to live together or die together."

Pauline said,"Amen," and heard a chorus of Amens behind her.

❖   ❖   ❖   ❖   ❖   ❖   ❖   ❖   ❖   ❖   ❖

Richard Kenworthy didn't like these bad feelings down inside him, but since the fall of Savannah and the report of the death in action of Clint Adams, he didn't seem to have any other kind. Now the Yankees were headed into the Carolinas. But the thing he couldn't stop thinking about was that he had failed to protect his own home. He went over and over it in his mind. That a nigger cavalry sergeant could go into his house and sleep under the same roof with his wife and children—it was just too much for a man to bear.

That and so much else didn't make sense. He'd marched off to war so proud and happy to protect the Southern way of life, and the very act of protecting that great and wonderful culture—the highest social form Western civilization had yet devised—had resulted in its destruction. And darky soldiers in his living room, giving his sweet Sue orders, putting their hands on her to restrain her! Somebody would have to pay for all this.

So it was with mixed feelings that he received orders—now that he could ride again—to report over in Louisiana to suppress the activities of the Negroes on some of the plantations. General Forrest assigning him to General Harrison's command over there was an admission that the Confederate cause in Mississippi was finished, and it was worrisome to have to leave Sue and the children so vulnerable. But one of the plantations in question was his sister's place.

Which meant he'd be able to kill two birds with one stone. Destroy some nigger enemy and renew his relationship with Pauline. Milly would be there, too. Joe's kid. The bastard had carried off most of his hard-earned money. It was stealing, never mind his damned Yankee receipt. And after he'd left Uncle Dan ten dollars for Zenobia!

   ✿   ✿   ✿   ✿   ✿   ✿   ✿   ✿   ✿   ✿   ✿

He specifically requested the assignment to the Cannon plantation when he arrived in Louisiana.

The general handed him the report from the scout about the Christmas party. "It's been a while, but the darkies are probably still up there. Get to it as soon as you can and get on back here. There's a Union cavalry detachment on its way down from the Arkansas border."

"It'll take me a few days to get together some horses and equipment and food. And the men are in pitiful shape. Rags for shoes."

"Yes, Grierson's boys did a job on the shoe factory over there. One of those regiments—the Third Colored—is on its way down here."

Richard slapped his gauntlet on the edge of the general's desk. "As soon as I destroy that band up at my sister's place, I'll be back to give you a hand with the Third. I've got a few scores to settle with them."

"So do a lot of people, Colonel. Montgomery still hasn't stopped complaining about that nigger who stole his horse."

   ✿   ✿   ✿   ✿   ✿   ✿   ✿   ✿   ✿   ✿   ✿

"Whoa, Princess," Joe said. "We got to wait a bit, see if Howerton can get over first."

The Third was in northern Louisiana, down near Oak Ridge, and wet as they could be. Joe looked at his hands, saw they were still trembling. God, he hoped nobody noticed. Not only that, but they were wrinkled like prunes. His and everybody else's in the regiment.

This time out, the main enemy had been the water. Some days he'd glance behind him and it would almost look like the men were wading instead of on horseback. All around was nothing but water, and wasn't nothing coming down out of the sky but more of it. The Rebs seemed to have melted away in the rain.

But he was expecting that to change soon.

In the meantime, a courier had come in before they left Memphis and brought word about the folks at the Cannon plantation needing help. Since Milly was there, Colonel Osband had given Joe permission to take a detachment of fifty men and bring everybody back into the Union lines.

Pauline was there too. What a story Luke had told him, about how at the last minute when it seemed like they were going to be sold into Texas, she'd persuaded Miss Cannon to step in and buy them. Luke showed how Pauline had taught him to write his name. Hard to say who was prouder— him or Luke.

What was he going to do when he saw her? He could still close his eyes and remember how happy he'd been when Momma had called him into the hut where she lay under a blanket. "See your baby sister." Before she went off to live in the big house, she'd followed him everywhere, crawling, toddling, walking, and sometimes running after him. Then one day when she was a full-grown woman with a golden brown body, Massa Richard—

"Look at Howerton!" A shout snapped Joe out of his daydream. Howerton had volunteered to try and get across that stream, and it wasn't going to be an easy thing.

He was edging his way down the bank of the river. The water was running fast, and ripples of white were breaking all around the legs of his horse. Logs and branches—all kinds of things—were coming down the stream.

"That's it. Just ease her down," Joe said. "And let her have her head."

Howerton looked back and grinned. "How the hell I'm going to do that the way this water's running?"

"You know how."

All along the bank of the river, the horse soldiers sat cheering him on.

"You bad enough to do it, man!"

"Sarge say there some fine young womens just a-waiting to sing you to sleep on the other side!"

"Look out!" Joe cried.

Howerton was dead in the middle of the stream, and a big-assed log was running straight at him. The horse must have seen the log the same time Joe did, because it almost looked like it tried to raise its legs out of the water to miss the thing. Horse and rider fell sideways and were swept away. Wasn't nothing anybody could do to help them. One minute they were there and the next, nothing but rushing water.

Everybody was quiet for a few seconds, and then all the men were looking at Joe.

❖   ❖   ❖   ❖   ❖   ❖   ❖   ❖   ❖   ❖   ❖

Should he risk their lives and keep trying to cross the river? Every one of the men in his command knew that the assignment had been given to them because Milly and Pauline were up there.

Logan, one of the best horsemen in the Third, rode up. "I'm next."

This time, almost as if the men thought their talking had jinxed Howerton, they kept silent. Except for Tucker, who said, "My turn next." Joe looked over his shoulder and saw eight men ready to try if Logan failed. Just when he had decided that if Logan didn't make it, he'd have to find another ford.

Logan was about halfway across when he stopped. He looked back at Joe, then bent down over the horse's mane and whispered something to her. She threw her head back like maybe she'd heard something flattering. One step, two steps, three steps, then she was out of the stream and on the bank, shaking the water off her mane.

"Form into a column, men!"

They lost a few weapons and some supplies, but in a little more than an hour everybody was safely across.

By the reckoning of the Union soldier who'd come down from the plantation, they were still about twelve miles away. With all this mud and water, it was going to seem more like twenty-five—and the crossing had taken a lot out of the men.

About a mile away was an abandoned plantation where they'd be able to warm themselves and bed down for the night. Just what they all needed.

CHAPTER TWENTY-TWO

RICHARD Kenworthy looked behind him at the ragged column that called itself the Fifth Louisiana Cavalry. This was a regiment? Why, it was barely more than a few squads. Half the men on mules, some walking, not a one of them in a real uniform. Nothing about them brought to mind the fiery-eyed legions that had set out just a few years ago on high-stepping mounts to whip the Yankees to a pulp. They were subsisting on wet Yankee hardtack, rotten and full of weevils. Enough to turn a healthy man's stomach, and given the condition of these men, it was worse than no food at all.

But, by God, when he'd asked for volunteers, seventy-five men had stepped forward. If there was one thing that could still stir them, make the poor devils forget their aching bellies, it was niggers with arms. Couldn't abide the thought any more than he could.

About four miles away from Dorothy's plantation he began to recognize the countryside, though this barren land was another sorry imitation of what had been. Close his eyes and he could see the rows and rows of white cotton stretching as far as the eye could see, line after line of darkies, backs bent, putting boll after boll into the sacks over their shoulders. Dorothy and the colonel and Sue on the veranda in the evening, children playing games. A good cigar, a fine wine, and the darkies' music . . .

A blast of wind blew stinging rain into his face. He looked around for Captain Brunson.

"With night coming on, and all this mud and wet, we'd best bivouac out here. Tell Sergeant Barclay to have the men up early and ready to hit them just about daybreak. And have the scouts report back to me as soon as they get in."

"Begging the colonel's pardon," Brunson said, "but it's going to be rough sleeping out here. Half of the men are already hacking and coughing, and some of them are coming down with swamp fever. I'd just as soon we pushed on and took the place tonight. They're nothing but some nigger slaves that have never had any military training. We could just walk in and take them, get us a good night's sleep."

Richard thought about the Big Black River Bridge and Franklin. "No, we'll do it my way."

✼   ✼   ✼   ✼   ✼   ✼   ✼   ✼   ✼   ✼   ✼

The captain was right about the conditions. Wretched. But the men were veterans, and Kenworthy knew they'd make the best of it. Somehow or other, they got a few fires going and set up some lean-tos. They'd make it, all right.

Just when he was about to fall off to sleep, the two scouts who'd been watching the plantation all day returned.

"Colonel, them niggers got pickets out all around that old place. Must be about forty or fifty of 'em living there."

"How many men in all, you reckon?"

"I'd say about twenty, the rest is women and children. No way to tell what's stashed in the house, but it don't look like they got many weapons—mostly old muskets and pikes. Won't be a problem at all."

"Well done. Get what sleep you can and we'll go in at first light. Better quarters tomorrow night, men!"

✼   ✼   ✼   ✼   ✼   ✼   ✼   ✼   ✼   ✼   ✼

Just before the sky lightened the next morning, the detachment was on the move. It was still raining hard, but the wind had diminished, and it had gotten a little warmer. As a matter of fact, here on the third day of February 1865, you could almost feel a touch of spring in the air.

As day broke, they approached the outskirts of the plantation. Richard

watched the men form into four squads—one for each side of the place—
and disappear into the near dark. He had kept the command of one squad
himself. They would face the front of the big house.

"Sergeant Barclay!"

"Sir!"

"We've got about fifteen minutes left. Have the men dismount and follow me."

Five men were left behind as horse holders. How strange to be approaching his sister's plantation with a group of soldiers to take it back
from a bunch of Negroes.

A row of hedges about thirty yards away grew around the perimeter of
the place. Perfect concealment for the attack. But to reach them, they
were going to have to walk down an approach road with woods on both
sides.

He motioned the men forward. They crouched down and just as they
began to move a volley of shots rang out.

"Son of a bitch! They bushwhacked us."

Two men fell. The rest quickly flushed out the woods on the sides, but
whoever had done the shooting had made their retreat through the
hedges. Probably running for the refuge of the house.

Shouts coming from the other squads confirmed that they had encoun-
tered similar resistance.

"Come on, men! "

Richard waved them into position behind the hedges, sent a runner
with orders for the others to hold their fire, then had a man approach the
house with a white flag.

   ✿   ✿   ✿   ✿   ✿   ✿   ✿   ✿   ✿   ✿

"Don't you go out there, Woodson," Pauline said. "They just want to kill
you."

"He says Colonel Kenworthy himself wants to parley with me."

Pauline's heart sank. "Him! Oh no, you mustn't go, he's ruthless."

"You see up there?" Woodson pointed to where two men stood on
boxes, their muskets aimed through the firing holes in the window frames.
"Anything happen to me, they'll shoot him dead. If nothing else, it'll gain

us some time. What with all this flooding and stuff, it may be taking an ex-
tra-long time for the Yankees to get here."

"If they even coming. You don't know that Josh got through."

"Pauline." He touched her mouth, smoothing her bottom lip with his
fingertips until she stopped biting it. "I'll be back in a little while."

❖   ❖   ❖   ❖   ❖   ❖   ❖   ❖   ❖   ❖   ❖

Milly stood with her at a peephole and watched Woodson and another
man bearing a white flag march out to meet Richard. They talked for
about five minutes, then Woodson came back inside.

"See, nothing happened. The colonel says if we surrender, he'll give us
safe conduct to the Yankee lines, even give us an escort to see we get there
safe. He carried on about how this the property of Colonel and Mrs. Cannon—'not a refuge for slaves.' Says the only thing they want is for us to
leave."

"What did you tell him?" Pauline asked.

The others had all crowded close.

"That we'd think about it."

"How much time?"

"Fifteen minutes, we all come out with our hands in the air, or they're
coming in here after us."

Everybody was quiet for a moment, then milling around, trying to talk it
out, see what was best to do.

Woodson called Pauline aside. "I'm have to tell you this—he offered
safe conduct to you and Milly even if nobody else surrenders."

She took Woodson's hand and called for silence.

"My husband just told me something I think you all ought to know—
Colonel Kenworthy has offered to let me and Milly go free no matter what
happens to the rest of you."

Milly's head was shaking back and forth.

"But I know that man out there. You have to do what you think is right,
but I have to tell you he can't be trusted and I, for one, will die before I
put myself in his hands again. Those white folks like to talk about how they
died at the Alamo—well, I pray it doesn't come to that, but we free now
and the only way to stay that way is to fight."

"Thank you, sister!"

"Tell the truth!"

"Amen!"

"Then let's get to work!" Woodson picked up a musket and walked over to where the ammunition tables had been set up. "We have to prepare the welcome table for Colonel Kenworthy and his men. Praise the Lord!"

❧   ❧   ❧   ❧   ❧   ❧   ❧   ❧   ❧   ❧   ❧

Joe looked out on the morning of February 3. Wasn't it ever going to stop raining? Josh had found them a good place to stay, and they'd dried off some during the night. The men wouldn't be too eager to get back out there in the wet, but it was time to get moving. Be lucky to make the plantation by nightfall with the roads the way they were.

"Send Josh out with the scouts, Zack. Give them the best mounts we've got—only way they going to deal with all this mud. If the way is clear, tell Josh to ride on in and let the people know we on our way."

The mud was so deep it hurt to see the men try to stay in column. The horses just sank in the imprints made by the mounts in front of them. Soon they were spread out over the fields on either side of the road.

By noontime, they'd made about six miles. Joe called a halt to feed the men and rest the horses. It was still pelting rain, and they were as wet and miserable as before. But when Logan, one of the scouts, came into view way down the road waving his hand, Joe was up immediately.

"A mile or so down the road, there's a crossroads," Logan said. "About fifty cavalry men come out of it. They got to be somewhere between us and the plantation. Jones and Jenkins have gone ahead with Josh."

"Boots and Saddles!" Joe didn't need to hear any more. "Good work, Logan. Zack will give you three more men and you'll make us an advance guard. Get going." He turned to Zack. "Flankers out. Get the men dismounted. I think we'll make better time that way."

It was definitely better for the horses, though the men soon had mud all over them. The column was moving faster, but no matter how they did it, he didn't see how they could get there before evening time. He tried not to think of Milly or Pauline—they had to be left in God's hands for now.

Logan was back at four. "Sir, we got firing in our front. Jenkins got down to the plantation and met back up with us about two miles down the road. Rebs all around it, and not much shooting coming from the plantation."

"How much further for us?"

Logan looked back over Joe's shoulder at the slow-moving column of men.

"I'd say—a two-hour march, sir."

   ✿   ✿   ✿   ✿   ✿   ✿   ✿   ✿   ✿   ✿

"Water, please." A mulatto man, bleeding badly from his stomach, lay on the floor looking up at Pauline.

"It will only hurt you. Here." She put a cloth into a bucket of water, wrung it out, then wiped his forehead.

She looked around the great room. Every last one of the chandeliers was shattered, and shards of glass lay all over the floor. Where boards had been nailed over the windows there was mostly nothing but splinters. Knots of little children lay flat on their bellies in a far corner of the room. One toddler, about three years old, held both hands over his ears. The women were busy with what few wounded there were.

About fifteen men had already been killed and their bodies piled in the corner of the room farthest from the children. Some women had picked up weapons—they had trained and drilled right alongside the men since Christmas. A total of eight folks were left to defend the whole house. Milly had been loading muskets, but with the ammunition almost gone now, there was little for her to do except help minister to the wounded and shepherd the children up the stairs. The firing had ceased for the moment, so she accomplished the latter task with haste. When she'd seen to it that all of the young ones were temporarily safe above, she returned to Woodson's side. He was putting the last loads into his revolver.

"I guess they'll be storming the place pretty soon. They soldiers, they know we down low now."

"Let them come," Pauline said.

"I just don't know what happened to Josh. I was sure he'd get through."

"We's just little people," said a man seated on the floor. "And we colored, don't count for nothing with nobody."

Woodson shrugged his shoulders. "Still, I thought—"

"Hello there in the house!"

That was Richard shouting out there. She'd recognize that deep, mellow voice of his anywhere.

"Hello, I say! *Pauline,* it's me, Richard!"

Woodson put his arm around her shoulder.

"Come on out, you and Milly. You and the rest of the women and children don't have to die in there."

Pauline took Woodson's revolver, cocked it, and walked up to the door.

"I didn't hear you good, Richard."

When he stepped out from behind the bush and cupped his hands to call to her, she fired.

"Damn you, you black bitch! We're coming in after you."

She slammed the door and leapt aside just in time. Bullets ripped through the door and into the staircase. And then they were tearing into the house from all directions.

Pauline had never heard such a racket in her life. It sounded although somebody had lit a bunch of rockets and thrown them into a room. She wanted to cover her ears like that little child had, but her place was next to Woodson.

Through a crack in the last intact board, she saw about twenty-five of them, running across the lawn, spread out a few feet apart. What a sight they were—hair below their shoulders, bearded, ragged, ugly, and wet, screaming their lungs out. Richard was leading them, his face still handsome but otherwise looking hardly better than the rest.

She took aim with the pistol, sighted along the barrel. Easy, now . . . there he was, right in the sights—

Missed him again!

Seemed as if she could hear her heart thumping wildly over the thud of feet on the porch, the splintering sound of wood as they pounded the butts of their guns against the front door.

"Upstairs, everybody." Woodson said. "They got to come up one by one, we can hold out a little bit longer. Use those muskets like clubs, when the ammunition is all gone."

Only six able-bodied persons remained. The floor was slippery with blood; the moans and cries of the wounded mingled with the sounds of exploding weapons, of breaking glass and cracking wood.

Pauline lay down beside Woodson at the top of the stairs, behind some desks and night tables taken from Dorothy's bedroom. She grasped his hand.

"Kiss me," she said. "Just one more time."

His kiss was sweet and long—enough for her to wish for what might have been, what—

A crash louder than anything yet shook the house. Must be the huge front door.

"Here they come!" Woodson said. "But praise the Lord, we going to die free."

❖   ❖   ❖   ❖   ❖   ❖   ❖   ❖   ❖   ❖   ❖

Richard was the first one through the doorway. They came in low, firing as they moved.

"Cease fire!" he called when he saw that the great room was empty.

In the stillness that followed they could hear babies crying. Sergeant Barclay pointed up toward the landing. With his revolver, Richard motioned the men up the stairs.

They were about halfway when Pauline and a big nigger sprang up, shotguns firing in unison. Two of the men on the stairway tumbled backward down the stairs.

Richard fired, but he would never know if it was a bullet from his gun that killed her. The other men were firing, too, and Pauline and the man staggered under the fire and collapsed together on the spot. Richard stood looking at her until fire from somewhere above brought him to his senses and they stormed the stairs, killing two more niggers at the top.

Once upstairs, they heard the sound of children crying again. It was coming from a room at the far end of the hall—Dorothy's old bedroom. At a signal from Richard, Sergeant Barclay cautiously made his way down the hall and kicked the door open. He looked, then turned around and beck-oned.

"Secure the house," Richard said, then walked down the hall to his sis-ter's room.

About a dozen nigger children ranging in age from about three to four-teen were huddled together with fifteen or so women. Most of them were staring at him, the whites of their eyes wide. He studied each face and picked out Joe's girl, who was crying without making a sound.

"Milly? Come here, child." He took her by the hand and pulled her away from the others. Why, she was almost a woman! Her hand was soft and her shoulders, too, even though he felt them tighten when he put his arm around her.

"Now, then, there's nothing to worry about. All the shooting's over. We'll get everything cleaned up and then get you to a safe place. In the mean-time you all just stay up here, nobody's going to hurt you."

By the time he got back downstairs Sergeant Barclay was waiting for further orders.

"First thing to do is get all those bodies out of my sister's living room. And send someone up to choose a few women to fix us something hot to eat. The rest of them—take them down to the slave cabins and lock them in. All except the one named Milly. Leave her upstairs under guard."

Some soldiers were already at the top of the stairs disposing of the bod-ies. He waited at the bottom and stopped the one who was carrying Pauline.

"No, wait a second."

She was beautiful, even in death. Could it be that he had really and truly loved her? Loved a nigger woman? He reached down and closed her eyes, then took her in his arms and carried her out the front door. When he had walked a ways, he called two of his men over and handed her body over to them.

"Bury her way over there, near where those rosebushes are."

He sat down on the front porch, unmindful of the falling rain, and watched. Half an hour later, he walked to the door and called for Barclay.

"Come outside for a minute."

They stepped back onto the porch.

"We've neither the time nor the supplies to deal with these nigger captives. We'll eat, enjoy ourselves a little bit afterwards, then lock them back up in the cabins and set the shacks on fire."

Teach niggers to take over other people's property!

Somebody had to pay.

❀   ❀   ❀   ❀   ❀   ❀   ❀   ❀   ❀   ❀   ❀

The firing had ceased before Joe's detachment got within earshot of the plantation. Minutes later, the scouts he sent out were back. The Rebs had taken the big house, and it looked as though they had killed all the men. Right now they were eating and drinking and playing around with a few of the women. They had locked the rest in the slave cabins with some children. There was a guard down at the slave cabins, but they hadn't posted any sentries.

Joe listened carefully, forcing himself to remain calm. The fate of his outfit depended on him. He called Zack and the other sergeants over and sketched out the plan of assault—kill the guard down at the cabins, then storm the house Third Cavalry style.

"Careful now, we don't want to hit any of our folks. Use the sabers as much as possible."

❀   ❀   ❀   ❀   ❀   ❀   ❀   ❀   ❀   ❀   ❀

He and Zack crept up on their bellies through the mud. From the sound of their singing he figured there must be about thirty of them in there. Having themselves a fine old time.

Joe nodded at Zack. The men took up positions at the doors and windows to await the assault signal, the firing of Joe's carbine. Joe slipped up to a window.

The first thing he saw when he peeked in the window was Kenworthy, with a woman in his lap. His pistol was laid out right on the table in front of him. The fucking bastard had a bottle of wine in one hand and the other—Oh, my God, that's *Milly* in his lap!

He stepped back from the window, took a position in front of the door. He kicked the shattered door open and fired away with his carbine.

Out of the corner of his eye, he saw Milly fall to the floor and bolt away behind a big overstuffed chair. Good girl.

In the second Joe stood watching her, Kenworthy had grabbed a carbine and was running up the stairs, firing as he went.

Rest of the poor drunken fools never had a chance. Not that they deserved one. One man on the sofa with his hand up a black woman's dress reached for his shotgun. Zack shot his hand off before it ever touched that gun. Rebs were running back and forth like the trapped rats they were. Any way they turned there was another big black man with a saber cutting into their arms, legs, bellies, necks.

Five of them who managed to get to their weapons dropped them, backed into a corner and begged for mercy. What did they know about mercy?

    ✫   ✫   ✫   ✫   ✫   ✫   ✫   ✫   ✫   ✫

"Prisoners!" Joe shouted. "Take cover, men, and cease fire."

The only one still armed was Colonel Richard Kenworthy, crouched at the top of the stairs with his carbine held crosswise against his chest. His eyes were red but still strong and mean, like he weren't licked yet. When he looked down and saw who was standing there, he shook his head slowly and the damnedest grin spread over his face.

"Well, now, it's come to this, hasn't it?"

"Sure has, Colonel."

"You don't intend to take me alive, do you?"

"Now, that depends on you. I done imagined killing you many a time, but I'm a soldier now and I obeys the rules. And lately seems like I'm losing my taste for fighting and killing. You the only one left, and if you put the gun down—"

"I'm tired of all of it, too. And I never meant for Pauline to die, that's a fact."

"You done that, Colonel? You sure enough done killed Pauline?"

"Colonel!" A Reb sergeant pushed his way to the bottom of the stairs and stood next to Joe. He was unarmed, but Zack kept a close eye on him anyway.

"Colonel, sir, please surrender, don't make them kill you!"

Kenworthy made a little bow.

"Sergeant Barclay, it's my deep honor and privilege to have served our

Cause with you and the other brave soldiers there behind you. Please give Mrs. Kenworthy and my children my dearest love. And see to it that my personal effects are conveyed to them. The Yankee sergeant here won't hinder you, I'm sure."

Joe nodded and for a moment nobody said anything.

"Joe, remember the time we treed that mountain jack?"

"I do, sir."

"Weren't those some high good times?"

"They was that."

The colonel looked down at the floor, like he had something heavy on his mind and wanted to think about it for a moment. Then he raised his head and looked Joe directly in the eye again.

"You're one hell of a soldier, you know."

Joe sprang to attention. "Thank you, sir."

"Now come get me!"

It was the strangest thing. Seemed like he took his time standing up in full view, brushing himself off. Only then did he raise his carbine and aim.

And only then did Joe throw the Choctaw knife.

It caught him square in the middle of the chest, and stuck there. He looked down and put both his hands on it like he might try to pull it out. And fell dead still holding it.

Joe walked across the room and wrapped Milly in his arms.

"You safe now, baby. Safe and free."

✧   ✧   ✧   ✧   ✧   ✧   ✧   ✧   ✧   ✧   ✧

In the morning, they dug a ditch for the dead and buried them all together, white and black.

"Going to put this Reb colonel in the same grave with the rest of the folk?" Zack asked.

"He an officer, ain't he? Bury him like one."

✧   ✧   ✧   ✧   ✧   ✧   ✧   ✧   ✧   ✧   ✧

A few hours later, after breakfast, when the column was all ready to move out, Joe walked over to Zack.

"Get going, I'll catch up with you. Me and Milly got something to do."

He took her hand and together they walked over to where the Reb sergeant told him Pauline was buried. The rain hadn't let up, and for once he was glad. He didn't want his daughter to see him crying as much as she was.

At the grave he got down on his knees in the mud with Milly right beside him. How was he going to say good-bye to Pauline, his sweet loving sister and the savior of his children in the dark night of slavery.

"Pauline, you hear me? Me and Milly, we kneeling here beside you, we praying hard for you, and I'm praying special hard you'll forgive me that I didn't get here in time to save you. I surely do wish I could have. But we going to see you over on the other shore. Every day will be Sunday, and Sabbath shall have no end."

He stood up, took his daughter's arm, and sang:

> "*Shine on me!*
> *Shine on me!*"

Milly reached over and wiped the tears from his cheeks, then her dark husky voice joined in.

> "*Let the light*
> *From the lighthouse*
> *Shine on me!*"

❖   ❖   ❖   ❖   ❖   ❖   ❖   ❖   ❖   ❖   ❖

Joe and Betty sat on their favorite hill outside of Vicksburg. Joe kept fingering the paper in his hand. He'd read it again and again, then had Betty read it, too, just to make sure it said that he was honorably discharged at Vicksburg on June 16, 1865. They'd also both read the letter from Captain Stiles about how he was starting a place over in Louisiana and wanted Joe as his top man.

Finally he folded the discharge paper carefully and put it in his shirt pocket. This wasn't going to get any easier, no matter how long he put it off.

"Betty . . ." He got up and stood for a moment with his back to her. "Damn!"

She looked at him but didn't say anything. Just raised her eyebrows and waited.

"I guess there ain't any way to say it good, but I got to do as my conscience tells me, got to do what's best for my children. Search for Zenobia until God tells me it's enough."

He sat back down, knees cradled between his arms. Betty laid her head against his shoulder.

"Think I don't know that? No matter what, Joe, you can go as far as life will take you, but you know I will always love you."

"You some fine woman. Luke and Milly, they done come to love you, too."

She smiled, her dimples pretty as could be. "Those children have been a blessing to have around. They so much like you, I can't help but love them to pieces." She kissed him gently on the cheek. "I've staying on as a volunteer nurse in the army for a while, then who knows where I'll go. You can always find me through them."

"And you can find me through Captain Stiles."

"Everybody going over there with you?"

"Well, not Zack and Lisa Mae. Now they married, they want to try and make it on their own. And Helen's going with them. But Ned, he'll be coming with me and the kids. That boy, he loves Zenobia something fierce."

"When you leaving?"

"Early in the morning. Figure it's a three-day ride from here, what with the kids and all."

"Put your arms around me, darlin'." Betty's eyes were wet. " I ain't going nowhere till I hear from you one way or another. You write me, hear, and let me know."

"I will, soon as I know anything."

✻   ✻   ✻   ✻   ✻   ✻   ✻   ✻   ✻   ✻   ✻

In the morning, Joe and Milly and Luke mounted their horses, then Ned got up behind Luke. The trip seemed long, even in the bright sunshine with the fields green again and the birds singing. And the guns all quiet. But Joe was grateful for the chance to get to know his children once again, to see how each one thought and looked at the world, to see Zenobia's strength in Luke's eyes, and her happy smile in Milly's face. And he laughed out loud when Ned said something that sounded just like Zenobia.

As he passed the places where the Third had fought so hard and where so many of his comrades had fallen, Zenobia seemed closer and closer to his heart. And it seemed like she took his hand when he passed by the spot where Lisa Mae said they'd left her, like she was riding with him. And singing, like she used to early in the morning, when the mist was still out on the field.

> *Oh, who'll go with me to that land?*
> *Who'll go with me to that land?*
> *Who'll go with me to that land where I'm*
>   *bound?*

Throwing her head back, ebony face shiny, eyes crinkling like she knew all about everything . . .

> *Oh, won't you go with me to that land?*

Strong shoulders rising and falling all the way down the cotton row in time with the song.

> *There's no kneeling in that land!*

Could be a quarter mile away from you on the way to the fields, but her voice would rise above all others.

> *Peace and happiness in that land!*

And when the sun got so high and burned down so hard, and the water boy didn't come . . .

> *There is joy in that land!*

Oh, Zenobia was sure enough with Joe and the children all the way up that road in the Yazoo Delta. And still there when Uncle Dan met them and pointed up to Someday, where her body lay in the moist Mississippi earth beside their darling Cally.

> *Where I'm Bound!*

AUTHOR'S NOTE

This book, first and foremost, is a work of fiction. Having said that, I'd like to note that most of the military events described in the book did take place, more or less as the author has described them. A key source for this book is Ed. M. Main's *The Story of the Marches, Battles and Incidents of the Third United States Colored Cavalry,* originally published in 1908 by the Globe Publishing Company, and reprinted in 1970 by Negro Universities Press. I also read each and every one of the Mississippi slave narratives (WPA) as background for the book, in addition to many dozens of other works on the Civil War, the war in the Western Theater, and on black troops in general. I was already well acquainted with the history of slavery, having done research on that subject for one of my previous books, *One More Day's Journey,* and having taught graduate history courses on the subject for many years now.

Ed. M. Main, the author of the book on the Third United States Colored Cavalry, was a major in that unit and drew both from personal knowledge and the *Official Records* for his well-researched regimental history. While devoting much space to his fellow white officers, many of whom had previously served with him in the 4th Illinois Regiment, Major Main had more difficulty in recalling the names of the black soldiers and noncoms who had fought with him. This is understandable, since he had served with the white officers before, and served with the blacks for only a period of two years. Major Main stated that "There were many men in this regiment who performed deeds of heroism entitling them to special men-

tion in the pages, but unfortunately their names cannot now be recalled."
Major Main was born January 1, 1837, and seventy-one years old at the
time of publication of his work.

However, Major or Main did recall the name of one black soldier, Al-
fred Wood, better known in the regiment as "Old Alf," primarily because
he was considered an "oracle, at least in the opinion of his own people."
The major wrote a sixteen-page sketch of the adventures of Old Alf, whom
he called the "Wizard of the Black Regiment" and the "Secret Service of
the Third United States Colored Cavalry." This sketch, containing almost
unbelievable deeds of daring by Old Alf, is the source for most of the personal escapades of Joe Duckett, duly elaborated upon and embellished by
this writer. In addition, Major Main, at another place in his book, detailed
the feat of two black sergeants, Washington Vincent and Isaac Trendall, in
carrying dispatches through to General McArthur. This too became grist
for this fiction writer's mill and part of Joe Duckett's adventures. The big
battles in which the regiment was involved, the most important of which
was the assault on the Big Black River Bridge, all took place, although I
have used fictional license in many places to make for a more dramatic
story line.

Zenobia, on the other hand, and all of those who accompany her on her
journey toward freedom are entirely creatures of the author's imagination.
Old Alf did in fact have a wife, Aunt Margaret, and she, with him, escaped
from slavery "undergoing many hardships and narrow escapes from capture, abandoning the horse and seeking safety in the swamps. They finally
reached the Mississippi River, where, after laying in hiding for a time, they
attracted the attention of a passing steamer, and were taken on board, and
safely landed within the Union lines at Vicksburg." Aunt Margaret, a
trained cook, became the head of the officers' mess, and in addition was a
nurse for all. Major Main says, "If any of us were sick or wounded, it was
the motherly hand of Aunt Margaret that ministered to us."

Colonel Kenworthy also is a creature of this writer's imagination but his
relationship to Joe Duckett is patterned after the relationship of Old Alf to
his former master, "one Doctor Wood, who lived on his plantation in Mississippi. The Doctor prized Old Alf largely on account of his many good
qualities, trusting him largely with the affairs of the plantation. While Old
Alf did his duty faithfully and well, his restless disposition led him into

many difficulties, which frequently involved him in *heated discussions* with the Doctor."

With regard to the siege of the fort at Yazoo City, the actual historical record should show that the commanding officer at the time of the first demand for its surrender was the redoubtable Major or J. B. Cook, and that at no time did he contemplate surrender. His actual reply to the Rebs was, "My compliments to General Ross and say to him that if he wants this fort to come and take it." Later command of the fort was taken by Major George C. McKee of the 11th Illinois Infantry, who likewise refused all efforts by the Confederates to get them to surrender the fort in this engagement of March 5, 1864. Both officers were commended for their gallantry and bravery in this encounter by Major General James B. McPherson, and this commendation was duly endorsed by Major General William T. Sherman and forwarded to the War Department on April 16, 1864. It should also be noted that the Third United States Colored Cavalry did not always bear that appellation. It was originally mustered into service as the First Mississippi Cavalry, African Descent, in October 1863. It was redesignated as the Third United States Colored Cavalry on March 11, 1864. In order not to confuse the reader, I refer to the outfit throughout the book by the designation Third United States Colored Cavalry.

At the battle of the Big Black River Bridge, the Confederate defenders did not use bloodhounds. But they did use them against the 1st South Carolina Regiment at Pocatalago Bridge, October 23, 1862 (Joseph T. Wilson, *The Black Phalanx* [New York: Arno Press and the *New York Times,* 1968, illustration, pg. 321]. See also Colonel Thomas Wentworth Higginson (*Army Life in a Black Regiment* New York: Penguin Books, 1997, p. 179]), which specifically refers to "dog companies" among the Confederates, on this occasion, "mounted riflemen with half a dozen trained bloodhounds." I couldn't resist using them. The trial and hanging of a cotton speculator by the officers of the Third Cavalry did actually take place. The offense that precipitated the action happened on board ship, but the actual hanging itself was done on land rather than aboard ship as I depict it. The man's name was W. B. Wooster, and he was "hanged by the neck to a telegraph pole until dead, by Major Jeremiah B. Cook and twenty-seven line officers" on April 24, 1864, less than two weeks after the April 12, 1864, massacre of black and white troops at Ft. Pillow, Tennessee, by General Nathan B. Forrest's men.

Captain William Stiles is likewise a creature of this writer's imagination. He is named after a college football and lacrosse coach of mine, William C. (Bill) Stiles, (1920–79), a much decorated and wounded Captain, USMC, during World War 11. He was a wonderful and brave man and a great inspiration to me and others of my classmates at Kenyon College in the late forties, although still suffering daily from the effects of his wartime wounds. In the year of my graduation from college, upon the appearance of a Marine Corps recruiter on campus and my then interest in becoming a Marine officer Bill Stiles said that he would be my reference for Platoon Leaders School. That was not an insignificant action on his part, for it was 1952 and I believe I would have been the first African-American to go through that school had I followed through on my initial interest. Instead, I opted to accept a Fulbright Scholarship to France, which came through at about the same time. I entered the U.S. Army a year later, fulfilling my military service from 1953–55 as an NCO at SHAPE Headquarters in Paris, but I've never forgotten Bill Stiles's action in support of me. He was the kind of person that I imagined Major Main and Major Cook must have been.

❖   ❖   ❖   ❖   ❖   ❖   ❖   ❖   ❖   ❖   ❖

I did consciously consider it to be my task to give a voice to those black soldiers who fought in the Third United States Colored Cavalry, so as to render Major Main's wonderful work of documenting the battle record of that regiment complete and whole. I have done my level best, both as historian and fiction writer, to tell their truths. The reader may judge how well I have succeeded.

ABOUT THE AUTHOR